*With thanks e best wishes,*

# SHADOWLAKE

*Olivia Rytwinski x*

## OLIVIA RYTWINSKI

ISBN: 9798711050575


PublishNation
www.publishnation.co.uk

*To my Family & Friends*

# Acknowledgements

Special thanks are due to my editor, A J Humpage, also Liz Best, Katy Everly, Kerry Newton and Shirley Jones. I couldn't have completed this book journey without them.

Also written by Olivia Rytwinski

*A Family by Design (2017)*
*I Never Knew You (2019)*

—

*The best way to find out if you can trust somebody
is to trust them.*

- Ernest Hemingway

*I will arise and go now, for always night and day
I hear lake water lapping with low sounds by the shore;
While I stand on the roadway, or on the pavements grey,
I hear it in the deep heart's core.*

- W. B. Yeats

# Prologue

It was mid-July and an afternoon I may never recall with any great accuracy or clarity. Even now, I'm not sure that I want to. Some details are better left in the shadows of our past. It's where they belong. At random moments, seemingly untriggered by anything related, and usually when my mind is calm and at rest, images and snatches from that day flicker through my mind like a scene from a black and white movie. Rarely, though, do they offer new insights, only phrases spoken, or the gestures and facial expressions of those I was with. And each time these come to me I want to press pause, take a hold and gather them up, so that I might alter the sequence of events that followed. A dream of sorts. No, a nightmare. But I've come to realise, as with so many other things in life, that we are merely actors in a drama - a drama largely written and set by someone else. Granted, we can think we are in control, and maybe to some extent we are, but it's always worth remembering that day to day we may only be moments away from an accident or a situation that could scoop us up and has the potential to change our lives forever.

Rarely, if ever, are such momentous life changing moments written on our terms.

# Chapter 1

*July*
*Ullswater - The Lake District, Northern England*

I turned my face to the bow of the boat and blinked against the glare of the afternoon sun.

Standing with legs braced and shoulders hunched, Jakob gripped the steering wheel while his eyes remained fixed on the water and the boat gathered speed. The underside of the boat bounced and dipped across the surface making us bump and slide on the moulded seats.

Inviting myself, husband Drew, and our two year old son, Harry, to take a ride in his boat had been a generous gesture by my colleague and friend, Jakob, and more importantly, it was an adventure for our little boy.

Drew turned to me and grinned, while Harry bobbed up and down on his lap and squealed excitedly.

Jakob had been through so much after losing his wife, Priya, who had died eighteen months previously, and it was good to see him embracing life once more. He'd even confided that he was thinking about dating again.

The sunlight bounced off the water, and lifting my hand to shield my eyes, I gazed across to the trees that lined the shore - their leaves richly green - glittered in the afternoon sun. Harry tore off his sunhat and with a cheeky look my way - before I could stop him - he flung it over the side of the boat and into the water. I twisted in my seat and watched it, sunflower yellow against the shadow black of the surface before it filled with water and was swallowed into the depths, never to be seen again.

Drew tipped his head back and laughed and I thought, we needed to spend more time like this as a family. Time away from work together with our little boy, when we could fully enjoy one another's company without any chores, urgent phone calls or emails to reply to.

'Harry!' I chided, but in the thrill of the ride I couldn't help but smile at his mischievousness. He'd recently celebrated his second birthday and had already pushed boundaries and revealed his feisty personality.

I pulled the hood of his fleece up and he promptly tugged it back down again with a non-negotiable, 'No!'

I pitched forwards as the front of the boat met another wave and Jakob turned to look at me. I saw something alarming in his eyes as the boat hurtled onwards before he turned back to the wheel and I watched him yank on the controls. Harry shrieked as the speed ramped up another level. I gripped the rail behind me to keep steady and Drew held Harry closer to him.

'Slow it down, mate,' Drew called across to Jakob.

But Jakob didn't hear him and we drew ever closer to the boathouse and shore at the far end of Ullswater. Without warning, Jakob jerked the steering wheel causing the boat to swerve, and a great gush of water splashed in our faces.

I peeled wet hair from my eyes and screamed, 'Slow down, Jakob!'

But when he turned, I saw the look of panic on his face.

'There's something wrong,' he yelled, and grappled again with the controls.

The boat careered across the water, and seemed to get faster and faster.

A feeling of terror rose up in me and instinctively I staggered the few yards to the front, as Jakob bent over and tussled with the throttle. I grabbed the steering wheel and tried to turn the boat, but at the same time realised we had no chance of swinging the boat round in time.

'Try the key,' I yelled over the scream of the engine.

Jakob's eyes grew wild with fear.

He wrestled with the key. 'It's fucking stuck.'

I reached down and pushed Jakob's hand away. 'Let me.'

But, moments later I recalled a sensation of falling, and of my body being thrown against something solid, back and forth again. Crashing sounds and screams filled the air. Pain pierced through me as a chilled blackness enveloped my body until I became weightless and beyond feeling. And after that, nothing.

4

# Chapter 2

*Six Weeks Later*
*Flat 2, Windmoor House, Keswick, The Lake District*

My body felt leaden with sleep beneath the bedcovers, but even with my eyes closed I sensed it was morning. Daylight dripped gentle and warm upon my face and I opened my eyes. The light dazzled and I squinted against the sun. The curtains were half open and even from here I could see the sky was a rare cloudless blue. I sat up and looked around at the strangely unfamiliar surroundings. It felt as if I was seeing the room for the first time, despite knowing full well that I'd picked out clothes from the wardrobe, stood before the standing mirror and sat at my dressing table to blowdry my hair many times before.

It was a peculiar sensation and a feeling of disorientation washed over me. I looked down at my hands and noticed the wedding ring on my finger, a smooth gold band with a diamond at its centre. I was married. And if that was so, where was my husband? And more startling to me still, who was he? The pillow beside me had no indentation where he might have laid last night and when I pulled back the duvet, the white cotton on that side of the bed appeared untouched and undisturbed. I swallowed but my mouth and throat felt impossibly dry. I needed water. I stood up and padded barefoot across the floorboards to the window. I looked down to the street below, to where an elderly gentleman led his two black labradors down the cobbled slope, with a view of the public gardens, and beyond, Derwent Water. The man's face seemed familiar but no name came to mind. Street scenes flashed through my mind - full with throngs of people one moment, and the next, empty, but with rain pounding the cobbles, streaming down the gullies and thunder rolling in the skies overhead.

I closed my eyes and when I pressed the heels of my palms against them a rainbow of phosphenes appeared. I looked out of the window again and beyond the shops and houses that led down the hill to the lake. The sun shimmered upon the water and on the far side a great hillside stood proud and clear of clouds with its jagged peak that glimmered and looked radiant. Had I walked that hill before? I had no clear recollection, only a vague sense that I had many times. To live in such a spectacular setting and not to have climbed it would be a crime.

The soles of my feet felt cold upon the floor and I turned to the room. A holdall sat on the end of the bed and I walked over and rummaged inside. Amongst the underwear, magazines and nightdresses I found a pair of fluffy socks. I bent down and slipped them onto my feet.

Water. I needed water.

Instinctively, I made my way to the bathroom. I ran the tap and lowered my mouth and felt the cool liquid wash over my lips and tongue and down my throat. It tasted divine and I swallowed until my thirst felt quenched. I dried my mouth on the towel that hung over the radiator then I straightened up and looked back at my reflection in the mirror over the sink. I wore a neutral expression as though I was alone with only my reflection to talk to. Being here felt strange and I noticed a peculiar stillness about the house.

My name was Orla. Long dark brown hair, which fell in waves and framed and sculpted my face. I looked fine boned, but my complexion seemed near translucent around green eyes with long lashes and unruly brows. I ran my fingers through my tresses to tease out the tangles. My cheekbones protruded and I pressed my fingers into the hollows beneath. My full lips looked pale and I realised I hadn't eaten properly in some time.

'Hello.' I spoke slowly to my reflection. 'Pleased to meet you, Orla.' My voice sounded curious and husky but the words curdled in my ears.

With a sense that I wasn't altogether who I thought I was and that I may not even belong here, I walked back through to the bedroom and onto the landing - an unlit corridor with three closed doors situated off it. I felt drawn to the second door and reached out my hand and touched the colourful letter 'H' fixed in the middle. Again, this seemed familiar but only vaguely so. I turned the handle and entered the room. It was smaller than the bedroom I'd awoken in and in near darkness, with a drawn down yellow blind. I walked across and pulled the cord and sunlight streamed in like a wave rushing up a sandy beach. For a moment it blinded me and I turned around and waited for the whiteness to fade. The sunlight cast across the walls and floor in a pale citrine yellow. The room was furnished with a matching cream bookshelf, wardrobe and chest of drawers and one single bed in the middle, too short for an adult and low to the floor. It was covered with a bold patterned black and white quilt and on the pillow lay two monkeys. I bent over and picked them up - one wore a floral dress with Mum embroidered across the front and the other wore a T-shirt and trousers with Dad similarly embroidered. How sweet, I thought.

But where was the child who slept in this bed? Another wave of confusion washed over me. My body began to shake and my mind fought against feelings and thoughts that tried to force their way in. I took some long breaths before I placed the two monkeys back on the pillow. Slowly, I turned a full circle and looked around at the four walls. I saw colourful prints of animals and children, but one framed photograph drew me nearer. It was of a small boy with dark curls, aqua blue eyes and pink chubby cheeks. This was a face I knew well, but I couldn't have named him or recalled where I'd seen him before. A beautiful child and certainly, this must be his bedroom. But if this was his bedroom and I'd awoken in the other room... a shiver jolted me and for some moments I felt lightheaded.

Something felt wrong, terribly wrong, and I sat down on the bed and tried to rearrange my thoughts which had become ever more chaotic and confused. The stretch of water and the hillside view from the window, the cobbled street, the man with the labradors, the untouched pillow beside me in bed, and the small boy in the photograph who made my head and heart ache with an intensity I could not comprehend.

These were all familiar things to me somewhere in the recesses of my mind, but equally, unknown.

# Chapter 3

*Sylvia*

I heard a door slam followed by footsteps approaching.

'Orla?' A woman's voice.

'Who is it?' I replied.

Seconds later a familiar face appeared in the doorway.

'Hey, you're up. I was hoping to get back before you woke up.'

She came and sat beside me on the bed and took my hand. 'Did you sleep?'

I nodded. 'Yes, I've only just woken up.' I knew her face which looked lovely but sad, with eyes the shape of mine.

She looked into my eyes. 'It's OK, Orla. It's me, Sylvia, your sister. Remember?' she said, with a warmness in her voice that I knew well.

'Of course,' I said. And I reached out my arms and embraced her. 'I'm so pleased to see you again.'

My eyes stung. I wasn't alone. That was all that mattered.

'I stayed here last night, but I had to nip out to buy provisions.'

'Is there no food?' I said. 'I'm sorry.'

I turned and picked up the Daddy monkey. 'What are these doing here?'

I sensed her hesitation and I searched her eyes that seemed to glisten against the sunlight.

She blinked as if to see better. 'It's OK,' she said. 'I'll explain once we've eaten breakfast.'

She took my hand and led me from the bedroom, through the living room and pulled out a chair for me at the kitchen table. She sat me down, but I got straight back up.

'I know where everything is,' I said. 'Toast or cereals?'

'Muesli if you've got some,' she said. 'I'll make us tea.' And she picked up the kettle beside the sink.

I reached down into the cupboard and lifted out a bag of muesli, then I found two bowls and spoons and set them on the table.

Sylvia reached into a carrier bag, held up a carton of milk and placed it between the bowls.

The muesli tasted sweet and delicious and I crunched hungrily one mouthful after another, without speaking or barely looking up. After I'd spooned up all the remaining milk, I looked across at Sylvia who smiled.

'You were hungry then,' she said.

I laughed lightly. 'I must have been.'

'You've been off your food recently,' she said, and lifted the teapot and poured tea into two mugs. She stirred in some milk and placed one in front of me. 'It's how you like it.'

'Yorkshire Tea?' I asked.

'Of course.'

I took a sip. 'What day is it?'

She paused and looked at me with a curious expression. 'It's Tuesday, remember?'

I shook my head. 'And what date is it?'

She watched me then gave a slight smile. 'The thirty-first of August.'

'Almost the end of summer,' I said, and had the strongest impression that I'd slipped through time.

'We have something important to do today,' she said, and her features softened.

'Oh?'

'We have a funeral to attend.' She swallowed and pinched her upper lip with her thumb and forefinger. 'But I'll be right beside you the whole time.'

I watched as she looked up at the ceiling and her eyes pooled with tears.

'Whose funeral?' I asked quietly.

Sylvia stood up and walked round to my side of the table. She drew out the chair beside me and sat down. 'It's Drew and Harry, remember?' Her hands trembled as she pulled a tissue from the sleeve of her cardigan.

'Drew and Harry?'

9

For a few moments she gazed towards the kitchen window, and blinked. She wiped her eyes, drew a breath and turned to me. 'It's OK.' She paused. 'I talked to you about them yesterday before we left the hospital?'

I shook my head but even as I did her words swam through my mind - disjointed and unfathomable.

'Drew and Harry were with you in the speedboat.' She waited for my reaction.

'I see.' But not seeing clearly at all. 'We lived here together?'

She nodded. 'Dr Malik said your memory should return in full, but I mustn't try to fill in the gaps for you. You'll begin to do that on your own, naturally.'

And then I could recall sitting up in a hospital bed and being told by a doctor who had smiled when she said I could come home. Sylvia had driven me home in her red Mini with my bag of nightwear and toiletries on the back seat.

I pushed back my chair and said, 'Then I'd better shower and dress for a funeral.'

'Let me help you find something. You told me you didn't want to wear black. You said children preferred colours.'

'Yes, Sylvia. I did say that. I remember that now.'

I wanted to ask her again how I knew Drew and Harry, but something prevented me. Something told me it would be safer not to say it aloud. For now.

I showered then sat at the dressing table and dried my hair. The ends felt rough and split. My skin looked almost translucent, with faded freckles across my nose, but no pink blush to my cheeks. I reached into my make-up bag and applied some bronzer, then a brush of eyeliner. I picked out a purple lipstick and swept it carefully across my cupid's bow. I no longer appeared ghost-like - a figure from my past.

Sylvia knocked on the open door and walked into the bedroom. She wore a lilac pleated skirt and white pussy-bow blouse.

'You look pretty,' I said.

'Thank you. Rick's going to meet us there. Amy's going to a friend's.'

I thought for a moment. 'Amy's your daughter?'

Sylvia nodded and looked pleased. 'Yes. That's fantastic. You couldn't recall her a few days ago. You're making brilliant progress.'

'Bring Amy over. I'd love to see her.'

'She'd love to see you, too.' Sylvia came over and hugged me. 'I love you so much, Sis.'

I looked up at her and into her honey brown eyes, beneath her wispy auburn fringe. 'You mean so much to me, Sylvia. We've always needed one another, haven't we?'

'Always...' It seemed as though she wanted to say more, but then thought better of it. Instead, she got up, walked across to the wardrobe and opened the door. 'Let's have a look.' She shuffled through the hangers. 'How about this?' She lifted out a white dress dotted with blue flowers.

'I'll try it,' I said and pulled my nightdress over my head.

'Do you want me to go out?' asked Sylvia.

'It's fine,' I replied, and dropped my nightdress onto the bed. I walked to the chest of drawers and picked out matching knickers and bra.

When I turned around, I noticed Sylvia watching me.

'You've lost a lot of weight, Orla.'

I looked down and placed my palm on my abdomen. 'Am I too thin?' I asked.

She shook her head. 'Not really. In fact, you look incredible. Given you've just...' she stopped. 'Well, you've lost all the baby weight and more.'

'I have a baby?' The bedroom with the colourful H came into my mind. The small bed and the yellow window blind. I looked into Sylvia's eyes. 'He's gone, hasn't he? It's Harry's funeral, isn't it?'

Sylvia drew in her breath then nodded slowly. 'Yes. Your memory is returning.'

I watched as her eyes filled with tears and silently she began to weep.

In contrast to her obvious emotion, I felt strangely hollow. It was as if my mind was filled with nothing but smoke - an infertile space where nothing could take root or grow.

'Let me try the dress,' I said. And I reached over and took the hanger from her.

11

# Chapter 4

*The Burial*

I thanked a woman who, through her tears and sniffles, told me how cruel life was and that she'd see me at the wake. She was dressed from head to toe in black and wore a solitary red flower in her silver-streaked, bobbed hair. I only vaguely recognised her, and didn't know what else to say in reply. Her eyes were pink from crying and a tall man dressed in a black suit walked up and put an arm around her shoulder.

'Come, my love. We'll talk to Orla later.' He smiled at me, but there was an intense anguish in his eyes. They walked away - their heads bowed.

'That's Drew's parents, Henri and Heather,' said, Sylvia. 'They came to see you in the hospital last week. They're heartbroken, obviously.'

She and all of these people around me had known Drew and our son, and by their devastated expressions it appeared they'd known them far better than I had. I felt only a veiled sense of affinity to my husband and baby, and of loss, as if they had been from my distant past - those I'd known well at some point, but had left me for good some time ago.

Nothing and nobody seemed quite real and although I knew I should have felt a gut-wrenching pain, I didn't and I couldn't pretend to. As we left the church, Sylvia hooked my arm and led me as though I were an invalid across the grass to where people had already gathered. They parted to allow us to walk through to the side of a grave with a mahogany coffin laid beside it upon a blanket of bright fake grass.

I turned to Sylvia. 'Where's Harry's coffin?'

She squeezed my hand. 'Do you remember, I told you his body hasn't been found? That can happen in such a deep body of water. But we'll have a memorial stone for him here and can remember him that way.'

'Then how do we know that he died?' It seemed an obvious question.

'After, at the wake, you can speak to Jakob. He's here and was there during the accident.' She paused. 'If you want to.'

'Yes. I want to know everything.'

I looked upon the coffin and tried to picture Drew - a man, my husband, lying inside with his eyes closed. But I could see nothing of him. Not even his face.

The name Jakob seemed familiar and I felt sure I'd know him. I had the strongest sense he'd visited me in the hospital a few times. Though I couldn't recall our conversations.

The vicar approached me and took my hand. He looked young - younger than me. 'God is watching over you. He has taken Drew and Harry into his embrace. I hope you can take some comfort from knowing they do not suffer.'

When I didn't respond, Sylvia replied.

'Thank you, vicar.'

He gave a brief smile and walked to stand at the head of the grave.

The coffin had been placed onto a frame above the grave and as I gazed upon the glossy wood, it seemed impossible to imagine that a man I'd lived with for years, lay inside. An image of his face flashed into my mind's eye - wavy golden hair, chocolate brown eyes above perfect halfmoon cheekbones - a classically handsome face. But the image didn't fill me with heartache and regret for someone who'd died too soon. For someone I must have loved deeply. His image smiled at me - his lips full and soft.

I turned to Sylvia. 'How old was Drew?'

'Thirty-seven.'

'And Harry?'

'Only two.' The words caught in her throat.

As the vicar began to speak I turned and looked at the faces that surrounded me - their gazes lowered.

'Give them, O Lord, your peace and let your eternal light shine upon your children, Andrew and Harry. Amen,' he finished saying.

'Amen,' repeated those around me.

As people began to disperse, I watched the coffin descend slowly into the grave and come to rest at the bottom. Two men lifted the lowering device and I took a step closer. I crouched down and picked up a handful of soil then sprinkled it onto the lid of the coffin.

I said quietly, 'I hope my memories return so I'll remember you for all that you were to me, and as a dad to Harry. I want to remember you, to know you, not to forget you.' The muscles tightened at the back of my throat and I could speak no more. I picked up another handful of soil. A long, fat earthworm slithered between my fingers and amongst the dirt - grainy and damp.

I felt Sylvia's protective hand upon my shoulder and as I moved to stand up, something caught my eye in the bottom of the pit. The side of the grave shifted and clumps of soil fell away.

I peered closer. 'What is that?'

But even as I spoke, the small pale bones and shreds of skin that jutted from the soil became clearer.

'A hand,' I whispered and sank to my knees. 'A child's hand.'

# Chapter 5

*The Wake*

When the door of The Anchor Inn creaked shut behind us, I looked around the bar and spotted one or two familiar faces amongst many others I could swear I'd never seen before.

'Come with me,' Sylvia said, and taking my hand she led me to a small table with four padded stools.

'I'll get us a whisky - medicinal,' she said.

A tall, slim gentleman in a navy suit came and sat beside me. He wore a colourful Mickey Mouse tie - and it was his tie that prompted my recognition of him, as much as his bristly beard and kind eyes.

'Would you buy me a whisky too, love?' He pulled a twenty pound note from his pocket and held it out for Sylvia.

'Uncle Ross,' I said, and reached out to hug him. 'I'm glad to see you.'

'I was in the pew behind you, you know, but we didn't get a chance to talk.'

'Then we can talk now,' I said, and felt comforted by his presence. 'Did you hear about the child's hand?'

'I've just been told. What a horrible shock for you. And on top of everything.'

'The vicar said it was rare for a casket to disintegrate, but that it happens from time to time,' I explained.

'Then I hope they rehouse the child. Whoever he or she was.'

'I read the headstone,' I said.

'And?' he asked.

'An eight year old boy called Christopher. He died thirty or so years ago. The vicar was mortified and they're going to sort it all out before they can fill the grave.'

Uncle Ross's brows came down and drew together. 'I've never heard of such a thing happening.'

15

'Maybe the casket wasn't sealed properly or the ground got soaked,' I said.

He scraped his fingers through his peppered black hair. 'They should inform the parents. I'll call the vicar.'

'Please don't,' I said. 'He seemed so sorry and it was upsetting enough.'

'All right.' His blue eyes sharpened and the lines on his forehead deepened. 'But next week I'll check the groundsmen have resolved the matter.'

Sylvia returned to the table with a tray of glasses.

'Now this, I need,' said uncle Ross.

'We all do,' said Sylvia, and placed a glass in front of me.

I raised the glass to my lips and sipped. Its fire warmed me, but strangely, the sight of the child's hand chilled me more than the thought that I'd said a final goodbye to my husband and son.

I knew I'd sustained a brain injury, although the doctors couldn't explain the irregularity of my memory loss. They'd reassured me my memory should return to its normal state, but I knew I was being told things repeatedly by Sylvia and still only able to retain random fragments. My doctors might not approve of my drinking whisky, but when my glass was empty and Sylvia got up to go to the bar for another, I didn't object.

When she returned she was with a man I recognised.

Jakob pulled out a chair to my other side. He took a long swig from his glass. 'I hope that wasn't too much to bear, Orla.'

For a moment I didn't reply as I tried to frame my words. 'Truthfully, it felt more unreal than unbearable, because I barely remember them.'

I knew what grief looked like. I'd seen it on the news and in movies. Hell, I could remember experiencing full blown grief myself as a teenager. When people lost someone close to them, they didn't sit in a bar and sip whisky and talk calmly to those around them. Or did they? Head injury or not, I felt like a freak, and the sympathetic looks and glances from those around the bar only seemed to confirm this.

When I turned again to Jakob he was watching me - with brows pinched and lips pressed together.

A flood of memories poured into my mind, of the office and sitting with Jakob at his desk.

'I've been thinking about returning to work,' I said to him. 'Physically I feel OK and familiar surroundings and colleagues will prompt my memories.'

'Surely not yet?' Jakob said, lowering his voice. 'You're still in shock.'

'I don't think the shock has hit me. When it does, I'll deal with it.'

'OK, why don't you get through today then see how you feel in the next day or so.'

'I know you're only thinking of me,' I said, 'but it'll be the best thing to speed my recovery. And moping around at home won't help.'

Jakob turned to Sylvia. 'Please reason with your sister.'

For a moment Sylvia remained silent as she thought. 'It should be Orla's call. And physically she seems well. Apart from her memory lapses, her doctor's said she's fit to go.'

'I will only come back if I feel up to it,' I said, and felt stifled by the gazes and opinions of those around me. I stood up. 'I'm nipping to the ladies.'

Sylvia stood up to accompany me.

'It's OK.' I smiled. 'I know where they are.'

And I did know. There seemed no rational explanation for what I could or couldn't recall right now. Everything about my work and career seemed clear in my mind.

I pushed the soap dispenser and a dollop of green soap dropped into my palm. I smoothed it into my hands and rinsed them beneath the hot tap then dried them on a paper towel. When I turned around I caught my reflection in the full length mirror. My dress looked too loose. I'd have to sort through what did and didn't fit me still. When I'd first awoken in the hospital I'd barely known who I was and even now, six weeks after the accident, whenever I looked at my reflection it often seemed I was looking back at a stranger, despite knowing my name, age, full address and occupation. Jakob was my colleague, and a friend since I'd started working for BioMedica. We worked on projects together - he was product development and I oversaw the marketing and research, so when a new drug joined the pipeline we'd team up with others to ensure every aspect of the product's manufacture and safety was thoroughly covered. Pharmaceuticals had been in my blood ever since I'd studied Chemistry followed by a postgraduate qualification in Marketing and Research at Liverpool University. I'd even travelled to America for my year out work experience with pharmaceutical giant, Glaxosmithkline.

A pretty woman with a neat, chocolate brown bob who I recognised, but couldn't name, came into the toilets. She offered a sympathetic smile and said she was sorry for my loss, then quickly walked into a cubicle and closed the door behind her. When I walked out of the toilets I saw Jakob leaning against the wall in the corridor outside the Gents.

'Orla.' He turned to me. 'I still feel responsible for this.'

'But why?' I said.

'Because it was my boat. And I know the malfunction was appalling luck, but it was me who'd invited you all for the ride.'

'I remember so little about the accident but I know you'll have done everything possible to prevent it. Please don't blame yourself.'

He looked down at the floor and shuffled his feet. 'If only it could have been me instead of Drew and Harry, you know I would have.' He rubbed his eyes with the back of his hand. 'My own Godson.'

I reached out and touched his arm. 'In time, I'll remember it all and then we can talk. But for now, I can't.'

Jakob rested his hand on my shoulder. 'I'm sorry. Ever since childhood I've blamed myself when bad things happen.'

'But I don't blame you, so you mustn't...' I took a step to leave. 'I'd better get back to the others.'

'Orla?'

I turned back to him.

'I wanted to tell you I'll be raising an official complaint at the way that poor child's grave was desecrated. You shouldn't have had to see that. None of us should.'

I felt my head rush and I leaned against the wall. 'It was no one's fault.'

'That boy is someone's son,' he said.

'Yes, and the vicar will see that it's sorted.' I closed my eyes and placed my palm on the wall to stop the corridor from turning around me.

Jakob took my hand. 'Let me help you.'

Slowly, the dizziness passed and I opened my eyes and felt Jakob's breath upon my cheek.

'Do you remember Dan Mace?' he asked.

'Our Director. Lives here in Keswick, off the square.'

Jakob looked steadily into my eyes. 'Well remembered.'

'What about him?'

'I was telling him you were out of hospital and about the funeral today. He was so relieved you're on the mend.'

'I'll call him and let him know my plan to return.'

'The thing is,' Jakob began, and hesitated. 'He mentioned he wants you to take a month off as a minimum now you're out of hospital, then he'll visit you and see how you're doing with regards to resuming work.'

'Doesn't he need me back? You too?'

'Of course. We all do. But your health comes first.'

'Surely I can be the judge of my health.'

'But can you?' he said, and his eyes searched mine.

I shook my head. 'What do you mean?'

'Given that your memory is patchy still and head injuries can lead to unpredictable behaviour. I mean, thank God you're recovering. But let's not rush things.'

My head began to swim again and doubt filled my mind. 'Maybe. I should ring Dan though.'

'Let me speak to him for you and see what I can do.'

I felt a well of emotion and my tears threatened. 'Everyone's being so kind. So supportive.'

He held out his hands. 'I think you need a hug.'

And he wrapped his arms around me and drew me close. I felt his hand move down and come to rest on my lower back.

'I'll make sure no more harm comes to you, Orla,' he said into my ear.

When I returned to the bar, Sylvia was looking over her shoulder and her eyes met mine.

'I was about to come and find you,' she said. 'You were ages.'

'I know it might seem doubtful, but I can make my way to the ladies and back,' I said, and sat back down.

'Good,' she said and smiled. 'I couldn't bear to lose you, too.'

19

# Chapter 6

Sylvia had packed her suitcase after I'd finally reassured her I would cope alone, not get run over in the street or drive somewhere and get hopelessly lost. We'd been to the supermarket and bought provisions and even cooked a few meals and portioned them in the freezer to make my life easier.

In the doorway I gave her a final hug. 'Go. Be with your family. I'll text you morning and night to let you know how I'm doing,' I added.

'OK,' she said, and flicked her fringe out of her eyes. 'But call me night or day if you feel confused or want to talk. Or if you feel down or upset. Even if it's a reminder how to work the microwave.'

'Stop it,' I said, but smiled. 'Give Rick and Amy a hug from me.'

After I'd waved her off I went to my laptop. Sylvia had discouraged me from logging in to check my emails and I could understand why, but I'd been itching to ever since talking to Jakob about work. I wasn't at all sure what I'd find or what would be familiar to me, but I knew my work had been a big part of my life prior to the accident. Pharmaceuticals had been a profitable but often controversial industry to work in. I'd been successful in my chosen career and having looked over my bank statements, I knew that without Drew's substantial income, money wouldn't be an issue, as it too often was for widows or widowers left alone suddenly. Sylvia had told me I mustn't rush back to work and that was after Jakob had said similarly, but I felt fitter each day, mentally as well as physically, and lazing around, watching daytime TV and reading book after book wasn't something I could tolerate for long.

When the login box appeared on the screen, I couldn't recall either my password or my email to reset it. I tried my phone, but that too asked for a password to access my emails. What a pain. Why hadn't I given automatic permission for saving password details? No doubt I'd had my reasons.

Damn it. Maybe I'd written them down. I pulled my notebook from my handbag and flicked through each page. There were various numbers, but they looked more like pin numbers. I tried a few, but none of them got me in.

Frustrated, I closed the laptop and ran a bath - hot, deep and full of scented bubbles. I hung my robe on the back of the door, stepped in and lay back, and felt the water fiery against my skin.

Since returning home from hospital I'd been bathing once, sometimes twice a day. It had amused Sylvia who reminded me that prior to the accident I'd been a strong advocate of showering whilst insisting that lounging in the bath took up too much time. I wasn't short of time right now. I had no work to do and more essentially, no child to care for. I looked down, placed one hand on my abdomen and moved it rhythmically in circular motions. For a few moments, as the water sloshed gently into my ears I felt the strongest sensation of a small but fully formed baby, a boy, floating and protected in his amniotic sac.

'I'm still here, Harry. You'll always be with me.'

I sat bolt upright and the water surged and splashed over the sides. I'd spoken to my son. A son who was no longer with me. I closed my eyes and pressed my palm to my belly. I waited, desperate to feel his presence again, but the sensation had gone. I released my breath, long and slow, and lay back again.

I reached for the shampoo, massaged some into my hair, and worked it into a thick lather. Then I tipped my head back in the water and ran my fingers through my hair, until the suds were rinsed away.

'Drew and Harry, Drew and Harry, Drew and Harry.' I repeated their names over and over. If I did this often enough, my memories of them would surely return and instead of seeing only distant and faded flowers, they would breathe life, colour and scent once more. And as their faces appeared, still blurred and distant in my mind, something else clicked.

Their names combined were my email password. Of course, it really couldn't be more obvious.

I towelled myself dry, wrapped my hair in a turban towel and dressed in a pair of denim shorts and a cream cotton blouse. The bedroom felt blissfully warm and I pulled up the sash window and looked down onto the street. The scene appeared as familiar as ever. Patricia, the owner of The Boathouse Bistro was putting out the blackboard that displayed the day's specials. She must have sensed my gaze and she lifted her head, spotted me and gave me a friendly wave. This morning life felt normal. And yet, how odd to perceive it as normal, when in truth, I should be on valium and weeping into my pillow day and night.

I went to the wardrobe to find a belt. All my clothes felt loose and the shorts slipped down my hips. I fastened the belt onto its tightest hole and realised I'd have to shop for some new clothes. I couldn't recall ever being overweight, but I'd obviously lost a few pounds. No doubt being unconscious for a few days had something to do with it, and not much of an appetite since.

A text link came through on my mobile and I successfully reset my password and logged into my emails.

I had dozens of unread emails, both personal and work related. There were messages from people sending their condolences and offering to do whatever they could to help. At some point I'd have to sit down, read them properly and reply to each - which could also help trigger some memories. I felt frustrated that I had no precise recollection of what I'd been working on prior to the accident. I read a few of the earlier work emails. Most of them had documents attached with various reports and research findings on a new drug - Hexprin, a drug to boost female arousal, but the emails stopped abruptly weeks ago, a fortnight after my accident. My colleagues obviously decided it would be pointless keeping me in the loop if I was recuperating with memory loss.

And they were right. Jakob had spoken to me again and we'd agreed it was too soon for me to return to work so why should I worry about emails that were no longer my concern? When I did return to the office I'd soon get up to speed without having to trawl through hundreds of emails and documents. If I read them all now they might overwhelm me and even hinder my recovery. No, I thought, small steps, heed Jakob's advice, and hopefully

22

my memory would soon return to full capacity. Each day I was remembering more and more and retaining new memories, too.

I ate a slice of toast and honey, laced up a pair of trainers and headed outside. On the cobbles I paused and looked back up at our first floor flat, one of three flats in a three story red brick house, detached and with the original sash windows dating back to 1880 according to the plaque beside the front door. In front of the door were eight stone steps and in front of these a narrow gully where rainfall would gather to form a stream and run on to drains and join more gullies in the streets down the hill. This was my home, the only place I still felt secure, and despite all that had happened and all that I'd lost, I experienced a sense of comfort from it.

I turned and continued on up the hill to the High Street. Twice, I checked that I had my purse and my mobile phone and that I could recall my pin number. All good. Our first floor flat was situated on a pedestrianised back street where tourists and shoppers often meandered through, stopping to go into coffee shops, the art gallery, a leather goods boutique and various eateries and bars. I loved the hustle and bustle of the area, always evident but softened inside the flat, especially during high season, and I'd often sit at the window seat with a cup of tea or glass of wine, and people watch - couples, families, groups of friends and lone shoppers. It seemed endlessly fascinating, and in warmer weather I could even listen in on some of the conversations. As the many times I'd sat there washed through my mind, I realised this memory had never left me. A simple pleasure - absorbing and harmless.

I hadn't heard any rainfall earlier but as I walked, drips fell in a slow and steady rhythm from the trees and gutters and sunlight made the cobblestones glisten. The air smelt sodden and sweet. As I continued up the street a tabby cat followed me and when I paused to stroke it it prowled around my feet and its tail curled into a question mark. Soaking up my attention, it purred and arched its back and its whiskers twitched against my bare legs. The air felt warming upon my skin and I took off my cardigan and tucked it into my shopping bag.

In the first clothes shop I entered there were endless rails of clothes on sale and I picked out a selection of skirts, tops and

23

dresses and three pairs of jeans. When I tried them on, they fit surprisingly well, apart from one blouse that felt too tight over my bust. After swapping one pair of black jeans for a smaller size, I bundled everything into my arms and queued at the till.

I recognised the woman behind the counter as she chatted to the blonde haired girl she was serving, and felt certain I knew her from elsewhere, too. When she spotted me, she gave me a friendly wave.

'Hi Orla.'

'Hi,' I replied, and felt awkward.

When it was my turn to be served, I placed the clothes onto the counter.

As she reached over the counter and took my hand, she watched my confusion. 'I'm Lizzie. It's so good to see you away from the hospital.'

The moment she told me her name, I knew her. 'I'm sorry. My memory is still patchy.'

'But you're out and about, shopping on your own.' She picked up one of the skirts and held it up. 'And choosing brilliantly, so you must be recovering.' She scanned and folded each item and placed them in a paper carrier bag. 'You'll look great in all of these.'

'I hope so. They seem to fit well.'

And then it came to me where I knew her from. 'We've known one another since primary school, haven't we?' I said.

'Since day one. And do you remember when we released that jar of red Lily beetles in Mrs Box's classroom?'

'Yes, I do remember that,' I said, and a bubble of laughter escaped me. 'What did she call us? The wild ones.'

'That's it. Caught on with the other teachers, too.' Lizzie threw her head back and laughed. 'Far too much curiosity and energy.'

'At least we weren't goody two shoes,' I said.

'No chance of that. Though you did do rather better in your exams than me. Hence, I'm working here.'

'I'm not back at work yet, but hopefully soon.' I took the bag of clothes from her, and was conscious of a queue of customers behind me. 'It's so good to see you.'

As I turned to leave, Lizzie said, 'Hey, Orla.'

'Yes?'

'I'm having a dinner party this Saturday. It's for my birthday. Would you like to come?' She wore an expectant smile.

'Ummm…' I hesitated.

'Only a few select guests,' she added.

'Oh, go on then,' I said, finally. 'And I remember where you live. Lilac Avenue. Still a red front door?' I pictured it in my mind.

'No.9. Fantastic! Seven thirtyish,' she said and clapped her hands. 'Hollywood dress is the theme. But come as you are if you prefer. No gifts - your presence is enough.'

'Then I'd be delighted to.'

As I walked back home I thought about Lizzie and remembered how when we were young we'd spend nights at one another's houses. We'd been best friends for years. When I went off to University, we'd still meet up during the holidays but later when I'd started working, we'd drifted apart. Had I been so engrossed in my career and so wrapped up in my life with Drew that I'd neglected my oldest friend? And then I remembered that she'd visited me in the hospital and brought a bouquet of roses and a basket of colourful fruit.

At the top end of my street I paused outside, Hair by Design. I peered through the window at the stylists busy with their clients. I felt certain this was my regular salon and given that it was so close to home and it wasn't, then it would at least be convenient. As I walked through the door, one of the stylists, a woman in a red dress that almost matched the shade of her hair, looked up and smiled.

'Orla.' She excused herself with her client and walked over. 'How are you?'

'I'm not sure.' I paused. 'Everything's so confused. But I can see that my hair needs a trim.'

She placed her hand on my arm. 'Let's see when we can fit you in.'

'Any chance before Saturday?' I asked.

# Chapter 7

I'd survived my first week alone. I'd showered and dressed by lunchtime every day. I'd gone through the fridge and binned a mouldy pot of Greek yoghurt and a jar of pasta sauce that must have been sitting there for almost two months, along with a few dry and limp vegetables. I'd re-stocked with fresh milk, cheeses and salads and under instruction from Sylvia, I'd prepared myself a meal every night - although eating it hadn't proved as easy. I'd even remembered my hair appointment. The only thing I hadn't managed to do was to step back into Harry's bedroom and I'd avoided looking in Drew's bedside cabinet, the drawers in his desk or the clothes in his side of the wardrobe. When I'd walked along the corridor to collect fresh sheets from the airing cupboard, I'd passed Harry's nursery, but when I glanced in and saw his bed, neatly made and empty, I'd reached for the door handle with a trembling hand and slammed it shut. I couldn't face it. Not yet.

Anything that belonged to Drew, a medical magazine, his running trainers by the front door, his black woolen jacket that hung on the coat hook - all of these things I'd bundled into the understairs cupboard. Avoidance seemed to me the best approach, for now.

There were framed photographs of Drew, Harry and me on the walls and bookshelves, that I'd tried not to avoid, and for a minute or two each day I'd sit with one in my hands or stand and look closely at them. Their faces grew familiar once more, but I still felt oddly numb and my memories of them only a shadow of real recognition. My mind seemed to be avoiding reality - a reality I was not yet prepared to acknowledge or accept.

Each night when I went to bed I'd fall into a deep slumber, only to awaken in the early hours feeling confused and I often wondered not only where I was but who I was. My heart would begin to race and I'd break out in a sweat, until I could say my full name aloud, 'Orla Louise Safian', and eventually I'd take some slow breaths, calm down and fall back to sleep again. Most mornings my head felt groggy until I'd brewed a pot of tea or coffee and sat collecting my thoughts for a few minutes while looking out onto the street. This had helped to clear the fog and made me feel almost normal once more.

Lizzie's dinner party had been preying on my mind and the moment I opened my eyes on Saturday morning, I felt a flutter of nerves in my belly. It could be quite a test - talking to people I probably didn't know and having to remember their names and understand what they were talking about. Lizzie had invited Dan Mace, my Director at BioMedica, and we'd always got on well ever since I'd started working for him five years previously. I had a vague memory of Dan visiting me in the hospital, but I knew he'd be sympathetic and at least understand my situation. I thought about mentioning to the others that I'd been in an accident that affected my memory, then they wouldn't think I was being rude at any point, or worse, crazy. As far as opening up about Drew or Harry, that was still a no-go area unless with my dearest Sylvia. Lizzie's guests might already know about the accident. Keswick wasn't a large town and bad news was always common news.

By mid-morning, I'd played some upbeat music and danced around in an attempt to loosen up and brighten my mood. When this left me feeling drained and breathless rather than invigorated, I read through more emails then tried to get to grips with my online bank statements and all the regular outgoings. I'd written an email to the bank and utilities to inform them about Drew, along with an attached copy of his death certificate. I hoped this would be enough and I wouldn't need to go in, too. When I read it through, it had the tone of a business letter and seemed somehow cold and inappropriate. I was informing virtual strangers that my husband had recently died in a boat accident, but without beginning to comprehend or to feel emotionally what his death really meant to me.

With all these thoughts rattling through my mind, I felt a restless energy that wouldn't dissipate. What would I normally do to occupy my time? No doubt I'd have played games with Harry, taken him down to the swings in Hope Gardens, spent time talking to Drew, cleaning, shopping and all the normal

27

things that a wife and mother of a young family did. When I'd spoken to Sylvia the previous night, she'd reminded me how much I loved to swim. That would be gentle exercise and help to relax and calm my mind, which continued to buzz with random thoughts I couldn't seem to place in any rational order. After some hunting, I found my swimsuit in my underwear drawer and put it on under my clothes like Sylvia and I always used to do whenever we went to the pool as children. It felt on the loose side, but it would do for now.

When I walked down the ramp to the changing rooms, the pool looked busy, and Queen's, *We will rock you*, echoed around the building.

I put my clothes into a locker and drank some cold water straight from the tap. My legs trembled as I stood at the side of the pool and watched as a father encouraged his son to jump in. The little boy perched on his toes at the edge, rocked back and forth with uncertainty, and after a long pause he took a huge leap and landed with a mighty splash. His dad clapped and lifted the boy onto his shoulders who bounced up and down with excitement.

My insides convulsed as an image came into my mind of Drew with Harry in his arms, bobbing him up and down in the shallow end. Then, as quickly, the memory disappeared and I was left with a thudding heart and a sickly feeling inside.

I took a breath, turned and walked to the far side of the pool where a strip of water had been cordoned off for lane swimmers. There were six or so swimmers gliding steadily up and down in a clockwise and orderly fashion. I sat down on the edge of the pool, dipped my legs into the water and wound my hair into a knot on top of my head and secured it with a hairband. I watched an elderly man swim towards me - his arms and legs moved rhythmically but painfully slowly through the crystal blue water. He held his chin above the surface and his eyes appeared half-shut. I slipped into the water which felt too cold and the skin on my arms pricked with goosebumps. I submerged my face and the water burbled in my ears. The music played - cushioned and distant.

My feet slid over the smooth porcelain tiles and I kicked off against the side. With an easy breaststroke I set off apace. As I approached the other end of the pool, I glanced up and saw a familiar figure walk out of the changing rooms and place his water bottle onto the bench. He scanned the length and breadth of the pool before he climbed down the steps into the shallow end.

I swam across, narrowly avoiding a man doing a violent butterfly crawl.

'Jakob. Fancy seeing you here.'

He stood up and the water ran from his shoulders and chest. 'A surprise to see you, too. Are you swimming alone?'

'I wanted to get out of the flat,' I explained.

He brushed his hair off his forehead and his brow furrowed. 'How are you doing, memory wise?'

I stood up and leaned against the side of the pool. 'Better each day. Moments when I feel dazed and especially when I wake up at night.'

He nodded, and I watched his eyes fall to my chest. I folded my arms and he lifted his gaze.

'Can you remember how to swim?' he asked, with all seriousness.

I swept a strand of wet hair off my face and his eyes slipped once more.

I felt uncomfortable - it was an unfamiliar feeling. I dipped down and the water covered my shoulders. 'Of course I can. I've managed to swim a length without swallowing any water or losing control of my limbs.' I tried to make light of his concern. 'Guess it's like riding a bike.'

He looked at me closely. 'It's just that with the accident... and the drownings...' he paused. 'It would be understandable if being in the water felt threatening.'

'I hadn't even thought of that,' I said, and rested my elbow against the side of the pool. I wanted to move the subject away from me. 'How are things at work?'

'A week from hell.' Then he quickly added, 'But nothing for you to worry about.'

'Why, what's happening?'

'Nothing I can't easily resolve.'

'I should come in to see how my projects are getting on. I know Hexprin is at a critical stage.'

He shook his head. 'Rest assured, I've taken over your role in that respect. All is well in hand.'

'I'll be seeing Dan tonight at a dinner party. He's the neighbour of a friend of mine.'

'Oh. Who's that?'

'Lizzie Arnold. We go back to primary school.'

Jakob tilted his head and narrowed his eyes. 'Do you feel up to partying?'

'I hope so,' I said. 'I've not been out at all, other than the funeral, which obviously doesn't count.' I gave an awkward laugh, and felt dreadful for making light of something I should be sobbing over.

'Shall we swim together?' he suggested.

'Wouldn't you rather go at your own pace?' I replied.

'I'll go steady and keep an eye on you.'

'Sure,' I said, although I'd rather have swum alone than adjust to anyone's pace.

We pushed off from the side and after only half a length Jakob had powered ahead. At the far end he did a swift turn and headed back towards me. Out of the corner of my eye I watched him flash a smile as he passed. I pretended not to see. How funny, I thought, given he'd suggested swimming at my pace. Despite the physical toll on my body from the accident, being in the water felt natural and my arms and legs surprisingly strong, especially since I hadn't swum in weeks. Jakob was going for it and he passed me again with a glance my way.

After only six lengths my limbs and lungs had to work harder, my heart pounded and my breaths grew laboured. The light and the water seemed to fold in and close around me. I heard a rushing sound as water ran into my ears. I paused, trod water and looked about me, swirling my arms and legs to turn on the spot. The surface of the water rippled, black and chilled, and I saw in the distance the dark shadow of a hillside that reached up into a sky thick with mist and clouds. There came a scream, a human cry, and I twisted around in the water. The cry came again - a child's high-pitched wail that seized and enshrouded me. His scream tore through me - it belonged to me as a part of my flesh.

My breath froze as all around me tipped on its side. The air seemed to press down on me and forced me below the surface. I sank, deeper and deeper. Water poured into my mouth and my nose, and my lungs felt tight and airless as I fell further still. The scream echoed around me and I spun full circle - desperate to catch a glimpse of the source. I saw nothing but blackened water. I stretched out my arms and clawed my way up, but my fingers only grappled at a void - an emptiness, just as some other force clasped my feet and dragged me down.

I opened my mouth and screamed as panic seized my heart and mind, but only strings of bubbles streamed from my mouth like black pearls.

Moments later, my head broke the surface of the water.

I coughed and sputtered the water from my throat and mouth, then gulped mouthfuls of chlorinated air into my lungs.

The space around me appeared clear and bright and the water became transparent once more.

Jakob trod water beside me - his hand gripping my upper arm. He looked panicked. 'Are you OK?' he asked. 'One moment you were swimming and the next you'd disappeared.'

'I need to get out,' I said, struggling for breath.

With Jakob's arm around me still, I swam with jerky strokes to the edge where a young lifeguard knelt down at the side. He took my hands and hauled me from the water.

I sat down with my head bent over and gradually my breathing eased and the terror subsided.

Another lifeguard, a girl, handed me a towel and I wiped my face and blew my nose. My hands and legs shook still but I felt safe.

I heard Jakob telling them how I'd recently been in an accident and was still recovering.

The young man said, 'Encourage her not to rush back.'

'Of course. We used to work together,' he said, hushed. 'I'll make sure she gets home safely.'

*'Used to work together.'* His words cut into me. Didn't we still?

I showered briefly and in the changing cubicle I sat on the bench with my towel wrapped loosely around me. I'd almost drowned and the bitter taste of chlorine still lingered in my throat and nose. I was a fool to think I could behave as though everything was normal. My new life was anything but normal.

31

I'd lost my husband and our only child - and by some extraordinary chance, I'd survived. And from what Jakob had said, it sounded like I'd lost my job. I sobbed quietly and my tears flowed. I didn't hold back, even when I heard a voice on the other side of the door ask quietly if I was OK.

'I'm fine,' I said, sounding quite the opposite.

I heard whispers but she and her companion moved away. When my tears finally let up and my body felt almost dry, I dressed and opened the cubicle door. A slim elderly woman, who combed her hair at the mirror, turned and looked my way. She smiled warmly.

I returned her smile to reassure her I was OK, then I towel dried and brushed my hair. I looked back at my reflection. My skin now had a healthy glow and to all outward appearances, I looked none the worse for my ordeal.

My memories of the boat accident were reemerging, but seemed chaotic and disorderly. I must brace myself for more unexpected revelations.

When I walked out of the changing room, I found Jakob leaning against the wall on the ramp that led to the exit.

He turned my way and slipped his phone into his jeans pocket. 'You gave me quite a fright in there.'

'I'm fine, really,' I said, and felt self-conscious and embarrassed for having created a drama.

'Let me buy you a coffee. It'll help with the shock.'

I nodded.

As we walked through the reception, the woman behind the counter looked up. 'Were the trunks the right size?'

Jakob appeared not to have heard her.

I stopped. 'Jakob?'

He turned to me.

I nodded to the reception desk. 'The lady asked you something.'

He turned to her. 'Yep. Perfect, thanks.'

'And,' the receptionist continued, 'I forgot to say there's a buy two towels and get one half price.' She had a sparkle in her eye, as women often did when they spoke to Jakob. He had that effect and I imagine he'd charmed her when he'd bought them earlier.

Jakob rolled his eyes and without looking at her said, 'I'm good, thanks.' He turned to me in explanation. 'I left my swim bag in the hall at home.'

'How inconvenient,' I replied. 'And costly.'

There was a coffee shop around the corner from the swimming pool that I'd been to many times, 'The Steam Room', appropriately named as it was next to the central train station. Inside it had a fascinating array of railway memorabilia and framed photographs dating back to Victorian times and through to modern day. Jakob headed off to order coffees and I found us a table in the window.

I sat down and Jakob came back to the table. 'I don't suppose you could sub me for the coffees? I forgot my wallet and spent all my cash on the damn swim gear.'

I pulled my debit card from my purse and gave it to him. 'Of course. It's contactless.'

'And my card's out of date and the bloody bank hasn't sent the new one. I've phoned twice this week to remind them,' he said, and gave an exasperated sigh.

'It's fine,' I reassured him. 'Hopefully they'll send it soon.'

When he returned from paying, he set our coffee cups down and sat beside me on the cushioned bench.

'How are you finding all this free time?'

'I don't see this as free time,' I said. 'Physically I'm OK and all the free time is giving me too much time to ruminate. I'd be better off if my mind was occupied. In fact, when I see Dan tonight I'm going to mention coming in on Monday. For a day or two to see how I get on.'

'Even after today? You might have drowned if I hadn't seen you.'

'Of course I wouldn't,' I said. 'I came to the surface myself.'

I took a sip of coffee. Maybe Jakob had a point about my not returning to work just yet.

'But I'm grateful to you.' I put my hand on his. 'I'll see what Dan thinks, too.'

Jakob turned his hand around and cupped my palm. 'Your job is waiting for you. But we can cope. Won't you rest some more - for me?'

'I'll bear it in mind. I promise,' I said.

We drank our coffee and chatted about work, though it seemed Jakob constantly tried to steer me away from the subject as if it might become too much for my delicate sensibilities.

As we stood up to leave I said, 'Oh I mustn't forget my debit card.'

'Of course.' He slipped it from his shirt pocket. 'Well remembered,' he said, with a wink.

I wondered how he'd managed to buy new swimming trunks and a towel without his wallet.

Although Jakob offered to walk me home, I insisted I felt well enough and we parted. I still needed to sort out my outfit for the dinner party and hadn't yet given it much thought. Hollywood - not exactly the sort of theme I could easily fulfil with my wardrobe.

When I got in, I rummaged through my coathangers and tried to envision a Hollywood star in a scenario where she might wear something underwhelmingly unglamorous or denim based. Plus, I only owned a few unexciting evening dresses, most of which would now look baggy and unflattering. Shoes - plenty to pick from. What I really needed was some inspiration.

I flipped open my laptop and googled Hollywood actresses and movies. Kate Winslet in The Titanic, Jennifer Lawrence in The Hunger Games - I'd loved the trilogy but there seemed little chance of rustling up a leather jumpsuit for tonight. Uma Thurman in Pulp Fiction. Her outfit looked fairly straightforward - cropped black trousers, gold pumps and a fitted white cotton shirt. Bold red lipstick. My hair didn't look a million miles off after my recent haircut and if I straightened it, plus I could avoid wearing high heels. Mia Wallace, yes, that would be fun. Stylish and tasteful - even with the drugs and violence. Also, appropriate, given my job in pharmaceuticals.

Perfect. I set to work on a pair of black trousers - I cut them down a few inches, stitched the hems and nipped them in at the waist. I found a wide collared white shirt, clean and ironed. As for gold pumps - I'd bought a pair a few years ago and had barely worn them.

I'd take along a bottle of decent red wine and some flowers for Lizzie.

# Chapter 8

I walked down Main Street and as I passed the old clock tower, it began to chime in the hour. Eight steady clangs. I'd always been a reliable timekeeper so it seemed I hadn't lost that capacity. I carried the wine in a gift bag and a bouquet of lilies and gypsophila. My pumps fell lightly upon the stone paving but my mind felt heavy with memories jumbled together with faces and events from the near and distant past. I glanced into the window of the Lava Java tearoom and caught sight of my reflection - tall, slim and walking with outward confidence. Appearances should never be trusted though, and I knew they could deceive the most astute amongst us. I considered myself to be reasonably extroverted, but I really didn't feel that way tonight.

As I passed, The Olde Inn on the Square, I felt a flutter of butterflies. This was the first time I'd been out socially. Hopefully, I'd be sitting next to Lizzie or Dan, which might put me at ease.

When I stepped up to the front door, music drifted through an open window and the scent from the rambling roses around the door hung in the air. I rang the doorbell and heard footsteps approach behind me.

'Glad we're not the only ones who are late.'

I turned around, surprised for the second time that day. 'Jakob! Hi Dan.'

'My date let me down last minute, and when Jakob phoned me about work, I thought I'd bring him along instead.'

'Only as friends though, eh pal?' Jakob joshed and punched Dan lightly on the arm.

'Never fear,' said Dan. 'Way too Alpha for my liking.'

I didn't believe a word of it. Jakob might be outright heterosexual, but I'd seen how Dan would watch him, in a quiet moment, and when he thought no one was looking.

'That's great,' I said and smiled. 'I feel less nervous already. Though I thought Lizzie said eight o'clock.'

'She said half seven to me,' replied Dan. 'But we're being fashionably late.'

The door opened and Lizzie beamed out at us with a flute of sparkling wine in hand.

'Wow! Look at you three. Did you coordinate outfits?'

Jakob and Dan wore black suits, black ties, hats and dark glasses.

'Not sure who they are, but I know who I am,' I said.

Lizzie held out her hand to Jakob. 'Pleased to meet you.'

He took her hand and gave a bow. 'Likewise, Lizzie.'

'Come on in. We're going to start with a guessing game.'

Heck, that might be a challenge for me, I thought.

We followed her down the hallway, lit up with a string of colourful lights, and into the living room, where it seemed we were the last to arrive.

'Friends, let me introduce you to Orla, my oldest and bestest school friend, and this is Dan and Jakob, who work with Orla. They deal drugs,' she said, and laughed. 'OK, more specifically, pharmaceuticals.'

She introduced the other guests, one or two whose faces I recognised, and then she poured us each a glass of sparkling wine. 'Are you OK to drink?' she asked me.

'The doctors didn't say I shouldn't, but I'll take it slowly.' I took a sip. 'Mmm. I've missed this.' I took another longer sip and the bubbles fizzed across my tongue.

'OK folks. It's guess the Hollywood star time,' announced Lizzie and she stepped into the middle of the room. She wore a silver flapper dress, a jeweled headband and diamante earrings. It suited her, but I hadn't a clue who she might be.

'Can only be the delicious Daisy from Great Gatsby,' called out Dan.

'Bravo! One point for you.' Lizzie did a few Charleston steps before she curtsied and stepped aside to allow the next Hollywood star to stand in.

Jakob draped an arm around Dan's shoulders and they stepped forwards.

'Too easy,' said a man in a top hat who held a shiny cane. 'Has to be The Blues Brothers.'

They grinned, took a bow and stepped aside.

36

The next couple - a man and a woman – looked obvious, even for me.

We all chorused, 'Batman and Robin.'

Robin was Batman's wife or girlfriend and she wore a short green catsuit, silver eye mask and the highest red stilettos I'd ever seen. Batman was built perfectly for the body-tight lycra top and trousers. They made a striking pair.

When Lizzie's friend, Hadrian, walked into the circle I felt emboldened and called out. 'Maximus from Gladiator?'

He grinned. 'Is it the gladiator sandals that give it away?'

'You look a bit like a young Russell Crowe, too,' I said.

'What size are the sandals?' Lizzie said. 'Only I'd quite like a pair.'

'Size 11, I'm afraid,' replied Hadrian, and bowed with a flourish and stepped back.

Jakob called out, 'Well remembered, Orla. Memory working OK tonight?'

I laughed, but when I caught one or two quizzical expressions from the other guests, I felt embarrassed. I turned and took a long slug from my glass.

When everyone else had taken their turn centre stage, I stepped forwards.

I looked at Dan who raised his eyebrows and gave a slight smile. Jakob looked me up and down and inclined his head to one side in thought.

After what felt like a minute's silence, during which I began to feel awkward that no one had attempted a guess, Lizzie said, 'Can you give us a clue? Maybe with a gesture or a phrase.'

'Should your hair be a touch shorter?' asked Dan.

'Yes, Dan - there's your clue.'

'Then I think you're Uma Thurman - aka Mia Wallace,' he said.

'I should be snorting cocaine and you'd have guessed straight away.'

'You do have a look of her, Orla,' said Lizzie. 'Equally as lovely and a figure to die for.'

I felt my cheeks redden and took another sip of fizzy wine.

'You're too kind, Lizzie, but I take my compliments where I can.'

'I'd better check nothing's burning, but here's the music selection.' She held out her phone to me. 'How about some Pulp Fiction?'

'I think I'd rather help you in the kitchen. If you don't mind?'

'Of course.' She handed her phone to Dan and I followed her down the hallway and into the kitchen.

'Sorry. I'm feeling a bit awkward.'

She pulled a bottle from the ice bucket and topped up my glass. 'You seem so confident. No one would think you're struggling.'

'I must be a better actor than I think,' I said, then added. 'I'm happy to be here, though.'

'What do you think of Hadrian?' she said.

'Hunky Russell Crowe, complete with sandals?'

'He's recently divorced and we've only been out a couple of times. I like him a lot.'

'He's handsome,' I said. 'Are you playing it cool?'

'Don't fear, I shan't be giving away how I feel. Not yet.'

'You deserve someone handsome and kind after what Brett did,' I said. 'Funny how I can remember all that. Last year, wasn't it?'

She nodded. 'At least he's stopped pestering me. As if I can just forgive and forget him sleeping around. Not a chance.'

'I'd never tolerate that either...' I felt a shudder of butterflies that stopped me speaking, but I couldn't form the connection in my mind.

Lizzie took my hand. 'I'm sorry for harping on about Hadrian.'

'Don't be. I'd hate anyone to feel awkward about their happiness. You deserve it.'

We reached out and hugged.

'This is why we've always been friends,' she said. 'You're special, Orla. Don't ever forget that.'

'I'm really not. I'm just trying to hide from what's beginning to feel all too real.'

And an unsettling feeling arose within me. A feeling that maybe there'd been an affair in my own marriage. Had it been Drew, or myself?

I heard a bubble of laughter and footsteps in the hallway and turned to see Jakob and Hadrian walk in.

'Do you have anything stronger than Prosecco?' asked Jakob. 'Whisky or gin, perhaps?'

'I've just the thing,' Lizzy said. She bent down and retrieved a bottle from the back of a cupboard. 'Jack Daniels any good?'

'Nice one,' Jakob said, and took the bottle from her. 'Any glasses?'

'In the cupboard over the sink,' replied Lizzie. She put her hand into an oven glove and opened the oven door.

I watched Jakob bring out four glasses and pour four measures. He picked up a glass and gave it to me.

Lizzy looked at me. 'Is that wise?'

'I'll only have the one,' I said, but placed it back on the worktop.

'Not for me,' she said. 'I can't stand the taste. A gift from last Christmas.'

Jakob took my glass of Prosecco and placed the whisky back in my hand. 'It's medicinal, remember?'

'OK, if you insist.' And I took a small sip. As far as whisky went, it wasn't bad.

Jakob and Hadrian returned to the living room with the bottle and I sat at the kitchen table as Lizzie tipped the potatoes and vegetables into serving dishes.

'Does it feel strange - coming out tonight?' she asked.

I thought for a moment. 'A bit. I'm struggling to clarify some things - the important things. I know Drew was my husband and Harry my baby, but I don't really feel it yet.'

'Maybe it's better that you don't rush those feelings.'

I took another sip of whisky. 'It does feel good to come out though and mix with other people.'

'I maybe shouldn't say this, but I get the impression Jakob's flirting with you,' she said, quietly. 'Which given what's happened, seems...I dunno, odd.'

'We're colleagues and he flirts with everyone,' I said.

'He seems like a full-on charmer. Handsome and gregarious too. I'm not suggesting you'd be interested.'

'I feel nothing like that towards him,' I said, knowing it was true. 'He blames himself for the accident. That's why he's being so kind.'

'It's good he's being supportive. You need your friends.'

'I do need friends,' I said, and my eyes pooled with tears. 'And I'm grateful.'

By the time we were onto the main course my mood had lifted and I was feeling more than a bit tipsy. Beside me, Dan cracked jokes and we all talked and laughed loudly.

'So, when would you like to return to work?' asked Dan, after he refilled my glass. 'Not that I'm rushing you.'

I felt myself frown. 'I thought you didn't want me back yet?'

'Whatever gave you that idea?'

'Something Jakob said.'

'Oh, don't worry about him,' Dan said in a whisper. 'He's being overprotective.'

'Then I'll be in on Monday,' I said and felt a rush of energy.

'Excellent. Can't wait to have you back on the team.'

Jakob who sat opposite piped up, 'Have you cleared it with your doctor?'

'You know I have. But I promise to go home if it gets too much.'

Jakob stroked his chin. 'You could start with half days?'

'Maybe,' I said, and turned to Dan. 'Could you send me the latest reports so I can get up to date with my projects?'

'Leave that to me,' said Jakob.

'Cheers mate,' replied Dan. 'All the latest on Hexprin, too. There's a lot going on there.'

'Of course,' I said. 'I'm keen to see what's happening.'

By the time we'd eaten Lizzie's tiramisu, I was giggling uncontrollably and felt well on my way to becoming sloshed.

When Lizzie placed a roulette tray of shots on the table, for a moment I considered making my excuses and heading home.

'Now anyone who doesn't want to play this, please sit it out,' Lizzie said and smiled across at me. 'Vodka, gin or lemonade. Eighteen glasses each with a number - two shots each. But you don't know what you're getting 'til we spin your number.'

Dan turned to me. 'I'll sit out with you if you prefer.'

'Think I'll give it a whirl. And who knows, I might get the lemonade.'

He leaned in as though to confide. 'You can always give your shots to me.'

Dan was being so sweet. He'd always been a thoughtful boss. Lizzie placed two randomly selected glasses in front of each of us.

'Come on, Orla,' she said. 'You spin the wheel first.'

I stood up, reached across the table and spun the wheel. I watched the ball roll round and round until it slowed and landed on red number thirteen.

Jakob jumped up and punched the air. 'Moi.' He hoisted his glass in a toast then knocked it back in one. 'Vodka. Huzzah!' He banged his glass back on the table and bowed to laughter and applause.

'My turn to spin,' he said, and with a flourish he spun the wheel so enthusiastically that the tray wobbled. 'Number one, black,' he announced, when the ball came to rest.

I looked at the two glasses in front of me. That was mine. Everyone looked my way as I bent down and sniffed the glass and grimaced. 'Gin.' I took a sip. 'Actually not bad.' I knocked it back and coughed as the alcohol hit the back of my throat.

We took turns to spin and drink until every glass had been emptied. The chatter grew louder and my tongue grew looser.

'So tell me, Dan and Jakob. What have I really been missing?'

'Oh, this and that,' said Jakob, with a one sided shoulder shrug. 'The usual day to day grind.'

Lizzie came round to me and bent her head to mine. 'That's enough work talk. Let's dance.'

'Me?' I said. 'You know I can't dance.'

'Don't tell porkies, Mia Wallace.' As she took my hand Chuck Berry's, *You Never Can Tell*, began to play.

Despite feeling pi-eyed and dizzy, I pushed back my chair. I pictured the scene from the movie, and we began to twist. It wasn't long before Dan stood up and joined us. He could really dance and a couple of the others got up too.

The track ended and Lizzie dashed over to her phone. 'How about, some Aretha Franklin?'

My head began to spin. 'God, I'm drunk,' I mumbled and headed out of the room to find the bathroom.

My face felt hot and I lurched my way up the stairs, tripped on the top step and landed on my hands and knees with a thwack. I stumbled to the bathroom in a drunken fog and closed the door. Then I leaned against the sink, jerked the tap and grasped the faucet. I bent down and pushed my mouth beneath the icy flow and drank thirstily. I straightened up and wiped my hand over my mouth then held both hands beneath the flow of the cold water, swaying where I stood. My face looked pink and blurred in the mirror. I was a fool to have come tonight and even more of a fool to have swallowed so much alcohol. It was too soon for this. My mouth filled with watery saliva, and my stomach rolled and heaved. I thrust my head over the toilet bowl without a moment to spare, and retched.

I should be at home with my baby. Not here getting legless. Harry needed me.

And I pictured him before me in vivid detail.

I could hear his cries when he awoke at night. All he wanted and needed was for me to scoop him out of his cot, take him in my arms and hold him close. To speak his name and to reassure him I was there for him. That I'd always be there. No matter what happened. To stroke his downy head and to kiss his pink cheeks. To wipe away his tears when he cried. To laugh with him when he giggled.

His face and round blue eyes filled my vision. My bonny boy. 'My baby.' I wept. 'What have I done to you?'

There came a knock at the door. 'Orla? You OK in there?'

I turned and faced the door, feeling disorientated for some moments, before remembering where I was.

Another knock. 'Orla?'

I opened the door.

Jakob stood there, his face full of concern.

'I know about Harry,' I slurred my words. 'What happened to him.'

He stepped in and closed the door behind him. 'We talked about it earlier, remember. It was a terrible accident.'

I leaned against the sink. 'I can see what happened.'

'What do you remember exactly?'

'I remember the boat going crazily fast.'

'The throttle jammed,' he said, blinking. 'I couldn't slow it down.'

Scenes from the boat flashed through my mind. The sense of panic as the boat hurtled across the water, the scream of the engine, the water splashing over the sides in the chaos. 'I tried to help turn it around,' I said. 'But what happened after that?'

Jakob stood closer and reached for my hand. 'As we neared the shore I knew it was too late to stop the boat and Drew jumped over the side with Harry. He did it to save Harry.'

I shook my head. 'But he didn't save Harry, or himself.'

'Because the water was bitterly cold. It was in Drew's autopsy.'

'Please. I must go home so I can remember more.'

'Of course.' He turned and opened the bathroom door. 'I'll help you.'

He took my hand again and led me down the stairs. My vision reeled and I couldn't focus on anything.

Lizzie was talking with Hadrian and Dan in the hallway.

'Orla,' she said. 'Are you OK?'

'I'm drunk and I'm sorry.' The words felt numb on my tongue.

'I'll walk her home and see she's safe,' said Jakob.

'Shall I come, too?' Dan offered.

'Let's not break up the party,' said Jakob. 'And I'll be back soon.'

As we turned to leave, Lizzie said, 'I'll call you tomorrow. Sleep it off and sweet dreams.'

# Chapter 9

When I awoke the following morning, my head throbbed as though it were clasped in a vice. I sat up and the blood pounded in my ears and white spots darted hither and thither before my eyes. I rubbed my palm against my forehead and tried to smooth away the pain. My tongue felt like sandpaper and I stood up carefully and headed to the bathroom for some painkillers. I popped two tablets into a glass of water and as they fizzed, I gulped from the cold tap to quench my thirst. As I sat and emptied my bladder, I drank back the dissolved tablets then returned to bed and curled back up beneath the covers.

I tried to replay the party in my mind. It had been fun up to a point and I'd enjoyed it more than I thought I would, especially the dressing up and dancing. That was until I'd stupidly drunk the whisky and those shots, which had dragged me well over the edge of sobriety. Throwing up at a party wasn't something I could recall doing in years. I felt deeply ashamed.

I drifted back to sleep and sometime later, my phone on the bedside table vibrated and woke me.

It was Sylvia. 'I'm outside. Are you up?'

I threw back the covers. 'I forgot you were coming. Is it eleven already?'

'Yep. I'm punctual as ever.'

I stood up and my head pounded. I pulled on my gown, padded to the front door and pressed the button for the main door to open. I heard the door slam and Sylvia's footsteps sounded on the stairs.

I opened the flat door. 'Sorry, I've only just woken up.'

'Ahh. The dinner party. How was it?'

'OK, I think. Until I threw up.'

Sylvia pursed her lips in a show of disapproval. 'Not sensible, but understandable.'

'I need coffee,' I said, and turned towards the kitchen. 'Want one?'

'Please. Black. I'm on a diet.'

'You don't need to diet, for goodness sake. You're anorexic as it is.'

'Says she who's lost about two stone and looks like a waif.' I laughed. 'Stop it. You're making my head hurt.'

'It's true. And I don't mind admitting I'm a teeny bit envious.' Then she quickly added, 'Not of anything else you've been through.'

Sylvia was like that. She'd say the most tactless things, but I never took it personally.

'Not sure if it was the alcohol loosening my mind, but last night I fully remembered Harry. For the first time, I really felt what he meant to me.' I sat down at the kitchen table. 'My darling boy.'

Sylvia sat beside me, took my hand and her eyes washed over with tears. 'We knew his memory would return.'

'I'm still blocking out the pain or I don't think I'd be capable of sitting here having this conversation.'

She said softly, 'What about Drew?'

'I'm so confused over him. I loved him, I know, but something feels out of place.'

'Take small steps, Orla.'

'I want to remember every detail. The accident. How it unfolded.'

Sylvia frowned. 'Are you sure that's wise?'

'I need to. So I can begin to accept and move on.'

'Of course.' She thought for a moment. 'Might it help if we go back to where it happened?'

I nodded. 'Please. Can we go today?'

'Do you feel well enough?'

'I need coffee, but my headache's easing, I think.'

I didn't feel like talking as Sylvia set off driving along the lanes to the far end of Ullswater. We listened to Lakeside radio - Classic Countdown, where listeners sent in their choices. Cerys Matthews was guest presenter.

'I love her accent,' Sylvia said, as we passed beneath the arch of a stone railway bridge.

'She makes the Welsh accent sound sexy,' I said, attempting one myself.

'Remember Mulder and Scully?'

'I feel a bit like Scully,' I said. 'Returning to the scene of the crime to hunt for clues.'

'Maybe see it more as a way to help remember Drew and Harry.'

'That's all I'm hoping for...' I said.

We pulled into a layby and set off walking along a pathway, laden with twigs and leaves. As we weaved between the trees and on down to the water's edge, the wind skirled through the branches overhead, and leaves, still green, fluttered down around us. We stood side by side on the bank and gazed out across the lake. Two hundred yards to our right lay the harbour wall that jutted twenty metres or so over the water. Two yachts and a handful of rowing boats were moored up and behind that, on the roadside, was the Lake Cafe and Long Gallery where local artists exhibited their work. I could picture the stunning panoramic view of the water and surrounding hillsides from that gallery window. We wandered along the pebbled shoreline and I recalled sitting in the boat beside Drew and Harry, with Jakob at the helm. But the images seemed murky as though I were viewing them through water. I remembered Harry being difficult about wearing his life jacket but relenting when I said that was the only way he'd be allowed on to the boat. At only two years, he'd understood my reasoning perfectly. I'd worn one too, but Drew and Jakob hadn't bothered.

Sylvia's phone rang. 'Rick.' She mouthed, 'sorry' and turned and walked away a few steps. 'I shan't be back for two hours at least. Can't you deal with it?' I heard her say.

The pebbles crunched beneath my feet as I walked along the shoreline until I came to some stepping stones that crossed a stream that flowed into the lake. I stepped carefully onto each stone, slippery with moss and almost submerged with pearly water, that twisted like glossy strands around the edges of the stones. On the far side of the stream there was a small bay with an outcrop of rocks. I scrambled onto the rocks and looked out over the water. I turned around and saw Sylvia, still on her phone. She threw her arm up with a wave. The rocks looked jagged but dry and easy enough to navigate in my trainers. On the far side lay a small stony inlet that narrowed into a gully between the trees and where another stream joined the lake. On the other side of the stream a flash of colour caught my eye - something that hung from a branch a few feet above the water. I leaped down onto the pebbles and tried to make out what the item could be. Turquoise blue. An item of clothing perhaps, although it appeared to have straps attached.

I caught my breath and my heart beat faster as I jumped off the rock, walked into the inlet and made my way to the far side. The colour and shape of the object seemed familiar, but it couldn't possibly be what I imagined it to be.

The item hung too far out for me to stretch my arms and reach and I stepped amongst the trees. I found a long stick, not too heavy, and stood at the water's edge. I held it out. The water lapped, and cold water seeped into my trainers and socks. I prodded the material and straps with the stick, but it was caught up around the branch and wouldn't come free. One of the branches looked low and sturdy enough and I found a couple of decent footholds on the trunk and clambered up. I stepped onto the branch, straddled it, then used my hands to steady myself and inched my way along its length. I heard the squawks of birds and I watched a flock of silvery wings as they rose up and drifted above the lake. It seemed as though they were calling me, urging me on.

The nearer I got to the blue item, the more convinced I became. One way or another, I needed to know if I was right.

Overhead the trees tossed in the wind and the branch beneath me swayed and creaked but I remained determinedly steady. When I was no more than two feet away, I leaned over and hugged the branch. Carefully, I raised my arm, gripped a strap and pulled. Now, I could see a label on the inside of the carrier and the initials in black marker pen - faded but unmistakable; H.S. We'd had it in the boat on the day of the accident. Seeing it there, close enough to touch, I felt it was the most important object in the world for me to hold in my hands. Nothing could bring Harry back to me, but I had to retrieve this. Perhaps this meant his little body was close by? I felt the bile rise in my throat. I tugged and pulled at the knot until one of the straps came free. I kept working at the knot, by easing and teasing it. Six or so feet below, the surface of the water purled inky and deep in the

47

shadow of the trees and overhead the wind babbled through the leaves - it sounded to me like the whisperings of the dead.

The wind rushed over me and a scream rent the air - it seemed to build in strength and grew louder in my ears. Then just as quickly, the wind dropped and the air fell to silence once more. Desperate now, I tugged and pulled the straps with all my strength but as it finally came free, the carrier slipped from my fingers and dropped into the water. Instinctually, I slipped sideways and plunged into the water. I kicked my legs, bobbed to the surface and searched around for the carrier. I saw only ripples across the surface and realised it had already sunk.

I dipped beneath and looked for a glimpse of turquoise. But the water appeared too black to see more than a few inches in front of me.

My clothes filled with water and dragged me down. I sank deeper until my feet touched the lake floor.

I pushed off the bottom and swam upwards. Through the gloom I saw daylight and when my face emerged, I gasped for air and trod water. I turned full circle, but the carrier was nowhere to be seen.

'Orla. Orla!' I heard Sylvia scream.

I watched as she sprinted across the stony inlet.

'Harry's carrier,' I called and swam further out.

I took a breath and dived again. The smooth and silent water surrounded me and for a moment I remained suspended in the near-black void until the chill seized my limbs and a lack of air crushed my lungs. I plunged deeper until my hands touched the stones on the bed of the lake. I grappled around amongst weeds and slime covered rocks. I could see nothing amongst the gloom, then growing hungry for air, I bent my knees and launched myself back up to the surface. The sound of water roared in my ears and I coughed and gasped for air.

I heard splashes and Sylvia swam towards me. She grabbed my sleeve. 'There's nothing here.'

With shaking hands I wiped the water from my eyes. 'I had it in my hands.' I began to sob. 'Harry was here.'

Sylvia pulled on my arm. 'Please.'

I relented and swam the few yards back to the shore.

Exhausted, freezing and breathless, I lay back on the stones and wept my frustration. My whole body shook as a chill gripped my skin.

Sylvia grabbed my hands. 'Stand up, Orla.' We must get to the car or we'll die of hypothermia.

'But Harry…'

'No, Orla.'

I saw the pleading in her eyes.

'There's nothing here,' she cried.

Back in the car, Sylvia reached for a blanket on the rear seat and switched on the engine. 'Take off your clothes.' She tugged at her jumper and pulled it over her head then threw it into the back. 'Come on!' She reached across and unzipped my fleece.

I turned to her. 'Don't you understand? It was Harry's baby carrier. His initials that I wrote.' My teeth clattered together and I could barely speak as I removed my sopping wet clothes.

Sylvia reached into the footwell for my sodden trainers and clothes and dropped them into the back. The air in the car warmed us, but we still shuddered with cold. We opened out the blanket, huddled together and drew it up to our chins.

I heard a vehicle approaching and moments later a silver van pulled into the layby in front of us.

'Shit,' said Sylvia. 'Hope they're not staying.'

'I don't care. It was Harry's.'

'Let's try to get warm. I think I've got a jacket in the boot. I'll get it once they've buggered off.'

She looked into my eyes. 'I thought you were drowning.' Her eyes were wet with tears. 'I couldn't bear to lose you, too.'

And the look of fear in her eyes made me realise what a fool I'd been. Even if it had been Harry's carrier, which I was convinced of, it didn't mean he was close by. The carrier could have floated away after the boat crashed. We hadn't even put Harry in it that day.

As we shivered together beneath the blanket, I looked into her eyes. 'I'm so sorry.'

The doors of the van swung open and three men clambered out.

'Maybe they're fishermen,' I said, and I watched two of them light up cigarettes, as the third, a lanky youth, walked round to the back of the van. He swung open the back doors, sat on the edge and pulled his phone from his jacket pocket.

The van was rammed full of boxes and rolls of carpet.

Sylvia sank lower in her seat. 'Oh bugger. Keep down.'

I followed her cue and hunched down.

'Rotten timing,' I whispered. 'Wish they'd get lost.'

'Probably stopped for a fag and phone break.'

'They'll be lucky to get any reception round here,' I replied.

The youth peered across then stood up to get a better look at us. He caught my eye and I scowled back at him.

He walked round to the other men. He said a few words and all three of them turned our way. Together, they casually crossed the few yards to our car. The two older men walked either side and the youth leaned his hands on the bonnet and gawked at us.

'Let's drive and risk them seeing us naked,' I said.

'I agree,' said Sylvia, and she lowered the blanket and tucked it under her armpits, to free her arms.

'Lock the doors, Sylvia.' I said, urgently.

But as I spoke the two older men stepped up and opened our doors. The man on my side, heavily built and almost bald, leaned in. 'Mind if we join your party?'

I reached for the door handle and the blanket slipped down.

His eyeballs bulged. 'Whoa! Look at the mamas on this one, lads.' He ogled and reached in to touch my breast. His breath reeked of stale alcohol.

I smacked his arm away and pulled the blanket back up. 'Get the fuck off me.'

I turned to Sylvia. 'Drive! Go!'

But she didn't move and shook uncontrollably.

I jerked her arm. 'Drive, Sylvia.'

The man on her side reached down, turned off the engine and pulled out the keys. 'Not so fast, girls.' He tucked the keys into his jacket pocket.

'And what's your name, pretty one?' The bald man at my door leaned in again. 'You been skinny dipping?'

'Get lost. If you go we won't prosecute you.'

'Nah. I want to see what you and your friend were up to. Give us a show, then we might go.'

'She's my sister. I fell in the water and she helped me out.'

'Sisters?' He slid his thick tongue between his lips. 'Even better! We got lesbos here, lads. And my old man's straining to get out.' He rubbed grotesquely at his crotch.

The man beside me tore the blanket from us, drew it to his face, sniffed it and cast it aside. 'Shall we take them for a romantic stroll in the woods - show them what a real man can do?' He called across to the others then snorted with laughter. 'We'll even bring your blanket to lie on. Make it all cosy and romantic.'

My tongue felt rubbery and dry in my mouth and my limbs felt weak.

He leaned into the car, grabbed hold of my arm and dragged me out. I tripped and he yanked me back up. 'Light as a feather, this one. Skin like fuckin' velvet.'

I saw them pull Sylvia from the car, then holding one arm each, they half carried her towards the trees.

'Sylvia!' I shouted and caught her eye but she seemed to have fallen into a catatonic state. Her eyelids drooped, her wet hair stuck to her face and her feet trailed uselessly behind her.

I knew what they wanted and I still had the presence of mind to look for an escape route, but one that must save Sylvia too. They hauled us down the same path we'd used, as I kicked, scratched and screamed to free myself. He grabbed both my arms and pulled them behind my back. I kicked out, but the youth came over to help him. Together, they wrenched my arms and dragged me along backwards. Before we reached the shore they stopped and looked about.

'This way,' the bald man called and they dragged me to a narrower path that led amongst a thicket of trees.

I wrestled to free my limbs, but they felt feeble and the chill sapped my energy. 'Sylvia!'

Her eyes were almost closed and the man lifted her by her arms. She whimpered, but her words made no sense.

I couldn't catch my breath as panic grew within me. Three men. Two of us. They were fully clothed. We were naked. We were in trouble and I couldn't see a way out.

Trees surrounded us, shielded us, and when I turned my head, I saw we were in a dip and neither the road nor the lake were visible. The younger man spread the blanket and the other dropped Sylvia onto it and she curled into the foetal position. Moaning, she covered her face. The young man grabbed Sylvia, turned her onto her back then forced her arms and legs straight.

The bald man shoved me to the ground beside her.

Then he unzipped his jacket and unbuckled the belt of his trousers.

Adrenaline fired through me - I rolled over, sprang up and reached for Sylvia's hand. 'Get up, Sylvia!'

'Shut up,' the bald man spat. He booted me in the hip and I stumbled over Sylvia and collapsed. The next moment he'd grabbed my arms and swung me roughly onto my back, then he held my wrists behind my head and pinned me to the floor - his colossal weight upon them.

When I caught the look of hate and violence in his eyes, I felt a rage burn inside of me.

I howled and the sound seemed to come from elsewhere - from an animal amongst the trees. I raised my knees and kicked my legs with every ounce of fury and strength I possessed. But the man laid his massive bulk upon me and I felt his stinking breath hot upon my neck whilst he wrestled my legs open with his hand and knees. I turned my head to Sylvia who lay catatonic and silent as the youth knelt between her legs and tugged down his pants to expose his swollen member.

I thrashed my legs again, gathered a mouthful of saliva and spat in his face.

'Bitch!' He slapped my face and my world turned white.

The next moment, a gunshot cracked the air.

Everything fell still and a ringing sound pierced my ears.

A man's voice bellowed. 'Stand away from the women.'

The man's beard brushed my face, but he knelt up and looked around.

I pulled my leg up between his thighs and kicked him full force. I hit my target.

He growled and toppled sideways - clutching at his groin.

I scrambled up and scanned the trees. The two other men had already backed away from Sylvia, pulled up their trousers and looked about them.

'Stand away, or I will shoot.' Jakob stepped into the clearing and aimed the gun from one man to the next. 'My aim is sharp and I'll blast you to fucking pieces.'

I reached for Sylvia's hands and pulled her to standing. I grabbed the blanket, draped it around her shoulders and led her out of the clearing and back along the path to the car. As soon as I'd sat her in the front passenger seat and I'd clambered into the driver's seat, I locked all the doors.

Sylvia stared ahead and sobbed in great heaving movements.

'It's OK. We're safe,' I said, breathing hard and looking back to see if any of the men returned.

'He has the keys,' she stuttered.

'Doesn't matter,' I said. 'They can't get to us now.' I shivered uncontrollably and I reached into the back and grabbed our wet clothes. 'Put these on. Quickly.'

As I struggled into my wet fleece and jeans, I watched Jakob follow behind the three men with his shotgun aimed at their backs. I heard him speak but couldn't distinguish his words. The men didn't appear to be resisting or talking back.

I opened the door a crack and shouted. 'The one in the red shirt has our keys.'

Jakob shouted to him. 'Give me the car keys. Now.'

The man dug into his jacket pocket and threw them at Jakob's feet.

Without taking his eyes or the gun off the men he picked them up, walked backwards to the car window and without looking my way, held the keys out to me.

I grabbed them and slammed the door.

Jakob shouted. 'Drive! I'll call you.'

I hesitated. Should we stay to help him?

'Orla,' Sylvia pleaded. 'Let's go.'

And I knew she was right.

I turned the key, revved the engine and glanced back at Jakob before I pulled away with a skid and a squeal of tyres on the gravel. I looked in the rearview mirror and caught sight of Jakob.

'We must call the police,' I said, as we careered around a corner and just missed a pheasant in the road. I spotted a layby ahead and slowed down. My head swarmed and I gripped the wheel.

53

'What if they turn on Jakob - get hold of his gun?' I said.

'We cannot go back.' Sylvia picked her phone from her jeans pocket. 'Useless.'

'Thank God I left mine in here.' I leaned over Sylvia and opened the glove box.

When I got through to the police, they told me they'd been alerted and officers were on their way. 'Jakob's already phoned them.'

'Does he live near here?' Sylvia asked quietly.

'Not far. But what a coincidence he found us.'

'Does he hunt for game?'

'I'll ask him. Bloody hell, I'll hug him. I'll forever be indebted to him.'

'Me too,' Sylvia said. 'That was too close…' her voice trailed off.

'I should never have climbed that tree. And what a fool to fall in.'

'Stop,' she said. 'You thought you saw something of Harry's. I'd have done the same if it was Amy's.'

'I did see it,' I said.

'Did he... hurt you?' Sylvia asked, and her eyes searched mine.

'He got close.' I shook my head, 'My arms and legs ache and I know I'll be bruised. But thank God, not that.'

I looked at myself in the rearview mirror. My cheeks were smeared with dirt and I had leaves stuck in my hair. 'How close did they get to you?'

'I passed out at some point. But like you, Jakob spared me that.'

'What will Rick do?' I asked.

'What would any husband want to do?'

'At least you have him to talk to.'

'You have me. And as Jakob was there -'

My ears caught the blare of sirens in the distance, which grew louder as they approached. Moments later, a police car screamed past us, lights flashing and siren screaming.

I revved the engine. 'Let's go.'

54

# Chapter 10

The alarm went off at six and I rolled over to turn it off. All that had happened the previous day flooded through my mind and for a moment I felt unsure whether to go into work as planned.

I texted Sylvia. 'Are you OK? I'll call you tonight.' I knew after talking to her last night she wouldn't be working today.

But if I delayed going in today, I knew returning could become an even greater hurdle, and work was one of the only constants I had left. I refused to allow myself to be beaten down. My nervous breakdown would have to wait.

I bathed, then ignoring my bruises and aching muscles, dressed in the clothes I'd hung out the previous night - a maroon pencil skirt that accentuated my slim hips and a long sleeved, cream silk blouse that didn't over embellish my bust. I blow dried my hair and fastened it into a high ponytail. Then I dug around at the bottom of the wardrobe and picked out a pair of black shoes with a modest heel that buckled up securely. When I stood in front of the full-length mirror, I looked far more prepared than I felt, mentally. I must feign confidence and fitness to convince Jakob I was ready to return full time. Any sign of vulnerability and I knew he'd grow concerned.

Yesterday, after Sylvia and I had given our statements to the police, Rick, Sylvia's husband had arrived and marched into the flat - his nerves on high alert and his cheeks pink and glistening with sweat.

He'd spent several minutes grilling the female police officer to find out exactly what was happening to the men. Though both Sylvia and I could have told him this. When the officers finally left he questioned us over every minute detail.

He looked at me and shook his head. 'Orla. You've been through so much but you need to sit back now and look after yourself. Not go searching for imaginary clues and almost killing yourself and my wife in the process.' He continued unrelenting. 'What do you think it looked like to those yobs seeing two naked women in a car in a quiet layby? It's hardly surprising they wanted to get involved.'

I opened my mouth to retaliate, but held back. Rick had already made up his mind that the whole thing was my fault. And who was I to argue with him? He was worried about Sylvia and had every right to be.

'I'm sorry.' I turned to Sylvia and felt my throat constrict again. 'I'm so sorry for putting you through hell. I'm sorry too that there are revolting men about who think it's OK to rape a woman because she's naked and vulnerable.'

'It's OK,' said Sylvia, with a sob in her throat. 'We're OK. That's all that matters. I want you to watch some feel good movies, go to a spa, drink coffee with a friend. But don't go back to work yet.'

I didn't dare tell her I'd already made up my mind about that.

Sylvia left wearing one of my long skirts and a jumper. Rick put a protective arm around her as they walked down the stairs.

At the bottom step, Sylvia turned around. 'Please rest and look after yourself.'

I nodded and forced a smile. 'I will.'

Rick looked up at me and his lips set in a hard line as he turned and led Sylvia to the front door.

The roads seemed unusually quiet as I drove the thirteen miles to Penrith between steep sided fells and woodland and open stretches of water. I turned to the news on Radio Four, which was my habit to do in the car each morning. The presenter was interviewing the prime minister - the Brexit deal was still an ongoing debate, as it had been prior to my accident. Some things never changed, and it felt strangely consolatory in its familiarity to me. This was followed by a reporter talking from China about a new strain of flu virus that was causing increasing concern. There was a suggestion that the source of the virus had originated in the wet meat markets where live wild animals were slaughtered alongside fresh fish and other meat produce. BioMedica had been one of many labs leading the research into a vaccine for the SARS virus back in 2009, but that was before my time with the company.

At the entrance to the BioMedica compound I waved my ID card at the barrier sensor. But the barrier didn't rise. I presented the card again. I glanced in my rearview mirror. A couple of cars had pulled up behind me. The security guard in the kiosk opened his door and walked over. He wasn't someone I recognised.

'Who are you here to see, Madam?'

'Hi, I'm Orla Safian, Head of Marketing here. I've been on leave for a few weeks and this is my first day back.'

'Let me ring through.' He leaned down to his walkie talkie and turned away as he spoke into it.

He returned and bent down at my window. 'No problem.'

The barrier lifted and he waved me through.

Stopped by security - not the best of starts.

My stomach fluttered with nerves as I walked up the stairs and through the doors into the open plan office. I looked around and all appeared reassuringly familiar. The same overgrown yucca plant stood outside my office door and another more modest in size outside the kitchen further along the corridor. Most of the desks were still empty - I'd arrived early to avoid walking into a bustling office and having to face everyone at once.

I spotted a woman I knew instantly with her glossy blond hair like a white frame around her elfin features.

She looked up, broke into a smile and walked over. 'Orla.'

'Kim.' I felt relieved to see a friendly face. 'How are you?'

'All the better for seeing you,' she said.

'You were at the funeral, weren't you?' I said. 'I'm sorry I didn't talk.'

'Doesn't matter.' She touched my arm. 'I'm only pleased to see you here. You know, you look pretty well, considering.'

'Which is weird, I know,' I said. 'I've missed being here.'

'First thing's first. Let's make you a coffee. We have a new machine which I suggested. And productivity has been equivalent to the increased caffeine intake.'

'Take me there,' I said.

In the kitchen, Kim turned to me. 'Do you feel up to being back?'

'I need work to occupy my mind,' I replied. 'Has your workload been crazy?'

She turned on the machine. 'You know we have Melanie - your stand in?'

'No. Really?' I said, surprised. 'Jakob gave me the impression he'd taken over my role in the projects - with your help.'

Kim worked as our Marketing Administrator but with her knowledge and expertise she could have covered my role for a period.

She turned back to me. 'Melanie started the week after the accident.' She came closer and said quietly. 'Between us, but don't repeat this, she's rather a cold fish towards women, so I for one am thrilled to have you back.'

'I hope she's been told I'm returning,' I said, with a grimace.

'I hope so, too. Jakob has her wrapped around his finger. She fawns over his every suggestion.'

'That doesn't sound good.'

'Not like you,' she said, with a wink.

'I suppose she is new and Jakob can be charming and persuasive.'

'Yes, but that isn't how cross teams should work, is it?'

I could sense Kim's unease and waited for her to elaborate. But she turned back to the coffee machine.

I didn't want to say anything against Jakob. Yesterday, he'd saved mine and Sylvia's lives. Who knew what state we'd be in had he not intervened.

'Jakob's a decent man at heart,' I said.

Kim snorted with derision. 'I'm glad you think so.'

Kim's attitude towards Jakob concerned me - I couldn't remember her having any issues with him previously, although she was outspoken, which I respected.

'Well, I for one am thrilled to see you back,' she continued. 'I've been worried about you and I'm so relieved that you're still you and you're surviving despite everything.' She spoke quickly and her eyes glistened. 'Sorry. It's been so different here without you.' She reached into the cupboard for some cups and set them on the worktop. 'Why don't you go and settle into your office. I'll bring these through and fill you in where I can.'

'Thank you. Can I have it black?'

'Sure,' she said. 'That's new.'

'I seem to have changed preferences in a few things.'

I walked along the corridor to my office - a path I'd walked so many times that it felt as familiar today as it had always been. I stood in front of my door and saw moving shadows through the glass. I turned the handle and walked in.

Jakob looked up, surprised.

A woman sat at my desk. The first thing I noticed was how pretty she was and her long rope of golden hair plaited to one side. She looked across at me through round, heavily made up eyes.

'Orla.' Jakob pushed back his chair, walked up to me and touched my arm. 'I didn't think you'd be coming in.' He grimaced, and rubbed the side of his nose. 'After yesterday.'

'I need to get back to normal,' I said, and turned to Melanie.

'This is Melanie,' said Jakob. 'Melanie, this is Orla.'

Melanie stood up and stretched out a hand with perfectly pink-varnished nails. I took her hand and she gave a closed lipped smile.

'It's good to meet you,' I said, and returned what I hoped to be a convincing smile.

Her eyelids fluttered. 'Likewise, Orla.'

I got the immediate impression that she wasn't in the least pleased to meet me.

'Mel has done a sterling job in your absence,' said Jakob.

I swallowed - already feeling like an intruder. The phone on my desk rang. I moved to answer it, but Melanie was quick to lift the receiver.

'Good morning, Mel speaking.' She listened then lifted her eyes to me.

She pursed her lips. 'It's for you.'

I took the phone from her.

It was Dan.

'I saw you come in. I wanted to say I have a meeting, but I'll be in to see you soon.'

'Great. I've met Melanie. Mel,' I said, and waited to hear his response.

Dan remained silent for a moment then said, 'OK. Leave that with me. Join her for now and she can share where she is with ongoing projects. Though hopefully you'll have had a bit of time to read the emails.'

'Yes, I have. I'll see you shortly.'

I sensed Dan felt awkward about Melanie being here - and so he should. They could at least have mentioned her on Saturday night. But, I supposed it might be useful for her to handover where things were at.

Kim walked in with the drinks, smiled my way and placed them on the coffee table by the window. Kim and I sat at the table and Jakob and Melanie pulled up chairs to join us.

Kim held out a file to Melanie. 'You said this needed submitting by lunchtime.'

Without a thank you, Melanie took the file, laid it on her lap and placed her hands firmly on top.

'Which report's that?' I said, immediately sensing Melanie's protective stance.

Melanie bit her lip and her eyes darted to Jakob.

Kim spoke. 'It's the launch article for...'

She was interrupted by Jakob. 'As time is pressing, let's leave this one for Mel to complete.'

I felt like an uninvited guest – my breath came faster and my heart thudded in my chest. I reached for my coffee, took a sip, and with a measure of irritation in my voice, said, 'At least the coffee's an improvement.' I placed my cup down, reached into my briefcase and pulled out my electronic notepad. 'I'll take a few notes. Oh, and I must talk to Dan about my emails. I know they were paused with good intention and you're sending through a few, but I do need to see everything I've missed.'

For the next twenty minutes or so, Kim ran through the two main projects I'd been working on prior to the accident.

The first drug was a new treatment for epilepsy containing a mild strain of cannabis. The years of testing and drug trials had been completed and we were taking the product to market. I paged through the latest report and although my memory of the drug wasn't as sharp as it should be, I knew all I needed to do was read up on the trial documents.

The second drug, Hexprin, Kim knew less about progress and it seemed Jakob and Melanie had taken full control of that. From the few emails I'd read I knew it was at a critical stage and in one of the last emails I'd sent to Jakob before the accident, I'd expressed concern that it wasn't ready to be marketed. But, I couldn't recall why. And neither could I find any of the reports covering the trials on our intranet.

Kim stood up. 'I'll leave you in Jakob's capable hands,' she said to me. 'Shall we have lunch - one o'clock?'

'Perfect,' I said, and felt incredibly grateful for her warmth and kindness.

Kim closed the door behind her.

'So, Hexprin?' I said, to Melanie.

'I've got the Hexprin reports on my laptop,' she said, but she avoided my eye as she stood up and returned to sit at my desk. She didn't look like she'd be giving up the driving seat anytime soon. I got up and sat down on the other side of the desk. Jakob joined me.

It felt like we were playing musical chairs and I was about to lose mine.

Melanie opened her laptop and looked at her screen. She seemed reluctant to speak and I was already sensing they were holding back on something. If they weren't, Kim would be well up to speed on the project.

'I realise your memories might be blurred, as a result of your head injury,' began Jakob, 'but Melanie has written the Hexprin marketing strategy. Myself and Dan have approved it and so we begin the roll out as of this week.'

Melanie looked up through thick lashes, which fluttered for a few moments. 'Thank you, Jakob.' Then she looked across to me. 'I hope you'll appreciate what I've come up with.'

'I hope so, too. Thank you, Melanie. I do appreciate your standing in but as I'm the one who'll be implementing the strategy, I must take a look at it before I can properly comment.'

'Ahh,' said Jakob, slipping his hands into his trouser pockets. 'I've agreed with Dan that as you're convalescing, Melanie will remain in post. Taking the lead alongside you to implement this particular strategy.'

I felt the heat rise through me and my neck prickled with sweat. This was the last thing I'd expected today.

'OK,' I said slowly, but my heart shuddered. 'Let me talk to Dan.' I pushed back my chair and stood up. 'I feel perfectly fit and my memory is improving each day. I'm ready to take on my full role again.'

'I'm only trying to help you out,' said Melanie, and folded her arms.

'I realise that,' I said. 'But it isn't that straightforward.'

I turned and left the office, closed the door behind me and headed down the corridor to see if Dan was free yet. I felt dangerously close to tears but that would only weaken my position. Melanie shouldn't even be here now and sitting at my bloody desk. I felt frustrated and angry. OK, maybe she should stay to do a handover for a day or two, but this was my job, my career, and it was obvious I was being pushed aside on the most important and potentially lucrative project BioMedica had worked on since I'd started here.

I'd talk to Dan to find out his thoughts and then I'd spend the next few hours reading all the data, reports and emails exchanged in my absence. And it wouldn't hurt to go through all the previous trial results. There was something niggling in the back of my mind - something of an obstacle in the project. But damn if I could recall it.

I peeped through the blinds into Dan's office. He was talking intently to a man sitting opposite him. I knew his face, but I couldn't remember where from. I didn't want to return to my office yet, and as I was about to head to the cloakroom, Dan looked up and saw me waiting. He beckoned me in.

'Sorry, I didn't want to interrupt you,' I said, and closed the door behind me.

'Not at all, Orla. We're about done. You remember, Adam, head of research in our Manchester Lab?'

'Of course.' I held out my hand. 'I haven't seen you for a while.'

When I'd first visited our Manchester branch, Adam had given me and Jakob a tour of the labs.

Adam looked momentarily confused. 'You don't recall our meeting early July? You wanted to talk about some drug trials,' he asked, tentatively.

But I couldn't recall any such meeting with him. 'Oh, yes.' I felt my face burn.

'It's OK, Orla. Adam knows about your head injury.'

'I'm remembering most things now but I appreciate the prompt.' And already our meeting was coming back to me. Back then I'd been concerned about some adverse reactions in the Hexprin drug trial.

Dan got up, pulled out a chair for me and I sat down.

'Since we spoke last,' Adam said to me, 'we've conducted a further full trial and the results were so positive that Hexprin has been cleared for public use.'

'So I hear. Melanie has already written the strategy.' I looked at Dan. 'And you've approved it?'

'You must read it,' he said. 'It's excellent. And she's written the articles to be published in the medical journals and to mail out to leading experts in this field.'

'Gosh,' I said, feeling more mean spirited and insecure by the second. 'I'd rather take it on myself though. I've been working on it for two years and I'd already drafted a strategy.'

'OK. Then might I suggest rather than Mel managing it alone, you work on it together?'

'Does it need two of us though? And think of the costs of employing two of me.'

'I understand your concern, but I think Mel is value for money and I don't want you placed under any unnecessary pressure yet. Let's keep her on and reassess in a month.' He rubbed his hand against the weft of his stubble and looked at Adam who nodded his agreement. 'And what's more, Hexprin is too crucial to us as a business not to get this right and on time.'

I felt defeated as I faced them while they awaited my reaction. I took a deep breath and swallowed the words I wanted to say. They'd made up their minds. Anything negative I said now would only make me sound emotional or unstable.

'Right,' I said. 'I'll go and talk to her.'

'Thanks, Orla,' said Dan. 'You'll like her. She's down to earth and super smart. Oxford graduate, I understand.'

I headed back to my office feeling sick and shaken. I'd have to make things work with Melanie and hopefully she'd be cooperative. They were still talking in my office - heads close together.

I walked in and stood in front of my desk. 'I've spoken to Dan and there's been a slight change of plan.'

'Oh?' Melanie blinked rapidly.

'Yes, we've agreed that I will manage the Hexprin roll out with you, Melanie. It's at a crucial step and I know the full history better than anyone.'

Jakob aimed glass-cutting eyes at mine. 'But do you?'

'It'll all come back to me once I've reread the background. It's a shame I wasn't included in the recent emails. Would you mind forwarding them now?' I looked from Jakob to Melanie.

'Yeah, sure,' said Jakob.

Melanie nodded her agreement but with discernible reluctance.

'I hope you don't mind Melanie, but as this is my office, you'll have to find somewhere else to work.' I looked at Jakob. 'Any spare offices right now? Or perhaps she could work opposite Kim? Lisa's still on maternity.'

Melanie puckered her lips and flicked her plait off her shoulder. She looked steely-eyed at Jakob who shifted uncomfortably in his seat. But he didn't speak or contradict me.

'Fine.' Melanie flipped her laptop shut, pushed her chair back and gathered up her handbag. And without another word she frowned at Jakob before leaving the office.

'Oops,' I said. 'Guess Mel doesn't like my returning. She did know the position was temporary, I take it?'

Jakob, picked an imaginary speck off his shirt sleeve. 'Of course.'

'How long is her contract for?'

Jakob hesitated. 'We weren't sure so we suggested three to six months.'

'That long? And it's only been seven weeks. That's awkward,' I said, and sat down at my desk feeling a small sense of triumph.

'With the launch, the extra support will be invaluable. Give her a chance. I'm sure you'll find her a tremendous help.'

'Of course. As long as she realises I've been working on this long before she arrived. I'll not be pushed aside, Jakob. I've been through enough without having to come back and wrangle over my job. I'll see how she responds to our working together and review the Hexprin situation with you next Monday?'

'Sure. But it was Dan who wanted her to stay, not me. He was concerned about your capacity,' he paused. 'And capability.'

My capability! Was Jakob deliberately trying to wind me up? I took some slow breaths and tried to hold onto my composure.

The moment Jakob left my office I sat down at my desk and logged into my emails. Either Dan or Jakob were being dishonest. Or maybe both genuinely distrusted my ability. I glanced at my watch. Only nine-thirty and I already felt frazzled and emotionally drained. Nevertheless, I had to keep up the positive facade or risk being sidelined for good. I'd heard about these things happening and could never understand how employers and bosses could be so focused on their business that they lost sight of the people who'd built it up for them. How bloody naive of me. Take any time off work at your peril, never mind the small matter of losing a husband and a child and suffering injury and memory loss.

I fired off an email to remind Jakob, Dan and Melanie to forward to me any documents or correspondence for Hexprin. I'd have to trust them to be thorough and fast.

My phone vibrated on the table.

A text from Sylvia. *'Are you at work? I've been ringing your home phone.'*

I sent my reply. *'I am, but I feel fine.'*

Seconds later. *'Please go home if you feel unwell, sad or tired.'*

Despite knowing Sylvia only had my best interests at heart, I felt frustrated that she too didn't think I was ready for this.

I sat forwards with my feet curled around the chair legs and rested my chin in my hands. I turned and gazed out of the window at the familiar view over the grey slated rooftops and chimneys of the town houses, and beyond to Blencathra Fell cloaked in sunshine and topped with cotton wool clouds. I looked about my office and at the frames that hung on the walls - mostly of landscapes and views across the lakes that I'd taken during my many walks with Drew. I noticed there was one photograph, similarly framed, that I couldn't recall taking. I walked around the desk to take a closer look. The frame was of a slightly darker wood. The photograph was of a large stately home, with a long drive that swept up through summer grass and leaf laden trees on either side. Where had I seen it before? My head felt hot and began to swim and I pressed my palms against the wall to steady myself.

Maybe Sylvia was right? Maybe I should head home before I made a complete fool of myself? But if I did, how would I later be able to face a return? Perhaps Jakob and Dan would prefer for me to go, and to leave Melanie to take over. Dan called her smart. She was an Oxford graduate. And she'd already written a great marketing strategy in the few weeks I'd been away. Perhaps instead of feeling insecure and even jealous, I should be grateful they'd brought in someone who was capable of moving the project forward.

But nauseating feelings of self-doubt kept coming in waves.

My dizziness subsided and I sat back down. I reached into my bag for my water bottle and took a long drink. I looked through the partition window to the open plan desks, where colleagues were greeting one another after the weekend, and no doubt sharing stories about what they'd been up to. I watched Tony from IT pause to chat with Kim and she smiled and laughed about something. I felt like an outsider and it wasn't a feeling I was used to. But no, I needed to rise above these insecurities and tackle my job with the professionalism I knew I was capable of.

So what if people doubted me?

I'd prove them wrong and they'd be relieved to have me back and to let Melanie move on.

# Chapter 11

I sat opposite Kim in Cafe Bean and stirred my fifth coffee of the day. My hands quivered with caffeine overload. I removed the cellophane from my chicken salad wrap, and rested it back on the plate.

'You could have got a muffin, too,' said Kim. 'I've got the real muffin top.' She laughed and pinched her belly. 'And you… are very slim indeed.'

'My appetite hasn't been up to much,' I said.

'You look great though and I'm a teeny bit jealous.' Then she quickly added, 'I mean, not of what you've been through. God, no. I wouldn't wish that on anyone as a way to lose weight.'

I smiled lightly. 'Please, Kim. I don't want people treading on eggshells. Be yourself. That's all I need. Especially after this morning.'

'I should have told you about Melanie when I rang last week. But I didn't want to make you anxious about returning and Jakob said he'd already told you about her.'

'Well, he hadn't, and he had plenty of opportunity.' I couldn't understand why he'd chosen not to.

'How are you finding her?'

I thought for a moment. 'I'm not sure. Who did she work for before?'

'Now there's a question. I've asked her a few times but she's been evasive. I didn't see her CV and Jakob recruited her - on his own. I'd have been suspicious about her experience if she hadn't given such an engaging presentation on Hexprin a couple of weeks back.'

'I've scanned through her strategy. Looks OK from what I've read, but I need to go through it line by line.' I felt an uncomfortable twinge behind my eyes and rubbed my forehead.

'Let's eat,' she said, and plunged her fork into her pasta salad.

My stomach churned but I picked up my wrap and took a bite. For a minute or two we ate in silence.

'How are you feeling?' asked Kim.

'Exhausted - in every possible sense.'

I had no hesitation being open with Kim. We'd often confided in one another and I could remember how she'd turned to me when she'd found out her live-in partner was having an affair with a friend - her best friend. Kim had been devastated but incredibly brave and immediately ended the relationship. 'Thank god we hadn't married or had children,' she'd said at the time as she'd wept into her glass of Pinot Grigio.

Oddly, I could recall every last detail of Kim's situation, which reminded me again how inconsistent my memory loss still was. More than once I'd wondered if I was being selective, subconsciously.

'Sylvia's been a massive help,' I said. 'But I still can't fathom losing Drew. I have moments of hell and devastation over Harry. I don't think I can face up to it and my damned memory loss is complicating it all.'

Kim reached over and took my hand. 'You will - in time.'

Her eyes watered and I swallowed and took some slow breaths to suppress an onset of tears.

After managing to chew through my lunch, Kim leaned closer as though to confide. 'Before we go back there is one more thing I must mention.'

I dabbed my mouth with my napkin. 'Sounds ominous.'

Kim nodded. 'It's only fair that you know what you're up against.'

I nodded for her to continue and felt my heart shudder.

'Jim treated me to a night away at The Glenridding Hotel a fortnight ago.'

'Sounds romantic,' I said.

'Yeah, it was lovely,' she said and paused. 'But guess who we bumped into on the stairs the next morning?'

And given the conversation we'd just had, I guessed precisely who she would say. 'Not Jakob and Melanie?'

'That's exactly who we saw.'

'Blimey! That must've been awkward.'

'Too right. But you know me, I gave them a smile and a cheery wave.'

'Did they say anything about it back at work?'

'It was hilarious. Jakob asked me into his office for a 'chat'. He made up this complete cock and bull story about how Melanie was staying with her mother in the hotel and their car had broken down. So he'd driven over to take them both home.'

'How do you know that wasn't true?'

Kim laughed. 'Because before they saw us coming down the stairs in the hotel, they were holding hands. I'd heard Jakob's voice - you know how loud he is, and I'd peered over the bannister rail from above. They let go of their hands the second they saw us walk round the corner.'

'I wonder how long it's been going on?' I said, then added, 'What if it was before she started here?'

'I wouldn't be surprised.'

'But I was at a dinner party on Saturday and Jakob came with Dan. Wouldn't he have brought or been with Melanie if they were an item?'

'They're not an item. At least, not officially.'

'In fact,' I said. 'Jakob didn't know Lizzie previously, and hadn't been invited until Dan's date cancelled and Jakob stepped in.'

Her eyes widened. 'Did you tell Jakob you were going to the party?'

I thought back to the cafe after swimming. 'I did actually. Party was OK until I got legless. It was Jakob who'd seen me home safely.'

Kim sniffed. 'Very gallant of him.'

'What's that supposed to mean?'

'You know he's always fancied you. Even before Priya died.'

'No way,' I said. 'I've never had that feeling.'

'Because you're too unsuspecting. A lot of men find you attractive, but you're too modest to notice.'

'They do not,' I said.

'I'm only telling you this because you're fresh prey and you don't want any love rats taking advantage of you given what you've been through.'

'OK. I'll keep that in mind. Actually, I'm not sure Drew liked me all that much.'

She gazed across the table at me then said quietly, 'You've never told me that before.'

I bit my bottom lip. 'I'm not sure I've really acknowledged it before, either.' I pulled my purse from my handbag and stood up. 'Let me go and pay.'

'Wait a minute,' she said.

I sat back down.

'I'm getting the impression, and I could be wrong, that this bang on the head might be throwing up a few surprises.'

I nodded. 'I think you're right.'

'I'm not suggesting you should go home. Far from it. But if there is anything more you want to talk about, I'm always here.'

'Thank you, Kim. I'm curious though - what makes you think Jakob sees me in that way?'

'The way he'd look at you. He's so transparent. Hopefully won't be an issue since he's seeing Melanie.'

'I'll keep it in mind though. Thank you.'

Kim continued. 'The fact that their relationship is a secret makes me suspicious of how she got the job.'

As Kim talked, I thought back to Saturday night. I couldn't remember anything past saying goodbye to Lizzie in the hallway. The next morning, I'd woken up naked in bed with no memory of getting home or undressed.

But something held me back from telling Kim this.

'When you're with them watch how she fawns over his every word. You must have noticed how she flutters and lowers her eyes. Doesn't matter what he says - he could be talking about buying more bog rolls - she'd still flutter away and agree it was a fabulous idea.'

'She is pretty,' I said, and felt as though I had judged Melanie before I'd got to know her. But Kim wasn't usually bitchy and I found her judgements of people were generally fair.

'And an Oxford graduate,' said Kim. 'Allegedly.'

'Yeah, Dan mentioned that.'

'Funny, but I Googled her and couldn't find any digital footprint,' Kim continued. 'What thirty year old doesn't have any online presence? Maybe Melanie isn't even her real name.'

I laughed. 'I think we might be getting carried away. She's maybe private and doesn't want to build a social media presence. Which would be wise and possibly even worthy of a place at Oxford.'

Kim raised her eyebrows. 'I'm not so sure. Now she's sitting opposite me, I'm going to super sleuth her.'

'You are funny,' I said, and crinkled my nose. 'And surprisingly wise.'

'Hey, less of the surprisingly.'

I looked down at my watch and stood up again. 'Better get back. Let me know what you find out, and I'll do likewise.'

'You got it, sister.'

# Chapter 12

When I got home that evening and after forcing myself to eat a bowl of chicken soup, I felt so depleted that I didn't bother changing out of my work clothes or washing the dishes. Instead, I melted into the sofa, lay back and stared up at the ceiling as thoughts played through my mind. The events of the past few days had doubled my mental turmoil. I selected a playlist of soothing piano music and reflected on my first day back. I'd spent the majority of the afternoon reading the emails that mysterious Melanie had sent across to me. Straightaway, I saw that there were gaps. Pages were missing but I couldn't put my finger on precisely what.

Damn my memory.

My head seemed to be shrouded in a fog and I realised I was deluding myself if I thought I could slip back into the job I used to do. It wasn't as though they even needed me now. My eyes pooled and I turned on my side. Could my life get any worse? Yes, I'd survived, but I was barely my former self. That was probably the only thing I felt certain of. Everyone kept commenting on my weight, not unkindly, but with concern, like I wasn't eating. But most of the time I couldn't eat. Each mouthful lodged in my throat like a lump of clay. It was hardly surprising I'd got so drunk at Lizzie's.

Who was I? Not a wife nor a mother. A sister, yes, and I felt so grateful to have Sylvia, still. I had a job, but for how long when it seemed they wanted rid of me?

I closed my eyes and took some slow breaths. Think, Orla. What was missing? Was it part of the drug trials? The only report I'd read had been the most recent trial, but I felt sure there had been more. They hadn't been on the BioMedica intranet, but I knew there must have been at least two previous trials to have reached this stage. Something was seriously amiss.

I yawned for the umpteenth time. Right now, I needed to sleep and when I closed my eyes I was lost in seconds to the outside world. I fell into a troubled slumber full of the faces of those who were no longer a part of my life.

Some time later, I surfaced from sleep to the sound of urgent rapping at the door. My dream washed away like water. The room was in near darkness now and I sat up and picked up my phone. Almost nine o'clock.

As I approached the door, I felt a sense of unease. 'Who is it?'

'It's Vincent. From upstairs.'

I released my breath. 'Hold on.'

I'd spoken to him briefly in the hallway when I'd returned from town on Saturday. That had been the first time I'd seen him since returning from the hospital.

I opened the door. 'Sorry. I fell asleep.'

The aureoles of his grey eyes widened, but he gave a warm smile. 'Then I'm sorry for waking you.'

'Actually, I'm glad you woke me.' I stood aside. 'Come on in.'

He turned to me. 'I hope you don't mind my coming down, but I heard you crying out and I thought you might be upset or in trouble.'

'Oh, was I?'

'As long as you're OK now?'

'I must've been dreaming,' I said. 'I'm sorry.'

'No need to be sorry. I saw Sylvia when you were convalescing. She mentioned you were still having memory problems.'

'Yes, it's odd. My memory is still quite random, but improving each day. Sylvia's been amazing.'

He nodded. 'I only wanted to say that as we've... as we've all lived in these flats for so long, I wanted you to know I'm here if you need me to jog your memory about anything.' He paused again. 'We know one another, Orla.'

I looked into his eyes with flecks of charcoal around the pupils, beneath brown hair that grew in whorls, and I knew that we'd been close. And that I'd shared personal things with him that I hadn't shared with others. I sat down on the sofa and he came to sit beside me.

Slowly, he reached over and took my hand and his lips curved upwards. 'Och, Orla I don't want to confuse you and I can see you don't remember everything from our friendship. But that's OK.'

The touch of his hand felt tender and supportive and I felt no awkwardness. 'Everything's coming back but I know I'm keeping certain memories at a distance.'

I watched the swell of his Adam's apple as he spoke.

'It'll come together when you're ready,' he said, and gave a reassuring nod.

There came a knock at the flat door.

'Are you expecting someone?' Vincent asked.

'Not at this time, no,' I replied. 'I didn't hear a buzz from the main door.'

He let go of my hand and stood up. 'Shall I see who it is?'

I nodded and he headed into the hallway. I heard voices and moments later Jakob walked in followed by Vincent.

'Jakob?' I said. 'Everything OK?'

Vincent sat back down beside me.

Jakob stood squarely in the middle of the room. 'Yes, everything's fine.' He looked at Vincent and gave a blatant frown.

'This is Vincent,' I said. 'A friend and neighbour.'

Jakob tilted his head. 'Nope. Don't think Orla's mentioned you before.'

'Actually, you came with me to one of his gigs,' I said. 'Last year?'

After a moment or two, Jakob said, 'Ah. Yes. Though I've never been much of a Proclaimers fan.'

Vincent let out a burst of laughter. 'Aye! I might well be Scottish but we don't cover any Proclaimers songs,' he replied in a more pronounced accent than was natural for him.

'Yeah, but you're Scottish, so that's how I remember your gig,' said Jakob, without returning the humour.

How rude, I thought. I turned to Vincent who, with a bemused expression didn't seem the slightest phased.

I turned back to Jakob. 'Was there something you needed?'

'Yes, but can we talk in private?'

'It can't wait until morning?'

'You did say you wanted to manage the Hexprin project and something urgent has come up.' His tone oozed matter of fact efficiency.

Vincent stood up. 'I'll go.' He smiled at me. 'I'll see myself out.' He gave Jakob a nod and walked out. In the doorway he turned around. 'Sleep well and sweet dreams.'

When I heard the door close, Jakob sat down beside me. He leaned back and laced his hands behind his head. 'Sweet dreams? What's his game?'

'Oh, nothing. Guess he knows I'm shattered after my first day back,' I said, and hoped Jakob might take the hint.

'I did suggest you take more time,' said Jakob. 'And especially after yesterday. I'm surprised you're not in shock.'

'I'm trying to block it out, along with every other shitty thing that's happened recently,' I said.

'Is that wise? Wouldn't it be better to take some time off to come to terms with it fully.'

'I'm overwhelmingly grateful for what you did yesterday and your concern is thoughtful, but no, I want and need to work.'

'OK. If you're sure. There's something that needs completing urgently. I can give it to Mel if you prefer?' He blinked several times in succession as he awaited my reply.

'No, of course I'll do it.' There was no way I wanted Melanie taking a job I should be doing.

'It's the article for The Harley Journal. They've brought the deadline forward. So it needs proofing and checking by first thing tomorrow.'

Why hadn't he asked Melanie to read it through given that she'd written it? Perhaps he genuinely wanted my opinion.

He upclipped his briefcase and drew out a slim folder.

'Jakob,' I said and paused, unsure. 'I wanted to apologise for Saturday night.'

He waved a hand. 'No apology needed.'

'But you missed some of the party.'

'I'd had enough anyway.'

'I hope I didn't make a fool of myself.' I stopped, uncertain how to continue. 'I don't remember much about it.'

'I'm your friend, Orla, and I was glad to see you home, safely. I still feel responsible...' his words trailed off.

'When I woke up in the morning, I was undressed.' I watched his face. 'But I don't even remember getting home or into bed.'

He opened the file and flipped through the pages. 'Really?'

'That's why I feel a bit embarrassed, you see?'

He looked at me and as he spoke, he cupped and scratched his chin. 'I saw you into the bedroom. You were quiet but coherent. You flopped onto the bed and said you were fine.'

'And yesterday. Those men. How might it have ended if you hadn't been there?'

He looked at me intently. 'Another reason why I'm worried for you. Too much pressure at this stage in your recovery. You need more time.'

He sounded sincere. But encouraging me not to return to work, then turning up at this hour to bring me an article to read through - was this a contradiction too far?

'I'm fine. Honestly. I've read the Hexprin reports and it's all in here,' I said, and tapped my temple.

Jakob's mouth twisted and for a moment he considered me. He held out the file. 'Good. I need it back first thing.'

'I want you to know I can do this,' I said.

I decided not to mention Melanie. Jakob's loyalties were undoubtedly swayed.

As I showed him to the door, he turned to me.

He tilted his head to one side then the other as if he had a crick in his neck. 'Your neighbour.'

'Vincent?'

He squinted and nodded slowly. 'I would advise you to keep a distance.'

'Why?'

'Because I saw the way he looked at you. Being a man, I notice these things.'

I gave an embarrassed laugh. 'But we're only friends and neighbours.'

'I'm sure. But without Drew, you're a target - an attractive young widow, living alone. There will be men wanting to take advantage of your vulnerability.'

I felt irritated by his overprotectiveness, which felt far more like jealousy than genuine concern.

'I assure you, Jakob, I can take care of myself.'

'I'm sure you can. I'm only sharing what I observed.'

The moment he'd gone, I locked and bolted the door. I went to the kitchen and made a cup of strong tea then sat back on the sofa with the article on my knees. It was finally sinking in that I was single and living alone - I no longer had Drew and Harry by my side to show I was a wife and mother. I'd long ago forgotten what it felt like to be a free agent and to date other men. Not that this was anything I was looking for. God, no. I hadn't felt a glimmer of desire, which for me was unusual. Thinking back, I hadn't had a period since the accident.

How ironic, I reflected, given the nature of the drug we were about to launch, Hexprin. It was the first drug developed that would perform a similar role to Viagra, but for women only. It was based around female hormones alongside natural ingredients to promote arousal. And it wasn't only to be promoted to pre and post menopausal women who were the main target market, but also women who experienced low arousal and who wanted to feel passion and excitement for their partner.

As I read through the article that Melanie had written and which had received the go ahead from Dan and Jakob, I saw she'd covered the pertinent points and done a good job of selling the product as effective and safe. There was a ten line paragraph on risks and this was one area of promotion that had to be a hundred percent accurate and relevant, not only for the suppliers but for the doctors and end users. These were the details that would end up enclosed with the product when supplied to the user. It seemed too brief, and again, I looked through my emails for the drug trials, and more importantly, the contraindications. As I continued reading, an uneasy feeling grew that this was being pushed without the full picture to support it. Jakob wanted this checked and with my approval by the morning, but I already knew I couldn't give this. At twenty to midnight, my phone pinged.

A text from Jakob. *'Still awake?'*

*'Yes.'*

*'What do you think?'* Then before I could respond another. *'All OK?'*

I typed my reply. *'There are a couple of issues. Perhaps we can talk about them first thing?'*

*'Can you tell me over the phone?'*

I dialled his number and he picked up. 'I don't think I've been given all the trials data. I'm sure there were some pertinent points not stated here.'

There was a pause before he replied. 'As far as I'm aware you've had it all. Melanie copied me in on the documents she forwarded to you.'

'OK, I'll double check with the labs first thing.'

'Fine, if you feel the need to.' There was an edge to his voice. After agreeing we'd meet in the office first thing, I hung up.

A pain twisted through my guts and I put the article down and headed to the bathroom. Something felt wrong. It seemed off that Jakob had asked me to give the article my approval when he and Dan had already endorsed it. Hexprin would be a huge earner for BioMedica and to delay it could mean a competitor getting their product to market first. We knew there would be massive demand for this drug, but only if it was fully tested and trusted. As head of product development, Jakob was responsible for safety and long term strategy.

# Chapter 13

*Seven months Earlier*

'Come on Harry,' I said, lying him back down in his cot and pulling the duvet up to his chin. 'You must be exhausted.' I glanced at the clock.

He kicked his legs and squealed in protest.

I stroked his forehead - a nice even temperature. 'Night, night, my darling.'

I turned away and switched off the light. I'd been back at work full time for over a year which had either caused or coincided with a prolonged period of broken nights. Harry caught up with sleep during the day at nursery, despite my asking them not to let him nap for too long, while I worked forty plus hours a week on top of managing the household and doing the majority of Harry's care.

Drew worked at Keswick General as an anaesthetist and at only thirty-six, he was working towards senior consultancy status. We had more money than we needed and had discussed both of us reducing our hours to allow Harry more time at home. But Drew had flatly refused and insisted that as his mother, it was only natural that I be the one to reduce mine. I went through the same routine with Harry most nights and couldn't help feeling I must be doing something wrong.

Unable to get Harry to sleep one evening, I'd relented to his cries and brought him back into the living room where he'd promptly fallen asleep on the sofa beside me.

On his way to bed, Drew looked down at Harry. 'We'll want a brother or sister for Harry someday. If you cut your hours, you'll be in a better position for pregnancy and for when we have our second baby.'

'I think we should wait a couple of years,' I said. The thought of another baby wasn't something I could contemplate. The exhaustion and workload might be doubled.

'Mum and Dad had me and David close together,' he continued, 'and because we were so close in age, we were great playmates freeing up Mum and Dad's time.'

I felt exhausted and irritable and wondered how I could even get pregnant again when we rarely made love. Then I thought, maybe I could pretend I wanted to get pregnant again but secretly keep on taking the pill. It might encourage more lovemaking on Drew's part and at the same time reduce my stress levels and help us feel fully connected once more.

'I'm worn out most of the time.' My eyes pooled with tears and as I leaned over to stroke Harry's head a tear fell onto his cheek. 'And sweet Harry. He never sleeps.'

'But he's sleeping now. Look at him.' Drew looked down at him and smiled.

Harry did look angelic but Drew slept so deeply, as though he'd anaesthetised himself, that he rarely woke up when Harry cried for attention at night. And in the morning when Drew bounced out of bed, I'd have to drag myself up to get showered and dressed, and pump myself with caffeine all day long. I'd feel even more depressed when I caught a look of myself in the bathroom mirror, my complexion dull with dark circles under my eyes. I'd attempt to conceal them with splashes of cold water and make up, but it was clear to Jakob and my colleagues that I wasn't sleeping. I tried so hard not to let my work suffer, but there were days when Harry was full of cold or had a sickness bug where I'd have to try and work from home. Drew couldn't phone in sick - operations were scheduled, people's health and lives were at stake if he failed to turn up.

I didn't ever resent Harry, not at all; I only wished that Drew helped out more. When he was home and not working on his laptop or sleeping, he'd play with Harry so that I could catch up with the chores. But once Drew fell asleep, that's where his parenting ended. Night-time feeds, nappy changes, preparing his meals and teething - that was all for me to handle.

I'd share and commiserate with the other mums in the postnatal group but none of them seemed to have a child as nocturnal as Harry. Some of them praised how hands-on the fathers were. Shamefully, I even joined in and said how wonderful Drew was - regaling scenarios and anecdotes and replacing myself with Drew as the doting parent. I'd sometimes wonder if they were putting a brave face on motherhood and hiding the full extent of their exhaustion. Not one of them looked as knackered as I did.

From the moment I held Harry in my arms after a surprisingly short labour of three hours, with only gas and air for pain relief, I'd fallen in love with our exquisite bundle of loveliness. When I looked into his eyes, both Harry and Drew looked adoringly back at me. Their faces became almost interchangeable such was their likeness. And it wasn't only me that noticed this. Everyone commented on their uncanny resemblance. Certainly, no one could ever doubt who fathered Harry. Of course, after stating how similar they looked, they'd follow by saying they could see me in his features too. 'He's got your nose and colouring.' Well, that was because he was a baby and Drew's nose was handsome and hooked. Anyway, I wasn't insecure about this - Drew was extremely attractive in a rugged and unique way, and I'd given birth to our beautiful son.

One evening at the beginning of March, I made myself a fruit tea and finally made it to the sofa. I flicked through the TV channels, but it was all Brexit news and soap operas. I fluffed up the sofa cushion, lay back against the arm and listened to Harry moaning in his cot still. His cries didn't escalate and I prayed he might nod off and give me a few hours rest. God only knew I needed it, if only to save my sanity.

The three story Victorian building we lived in, with a large flat on each floor, had elevated ceilings, pretty architrave and the original wooden floorboards, stained or varnished, even out on the landings. This meant that we'd often hear the footsteps of people coming and going. I heard the key turn in the door of the flat above and Vincent coming down the staircase. I expected him to continue past our door on his way out, but was surprised when the footsteps stopped and there came a knock. Weary, I got up and went to open the door.

In one hand Vincent held a bottle of wine and in the other a box of Roses chocolates. He held them up.

'Hi, Vincent,' I said.

'Fancy a glass?' He looked past me. 'Is the nipper in bed?'

'Yes - touch wood.'

'Drew in?'

I sighed. 'Nope, he's late again.'

He followed me through to the living room.

I heard a shrill cry from Harry's room and stopped still.

'Harry still not sleeping well then?' he whispered.

'Don't you hear him crying?'

'Only occasionally. I'm usually out like a light.'

'I am, too, when given the chance.'

I collected two glasses from the kitchen and set them on the coffee table.

Vincent opened the bottle and poured some wine. 'Is that enough?'

I shook my head. 'To the brim. Maybe if I'm in a drunken stupor I won't hear Harry and Drew will have to get up.'

Vincent looked up. 'Doesn't Drew pull his weight?'

'From the moment we brought Harry home, Drew seems to fall into a coma each night. Since I went back to work and gave up breastfeeding, he promised to take turns getting up at night, but...' I felt guilty for talking about Drew this way.

'Hey, he's sleeping now so what say we enjoy a wee drink and when Drew gets home you can tell him it's his shift?'

'You're right, Vince. I'm going to be more assertive.'

'I can't wait to have kids, but Sadie's not ready yet.'

'How is Sadie?'

'Not sure actually. She's busy with work and we haven't chatted much this week.'

'Dubai isn't it?' I asked.

'Now in Tokyo, covering more news about Fukushima.'

'Hope she's in a radiation safe zone.'

He passed me my glass and took a sip from his own. 'WHO have designated it as low risk in terms of radioactive strength, mostly because the nuclear reactors were contained in specially built structures, unlike Chernobyl, which had no such protection. She's been to the Fukushima site anyway and not the least concerned about the radiation despite knowing the radioactive waste hasn't been disposed of.'

'Blimey. You wouldn't catch me getting close.'

'We all take risks in different ways,' he said.

Vincent was a journalist and currently reporting on national affairs after returning from weeks away covering the conflict in Israel. From what I could gather, he'd seen some horrific war crimes and had returned to 'recover'.

'I can only imagine what you saw in Israel. Are you feeling better about it now?'

'A bit because I'm not there. But I still read the news and see the suffering and pain of those caught up in the conflict. I've got a couple of mates working out there still. Someone we knew was killed last week. You might have read about it.'

'God, yes. I did. And only in his thirties - a dad to young children, too. Were you close?'

'Not really, but we'd spoken plenty. And you just think - it shouldn't be happening. Nor should any of the violence and violations of human rights going on there. And all in the name of religion. It's sick. It's a bloody holocaust.'

'Don't ever go back there.'

'Sounds cowardly, but I don't think I will. Fortunately, there's plenty for me to work on here with Brexit. Not that I'm in any way thankful for these, if you know what I mean.'

I laughed. 'We need reporters who present the truth and I know we can count on you.'

I'd seen Vincent on a few TV news reports since he'd returned home and he was smart and astute in his questioning - able to prize out information and put politicians on the spot as and when necessary.

'Thank you. In fact, I've been asked in for an interview with our Director of News.'

'What's the role?'

'Ahh, there isn't a job advertised but I've heard whispers of my manager upping sticks.'

'So potentially a promotion?'

'I'm not getting excited. Not yet. But I'll let you know.'

'You're good and I'm sure they can see that.'

'I could do with the money, too.'

'Do you still like living here?' I realised how much I appreciated having him as my neighbour. I'd hate for him to move on, but the flats weren't ideal for young families if he and

Sadie were thinking of heading down that route. She was a little younger than me and Vince was almost forty.

Vincent had moved in not long after Drew and I, four years ago, and Sadie had moved in with him about a year ago.

'I'm not wanting to move anywhere. But I'd like to be able to do it up a bit, maybe a walk in shower and a smarter kitchen. A new guitar or two.' His eyes sparkled.

'Yeah, cus you've only got half a dozen guitars,' I said, and laughed.

He laughed too. 'I have just sold one to a mate.'

'Got any gigs lined up?'

'We're playing at the Goat and Gill on the eighteenth if you fancy it. Bring Drew.'

'You bet. I'll ask Sylvia if she can babysit.'

Vincent sang and played lead guitar in a band. I'd seen them a few times and whilst they mostly performed covers Vincent and the keyboardist had written a couple of gorgeous ballads. Vincent was a natural performer with a wonderful voice - deep and gravelly. At his last gig I noticed there were a few women who gave his performance their undivided attention, and I was no exception.

We chatted for a while and as the wine took effect I talked about work and the drug we were working on.

'Will the drug be for older women?' Vincent asked.

'It can be used by women of any age, just as Viagra can, though I imagine the older female market most likely.'

'Would you ever try it?' he asked, with a grin.

I thought for a moment. 'I have considered that. But right now, definitely not. The recent trial has thrown up a few contraindications that in my mind should delay the product.'

'Should?'

'Mmm. Yes, Jakob, he's Product Manager and has given it the go ahead, despite this.'

'Isn't that dangerous? Not only for the recipients, but for suing or litigation?'

'The contraindications were linked to existing heart problems and mental health issues - at least that's Jakob's argument. Therefore, not a reason to hold off or demand further testing.'

'And are you in agreement with that?'

'We've disagreed. But as he and Dan have final say, I can only argue my concerns and hope they'll listen.'

'Then, I shall watch this space with interest,' said Vincent.

'It'll most likely be months before it's launched. You can't imagine the hoops in pharmaceuticals.'

'Good. It's important that drugs are as safe as they can possibly be.'

I knew Vincent well enough to know that in his job he was always in search of the truth and would never allow unethical arguments to hold him back from exposing cover ups or dangers to the public. I admired his integrity.

I checked my phone - nine o'clock and neither a text or call from Drew to explain his lateness.

'Top up?' asked Vincent.

'I'd like to but better not. It's hard enough to get up in the morning as it is.'

He screwed the lid back on the bottle. 'You're right, drinking on a school night is not so wise.'

I lifted my feet onto the sofa. 'It's kind of you though, Vincent.'

'My sister had her first baby last year and she's always saying how exhausted she is,' said Vincent. 'And their baby sleeps through, so I can only imagine what it must be like to have night after broken night, and be back at work full time.'

Right on cue, I heard a loud wail from Harry's room. I gave an exasperated sigh and untucked my legs.

Vincent stood up. 'Why don't you let me go? Does he need feeding?'

'I'm trying to only give him water at night now. That's advice from my doctor.'

'OK, where's his bottle and let me try.'

'Are you sure?'

'I've babysat for Helen and nursed baby Tina a few times.'

'All right,' I said. 'His water's beside his cot.'

And he set off in the direction of Harry's bedroom.

'Good luck,' I called.

He turned back and with a smile said, 'I'll do my best.'

I lay my head back in the vague hope that Harry might settle for Vincent. The wine had made me sleepy and as Harry's cries silenced, I closed my eyes and dozed off.

A while later I awoke to the touch of a hand upon mine.

'Sorry I'm so late.'

I opened my eyes. 'Drew. What time is it?'

'Almost midnight.'

'Harry was crying.' I pushed myself up off the sofa.

'All quiet now. Guess he must be sleeping.'

I yawned and stretched my arms. 'Let me check.' I went to Harry's room then peered through the gap in the door. I could see Harry sleeping peacefully - his breaths soft and slow.

I went back into the living room. 'He's sleeping like an actual baby. Why doesn't he ever do that for me?'

'I'm assuming he did sleep for you - tonight.' Drew looked at the two glasses and the bottle of wine. 'Needed a drink, or two, I see? Chocolates too.' He unwrapped one and popped it in his mouth.

'Vincent brought them down. He kindly settled Harry back to sleep. He obviously slipped out when he saw I'd nodded off.'

Drew's brow furrowed. 'You let Vincent put Harry to bed?'

'No. I bathed him, as I always do.' I paused. 'But he woke up and Vince offered to help. I could hardly refuse - I'm on my knees.'

Drew shook his head and sighed with obvious disapproval. 'We knew it would be exhausting having a baby, but to leave him with a man who's never had children feels negligent to me.'

I felt my irritation build. 'Perhaps you'd like to help out more then?'

'I do. All the time.'

'When you're awake, Drew. And when you're bloody well here.'

'I can't help it when someone phones in sick and I have to fill in for theatre,' he said, his voice rising.

'Why don't you even text me?'

'Isn't it obvious? It's not like I'm swanning off to the pub like some dads do.'

I slumped back onto the sofa. 'I'm sorry. I'm just knackered, and work is mental too.'

'You know you could give up for a while - or at least go part-time?'

'You know I don't want that.'

'You'll still be able to work your way up.'

'That isn't how it works,' I said. 'And I'm sure you know that. We should be able to cope with one child between us, but the minute you're asleep, you're like a corpse 'til morning. You never hear him.' And I added. 'Or you choose not to.'

'You know I need to be fully alert during the day. I can't afford to make mistakes in my job. It's people's lives.'

'Female doctors and surgeons have babies and still work. Fathers still help out and perform brain surgery.'

'Fine,' he said, and relented. 'But you'll probably have to wake me up.'

'I will,' I said, determined that from now on Drew would pull his weight.

For the first time ever Harry slept right through until morning and I awoke with a clear head and more energy than I'd had in ages. Unfortunately it wasn't a trend and only the next night, after a nine hour crazy day at work, it took me over an hour of lying down beside Harry's cot and holding his hand through the bars, for him to fall asleep. Rather than sit with Drew and watch TV, I'd gone straight to bed. Then just as Drew had slipped into bed beside me and turned his back to me, Harry awoke with a scream that demanded attention.

Drew sighed and huffed. 'I'll go.' And he threw back the duvet, leaving me exposed.

I hauled the duvet back up to cover me.

I heard Drew march down the corridor then over Harry's shrieks, he talked to him in a voice that seemed too loud, too stern and unlikely to soothe him. 'I'm not getting you out so you can cry all you want.' I heard him say.

Exasperated, I threw back the duvet and hurried through. Harry was standing up, balling his eyes out as he reached his arms out over the rails. Drew stood a foot away with his arms folded and looked down on him.

'What are you doing?' I said to Drew.

'I thought if he knew I wasn't going to pick him up he'd soon realise and lie back down.'

I scooped Harry up and held him close. 'For goodness sake, you know babies don't think that way.'

'But he's old enough to understand more of what we say.'

'Even if he understands he can't rationalise how he feels.' I kissed Harry's cheek and went to sit on the armchair. 'It's OK sweetie.' I held his soft downy head against my breast.

'Go back to bed,' I said to Drew, feeling resigned.

'But you wanted me to help out more. So here I am and you're now telling me I'm doing it all wrong. I can't bloody win.' Drew's voice rose and Harry let out a sob.

'Please. Not in front of Harry.'

'Fine, I'll leave it to she who knows best.' And he turned on his heel and stomped out.

And there we were, back to square one. When I finally settled Harry to sleep, forty minutes later, I slipped back into bed feeling weepy and frustrated over Drew's reaction. It was almost as if his ineptitude was intentional.

# Chapter 14

*Four Months before the Accident*

In the weeks that followed, I continued to battle through work, whilst in between caring for our little boy. Many times, I wondered if I should jack it all in and become a stay at home mum. Harry would no doubt be happier and might become more settled if I could get him into a proper routine. I'd be able to join all the playgroups and toddler groups, go for walks and picnics beside the lake with the other mums and dads. Most importantly, I'd be less stressed and annoyed with Drew.

Drew earned a good salary and we could probably afford for me to take a year or two out of work. But would I have a job to go back to, and if I did, would I have to take a step back in my career? I'd heard all these stories before and long resolved that raising a family wouldn't interfere with my career, but the reality seemed so much harder than I could have ever imagined or anticipated. If only Drew was a more hands on dad. These things a woman could never know prior to having her first child. It was Drew who'd been keen for us to start a family soon after we married. I'd have been content to wait another year or two. Of course, now that I had Harry, nothing on earth would tempt me back to living without him. Our bond was strong and beautiful, and I knew nothing could ever break that. And he adored me - the way that he gazed into my eyes when I held him - the way that he handed me his favourite toys so that I could enjoy them as much as he did - the  way he'd stroke my hair and my cheek when he lay beside me on the bed. All of those things and much more made me love him completely and unconditionally.

One Sunday evening, I was at home alone with Harry and playing a game on the living room rug. He'd had his bath, was in his pyjamas and we were building block towers as high as we could make them. Each time our tower toppled over Harry shrieked with laughter and began to build it back up again. My phone rang and I got up to retrieve it from the mantlepiece. It was Drew ringing to say he had to cover another emergency operation and might not be home until midnight.

I sighed. I'd barely seen him all weekend. 'You must be shattered. Is there no one else to step in?'

'Holly's still off sick with this damned flu and Simon's not back from New Zealand for another week. I'll get the time back and I'll make up for it, I promise.'

'I know you will. Take care, my love.' Poor Drew, he'd been on an almost constant shift for the past five days. He was catching a few hours of sleep here and there at the hospital, but had barely been home other than to shower, pick up clean clothes and to say hello to Harry and me.

As I set my phone back down, I heard Harry coughing. When I turned around his eyes were dilated and bulging and I could see instantly that he was choking. His mouth was open and his fingers clawed at his tongue. I ran over, picked him up and moved his hands away from his face. He made horrific gurgling and gagging sounds as I tried to see into the back of his throat.

Quickly, I bent him over my knee. I patted his back firmly, but he gasped for breath. I sat him upright and peered into his mouth again but there was nothing to see, only his face growing redder and his lips already turning purple. I picked him up and gripped his legs, and in the hope that gravity might work I held him upside down. Nothing came out and equally as worrying, Harry no longer made choking noises, but had gone floppy and quiet.

My heart was hammering in my ribcage and I knelt down and turned Harry round to face me. His head flopped forwards. 'Please, Harry!' He remained unresponsive and my mind reeled with panic. I lifted his chin and his eyes rolled back in their sockets.

I cupped his cheeks. 'Harry!'

What to do?

And then I remembered Vincent upstairs. He'd recently told me he'd been on some medical training for his job. I carried Harry in my arms and hurried out of the flat and up the stairs to the top landing.

I hammered on Vincent's door. 'Vincent! It's Orla. Help me!'

Moments later I heard footsteps and the door opened. Vincent took one look at Harry. 'What's happened?'

'He's choking. He swallowed something. I've tried everything.'

'Come in,' he said.

I carried Harry through.

'Let me hold him.' Vincent knelt down on the floor and I placed Harry onto his lap.

By this time Harry looked lifeless and his eyes were barely open.

Vincent clenched his hands around Harry's tummy and in one small movement jerked his fists into his belly. Harry spluttered and a small object jettisoned from his mouth. It landed with a clink upon the floorboards and rolled slowly towards me. I opened my hand and picked it up. A pound coin. Harry coughed, but in between he gulped mouthfuls of air. His round eyes looked into mine and he reached out his arms.

'Mumma.'

It was the first time he'd said my name.

I gasped and burst into tears then lifted him from Vincent's lap. 'Thank you, thank you.' I cradled Harry against me. 'I thought he was going to die.'

Vincent stood up. 'The Heimlich manoeuvre works every time. Or so I've been told.'

I looked into Harry's wet eyes and watched his skin begin to regain colour. 'I've seen it demonstrated on TV, but I panicked and it didn't occur to me.'

'I've only ever done it on a dummy, but I know you must be careful with small children. I hope he won't be bruised.'

Harry breathed normally and he pulled a strand of my hair and gurgled. Vincent looked on and smiled so warmly that I wanted to hug him too.

I let out a sob of relief. 'He doesn't seem hurt.' I lifted Harry's pyjama top and touched his belly. Soft and pale pink as always. I propped him on my hip and followed Vincent through to the living room. Exhausted by the drama Harry rested his head on my shoulder. 'Do you have a small cup so I can give him a sip of water? His throat must be so sore.' I looked down at the pound coin in my palm. 'I always keep a pound in my jacket pocket for the trolley. It must have slipped out when I threw my jacket onto the chair.'

I cradled Harry against me and touched his face, which felt reassuringly warm. Recovering still, his eyelids drooped and his breathing relaxed. Vincent returned with a plastic beaker and placed it in my hand, but as I held it up to Harry's mouth, his eyes flickered and closed.

'Poor little man's worn out.' I stroked his cheek and felt overwhelmed with relief that he seemed OK.

Vincent ran his hand over Harry's head. 'I'm sure he'll be fine.'

'I'll take him to the doctor tomorrow for a check though.'

Vincent nodded. 'Sensible.'

I reached over for a cushion and eased Harry onto the sofa. He sniffled and yawned then lay peaceful and still.

I turned to Vincent who smiled and I felt a rush of emotion.

'He could have died,' I said, and my eyes filled with tears. 'Thank God you were in.'

Vincent sat beside me and took my hand. 'You did the right thing and because of that he's fine. Children do things like this all the time. Seeing what my sister and brother in law are like with their little one, I sometimes think these accidents occur to strengthen the bond between the child and parents.'

I wiped my eyes with my fingers. 'I suppose that's a better way to look at it. Though I don't think I could love Harry any more than I already do.'

'Shared experiences,' said Vincent. 'Or should I say, shared dramas.' He gave my hand a squeeze. 'Harry is a lucky boy to have you as his mum.'

'Is he though?' I said. 'I work full time. And I've got precious little energy to look after him properly when I am with him.'

'But you've got Drew to help. He's got two loving parents.'

'When Drew's home,' I said.

'The medical profession, like many others, does make tough demands on their employees.'

'I should be more understanding, I know. It's only that I'm trying to do everything, and as you know, Harry doesn't sleep well.'

'Why don't you leave him here to sleep it off, and we'll have something to settle our nerves in the snug. A wee dram perhaps?'

'Perfect, thank you,' I replied.

I walked into the corridor and through the opposite door. It wasn't so much a snug - more like another living room. It had a plush grey velvet sofa and antique shelves full of neatly organised books and files. I crossed to the desk in front of the window and looked down onto the street. I noticed a pair of binoculars beside a bonsai tree. The views from up here that looked down to the water and beyond to the fells were too splendid not to take advantage of. Drew had once laughed and said I looked like a peeping Tom or espionage agent peering out with my binoculars from our window seat.

'I wouldn't dream of peeping through neighbours' windows,' I'd said and laughed in reply. He definitely had a point, but I didn't allow that to stop me.

Outside, the street lamp flickered on, and over the road in the flat above her bakery, I could see Nora Grant sitting watching the television.

I looked at the framed photographs on the walls, mostly black and white art prints that I imagined Vincent or Sadie had taken. One or two were of them both on holiday, or they may have been working in far flung destinations. I knew they'd met through their work as journalists. There were a few ornaments that looked to be of African tribal origin - colourful figures, animal carvings and masks. I popped my head back round the living room door to see Harry still soundly asleep as Vincent returned with two tumblers of whisky.

Vincent nodded back at Harry. 'All the excitement's got to him.'

We sat beside one another on the sofa and I raised my glass. 'Here's to Harry and to you!'

We chinked glasses.

'And to his mum - who can think on her feet in a crisis.'

The whisky bristled in my mouth and felt comforting as it slipped down my throat. 'I really need this.'

'Me too,' said Vincent, his expression turning serious. 'I might have appeared calm but it was a frightening sight.'

'Awful. I remember my mum turning me upside down once when I choked on a boiled sweet.'

'Hopefully Harry will be too young to remember it all.'

'Sorry if I interrupted your evening.'

'Honestly, now he's OK, it's good to have some company.'

'When's Sadie home?' I said, and tried to recall the last time I'd seen or heard her about.

'She isn't, or at least, she won't be.'

'Oh?'

He nibbled his bottom lip. 'She's not coming back. I guess she will, but only to move her stuff out.'

'Oh no. I'm so sorry.'

He gave a deep sigh. 'I'd not heard from her all week, and her calls were becoming less and less frequent. So I rang her Friday night and she finally answered.' He sighed again. 'To cut it short, she's met someone. Her soulmate apparently, and she's moving in with him.'

'Has it been going on a while?'

'A few weeks, so she claims.' He sniffed with disbelief. 'But I reckon longer. Last time she was home, she was distant and constantly messaging on her phone. I suspected, but didn't want to believe it.'

'How long have you've been together?'

'Two and a half years.' Vincent swallowed back his drink. 'Want another?' He stood up.

I drank mine back too. 'Go on then.'

I could see he needed to talk and as I'd barely been in adult company all weekend, I felt glad to have someone to talk to. The whisky had done an excellent job of dulling the shock of Harry choking, too.

Vincent returned with the bottle and poured a splash into each glass. 'I don't generally use alcohol as a prop.'

'No excuses needed tonight,' I said.

Sadie and I had never hit it off. She was super career driven, as was I, but it felt as if she wanted to brag about the stories she'd been covering, even trying to get one up on Vincent. Of course, I didn't try to compete. I worked in an office researching and marketing drugs which could hardly compare with travelling the world to report on war torn countries or natural disasters. She'd once told me she despised big pharma, as she called it. Said it was corrupt as hell and anyone with an ounce of integrity would steer well clear.

94

I hadn't retaliated, although I had defended my position as rationally as I could. I loved my job and knew full well that I worked with strong principles. Vincent had come to my defence and said that without drugs, some people would be dead rather than able to live normal lives.

'Name one drug,' Sadie had said, and placed her finger on her chin.

'Insulin, for one,' he replied.

'Most people have diabetes because they're either morbidly obese or have rotten diets.'

'Not strictly true,' he said, 'I don't know the statistics, but many are born or grow up with the condition. Children, who wouldn't be here if it weren't for insulin.'

'Well, there aren't many other drugs I can think of that people couldn't avoid with a healthier lifestyle and more exercise,' she'd retorted.

'OK,' I said, feeling my irritation rise to the challenge. 'My sister had to have her thyroid removed due to a benign tumour and now has to take thyroxine daily. She'd have become a cretin in her twenties if it wasn't for her daily medicine. Most likely dead by now. And given that my parents died in our teens, we're pretty grateful for this.'

'Fair enough,' Sadie had admitted with a detectable sneer. 'I still maintain that most drugs are unnecessary and certainly in many countries are marketed and sold unethically and at extortionate prices so that the poor die if they can't afford insurance - look at America.'

I nodded. 'Yep. America's healthcare system is dysfunctional, to say the least.'

'But you've seen first-hand how anti-malarial drugs and vaccines for children in third world countries have saved millions of lives,' said Vincent.

'Of course, these are life saving drugs for those who need them most. I just think that in first world countries, too many doctors hand them out willy nilly and people are only too willing to take them rather than tackle the root cause of their problems. Antidepressants, blood pressure drugs and statins for instance, HRT's another.'

'But again, Sadie, you've never suffered from anxiety or depression or been through the menopause. Plus, you take the oral contraceptive pill, which you could avoid,' said Vincent.

'I know you'd like me to,' she snapped. 'I don't want a screaming baby yet.' She glanced my way and I knew she meant Harry. 'I might never want one.' She gave a defiant look.

'Anyway,' I'd said, hoping to diffuse the tension. 'I agree that people shouldn't take drugs unnecessarily, but for some they are the very best and often, life-extending or life-saving option. Which is why I maintain a lot of respect for my industry.'

'And the pay packet,' Sadie had muttered under her breath.

I'd had a bellyful of her pompous attitude and arrogance. 'We all need to make a living, Sadie, so come on down from your high horse. What we do benefits and saves lives - end of argument.'

I glanced at Vincent who visibly repressed a smile.

Neither of us disputed further. She was an investigative journalist and smart enough to see all things as they were but with an extra helping of cynicism. No wonder she did so well in a highly competitive environment and had raced up the career ladder. Vincent was super intelligent, but he seemed more sensitive to those around him.

When Sadie first moved in with Vincent I'd invited them both round for dinner. The wine flowed fast and Sadie and Drew had got talking about one another's work. I could see she was flirting with Drew and he was quite obviously loving the attention. She was petite, with curves, pretty and wore a short summer dress and high heeled sandals. What straight man wouldn't enjoy her bestowing her time on them? I hadn't felt the least bit jealous, and had enjoyed chatting with Vincent about all sorts of things other than work. We were both keen photographers, and although Vincent had received training for his work, I'd shown him my recent efforts of local landmarks and landscapes taken on my phone and together we'd added a few filters to enhance them further.

'You should print and frame that one,' he'd said of one shot I'd taken of Castlerigg Stone Circle. He looked around the room. 'That space above the fireplace is crying out for a view like this.'

'I think I will. I took it on midsummer's eve. We were going to camp overnight, but Harry had other ideas.'

Vincent laughed. 'Funny how parents say they'll never allow a baby to stop them doing things - but it doesn't really work like that, does it?'

'I was probably one of those parents. But no, you have to do what's right for your child if they're ill or not in the mood.'

And I couldn't help but consider the difference between Vincent's perspective on parenthood and encouragement of my photography, and Drew's complete lack of understanding or interest in my hobbies. Is that what marriage did? Weren't we supposed to support our spouses in whatever they chose to pursue work or hobbywise? Drew didn't really have any hobbies. He did read medical journals and papers and would join me on the many picturesque walks in the area, but he was fairly work obsessed and liked to come home and tell me all about his day. Whereas I preferred to leave my work behind me. Not that I didn't love my work, but I wasn't convinced it sounded all that exciting to those outside the industry. Or perhaps that was the perception I'd gathered from Drew, who never seemed attentive when I brought up the subject of drug trials or therapy or wanted to talk about an aspect of work that was bothering me. Surprising, given that he worked with medicines all day long.

Drew was smart and made everything he spoke about sound fascinating. And he was charismatic too - no doubt one of the reasons I was so strongly attracted to him in the first place. As he chatted with Sadie, oblivious to my watching him, I thought how handsome he was. And as he topped up our wine glasses and smiled down at me briefly, it suddenly seemed as though I didn't know him well at all. If an outsider had walked into the room, I'm sure they'd have thought that Drew was with Sadie and I was with Vincent. Tonight, the chemistry seemed switched. Or perhaps that was the purpose of dinner parties - to get to know others better.

In the study, as I sipped my second shot of whisky, Vincent selected some music and set it at a soft volume.

'I don't know this band,' I said. 'Who are they?'

'The Civil Wars. It's their new album.'

'This track's gorgeous. How is it I've never heard of them?'

He sat back down beside me.

He rubbed his hand through his hair in a circular motion. 'I don't think they're well known. Which is surprising, given how amazing their music is - the lyrics, their voices and harmonies. We play a couple of their songs at gigs.'

'Have you seen them live?'

'I haven't but I follow them on social media, as with other artists I admire. I've been looking out for when they set any dates up north.'

'I'd love to see them.'

'Then I'll let you know.'

I held the glass on my knee, rested my head back and hummed along quietly to the tune.

Vincent did the same and began to sing along, softly. He knew all the lyrics.

As the whisky soothed my senses and the rhythm of the sounds and words swept over me, my eyes watered with emotion. I turned my head to look at Vincent, who, with eyes closed, continued to sing along, soft, sweet and melodic. I don't know what made me do it, but instinctually, I reached out and with the back of my hand I caressed his cheek. He murmured and his eyes flickered but remained closed and when I ran my finger slowly across his bottom lip, he opened his mouth slightly. I slipped the tip of my finger into his mouth. I sensed him tense for a moment before I felt his tongue, warm like silk, swirl around my finger. He sucked lightly and drew my finger deeper. Vincent opened his eyes and I withdrew my finger. He turned and looked into my eyes and without a word leaned across and pressed his lips upon mine. As we kissed, adrenaline coursed through me and we remained there, kissing deeply and sensually. I floated in a pool of the purest pleasure - weightless, and as his arms enfolded me, my core melted and my thoughts ran wild.

I didn't hear footsteps on the stairs, nor did I hear Drew enter the flat. But thank God I did hear him call through from the living room. 'Anyone in?'

We sprang apart and I jumped to my feet. 'I'm so sorry.'

Vincent looked intently up at me for a moment. 'Don't be.' And he stood abruptly and left the room.

I straightened down my hair and jumper, my cheeks simmering, and walked through to the living room where Harry still lay fast asleep.

# Chapter 15

*Present Day - Tuesday*

The following morning when I drove into the car park at work, I spotted Jakob's black Mazda already parked up next to a mustard yellow Nissan. I had a hunch it must be Melanie's car. After what Kim told me, I imagined they'd spent the night together and followed one another into work.

I'd slept surprisingly well despite staying up late, and this morning, for probably the first time since the accident, my head felt clear and my mind sharp. I'd even managed to eat two slices of toast and honey as well as drinking my usual strong coffee before setting off. When I walked through reception, Natasha, who hadn't been at the front desk yesterday but who I knew as our receptionist, gave a broad smile.

'It's wonderful to see you back, Orla.'

'And I'm pleased to be back.' This was a great start. 'How's Isabelle?'

When Natasha was pregnant with her first baby, Isabelle, I'd shared my experiences with Harry, the birth, his milestones and when he'd taken his first steps. I hadn't moaned on about the sleepless nights and exhaustion - all babies were different. As it turned out, Isabelle had been an angel at night and Natasha had breezed back to work after five months, full of the joys of motherhood, and complete with the perfect hourglass figure she'd had prior to her pregnancy.

'Isabelle's doing great, and you look well,' said Natasha, then added, 'Sorry. Stupid thing to say. How are you?'

'Slowly getting there. Too much to come to terms with.'

She stood up and walked around the desk. Her eyes were glassy as she came forwards and embraced me. I hugged her back and we remained this way for a few moments.

She drew away. 'I know you've got supportive friends. But remember me if you want to talk. About anything.'

Natasha and I had exchanged our experiences of the births of our children which had created a bond that grows between mothers who understand. I knew she'd be thinking about Harry - the sheer impossible magnitude of losing a child. And how she might feel if it was Isabelle.

I swallowed hard. 'Everyone's being so kind, but I need to work - I think being here will help me cope better.'

She placed her palm on my arm. 'Jakob and Melanie are already in.' Natasha lowered her voice. 'I shouldn't say this, but Melanie is Jakob's bitch - sniffing eagerly at his heels. Or should I say, his privates.' Natasha sniggered.

I suppressed a smile. 'I'll look out for that.'

'At first Melanie seemed friendly,' she continued, 'but Jakob's got her under his spell. I mean, I know he's attractive and charming but...' the reception phone rang and she broke off. 'Anyway, you'll maybe win her over.'

'As I'll have to work with her for a bit, I'll do my best,' I said.

After giving me a final look of sympathy, Natasha picked up the phone and I headed up the stairs.

I dropped my briefcase in my office then headed straight for the kitchen for an extra shot of caffeine. As I walked with coffee in hand down to Jakob's office, the main office seemed quiet and only a couple of the IT guys were in.

A familiar face looked my way. 'Came back for more then?' said Tony.

I laughed. 'A glutton for punishment.'

'Aren't we all?'

Everyone enjoyed the office banter. But the truth was, most of us absolutely loved working here. The pay was excellent, but that wasn't the reason people tended to stay. It was down to Dan, our Director, who was about as inclusive as any boss could be. He recruited well - genuine and competent people, most of the time, but he also fostered an atmosphere where staff were encouraged to come forwards with their opinions and ideas on things. Dan always listened. He might not change his mind, but this was generally justified because he had sound business sense and considerable experience. He spoke kindly to staff, from senior managers to the cleaners, resolved problems as and when they arose, and he didn't have favourites or cliques with any of the staff. I thought he was a brilliant leader and I think most of us recognised this.

But had Dan taken his eagle eye off Jakob and the Hexprin project and had he even been included in Melanie's recruitment? All would become clear in time, I felt certain.

As I passed Jakob's office I saw Melanie with him. I watched as she sipped her drink then laughed in an exaggerated fashion as though he'd said something hilarious. I stood before his door, braced myself and took a breath.

Be straight, be honest and be assertive, I said to myself.

They were both still chortling away as I walked in.

'Morning,' I said.

'Do take a seat.' Jakob's expression instantly dropped any suggestion of humour, and gestured to the seats as if it was the first time I'd been in his office.

I sat down, placed my coffee on the table and rested the file containing the articles onto my lap.

'How are you feeling this morning? Any headaches or dizziness?' asked Jakob.

'I'm good, thanks,' I replied, determined to give a reassuring impression. 'Fit as a fiddle, actually.'

Jakob raised his eyebrows and pressed his lips together as though he doubted my reply.

Melanie came to sit at the table beside me.

I turned to her. 'How are you?'

'I'm excited,' she said. 'So close to the launch. I'm literally buzzing.'

'I wouldn't get too excited yet,' I said. 'There're a couple of fairly substantial issues we need to resolve first.'

'Oh?' said Jakob, joining us. He rubbed his forefinger over his bottom lip and I felt his gaze on me like a weight. 'What seems to be the problem?'

I didn't reply but turned back to Melanie. 'I know you said you'd sent all the research findings, but you haven't sent all the previous trials data. I recall a problem with the results.'

Melanie's hazel eyes flickered beneath pinched brows, and she looked to Jakob.

'You don't need them,' he said, and his eyes ping-ponged between Melanie's and mine.

101

'Of course I do,' I said. 'I need to compare the differences in the drug and how the trial was administered.'

He looked at me squarely and his chin jutted forwards. 'That's not your remit. Never has been. You only need the results of the last trial. Any previous issues have been ironed out and resolved.' He shook his head slowly. 'Your memory is obviously playing tricks and you've remembered incorrectly. The results of the previous trials were sound. Nothing much to sort out. You'll have to trust me on this. As Melanie does.'

Melanie pouted and nodded with enthusiasm. 'I've studied them and it's all good. You'll have to trust us, Orla,' she said, parroting Jakob.

My temper was fraying at the edges and I took a breath. 'How long have you been in this role?'

She tilted her head and fluttered her eyelashes. 'Don't you remember?'

'Of course I do,' I replied, and felt an urge to slap her patronising question back in her face. 'What I'm suggesting is that as I've been Marketing Manager here for five years, I think I know the correct protocols.' I turned to Jakob. 'As should you.'

I crossed my legs and as I did I accidentally kicked the table. The coffee cups upended and splashed across the surface. 'Oh, for fuck's sake.' I said, and instantly regretted my outburst. I stood up and looked around for something to clean up with.

'Please calm down,' said Jakob, and tutted and shook his head at the spilt coffee. 'The only thing I need to know from you is, are you satisfied with the articles so I can get them signed off and circulated to the journals?'

I felt a vein throb in my neck. 'I could say yes, but that would be irresponsible, given that I don't have all the relevant information. So no, I can't sign them off.'

'Then myself and Melanie will authorise them without you. It's a pity as I was hoping you'd be fully on board upon your return. But it's evident you are still unwell. That you are becoming hysterical only confirms my concerns.'

I raised my voice and the words tumbled from my mouth. 'What are you talking about…?'

At that moment Dan walked in. 'What's going on?' He stood with a wide stance and looked from me to Jakob.

Jakob stood up and walked around the table to me. He put his hand on my shoulder. 'It's all right. I understand. You've been through so much. You're not ready for this level of responsibility.' He looked at Dan. 'This isn't fair on Orla. We should never have agreed she could return yet.'

'I did suggest it might be too soon,' agreed Dan quietly. He stepped forwards, his expression kind but annoyingly sympathetic.

'You sustained a serious head injury,' Jakob said. 'You can't expect to recover from that overnight. And I'm surprised at your doctors for having cleared you for work so soon.'

I sat back down, feeling suddenly outnumbered and unsure. 'But on Saturday night you were keen for me to return, Dan. And my consultant said it was up to me if I felt well enough.'

'But your memory is causing you to doubt your judgements,' said Melanie.

My eyes blazed. 'Not at all. In fact, my memory is virtually back to normal.'

'Really?' asked Jakob. 'You're only now beginning to grieve for your dead husband and only child…'

I wasn't fooled by his sympathy, but the significance of his words made me choke. My voice cracked. 'I haven't fully accepted what happened, naturally, but that's not my memory at fault.'

'But could it be a combination of memory problems and shock?' asked Dan.

The three of them fixed their eyes on me and I suddenly felt my strength and resolve fall away.

I let out a long breath. 'I only want to get back to normal and to doing what I love.'

'And you will,' said Jakob, and he perched on a dry corner of the coffee table. He touched my hand. 'I think you should consider talking to a counsellor. We can provide one through work. Can't we Dan?'

'Absolutely.' Dan nodded. 'That's wise, Jakob. I should have suggested that myself.'

'Fine,' I said. 'I'm willing to talk to someone, but I still want to be here.'

Dan took a step closer. 'Why don't you see the counsellor, and when you've talked it through, together you can decide if you're ready for full-time work again?'

'No, Dan, I need to be here. It's a crucial time for Hexprin.'

'That's why we're keeping Melanie in post,' Jakob intervened. 'To take the pressure off you.'

Their arguments rendered me flailing and dumb. All three of them looked at me with concern on their faces. They might have looked genuine, but I doubted it. Did they merely want me out of the way?

'When can I see the counsellor?' I said, and felt confident I'd convince them I was fit for work.

'Let me or Jakob talk to HR.' Dan paused. 'But in the meantime, I want you to go home and put your feet up. Relax, meditate, go shopping. Whatever you need to do to recuperate.'

I stood up. 'I realise I'm not being given a choice. But I will go home and relax and see you tomorrow.'

'Orla?' said Dan.

'Yes?'

He lowered his voice and spoke deliberately. 'I want you to stay home until you've seen the counsellor and they've made a full assessment. You must trust Jakob and Melanie to take care of Hexprin. Don't try to control everything when it's yourself you need to be controlling - looking after.'

'You're kidding me, right?'

Dan gave an exasperated breath. 'It's for your own good. Trust me on this.'

'Then please can you get me an appointment asap?' I turned to Jakob. 'I'm well enough to be here and the sooner I see the counsellor, the sooner I can return.'

Jakob's brow creased. 'Let's wait and see. There really is no rush.'

I pulled out of the car park with a squeal of tyres and headed out of town before I pulled into a layby and thumped the steering wheel. My frustration erupted in a torrent of tears and I remained there replaying the scene through my mind and tried to work out how it had gone so badly wrong. So this was payment for disagreeing with my manager - for refusing to ignore real concerns so that they could tick their boxes. They'd accused me of being some sort of control freak who couldn't even control myself. I wasn't prepared to let this go, even if it did mean being humiliated and cast aside. No doubt I could have handled myself better and responded more assertively and calmly, but against the three of them what chance did I realistically have? A bloody counsellor!

Was it their plan to render me incompetent and unfit for work?

# Chapter 16

I turned towards home and tried to view my situation objectively. Jakob seemed to be undermining my capability. But why would he want to do this? Yes, Kim had told me he was having a relationship with Melanie and so no doubt he wanted to protect her position. But Jakob and I went back a long way, we'd always got on well, both professionally and personally. Previously, he'd behaved honestly, was an understanding manager and had been businesslike and thorough in all things work related. At least, that had been my perception.

But perhaps my ever rational mind had been blinded by his confidence and intelligence. Or had it been arrogance? He'd consistently made arguments for the decisions he made and seemed able to back them up with logic and reasoning. So what had changed?

The fact that he'd withheld information was the key here. If there hadn't been a problem with the previous trials, he'd have sent me the files or allowed Melanie to. I was convinced they'd been deliberately hidden.

When I got back to the flat I made a cup of tea, sat on the window seat and hugged my knees to my chest. A pigeon fluttered down and landed in the tub of begonias I'd planted in the spring - now neglected and withered. The pigeon scratched around in the soil before it perched on the edge of the box and peered in at me. He cocked his head to one side, curious, before he turned around, lifted his tail and left a dropping in the soil.

Down on the cobbles I saw a few locals walking past and I spotted Mr Holden, the retired headmaster from my primary school with his two black labradors, Mabel and Mac. He'd routinely take this route down to the water where I'd often seen him down on the beach throwing sticks into the water for the dogs to swim out to. We'd chatted many times and I cast my mind back to the first conversation I'd had with him after the accident. Unlike some who seemed afraid to mention Drew and

Harry, Mr Holden was direct but sensitive as he asked me how I was. He'd mentioned Drew and Harry by their names and asked how my memory was coming along. I'd admitted that it was terrible, at the time, but now I could recall our conversation almost word for word.

What I still had to do was face up to losing Drew and Harry. Not only in the fleeting moments when I felt strong enough, but to fully accept and to allow myself to grieve for them. Until I did, I couldn't move forwards in any areas of my life. It seemed an unlikely way to come to terms with grief. Had others experienced loss this way? I suspected my head injury was the underlying cause.

I reached into my handbag for my phone.

There was a message from Kim. *'I hear you've gone home. Are you OK?'*

I typed a reply. *'I'm furious. Dan and Jakob sent me home. I've got to see their counsellor before I can return. Keep this confidential though. Let them talk to you about me if the opportunity arises. If you don't mind? I'm interested to hear what they say. You're the only one I can trust - Love, Orla xx.'*

I rang Jakob's office number.

'Hi Jakob,' I kept my voice deliberately upbeat.

'Sorry about earlier,' he said, and didn't sound in the least apologetic.

'I wanted to ask if you've arranged the counsellor yet?'

There was silence from his end.

'Jakob?'

'Not yet. But I will. Today if possible.'

'I'll hear from you later then?'

'Of course. Now please forget about work.'

I restrained my frustration. 'I'm not an invalid.'

'Of course not. I want you back here asap. That's all.'

'Glad to hear it.'

He was lying. He didn't want me back at all.

Fact. I was about to lose my job. Unless I was clever. Unless I took the right steps. Which didn't mean that I was prepared to compromise my ethical principles.

My phone buzzed. Text from Kim. *'I've got your back, sister.*
*I'll work on Melanie/Jakob/Dan today. With all the subtlety and*
*deviousness I can muster! Love you. Kim xx.'*
At least someone was on my side. Without her confidence in
me or her support, I'm not sure I'd have had enough courage to
fight for my position.

# Chapter 17

I had a plan. It was risky, but if it worked it would pay off and put me in a far stronger position.

It wouldn't be dark until tenish. I pulled on some leggings, trainers and a fleece with a zip up pocket for my phone. If I bumped into security or anyone, I'd say I'd been to the gym, but had left my mobile at work. No one could manage without their phone so I felt sure that would win me some credibility. Hopefully, everyone would have left work by that time.

At nine o'clock, and after one more check through my emails, I set off for Penrith, for the second time that day. I played through possible scenarios in my mind as I drove - like meeting the security guard or a member of staff. The only person I dreaded meeting was Jakob. When I drove slowly past the office car park, I saw it was virtually empty. I didn't recognise any of the remaining cars so at least Melanie, Jakob and Dan must have gone for the night. I still had my key and security pass and pretty much everyone knew my face so even if I did see someone, I had a perfectly legitimate excuse to be there. I pushed aside my nerves and refused to feel intimidated entering my own workplace.

I waved my card and the main doors slid open.

A security guard I recognised from the main gate sat at the reception desk. He looked up from his phone and I approached the desk.

I showed him my ID card. 'I stupidly left my phone at my desk. At least, I'm certain that's where it is.'

He nodded, and his phone pinged. He glanced down at it and without looking up again, said, 'Hope you find it.'

Instead of heading down to the labs, I jogged up the stairs to the offices. Damn. I should have realised there'd be security at the desk. I wondered if he'd be watching the security cameras and expecting me to return quickly. The offices appeared eerily empty, but I made my way directly to the far end of the corridor and straight through the door to the emergency fire exit staircase. Thankfully, there were windows to allow sufficient light to guide me safely down the concrete steps. I moved silently and swiftly. The final flight of steps that led to the basement were pitch black and as I stepped I slid my hand against the wall to keep steady. At the bottom and with my hands outstretched I felt for the door to the labs and found the handle. For security reasons there was an access keypad positioned to the side. I knew my personal staff code without a moment's hesitation but I couldn't see the keypad clearly and couldn't risk an error. I pulled out my phone and shone the screen at the numbers. I keyed in my code, heard the door release click and I headed through to the corridor.

Three laboratories led off it and each served a unique purpose. The first was the largest and had the tightest security. I could only enter if I was with the lab manager or his designate, and was fully dressed in clinical wear. This was where the lab rats and live animals were housed. It wasn't a space I often entered, mainly because I felt uncomfortable seeing the helpless creatures in cages. I knew they were an essential part of many of our testing procedures, prior to trialling on humans, but I also knew that ultimately, the animals sometimes suffered and died as a result of the medication and conditions they were kept under. It was one aspect of my job and industry that I could never fully come to terms with, although the fact that our drugs were produced to improve the lives of humans suffering from illness or disease, ultimately enabled me to see beyond this.

Our lab manager, Lucas, was stern with an air of arrogance that tended to aggravate the female members of staff. I'd never warmed to him, but the animals were well fed, the cages kept impeccably clean and he never allowed any of the animals to suffer for longer than they needed to.

In the dimly lit corridor, I passed the animal quarters and peered through the glass square. I heard a soft mewling sound and couldn't imagine what creature it could be. I felt a shiver run through me. Otherwise, all appeared still amidst the near darkness. I continued towards the records and results room, where I hoped to locate the information which had been deliberately withheld. Despite advances in technology and the move over to digital storage, we were still required by law to hold all results in paper form and to keep them secured for twenty years. Consequently, the room was vast and with hundreds of shelves stocked full with files and reports.

The files manager, Phoebe Tonkin, was also Lucas's Personal Assistant. They were both in their fifties and had worked as a team for the past twenty years, ever since the Penrith office and laboratories had opened. I'd talked with Phoebe many times, often eating our lunch together in the work canteen. She was pale and slim and reminded me of Princess Diana in her voice and manner. She lived alone, never mentioned an ex-husband or boyfriend and spent far longer in work than she was paid for. Her devotion to her job, and the animals, was one of the reasons the lab side of the business ran so smoothly and never seemed to run into problems, despite the controversial nature of the work. She was super intelligent too, and Dan and Lucas would praise her ideas and methods for introducing and improving processes and systems.

What I was about to do wasn't without risks. Accessing the files was strictly monitored and although I'd been allowed sole access to the room previously, Phoebe always insisted that no one be allowed to go in alone.

'We're protecting our staff, just as much as our files,' she'd say.

And in one way, here I was about to prove her theory. My counter argument, if necessary, would be that I was trying to protect our business and staff too. The intentional concealing of any results was potentially unethical and risky in the long term. Not least to the recipients of the medication, who were in the initial stages, our guinea pigs.

The nerves in my stomach jangled as I stopped in front of the code panel beside the door. This required a separate code - our individual date of birth - and a means of tracking our use in the room. I closed the door silently behind me. The store was dimly lit and I headed down the main footway between rows of floor to ceiling shelves.

A sound came from somewhere close by and I paused.

I remained still and listened. A scuffling sound and whispered words.

Without a sound, I moved down an aisle and waited and listened, hardly daring to breathe. My heart thundered in my chest. I hadn't expected anyone to be here. The air felt suddenly hot and stuffy. Had I only imagined the sounds?

I waited.

Then the sound of shuffling again, and this time a voice. A man - but his words were indecipherable. I moved further into the aisle. At the far end another, narrower aisle led either back to the front of the room where I could creep out quietly, or deeper into the store. Had they heard me? Either way, I was entitled to be there, although sneaking around at night could be hard to explain, especially as I'd been sent home. The H - Hexprin files I needed access to were a few aisles away and I peered around to see if anyone was there. The noises continued and I moved on, and peered round each aisle as I went before I crept past.

Whoever was here, was only feet away and I couldn't afford to be seen or heard. The lights were low and I crouched down. There were slim gaps above the files to peer between the shelves and into the aisle beyond. I crawled on my hands and knees. Shuffles and shadows of movement flickered through the shelves. Then between the slither of a gap I spotted flesh and hair in the semi-light. The chin and nose of a face I recognised. It was Phoebe, and further movement exposed her naked form. She was with a man. And from her movements it was clear they were making love. Quietly, sensually.

I felt like a voyeur, but I couldn't look away.

'My love.'

A voice I knew well - Lucas. Lovers - secret lovers. How many times had they been here like this? Lucas was married. Happily, as far as I'd been aware. I should leave quietly and return later, once they'd finished and left. Their moans grew louder and more urgent, and slowly I stood up. I tiptoed to the end of the aisle and headed back down the space between the shelving.

I reached the H aisle and spotted a box file labelled Hexprin. I pulled it off the shelf and clasped it under my arm. I could still hear Lucas and Phoebe, and I realised their affair must have been going on for years. I'd heard no rumours around them, and saw them as friends and co-workers. Phoebe was such a sensible and reserved woman that I couldn't imagine anyone would suspect her of having an affair with a married man.

Near the door I passed the line of tall cabinet fridges where we kept all drug samples. I paused. It might prove useful to take one sample of Hexprin from each trial stage, and especially given that I might not be allowed back into work any day soon. They could come in handy for evidence at some point, and in that moment, it seemed a logical risk.

With the greatest care, I placed the box file onto the floor and went to the fridge marked F-J. I knew precisely which shelf they were on, unless they'd been rearranged in my absence. With a click the door opened and the light shone out. On the top shelf were metal trays of glass vials, sealed with rubber stoppers. Beside each tray were the drugs in tablet form in small coloured plastic boxes and labelled with each sample and date. All I needed was one foil strip of each sample and hopefully no one would check the exact contents and notice that any were missing. Deftly I opened each box and pulled out a strip. I kept them in order with the most recent trial drug on top and slipped them into the small inside pocket of my top. I rearranged the boxes neatly and closed the fridge door.

When I bent down and picked up the Hexprin box file my phone dropped out of my pocket and landed on the tiled floor with a thud.

I snatched it up, held my breath and listened.

I could no longer hear Phoebe and Lucas and the silence seemed to stretch before me. I didn't dare move towards the door, which would mean crossing the gap between the shelves.

I remained still. I heard Phoebe - louder whispers. There was nothing I could do other than risk heading for the door.

'Orla?'

I jumped and turned as my heart juddered in my chest.

Lucas walked towards me. Fully clothed. 'What are you doing here?'

'Lucas,' I said, 'I wasn't expecting anyone to be here.'

'Clearly.' His tone was unyielding. 'What are you after exactly?'

Immediately, I sensed he knew that I'd been sent home.

'I wanted to check out some information on the research for Hexprin.' Honesty seemed the best approach.

'But why sneak around at night?'

'Because I was working on something at home and it couldn't wait. You know Hexprin is close to launch?'

'Of course. But Jakob told me you went off sick again after only one day back. Therefore, why are you here at this late hour?'

'Because I care about my work and the matter is urgent.'

'I've been notified that you're no longer responsible for Hexprin. Melanie's taken over.'

What a total jobsworth, I thought. Had he forgotten or did he even care that I'd just lost my husband and baby.

'Was this before I returned?' I asked.

'I'm afraid not. Jakob sent an email to management this afternoon.'

My throat felt dry and I swallowed hard. So Jakob had no intention of allowing me back to work. I had to think fast.

'OK. The thing is, I'm waiting to see the counsellor and until then I've been told to rest. But that doesn't mean Melanie has taken over. In fact, the opposite is true. I have every intention of seeing this project through and I have concerns over aspects of the research.'

His features blackened. 'I can assure you that as manager of this project I have been through all the research findings and if I thought anything was in danger of compromising the safety of the drug I would highlight and report it.'

'That's reassuring to hear. I only want to borrow this file and I'll have it back to you by tomorrow evening. And if there's nothing concerning or untoward then no one should mind me looking over it again.'

'I can't allow you to take the file from this room.'

'But I might need to take notes and it's lengthy.'

Lucas shook his head and I knew he was going to be difficult. I knew too that he'd probably report me to Dan and Jakob tomorrow.

'Why are you working so late?' I asked.

His fingers moved to the biro in the breast pocket of his jacket and he twisted it round. 'You know me, I can't switch off and there's always too much to do.'

'But doesn't your wife prefer you to come home?' I asked.

He raised a brow but didn't reply.

'And you do have Phoebe to help lighten your load.' I smiled warmly. 'Where is she tonight?'

His face reddened. 'Phoebe's at home, obviously.'

'Only I thought I heard her.' I nodded towards the aisle. 'Back there. Talking to you and...' I paused.

He opened his mouth to speak then seemed to think better of it. He thought for a moment before he spoke. 'You're mistaken. I was listening to a podcast on my phone.'

I fixed my eyes upon his. 'Come on, Lucas, we both know that's not what you were doing.'

His mouth opened and closed as he considered me through narrowed eyes. His cheeks turned puce. 'However, I will allow you to take the file on condition that you return it to me tomorrow - tidy and complete.'

'I'll return it when I'm ready - tidy and complete.' I took a step towards the door then turned back to him. 'Oh, and how is your wife doing?' She'd had a breast lump removed earlier in the year which had been followed up with chemotherapy.

'Doing well, thank you. Given the all clear and enjoying life again.'

'I'm pleased to hear that. You must both be so relieved.'

'We are. Extremely.'

I nodded, smiled and walked swiftly out of the store. Hopefully, his indiscretion would keep him from running to Dan or Jakob. When I hurried back down the stairs from the office, the security guard looked up.

'Any luck?' he said.

'Yep, eventually, thanks.' I held it up. 'Took a bit of finding.'

'Have a good night,' he called after me, as I headed out through the main doors.

I turned and lifted my hand in a wave. 'You too.' I felt a tiny pang of guilt as I got into my car and placed the file on the passenger seat. Mostly because if they checked the security cameras, I'd be well and truly rumbled.

I drove home too fast and too eager to read through the documents. And I had the drug samples too. Result!

# Chapter 18

And here it was - right in front of me.

I knew there'd been a complication with the tests. I could also see why it might have been dismissed as irrelevant, but whichever way I viewed it, it could potentially be a real danger for some users. The second trial had involved a small sample of twenty-five women who had taken the drug once a week for one month. Their ages ranged from twenty-five to sixty-eight. Twenty-three of the women had been ecstatic about the drug. They reported having the most vivid and intense sexual experiences with their partners. One or two had said they'd never fully enjoyed sex or climaxed before taking the drug, but that Hexprin had made them crave their partner in a way they couldn't recall previously. A handful of the older women in the study said they rarely had sex but the drug had made them want it instantly. Their partners had reportedly been similarly thrilled with the results with one reporting he never realised, even after thirty years of a happy marriage, that he'd married a raging nymphomaniac. I couldn't help but smile at this comment. I'd read all of this prior to my accident.

However, it wasn't these positive reports that had concerned me. The two women who had reported side effects after taking the drug - they were my worry. And they weren't minor side effects. One of them reported that the first time she'd taken it she'd been fine until about half an hour after making love at which point she'd begun to see white spots and then her vision had turned almost entirely white. She'd felt faint and experienced horrendous griping pains and diarrhoea. This had passed after an hour or two, but it had frightened her so much that she'd refused to take the remaining three tablets. Unfortunately, because she hadn't reported this to the trials manager immediately, when she had undergone tests, her health had returned to normal. In her words, *'This drug quadrupled my arousal, but the side effects were terrifying and dramatic - so much so that I could never risk taking it again.'* The woman was in her mid-fifties and otherwise in excellent health. She'd been going through the menopause at the time and the trial doctors concluded that it was her hormonal fluctuations that had caused her fainting, not the drug itself.

The second reported side effect had been even more alarming. The woman was in her thirties and had never experienced orgasm through intercourse. She loved her partner but said their relationship had suffered due to her lack of arousal and satisfaction during intercourse. Once again, she'd taken Hexprin and reported that initially she'd become hyper aroused and desperate to jump into bed with her partner. She reported climaxing multiple times, which had made her emotional. After resting for a while, the couple had begun to make love once more. This time her partner was able to keep going for much longer and the woman again climaxed multiple times. Her partner reported covering her mouth to quell her shrieks of pleasure, but otherwise he'd been similarly elated by the experience. That was until the woman climaxed for the umpteenth time and passed out. Her partner had tried to rouse her, but the woman remained unconscious for over five minutes. He'd been about to call for an ambulance when the woman regained consciousness and began calling her partner all sorts of abusive names. She accused him of raping and abusing her. Of course, this had resulted in her abandoning the trial and attempting to claim compensation. As she'd signed a waiver, she had no grounds for compensation and the couple dropped the case. Because the woman had previously suffered from postpartum psychosis - a severe form of postnatal depression which had not been picked up in her medical notes prior to the trial, her adverse reaction had been linked to her propensity for depression, and not as a result of taking Hexprin.

These two reactions were more than enough to demand another trial. The third and final trial had been a smaller sample and all participants had had their medical records thoroughly examined and gone through a number of health tests, prior to allowing them to participate in the trial. The results were impressive and each woman reported feeling elated with their experience. One or two women had reported that they were keen to continue taking the drug, even though it hadn't yet been opened to the drugs market.

Here was the problem.

These women had all been thoroughly vetted and checked over before being allowed to take part in the Hexprin trial. In the real world, this was unlikely to be done thoroughly enough to avoid a few women experiencing problems - potentially.

So the drug had been passed as safe with enough medical evidence and authority to back it up. From my experience of assessing drug trials results, I'd seen lesser reactions preventing a drug from being approved, but instead to undergo ingredient adjustments and trials on animals. Usually, and eventually, the drug would be approved.

Another factor with Hexprin was that it contained only 'natural' ingredients, although they were highly condensed and processed to heighten their effects. That it was labelled an all-natural ingredient product had been another persuading factor for approval without necessitating additional testing, and it was even suggested the drug could eventually, at some point in the future, be bought over the counter or online.

I made photocopies of the results and filed the originals neatly back into the box.

I reflected on Lucas and Phoebe. I liked Phoebe and I couldn't help but think Lucas had taken advantage of her kind nature as well as the obvious sexual gratification. But I could also see that working together, downstairs in the labs for days on end, they must have come to know one another well. Was it poor Phoebe? Or maybe, good for Phoebe? I'd never had an illicit relationship with a married man and failed to understand why single women fell for such men and stayed with them. But it wasn't uncommon and no doubt men got caught up with married women in the same way, too. But it wasn't my problem or my position to judge them, and the fact that I'd caught them at it had at least allowed me to get away with what I'd snuck in for. I'd have to play it carefully and let Lucas know that if he told of my night-time visit, I'd repay him in some way he'd regret. God, not that I'd ever tell his wife. Not after what she'd been through. But I could make his life difficult with Dan. Dan would never ignore or allow an affair to be conducted downstairs amongst the archives. Lucas would be mortified that people knew of his affair. Outwardly, he appeared such a proper and respectable fellow that his personal reputation would be in tatters and his professional reputation may be damaged, too.

Besides, that was for tomorrow. It was past midnight, I felt ready to drop and needed to sleep.

# Chapter 19

*Wednesday*

Now that I had the information I'd been searching for, I needed to think through my approach. I rang Jakob first thing the following morning to ask if he'd arranged the counsellor appointment. Again, he said he was waiting for him to get back with a date and time. I felt mistrustful. My gut feeling was that Jakob was stalling, and I always trusted my intuition.

'Have you been up to the cemetery again yet?' he asked, trying to change the subject. 'I know you said you were going to.'

'I've been putting it off but I had thought I'd walk down this morning.'

'I wish I could come too. To support you.' Again he sounded all too sincere.

Jakob had been my friend for so long. Since recruiting me at BioMedica, we'd developed a close working relationship. I'd respected his knowledge, intelligence and work ethic, too. But in stark contrast, I now had mixed feelings about him. I doubted our friendship would survive this. His words blew hot and cold, which left me confused one minute, then I'd give him the benefit of the doubt the next. He was playing a game and I sensed he wanted me out of my job for good. And what sort of friend wanted that? No, to believe anything he said now would be a gamble and I refused to be drawn in.

'I need to speak to you and Dan about something important,' I said. 'Can I come in today or tomorrow?'

'What about?'

'I'd rather not say over the phone.'

'OK,' he said, with a distinct edge to his voice. 'Let me ask Kim if she can rearrange a meeting or two.'

'Please,' I said, not caring if I sounded desperate. 'I'll come after work if necessary.'

'Leave it with me,' he said after probing once more for me to give him an idea of what I needed to discuss.

'I must speak to both of you together,' I insisted.

The sun shone through the living room windows and I sat on the armchair in a warm square of light. It had been sunny almost continuously for the past week. An Indian Summer, as we were sometimes lucky to experience in September. The number of times I'd sat here looking out at the endless rain made me feel grateful for these remaining days of summer sun.

It had been two weeks now since the funeral. Two weeks more for me to think about Drew and Harry, the accident, their deaths and the possible location of Harry's missing body.

A glimmer of light dazzled me - a shaft of sunlight that reflected on a glass bowl on the bookshelf, half-filled with smooth stones and glass fragments Harry and I had collected during our walks down by the lake. Something drew me to the row of coloured photo albums behind the bowl and I got up from the chair and withdrew the pale blue album I knew to be full of Harry's first baby photos. My heartbeat pulsed in my ears as I carried it back to the armchair and laid it on my lap. My fingers trembled as I placed them beneath the cover, but something prevented me from opening it - the thought of his first photos and early days arousing only memories that could never be followed up with new experiences.

A shriek from outside startled me. I got up and with the album in my hands I went to the window and looked out. Down below, I saw a child, a girl of about three, running in circles and waving a colourful windmill above her head.

She ran and laughed as the windmill whizzed round and round.

I went to the coat stand at the front door, unhooked my canvas bag and slipped the photo album inside, then I grabbed my keys from the sideboard. Down on the street the girl was still laughing and playing whilst her Mum, with a tiny baby in her arms, sat on the bench. As I walked past, I felt a stab of envy and regret but I smiled their way and the mother smiled back.

I slung my bag over my shoulder and walked on down the street. As I headed towards the cemetery, nerves flitted through my insides. But I knew I must do this. I'd received a letter from the funeral director to say the two headstones had been set. The flowers would still be laid out. Sylvia had helped me to compose the words for the inscriptions, which I hoped had done them justice.

As I walked through the streets and amongst the tourists who paused and peered into shop windows or headed in and out of doorways, I reflected back on my thirty six years - the memories of which had grown ever sharper the past few days. Death had become a significant part of my life and far more than most would be unlucky to have experienced by my age.

My parents had been on a working trip abroad together when an earthquake struck off the coast of Thailand and they'd been caught up in a devastating tsunami that had destroyed entire towns and villages along with many lives of those living or visiting there. They'd only decided to go together at the last minute when Sylvia and I had assured them that at sixteen and eighteen we were perfectly capable of looking after ourselves for a week. I'll always regret not saying that we'd rather one of them stay behind, especially Mum. They hadn't both needed to go but had seen it as an opportunity to have a holiday alone, too. Together, they'd run the family business - two furniture stores - one in Penrith and one in Keswick. The shock of their deaths at the time had been overwhelmingly harrowing for both of us and twenty years on, the memory of the moment we'd found out and the alternating feelings of numbness and pain in the days, weeks and months that followed continued to haunt me. Their business had been sold and Sylvia and I had remained in the family home. Thankfully, our parents had also taken out generous life insurance policies that helped to see us through the rest of our schooling. Sylvia and I had raised ourselves from that moment onwards. Looking back, I could see both of us had gone off the rails for a while - we held all night parties and slept with more boys than was wise for our fragile emotional states. In the end it was my sixth form teacher who'd suggested we have counselling and it was only from this point on that we really began to turn our lives back around again.

Initially, our uncle Ross, Mum's older brother, and his wife, Emma, had invited us to live with them. But they lived in Cornwall and neither Sylvia nor I had wanted to leave our lives and our friends in the Lake District. Sylvia and I had held one another in our grief. We'd grown incredibly close and cared for each other in all things. Sylvia deferred going to University until I was eighteen and headed off to University, too. We'd chosen the same University in Liverpool so we could still meet up regularly. And it wasn't too far from our home where we'd return at the end of each term.

We'd both worked part-time to help support our studies and I think we'd worked harder than we might have had we still had parents to support us. Sylvia had studied psychology and after several years working in mental health support, she was now an independent life coach and highly successful. She was in such demand that she frequently had to turn down new clients. Her real-life experiences had helped equip her for that role. The reason I'd gone into pharmaceuticals had been because I was naturally good at and enjoyed the sciences. I loved all the research and lab experiments. As a teenager, my bedroom had been a haven of chemistry sets, test tubes and scientific texts, along with samples of insects, rocks and plants I'd collected during outdoor explorations. My fiction preferences were for Sci-fi and H G Wells, Arthur C Clark, Ursula le Guin and Jules Verne. At University I'd combined my science studies with a postgraduate marketing qualification and after six months of working as a barista in our local Starbucks and applying for jobs and attending interviews, I finally stepped onto the first rung of the ladder in the pharmaceutical industry. So, despite our significant setbacks and difficulties, we'd each found our way and our careers.

At the gateway to the cemetery, a breeze whipped my hair across my face. I brushed it from my eyes and looked up at the slope of sun dried grass and row after row of headstones. The sight seemed a stark reminder of how temporary and fragile all human lives were. The average lifespan might be eighty years or so, but that number bore no relation to those people that I'd loved the most. A feeling of dread made me falter and almost persuaded me to turn around and return to the safety of home, where I could instead look at their smiling faces in the photograph albums and put off the inevitable pain I knew I'd feel at their graves - distant and lifeless, but all too solid proof of their demise.

A middle-aged couple, wrapped in overcoats, despite the warmth of the day, walked towards me. They looked to be in their sixties and about the age Mum and Dad would have been if they'd lived. It was obvious the woman had been crying. She dabbed at her eyes and the man held a protective arm around her shoulders and wore an expression of quiet but mournful acceptance. The woman blew her nose and then as if she'd only now spotted me there, turned her eyes to me.

'Hello dear,' the man said and gave the slimmest of smiles. 'It's a fine day.'

I nodded. 'And does the sun make the cemetery a friendlier place?'

'I'm afraid not,' the woman said and they stopped beside me on the path.

'Of course not. I'm sorry,' I said.

'You look reluctant to enter,' she said. 'Or perhaps you're waiting for someone?' She looked beyond me and towards the town.

'I am reluctant.'

'Who have you lost?' the woman asked with a kind expression.

I took a breath and spoke what seemed to be impossible words. 'My husband and my baby.'

The woman's hand went to her mouth. 'Recently?' There was a crack in her voice.

'Eight weeks ago. I've not been back since the funeral.' I paused. 'I've had trouble with my memory.'

The man took a step closer. 'My dear, are you the young lady from the boat on the lake?'

I nodded again.

'And do you have other family nearby? Friends?'

'My sister Sylvia and I are very close. I have some friends, too.'

'Would it help for us to accompany you? We wouldn't intrude.'

'That's so kind, but no,' I said. 'I'll be OK.'

The man nodded. 'Of course you will.' He turned to the woman. 'Let's go home, Betty.'

123

He turned again to me. 'The only thing we can all be sure of in life, is that at some point or another, we are going to lose someone close to us. But their pain is gone. They are free in every respect. But in us, in our memories, they live on. As does your husband and your baby. Take care my dear.'

I smiled lightly. 'I hope you are right. And thank you for your kind words.'

They wished me farewell and walked on their way.

I took a breath, straightened my spine and walked on through the gateway. I continued up the gravel footpath to the top of the embankment and down again to where the pathway dipped prettily between a cluster of Yew and Beech trees and what looked to be the oldest burial sites. Some of the gravestones had been laid down flat and others jutted from the ground, and listed at ungainly angles. A small chapel was set back from the path between a clutch of trees and two hundred yards further still, at the bottom of the hill, stood the larger medieval church of St Paul's. To its right stood the main gated entrance from the top end of Keswick town.

As I walked, I thought back to our wedding, almost four years ago. It was such a stunning setting with Derwentwater in view, that it seemed natural to choose to marry in this church despite neither of us being religious. Several of our friends had similarly married here at a time when marriage seemed contagious. The girl in me had wanted the fairytale white wedding - the wedding that our parents had had in the same church. And today, where they were both buried, not far from Drew and Harry. I still had their silver framed wedding photograph on my mantelpiece - in it Sylvia stood beside them, their two year old flower girl born out of wedlock. Sometimes I wished I'd been their first born to have been at their wedding - a far preferable memory to being at their funeral. They made a striking couple. Dad, tall and handsome with long legs, olive skin, roman nose and chiselled cheekbones. Mum, graceful and slender despite being five months pregnant with me and with her long black, pretty curls coiled around her face. When they'd first met, Mum had been performing in a production of Equus at the Edinburgh Festival. Dad had been in the audience and told how he had been mesmerised by her performance. Mum would laugh and say,

'You know it's because I had to perform one scene completely naked.'

Dad would chortle and reply, 'But the lights were too dim and I gazed only upon your face, my dear.' Dad had taken to calling her his darling thespian as a term of endearment which would always make mum smile.

I remembered Mum vividly, with her colourful sense of fashion, wonderful singing voice and ever warm embrace. She'd sing us lullabies at bedtime, and when doing chores, she'd sing loudly and confidently along to the radio. I'd inherited her tuneful voice whilst Sylvia had inherited her daring sense of fashion. Gazing at Mum's photo I was often struck by the remarkable likeness of her features to form mine and Sylvia's - Sylvia and I could almost be twins if it weren't for the two year age gap, despite our differences in colouring.

I followed a bend in the path and drew closer to their stones, and the mounds of colourful flowers came into view. In contrast to the sound of birdsong in the trees and the distant rumble of cars and the bustle of the town, my heartbeat throbbed in my ears, and my mind and body felt in a state of high alert. I drew closer and saw their gravestones in place - burnished black with gold engraved lettering. My legs felt weak in front of the stones and I sat cross legged on the grass - cool and damp against my bare legs. I inhaled deeply, but my heart rattled faster against my ribs. I pulled my sunglasses up onto my head and read the words on Harry's stone.

*Harry Safian*
*Born 18 June 2017, Died 15 July 2019*
*The sun beamed on us the day you were born*
*and in our memories you shine on still*
*Sleep well, sweet boy,*
*beside your father who protects and keeps you near*

My breath shuddered and through the blur of my tears I sensed Harry, sitting beside me with his toy truck, pushing it over the tufts of grass while he made engine noises. I reached out to him and my hand came to rest on the grass. I felt the lightest touch of his tiny fingers upon mine. I turned my palm and clasped them and heard his laughter echo in the trees above me.

'Harry,' I said aloud. 'Are you here?'

His absence seemed unreal. I knew that he'd gone, but at the same time, I couldn't accept the reality of this.

I waited for his voice in reply, but only silence followed - cruel, empty and unforgiving. An image of the child's fingers that had reached through the soil at the burial came into my mind. What illness or tragedy had befallen the child? I looked across at the engraving on his memorial stone.

*'Christopher Jones. 1978-1986.'* Only eight years old. A bouquet of white roses had been laid upon the freshly rearranged soil at the foot of the small stone cross. No doubt the family had been informed about the disintegration of their child's coffin.

Another boy. Too young to be taken from his family and denied a longer life.

But at eight years old that would have given me six additional years to watch Harry grow into his boyhood. To see how his features changed day by day, his voice and the words he could use, his personality to continue to shape and grow. To strengthen our bond further. Would that extra time have made losing him any easier? It would have meant more photographs and memories, but if anything, it might have made losing him even more agonizing. I placed my palm on the photograph album.

I wiped away my tears and turned to Drew's stone. Compared to Harry's stone, it seemed to take on a very different stance. Did I imagine there was something sinister in the way it looked back at me?

Drew had been in the year above me at school, although we'd attended different schools. He'd boarded at an exclusive public school in North Yorkshire. Both of his parents were doctors. His Jewish father, Henri, was French born but had done his medical training in London where he'd met Drew's mother, Heather. She was an outspoken atheist and now an eminent professor at Durham University. Drew had turned thirty seven only a week before the accident. Ironically, the boat trip had in part been to celebrate his birthday. We'd booked a table at, The Gables, a restaurant in the town with an a la carte menu. We'd invited Jakob along, but he said he'd have to head off to see his mother

- she lived nearby. Jakob was close to his mum and he often mentioned her and received calls from her at work.

My insides spasmed and I took some slow breaths until the pain subsided. I had no trouble seeing the Drew I'd loved for over fifteen years. Almost six feet tall, dark auburn hair that curled to his shoulders. Muscular, but not in a bulky way - more lean and angular. For work he'd tie his hair back in a ponytail but refused to have it cut into any conventional styles. It suited him and enhanced his cheekbones and his wide, bow tipped lips. His eyes were the colour of the finest ale and he had the most enviable eyelashes, courtesy of his father. Drew was handsome in a very masculine way. Sometimes, I'd call him my Apollo. But although he was gorgeous, he wasn't arrogant with it. He never spent longer than necessary dressing or shaving, and any sense of vanity had completely bypassed him. He must have known he was handsome. For one thing, I was always telling him so. I could hardly believe that he'd wanted me - that he'd chosen me to be his life long partner. I'd always felt like an eight compared to his ten. But whenever in a rare moment I'd voiced this to my friends, particularly after Harry came along, they'd dismissed my concerns. 'You're stunning, Orla. I'd swap my face, my body, my entire life for yours in a flash.' Kim had once said. 'And not only because Drew's drop dead gorgeous,' she added with a laugh. I knew she was only being kind but she was the sort of friend to always bolster my confidence when I needed it.

Since Harry came into our lives, I'd come to know a very different side to Drew. Maybe even from the moment I discovered I was pregnant. Rather than strengthening the bond between us it was almost as though Harry, our sweet beloved Harry, had begun to build a wall between us - a wall that grew taller and broader each day, brick by brick. It wasn't that I saw our baby as more important than Drew either before or after he was born, it was more that Drew viewed me differently.

I'd loved how my body had changed from the moment I conceived. My breasts, my complexion, my belly. I hadn't put on a huge amount of weight, but I'd become more curvy, more womanly in my eyes. I'd always been on the skinny side - my legs and arms too slim, despite my exercising regularly. It was

127

how I was built. But with pregnancy I finally had full, round buttocks and curvaceous thighs.

My friends made admiring comments about my new curves and Drew would join in, though he never convinced me. I knew from Drew's dwindling lack of interest in me sexually, that he didn't find the new me desirable. With reluctance, he'd put his hand on my belly when Harry kicked or when I encouraged him to talk up close to my stretched skin so that our baby could get to know his Daddy's voice. I felt frustrated and rejected physically even before Harry was born. And once I had Harry at my breast, the distance between us only lengthened. Prior to my pregnancy we'd made love most nights or would make love spontaneously on the living room floor or even al fresco. Drew had always been insatiable, as had I, with him. I loved his body and his raw masculinity and how desirable he made me feel.

But his lack of attention left me feeling unloved, frustrated and resentful - and it was Drew who had persuaded me to get pregnant. I was overwhelmed with joy to finally have our darling baby boy, but I'd felt increasingly hurt when motherhood had destroyed the intimacy in our relationship.

Sitting here now, in front of his grave, I wondered if our relationship had already died before he had. How cruel that I was looking at my husband's grave and the only real sense of loss I felt was that he hadn't really loved me in the way that I'd loved him, or at least had loved him before we'd had our child. That was the only loss I could truly admit to.

'Where did we go wrong?' I heard myself say. 'What did I do wrong?'

I wiped at my tears. There was nothing wrong with my memory. All of my past, our relationship from the very start, giving birth to Harry - it seemed only too clear for me to see now and in vivid technicolour.

I got up and looked down at the wreaths of flowers wrapped in cellophane and tied with shining ribbons. I crouched down and read the messages. A fresh bouquet placed next to Drew's stone caught my eye. It was small with delicate blue and lilac flowers and white gypsophila. It must have only been laid within the past couple of days such were the flower's freshness. I picked them up. A small card lay almost hidden amongst the stems and I reached my fingers down to retrieve it.

When I read the words the world teemed around me and my legs gave way.

I sank to the ground.

*'Darling Drew, I miss you. S xx.'*

I turned the card over. That was all it said. Who was S? And I knew instantly, by the cryptic 'S' and the kisses, it was a message from a lover. I wasn't so naive to think it could be anything but his lover. So, that was why Drew had no longer wanted me in that way. No longer desired me in the way that I'd desired him. Despite our relationship losing its spark, I'd never suspected him of being unfaithful. What a fool. It all made perfect sense now. But who was she and how long had the affair been going on? How would I ever find out? Should I talk to his colleagues at work? And was there any point in doing so? Perhaps he was planning on leaving me. Leaving Harry and me. If he had stopped loving me, and I felt certain of this now, he'd have had no trouble making another woman fall for him. Drew was attractive in every sense. Intelligent, cultured, athletic build, a confident conversationalist and a bloody doctor, for God's sake. What single woman wouldn't find him irresistible, other than that he was married?

I slipped the card into the pocket of my shorts and resisting the temptation to dump them on the nearest compost heap, placed them back in the same position. I looked all around me. The hairs on my skin prickled and I felt a chill seep through me. Was she close by, watching me? Perhaps I could fix a surveillance camera onto a tree to see who visited the grave? But whoever she was, there was every chance she may never return. Or at least, not for weeks to come. Jealousy wasn't a feeling I'd experienced often but now it burned through me. My mouth filled with saliva and my bowels turned to liquid. Drew had turned against me. I'd never once rejected his love or affection. I'd vowed to love him forever. His vows had clearly meant nothing to him. Maybe 'S' was prettier and more interesting than me. For certain, I knew she didn't have children. Many times during the past year I'd tried talking to him about how he felt about 'us', but he'd insisted that he still loved me and that he felt overwhelmed with work and being a father. But even though I'd tried not to pressure him with housework or caring for Harry, it hadn't made him any more affectionate towards me. And now he was gone, and I'd never be able to talk things through with him again. And as for who S was, I'd probably never know either. This would leave me in limbo about my feelings for him and our marriage. Grieving for Harry was going to be painful enough on its own, but coming to terms with what I had or hadn't meant to Drew, and of letting go of him, would be something else altogether. Did all the years we have together amount to nothing more than a lie?

# Chapter 20

*Wednesday*

I knelt before Harry's grave and leaned in and kissed his name. 'I love you so much, Harry. Do you hear me? I will always love you. Don't ever forget, my beautiful boy.'

I cast a final glance at the fresh bouquet then I turned and stumbled my way across the grass. By the time I'd reached the gates of the cemetery I'd already decided what I would do next. Angry tears streamed down my cheeks as I made my way back up through the narrow bustling streets towards home. The warmth of the afternoon sun did nothing to brighten my mood and I didn't care what I looked like as I wept, with my head bowed and watching my feet step one in front of the other. I glanced up every now and then as I passed people, and their faces turned to me with concern.

I slammed the front door to my flat behind me, sank to my knees and retched. I stayed this way, releasing the pent up pain and yearning for two people who filled me with such mixed emotions - grief, regret, loss and utter confusion. I remained there until I had nothing left. This was my life now - no husband - a husband who for the last two years or more hadn't loved me, and who was most likely planning on leaving us if his life hadn't been snatched away.

For some time, I sat with my back against the door, and grew increasingly angry with Drew, and with an ache in my belly for my lost baby. If only I'd realised he was having an affair months ago and confronted him full on - no treading lightly around how he was struggling with being a new father. He was nothing but a coward unwilling to face up to his responsibilities and instead sought solace with another woman - a free agent completely at his beck and call. What about me? Couldn't he see that I'd been struggling, too?

A long horn blast out on the street finally brought me back to the present. Most likely another frustrated delivery driver unable to get through - it happened too often down these streets. I got up and walked to the kitchen for a glass of water. My legs felt unsteady and the back of my throat felt raw. I twisted the tap and let it run cold. If Drew had been having an affair, surely there must be evidence. Perhaps a lover's gift or a letter. Or some online evidence! Yes, that was where affairs took place these days - loving texts, sexting, and photos, too.

I walked across the living room and through to Drew's study - the smallest room in the flat but large enough for a desk, a set of shelves and a rocking chair. The room looked out across the back yards and gardens. We shared a small lawned garden with Vincent above, and Polly Jameson, a recently retired social worker, in the flat below. She was a single lady who never seemed short of visitors. I looked out and saw her sitting on the garden bench with a lady friend I'd seen her with before. They both had books in hand and hot drinks resting on the table in the middle. Drew had occasionally raised a brow and pointed out when yet another lady came to stay, and once or twice suggested she was a lesbian with numerous lovers. I'd laughed and told him he had a one track mind, though in truth, I did wonder if he might be right, only because I'd once seen her kiss one of her friends on the lips as they'd talked in the garden. Not that I'd judge or begrudge her any enjoyment on that score. Quite the opposite. I also knew Drew had only been teasing with me and in no way judged others' sexual preferences.

I went to his desk and looked down on the piles of papers and the pot of pens beside his closed laptop, untouched from the last time he'd sat here. I couldn't recall ever looking through the desk drawers. I'd had no reason to. No reason to mistrust him. I pulled open the top draw. Drew wasn't the sort of person to accumulate junk and papers he no longer needed. Other than some loose paper clips, more pens and various stationery items, there weren't even any notebooks or papers to read through. I sat down and pulled the largest pile of papers towards me. There was a letter from our bank notifying us of mortgage charges for the year, a receipt for his latest car service and a form for him to complete for his annual performance review at work. According to the date at the top it had been due in a few days before the accident.

Why hadn't he completed it? Or maybe he'd done it online. There was nothing much else of note amongst the pile and I pushed the chair back to stand up. As I did, I kicked the waste paper bin beneath and it toppled over and spilled some of the contents. I knelt down to clear them up. Amongst them I noticed a tight bundle of paper and I unravelled it and flattened it out on my thigh.

It was another copy of his work review form but this one was half completed. Most of it was blank but he'd handwritten under the heading, 'Highlight any areas of difficulty this year'.

I read his written reply.

*'Becoming a father has been a harder transition than I could have ever anticipated. I genuinely don't know how Orla does it, but she does so in a way that has shown her in the best light I've ever seen her. She gets up for him at night whereas I lie exhausted in bed too drained to move. I've failed as a father from day one. If our baby relied on me alone, I could never have held down my job as well. But the truth is, I wouldn't have wanted to care for him full time. I love my son. How could I not? But many evenings I find an excuse to avoid going home so that he'll be in bed by the time I get in. I know Orla's frustrated with me, but she doesn't get angry. I know I would in her shoes.'*

There were furious black scribbles and doodles down one margin.

Drew had no intention of handing this handwritten form in. He was using it to express his frustration and unhappiness. I'd known all along that something was terribly wrong between us. I should have tried harder to encourage him to open up. But I could only recall him muttering and turning away to avoid any of the real conversations I'd tried to initiate. I should have insisted he see a counsellor. Both of us together. But I couldn't help feeling angry that he'd been too weak to cope with the responsibility of parenthood. He should have tried harder. He was a doctor, for God's sake and responsible for people's lives at their most vulnerable. It wasn't as though my job was a breeze. Far from it. And although this confession had shown he'd appreciated me, he'd barely shown it in person.

Why hadn't he told me how he felt?

I'd opened up to him about how I was struggling. And it was poor Harry who had borne the brunt of our marital problems. And maybe that was in part the reason he rarely slept through. He wanted our attention. He wanted more of his Dad's attention. Only now, I'd never know or be able to alter the past.

That didn't explain who'd left the flowers and card at his headstone. I flipped open his laptop and the screen sprang to life with the login boxes. I had no idea what his password could be. I'd never considered either checking his phone or trying to spy on him in any way. I knew people did spy on their partners if they suspected them of an indiscretion or an affair. I'd been too trusting - too busy to be suspicious. Could his password be Harry? Too obvious but worth a try. I typed it in but after only a moment it returned with an error. Maybe Harry1. I tried that, but again, incorrect. If I kept trying and failing, I'd be locked out. I stared at the screen.

Think, Orla.

What I needed was an IT expert, or more realistically, a hacker. The BioMedica IT team and Tony in particular came to mind. Tony had often helped me out with technical problems and whenever I'd stood aside as he worked on my laptop, we'd shared stuff about our personal lives. Unlike some men, or women for that matter, he was forthcoming in that way. He'd told me all about his father who'd been diagnosed with early onset Alzheimers and admitted he was terrified at how quickly his dad was deteriorating and how his Mum was suffering a near breakdown as a result. I recalled his extension number and called him at work.

'Sorry we didn't get to chat properly when you were in,' he said, and his voice softened. 'How are you?'

'Not brilliant, but getting there, I think.' I paused. 'As you know I'm not fully back in work yet.'

'I heard. I asked after you and Jakob said you decided you weren't quite ready.'

There's a surprise, I thought, and felt my irritation bubble up. 'I'm hoping to be back properly soon though.'

'Cool. I miss our craic.'

'Bet you don't miss me dragging you in to sort out my techy problems though.'

'Course I do. You're my favourite technophobe,' he said and laughed.

'Hey! I'm good on computers.'

He laughed. 'You know I'm kidding.'

I laughed too. 'I miss you guys.'

'Now what can I do for you?'

We hung up after Tony kindly insisted he'd drop over after work to sort out access to Drew's laptop, emails and messages. Tony was one of those colleagues that made work life infinitely easier and richer for everyone.

'Did you manage to park OK?' I said, and stood aside to let him in.

'Yeah, I snuck in as someone pulled out. Lucky timing.'

We headed up the stairs.

'Evenings can be difficult if you don't have a permit,' I said.

'It's a pleasure to help you and I was only going home to play Minecraft.'

'Really?' I said.

He guffawed and scratched his beard. 'No, but that's what most people at work think I spend my free time doing.'

I laughed. 'I'd be more inclined to think you'd want a break from technology.'

'Truthfully, I just move over to different technology - playing my synth and social media mostly.'

I led him through to the study. 'It's really only because I need access to some of the letters from our utility providers and some information on Drew's will.'

'How about his phone?'

'That was lost in the accident.'

'iPad?'

'Actually, yes. I think it linked to his phone, so that could be useful.'

Tony didn't seem in the least suspicious of my motives for wanting to read Drew's messages or emails.

'You're a lifesaver, Tony. Can I get you something to eat and drink?'

'Wouldn't mind, thanks, I'm ravenous as always.'

135

'I'll phone for a pizza,' I said. 'Maybe some cheesy carbs will perk me up too.' I felt hollow after barely eating and throwing up after my visit to the cemetery.

'Cheesy carbs are always a staple, in my book,' Tony said, as he opened up the laptop.

I collected Drew's iPad still on his bedside table and handed it to Tony.

I left him leaning over the screens and went to order pizza and to brew some tea.

When I returned, I set Tony's mug beside the laptop.

He looked up at me and grinned. 'iPad all sorted.'

I took it from him. 'Blimey. That was fast work.'

'I have my uses,' he said. 'I recommend you try clicking his gmail, and text messages. WhatsApp, too.'

'Yes, he used WhatsApp. Will I need a password?'

'His new password is Orla.'

'My kind of password. You're brilliant.'

'Not really. A smart ten year old could hack in as fast.'

'I wouldn't know where to start, so I'm grateful.'

'No probs.' He paused for a moment. 'Must have been strange losing your memory, on top of everything else.'

I nodded and leaned against the desk. 'It's been horrible, and I veer between feeling OK-ish one minute, to frightened and confused the next. And now my memory is back, I have to face up to everything.' I felt a painful twinge behind one eye and massaged my forehead.

'You OK?' he said, with a look of concern.

'I think so. I still get the odd twinge and headache. Doc said it's common after a brain injury.'

'I'm sure,' he said.

'I visited the graves today, for the first time since the funeral.'

'Did you go alone?' he asked.

'Yes, and I needed to.'

'And how did you feel?'

'Dizzy. Ill. Angry. Partly in denial still.'

'I can imagine. I'm always here to talk if you want a sympathetic ear.'

My eyes watered. 'You're so kind, Tony. And I will.' I felt tempted to mention my problems with Jakob and Melanie, but it didn't seem fair to involve him. 'How are you finding working with Melanie?'

He sniffed. 'You really want my opinion?'

'Yes, I do.'

'I dunno. If she has her own voice, she's hiding it. She's maybe inexperienced or daunted by Jakob.'

'Mmmm. Kim said something similar. I don't know her well enough to comment yet.'

'Hopefully, when you're back, she'll move on. She's not a patch on you - professionally or personally. The whole office would say the same.'

My eyes welled. 'Do you know, Tony, I really needed to hear that today. Thank you.' I leaned over and gave him a hug.

'Important to know who your friends are at times like these,' he said.

'You're not kidding.'

'How's Jakob being with you returning, given it was his boat?' he asked.

I chewed my top lip. 'I'm not sure. He feels terrible about his part in the accident so in one way I can see he's being over protective and cautious.' I thought back to the men down by the lake. 'And he's been a life saver in ways I can't begin to explain. But, he's singing Melanie's praises and I'm feeling insecure.'

'They do seem pally,' he said. 'Maybe too close.'

I nodded. 'But soon I will prove to Jakob and everyone else that I'm fit enough for my job.'

'I don't doubt it,' he replied and took a long slug of his tea.

I picked up the iPad and typed in my password. A screen full of apps sprang to life. I clicked on the email icon which opened fine. I didn't want to probe them right now, so I closed it again and found the message and WhatsApp icons. Similarly, both opened without a hitch. 'All seems to be working fine, but I'll peruse later.'

I heard the downstairs door bell. 'Pizzas were fast!'

I hurried into the living room, grabbed my purse, ran down the stairs and opened the front door. My heart juddered, and everything stopped for a split second. The pizza delivery girl stood beside Jakob who raised an eyebrow.

137

The breath caught in my throat, but I dared not show any reaction to his surprise appearance. I paid and thanked the girl and gave her a tip.

Jakob eyed the box with a creased brow. 'That's a mighty big pizza for one.'

I wasn't pleased to see him. 'It's because I've had too many comments about being skinny.'

'You know you look stunning, and anyway, you should eat for nutrition - rather than empty carbs.'

I felt like throwing the box at him, but I refused to react.

'Mind if I come in?' he said, and took a step closer.

I moved into the middle of the doorway. 'Actually, I'm tired. Is it important?'

'I dropped by on my way home to let you know the counsellor, Mark Winters, can see you on Friday.'

'OK. What time shall I come in?'

'No need. Mark will come here - 10am. Said it would be helpful to see you in your home setting.'

'Isn't it my work setting that matters?'

'Mark's the professional, so…' Jakob's words trailed off.

I took a deep breath. 'Then I look forward to meeting him.' I had no intention of inviting Jakob in and wasn't in the mood for polite conversation. I remained mute and waited for him to leave.

Not getting the hint he asked. 'Did you go to the cemetery?'

'Uh huh.'

'How was it?'

My voice rose. 'How do you think? Horrible.' I didn't add that included his resistance to my returning, or the mysterious card amongst the freshly laid flowers.

'Sorry.' He held his hands up. 'I didn't mean to upset you.'

'Now my memory's returned, it's all too real,' I said, my voice deliberately blunt.

'Which is why I want to give you more time to come to terms with it.'

'Which is why I need to be working,' I said, but my throat thickened and my voice cracked.

'I'll leave you to eat your pizza, alone,' he said, and frowned at the box again, 'and hopefully we can fix a time to see you about whatever it is you need to discuss.' His eyes bore into mine. 'If you can't tell me what it is now?'

It wouldn't hurt to keep him guessing. 'I must speak to you and Dan together.'

His eyes narrowed and he sighed. 'I hope you trust me, Orla?'

About as much as my dead unfaithful husband, I thought.

'I'll wait and talk to you both.'

His jaw clenched. 'This is ridiculous. We've worked together for years. You're behaving completely out of character for me.'

'As you keep trying to imply, so why are you so surprised?'

'Because I want to know the Orla I knew before.'

'Then let me come back in and do the job you and I both know I can do far better than Melanie. Then you'll see the real me.'

'You're making that impossible right now.'

'Impossible because I won't comply with your wishes?'

He scrubbed a hand through his hair. 'I give up, Orla.' And without a goodbye he turned abruptly and walked away.

I was shaking, but I felt a sense of achievement that I'd wound him up.

When I walked into the flat, Tony stood looking out of the living room window. He turned to me. 'Everything OK?'

'You saw Jakob?' I said, and placed the pizza box on the dining table.

'I did.'

'I have to see a counsellor on Friday. In fact, our head of HR, Mark Winters. To see if I'm fit to return to work.'

'And do you want and need to talk to him?' Tony enquired.

'Not at all. But it seems I have no choice.' I laid two serviettes on the table. 'Let's eat.' I tugged a chair back, sat down and opened the box. 'It does smell delicious.'

Tony sat opposite me and we each tore off a slice of pizza.

'Could be HR policy,' said Tony. 'To see someone after so many weeks off.'

'I'm not so sure,' I said. 'If it was, he'd have organised for me to see someone before I returned.'

'True,' replied Tony, before taking a bite.

'But, it's OK. I know I'm fit enough and I can convince the counsellor of the same.'

'If you need someone to back you up, give me a shout.'

'I will, thank you. But I don't want to drag you into any tussles.'

For a while as we chatted and ate, my mind became distracted.

'Thank you so much for this, Tony. And not only the computer stuff,' I said, as he gave me a quick hug in the doorway. 'You've been such a friend in more ways than you can imagine.'

'I'm glad. Show that HR guy how strong you really are. We want you back.'

When Tony had gone, I carried Drew's iPad and laptop through to the living room. I selected some Chopin and poured a shot of Jack Daniels. My stomach turned over as I opened Drew's WhatsApp messages.

# Chapter 21

At the top of the screen there were ten unopened messages from, 'S'.

My heart pounded - they'd been sent the day of the accident.

Was she a Simone, Susan, Sally? No surname and not even a full forename which sent my suspicions skyrocketing. Damn it - no photo either, only the head of a brown dog. I took a sip of whisky and tapped the screen with a trembling finger.

The words merged as my eyes raced to take them in.

*'Where are you?'*

*'Why won't you answer your phone?'*

*'Please, Drew, pick up - I have to talk to you.'*

*'I'm worried.'*

The messages had been sent the evening on the day of the accident, no kisses or love hearts, and there were no messages prior to that. Drew must have deleted them all. Covered his tracks. Avoided discovery. She'd see that they'd been read now. But she also knew his fate, hence no further messages.

My head spun. I could ring the number. Send a text.

Instinctually, I keyed her number into my phone. After five rings, someone answered. I waited for her to speak but there was only silence.

'Who is this?' I said. I heard breathing. 'This is Orla. Orla Safian.'

The line went dead. I called again, but this time it was left unanswered. I threw my phone onto the sofa. If their relationship was innocent, whoever it was would surely have spoken.

Had Drew mentioned a woman at work whose name began with S? I'd been to one or two of the hospital functions, but that was prior to Harry. Drew had been to a few parties and functions since then, but because of Harry's sleep patterns it was almost always me who'd stay home. Drew and I had barely had a night out together in the past two years. That hadn't helped our relationship. I wouldn't make excuses for him, though. No. I

141

wanted to know the full extent of his deceit. I wanted to know exactly who I'd married. Who'd fathered our child. When I thought back to our relationship before Harry, I could never have imagined Drew doing the dirty behind my back. He'd been sensitive, shared his worries with me, far more open about his feelings than any of the boys I'd dated prior to him. Of course his looks often attracted admiring glances from women and I could always tell when someone was flirting with him. But he'd take my hand, bring me into the conversation, and make it perfectly clear that I was his and he was mine.

So, why had our relationship gone so horribly wrong? Had I really been so attentive to Harry that I'd ignored Drew? No, I don't believe I had and I wasn't prepared to take the blame for his philandering. If that's what it was. I'd be naive to think it was anything less.

The only other messages were from me, his parents and brother and a few of our mutual friends.

What about photos? My WhatsApp images automatically saved to my photo gallery, but did it work on an iPad? Drew had been a keen photographer with a decent following on Instagram. I wondered who he followed. That might hold a clue. My mind whirled and clicked with all the places I could search. My stomach churned as I looked through the gallery. Mostly, they were of Harry. So many of these I'd never seen before, and there were one or two where I was playing with or walking with Harry clutching my hand. I didn't know Drew had taken them. I ached at the sight of Harry beside me. Photographs and videos were all I had to remember him by and these of Drew's would add to my memories. To watch Harry crawl across the kitchen floor and pull himself up against the kitchen cabinets. To see him climb onto our king size bed which he'd only recently managed to do, such was its height. To hear his giggles. Even to hear him wail, something that had always grated upon me previously, but now I needed to hear more than anything. The lump in my throat hurt as if I'd swallowed a stone. It choked me and for a few moments I couldn't catch my breath.

I poured another shot of whisky. As Chopin's nocturnes played, the melodies did nothing to calm my thoughts which darted like needles through my mind. I worked my way through his most recent emails. In his sent file I spotted an email to a S.O'Neill. I wondered how old she was or what she looked like. I Googled S.O'Neill and it didn't take long to find a photograph of her on their hospital website. Dr. S. O'Neill - no forename. She looked a similar age to me, slim freckled face, blue eyes, and her hair was smooth, flaxen blonde tied into a bun on top. Natural looking and definitely attractive.

I copied her email address into the search bar. He'd received several from her. I read through the first three sent a couple of months ago which appeared professional and to the point. Their exchange regarded a drug that would be replaced by a newer version.

When I searched through his online calendar there were a number of appointments with no name or description - a few of them were around lunchtime whilst others were early in the evening.

Then as I cast my mind back, like a net capturing what I needed to know, I recalled that Drew kept a pocket diary which he'd slot into his suit pocket. I'd never looked in it but had asked him why he still kept one when he could have everything synced online.

'I like having one. Writing in it. I'll always keep one,' he had said.

I stood up, walked through to the bedroom and opened Drew's side of the wardrobe. He had half a dozen suits, all neatly hung and orderly. I hadn't considered going through his clothes yet. Seeing them again made me picture how each morning he'd pause in front of them for a few moments before he picked out a hanger - a different suit each day.

I took a breath and pushed the image of him aside, before I slipped my fingers into the pockets and pulled out the odd tissue and receipt. When I slid my hand into his black pinstriped suit pocket my fingers met the hard rectangular outline of a book. Here it was, presumably the last jacket he'd worn. I sat down on the bed and turned to find his last entry. My hands trembled as I turned the pages. Dated a week after the accident he'd drawn a star beside the time, 5.30pm. No names, places or anything to explain the nature of the appointment. I flipped frantically through more days. There were plenty of times with names for meetings or reminders of things he needed to do. Most concerningly, there were other little stars that indicated appointments in the evenings, but with no names and no mention anywhere of an S or Dr O'Neill. I closed the diary and placed it on his bedside table. I wondered how many other widows and widowers went through their partner's papers and possessions and discovered things they wished they hadn't. Or perhaps glad that they had. We all had secrets. Things we preferred not to share.

Dared not share.

At least I imagined most people did. In truth, I hadn't been whiter than white throughout our marriage. There had been that kiss with Vincent that evening. If it had only been a kiss with no feelings involved, I could easily forgive myself. But we'd never repeated it, and when Vincent had come round to talk about it, I'd been quick to dismiss it as a foolish moment, suspecting that if I dared to admit it to myself or to him, my mind and body had taken over where the kiss had ended.

And if I was being brutally honest with myself, there had even been odd moments with Jakob. Moments that might easily have slipped into more than friendship if I'd allowed them to. After his wife, Priya, had died, he'd opened up to me, even said I was the only one he could talk to properly. Intuitively, I know Jakob would have responded if I'd shown a willingness that would have allowed him in, but I'd always taken a step back. Although Jakob was physically attractive, I had never been attracted to his personality or physicality in a sexual way.

One day at work, a few months after Priya passed away, I'd seen Jakob struggling. He'd been cutting and rude with colleagues and after one overreaction he'd slammed his door and booted the waste bin scattering papers across the office floor. When everyone else had gone for the night I went into his office and sat beside him on the comfy chairs.

'Talk to me, Jakob.'

'What for? Talking won't bring her back.'

'I'm a good listener.'

'You're more to me than that, Orla,' he said, and held my gaze. 'I don't want to burden you over and over like this.'

'We're friends aren't we?'

'I hope so.'

'You know so,' I said.

'It's not only losing Priya, it's Mum.'

'You're staying with her at the moment?'

'She says she needs me there.'

'Maybe you need her, too?'

He shook his head. 'She's not easy to be around, but she adored Priya.'

'They were close then?'

'They didn't always get on, but in time, they found things in common. There were times I felt like I was invisible when they got talking.'

'Did that bother you?'

'Yes, and no. Mum knew about our difficulties conceiving. She'd offer advice on Priya's cycle, the right things to eat to improve our chances.'

'You were an only child, weren't you?'

'It was a huge disappointment to Mum that she could never have another child. They tried. I think there may have been miscarriages. There were times she'd lie in bed for days at a time refusing to see anyone - even me, her only child.'

'That is sad. I can't imagine not having Harry now I have him. And one day, we'll hopefully have another child. Once Harry's sleeping well and I've slept properly for a year. At least. And if I'm still fertile.'

He nodded. 'So you see, Priya and Mum had that in common. I desperately wanted children too, but I didn't want that to become our sole goal together.'

'I can understand why women feel that need for a baby. I might not have experienced this myself, but if I couldn't conceive, I'm certain I'd have become obsessed with the idea of a baby of my own.'

Jakob reached over and took my hand and looked into my eyes. 'You're astonishingly beautiful. Do you know that?'

I'd felt my cheeks redden. 'No I'm not.'

'I don't only mean your face. Though you surely see that each time you look in the mirror. But in the way that people treat you and admire you. Beauty is incredibly powerful. But equally, it's your soul. Your mind - your kindness and empathy.'

145

I felt my eyes moisten. 'To me, there's nothing more important in a human being. We are all here sharing this world. And most of our problems stem from humans failing to see that we are all one and the same.'

'That's why you're so attractive to me, Orla.' Jakob lifted my hand and raised it to his mouth. He pressed his lips to my fingers - softly and sensually.

And in that moment, I wanted to hold him. I'd wanted him to put his arms around me. But the moment was fleeting and I lowered my hand to my side.

'Do you ever feel that we've known one another in a former life?' he asked.

I felt taken aback. 'I don't think that's occurred to me.'

'I often get that feeling when I look at you,' he said. 'It's most likely because you understand me better than anyone else I know.'

I didn't want to give him the wrong idea about our relationship, and I shifted back in my chair and changed the subject. 'I know, why don't you come over for dinner on Saturday? Drew and I would love the company and I can invite a female friend, too. It'll give you the chance to spend some time away from your Mum.'

Jakob had accepted graciously and apologised for kissing my hand.

'I don't think I've ever had a man kiss my hand before.' Though it had felt far more than a gentlemanly gesture.

We smiled and laughed about it and established again that friendship was as far as our relationship would ever go. At least, that was my impression.

Right now, I had enough to cope with, without obsessing over who 'S' might be. All I needed to know was that Drew had been having an affair. Had I ever neglected him? No, I don't believe I had. I'd tried so hard to keep us close whilst trying everything I could think of to cope with Harry at night and keep on top of my job. But the realisation that for the last god knows how long our marriage had been a lie, made me feel physically ill.

I fell back onto the pillow. 'Damn you, Drew.'

I wept, and it felt cathartic to release my grief and frustration.

146

Worn out from crying, I dozed off and woke up some time later to the sound of a pigeon cooing out on the window ledge. The bedroom had a peculiar stillness about it with strange silvery shadows on the walls cast by the streetlamp outside my window. I felt too miserable and exhausted to wash, and I undressed and left my clothes in a pile on the end of the bed, then crawled under the duvet and fell back into a dream-filled sleep.

*I pace the length of the living room back and forth. Harry continues to wail as I hold his compact and warm body close to me and smooth my palm over his back.*

*Drew, who's reclining on the sofa with his feet up on the coffee table, folds his newspaper and stands up. He huffs with irritation and walks away to the bedroom.*

*I quell my tears and try everything to soothe Harry. I feed him - again, change his nappy, check his temperature - again, leave him to cry in his cot, pick him up and carry him round from room to room.*

*Downstairs, I pull the pram from the alcove and lie Harry down. He looks up at me with wet, pleading eyes and his wails intensify.*

*Out on the street, and with the movement and the marbled grey of the sky to gaze up at, Harry's cries quieten. I pray that he'll fall asleep so I can return home and rest, finally. I turn the corner at the end of the street and on through the gate into Hope Gardens. People are out for an evening stroll - couples holding hands, teenagers hanging out on the grass, and dog walkers. A hundred yards into the park, I spot a familiar figure. He's walking away but I know his broad shoulders and dark auburn curls. When I call his name, there is no sound. I watch a woman, petite and shapely with blonde hair, walk across the grass towards him. When he turns to her she smiles and he hurries to meet her, takes her in his arms and kisses her deeply.*

*I stop dead.*

*I call his name, but I hear no sound. I break into a run - trundle Harry's pram down the path and thread through a crowd of tourists. The distance between us seems to lengthen as Drew and the woman pause, turn around - see me, then exchange looks of recognition with one another. They clasp hands and set off running in the opposite direction.*

*I run, determined to keep them in my sight. But swarms of children are in my way with their bikes and scooters, and elderly people are walking in the middle of the path.*

*'I need to get past,' I say, and skirt around them.*

*I watch Drew and the woman pass through the gate and turn left up the footpath. They disappear behind a tall privet hedge. At the gateway I swing Harry's pram and look towards the town. I see them run across the road and into the ginnel between the library and The Waterhorse Hotel. My feet drag beneath me and it feels like I'm moving nowhere. Harry is silent and I look down. His blanket hangs over the edge of the pram and only one of his red socks remains where he'd lain only moments ago.*

*'Harry!' I scream. 'Harry!'*

*I scream again and again until my tongue won't work and as my vision turns white I fall to the ground.*

I awoke, soaked in sweat and with an unbearable and agonising ache that tore through my throat and heart. 'Harry...'

I continued to weep.

# Chapter 22

The nightmare loomed in my mind like an apparition - with disturbing images and facial expressions that refused to melt away. I tried to fall back to sleep, but my mind churned with pictures of Harry and Drew and the mystery mistress. It might only have been a dream but it was one that reflected my reality through a broken mirror.

Eventually, feeling a mixture of yearning, frustration and sadness, and sensing daylight nearing, I climbed out of bed and pulled on my gown. I headed to the kitchen, brewed a cup of tea, and sat in the window seat. As I sipped my tea, hot and strong, I watched the sky work through its tints of dawn. When the pale sun had risen but the light remained muted and yellow - it seemed as though I was seeing our street in sepia tone, from a century ago. There was barely anything out there that set it apart from that period - no cars, and the old brick and stone buildings still had traditional shop fronts. The cobbles, the slate roofs and chimney tops completed the scene. I raised the sash window and a cool breeze swept in and rushed against my cheeks and through my hair. I sat back down and breathed in the familiar scent that blew up from the lake shore, of silt and water - calming, refreshing.

I'd always loved that our street was mostly vehicle free, despite the inconvenience this caused since we'd had Harry. Now that was no longer an inconvenience, but one I'd have back in a breath along with sleepless nights for all eternity, if only to hold him in my arms again.

I picked up my laptop from the coffee table and opened my emails to see if Jakob had set up a time for me to meet with him and Dan. I hadn't received any emails from work and I sent a brief email to Kim, asking if she'd had any instruction from Jakob about not copying me in. My eyes stung with frustration and I sighed and flipped the lid back down and put the laptop aside.

I got up and went to stand at the bay window. The sun appeared from behind the clouds, and a brisk breeze swept up leaves from the Elm tree outside, yellow, crisp and pale. They tapped against the window panes and three leaves fluttered in and came to rest on the floorboards. I drew the window down, and after getting dressed, put on my red leather jacket and headed outside and down to the lake. I walked past the crazy golf where two elderly couples appeared to be the first customers of the day, and past the theatre by the lake.

There were serious looking walkers setting out for a hike and dog owners in no great rush, a few of whom I recognised. I'd often talked to Drew about getting a dog, although I knew this would be impractical given we could barely cope with one child, let alone walk a dog twice a day and leave it whilst we were at work. This had been more wishful thinking and nostalgia for my childhood days than a serious notion.

This morning, as I walked and zipped up my jacket against the breeze, I thought back to when I'd walked this route as a child. After years of pleading, Mum and Dad had finally bought me a puppy for my twelfth birthday - a miniature Schnauzer I named Jess. I'd been given her on the proviso that I'd walk her every morning before school and again when I got in. Receiving her as a gift had been more than I'd ever dreamed of and I'd set my alarm early each morning to allow time to walk her down to the lake before I settled her back at home and cycled to school. At weekends, Sylvia and I would go on hikes with Mum and Dad up the fells or follow the rivers along the valleys. Taking Jess along made this all the more pleasurable, even when the rain was persistent.

Mum and Dad had been great hikers, especially before Sylvia and I were born. Sylvia would occasionally walk with me and Jess in the mornings before school but mostly she'd lie in bed while I'd go off on my own and pay no attention to my parents' warnings that I was to stay on the main paths. I'd trained Jess pretty well, but she was a devil for following the scents of squirrels or rabbits and disappearing amongst bushes and behind mounds and hillocks. I'd hear her barking frantically at the foot of a tree or at the entrance to a rabbit warren. Of course, she'd never managed to catch anything, but she loved the thrill of the chase.

Mum always said I should keep her on a lead but I knew how much Jess loved to run freely and so I didn't follow her advice.

I lived to regret this.

One spring morning I'd awoken early, even before my alarm had gone off, and when I'd gone down to the kitchen, Jess had climbed out of her bed and greeted me with a yawn, a lazy stretch and a wagging tail. She scampered away and returned dragging her harness and lead. I'd already decided that because I had an extra twenty minutes, that we'd take the path up to Whispering Crag. On a clear day I could stand at the top and see out to the far end of the lake and beyond that to stretches of farmland and wooded valleys or hillsides. If the sun was shining, which it was on this particular morning, we were occasionally lucky enough to see an upturned rainbow appear between Summary Gill and Cargale Heights. Dad had tried to explain this rare rainbow phenomenon, but I didn't need to understand the physics of it, only to see the magnificent illusion of it. The sight was better than any regular rainbow or sunset I'd ever seen. Even more thrilling than a murmuration of starlings, which we were sometimes lucky to see down by the lake at eventide.

The path beside the lake had seemed quieter than normal that fateful morning, many years ago, and I let Jess off her lead and she charged on ahead, glancing back every now and then to check that I was keeping up with her. When we reached the fork in the path that led to Whispering Crag, Jess continued trotting along the main path. I called her back and we set off up the incline towards the crag. The wall of granite shone, golden and beguiling.

Mum and Dad had been keen climbers and occasionally, they'd bring along their ropes and hooks and the four of us would spend an afternoon climbing the crag and abseiling back down again. It was a rock face that didn't immediately look as if it needed ropes, but I knew this was deceptive as there had been a few fatalities with people who had taken risks and had climbed the sheer drops without the proper equipment. There were a couple of routes to climb safely and under parental supervision, Sylvia and I had been allowed to do this.

151

When Jess and I reached the foot of the crag I was breathing hard and I sat down on a rock at the edge of the path to catch my breath. I glanced down at my watch. Still enough time for us to walk the short but steep path to the top. I tipped my head back and looked up. The cliff was always an imposing sight - sheer in a few places. I got up, jogged around the base of the rock, with Jess leading the way, and on up the incline that led to the far side.

I wished I'd brought my camera - the sky, with rain clouds dotted on the peaks, looked ideal for a chance of spotting the smiling rainbow. Trees lined the path and because they seemed so perfectly aligned and spaced, I felt sure they must have been planted that way. Dad said it was because it was the only part of the rock where the soil was deep enough for trees to have taken root and survived. Whatever the reason for their being so placed, they offered Jess further opportunity to hunt for unsuspecting creatures. I leaned forward and marched onwards - the only way to get to the top without making a meal of the incline.

'Come on Jessie,' I called when I heard her barking amongst the trees. Her yapping grew more frantic and I stopped and looked back. 'Come along, Jess. No time for squirrels.' I walked back a few yards and peered amongst the undergrowth and trees. I heard rustling and a squirrel darted from a bush. A moment later Jess followed in hot pursuit. She disappeared amidst more rustling and yowling.

'Jess,' I hollered. 'Come back, right now!'

But she was on the scent and oblivious to my calls. Jess's barking told me she was heading across the top of the crag and I felt fearful. I knew from experience that the drop appeared unexpectedly. In patches, the grass grew tall and in some places the bushes hung over the ledge. I stepped between two trees and stomped through the undergrowth. Brambles tugged at my navy tights as I pushed aside twigs from the undergrowth, all the while calling Jess. But my calls went unheeded and I heard her scrabbling around, snuffling and whining.

When I neared the edge to where the rock fell away to a hundred foot drop at least, I paused and listened again. No scurrying or barking. My heart was jumping in my chest so hard as I looked down to the lake and beyond, and I felt momentarily dizzy. Just here, the drop was sheer, and I got down on my hands and knees, as Mum always insisted we do when near to the edge.

'It only takes one misplaced foot for you to trip and fall.' Mum's words rang in my ears.

She was right. The topsoil was uneven, gritty and loose.

'Jess,' I called and felt certain now that something terrible had happened. 'Jessie.' My voice wavered.

I heard a whimpering and scratching and knew she had to be close by. I lay down on my stomach and peered over. My heart lurched. There, seven or so feet below, on a narrow ledge no more than three foot long and a foot wide, crouched Jess. How she'd landed there and not plunged to her death, I will never understand. Nothing less than a miraculous stroke of good fortune.

'It's OK, baby. Stay still. I'll help you.'

She looked up at me and pleaded with fearful eyes, but she seemed to understand. She remained still and if she stayed like that she couldn't fall. There was no chance I could reach her from my position. But I did have her lead, one that extended several feet. I looked around for something to secure the end to. Behind me, a rock jutted up about a foot. I crawled back and slipped the collar clip through the handle. I hooked a length of the lead around the rock and tugged it hard to judge how secure it felt. As long as the lead didn't slip upwards, it would hold me. I gripped onto the lead and inched backwards towards the ledge, then checked again to see where Jess lay. I gripped the lead and lowered myself down. My hands slipped down the cord just as my feet touched the ledge. I held on for my life and I glanced down at Jess who whined and stood up.

'Lie down, Jess. Stay.' I said, firmly.

She hunkered down, obedient for possibly the first time in her life.

'Clever girl,' I said, and tried to sound as calm as I could given that my heart raced like a bullet train and my head whirled. My palms grew damp with sweat against the lead and I wiped each in turn on my skirt, while I kept a life-saving grip with the other.

I pinned my body against the rockface and crouching down I reached for Jess and her harness. I felt the hook along her back and managed to clip the lead. Jess tried to stand up.

'Stay.' I urged her again.

I heard a loud squawk and looked up to see a huge bird, an eagle or Red Kite, which circled above and looked down on us. We weren't carrion yet and I had no intention of us becoming so. But its presence only heightened my fear.

Before I could pull Jess up, I had to climb back up myself, somehow. I clung to the lead, pressed myself against the rock and eased myself to standing. The top of my head looked at least two feet from the top. I reached up, but as I did the ledge crumbled beneath my feet. For a moment I hung by a thread and as my hands slipped, I swung my legs to the side and felt the firmness of the ledge once more. Jess yelped and I knew I'd either kicked or trodden on her. I could barely breathe or focus and I pressed my cheek against the rock and closed my eyes.

'Breathe, stupid. Breathe.' I counted slowly to ten and down to zero.

I moved my hands up the lead and tried to heave myself up, but I realised it was hopeless. The nylon cord was too thin and slippery to gain a secure grip. Shivers ran through me and my legs trembled making me feel even more in danger of plunging to my death.

We needed help. I craned my neck and looked down the hillside. My vision staggered and I turned back to the rock face and took some breaths.

'Get a bloody grip,' I cursed myself.

Jess's life and my own depended on me keeping a cool head. I'd never suffered from vertigo, but I'd never before been stranded a hundred metres high on a sheer rock face. I kept breathing deliberately and steadily.

'HELP.' I called. 'PLEASE HELP US.'

But my cries only echoed into a seeming endless emptiness. No reassuring voices or replies returned. Even the birds had silenced. Only my breath came in gasps as I tried to figure out what to do next. I pulled on the lead once more to see if I could gain any leverage, but again my hands slipped.

'Shit, shit, fucking shit!'

At school I was one of the fastest to climb the ropes. I was skinny and long limbed, which helped. But I realised I'd been stupid to attempt to rescue Jess alone.

At least Jess was safe, as long as she didn't struggle. What a sensible creature. Unlike me. My fear and frustration spilled into tears and I felt a sense of hopelessness enclose me.

'Please help,' I cried again, with my chin pressed against the rock.

I craned my neck to look at my watch. A quarter to eight. Mum and Dad must have noticed I wasn't back yet. Surely they'd come looking for me. They knew where I walked. Though they won't have known I'd come up here and I might be too far from the path for them to hear my cries.

'Don't move,' a woman's voice, faint but urgent, called from below. 'We're coming to help you.'

'Please hurry,' I shouted back.

I clung tight to the lead and my body shook as I dared to glance down. I saw a distant female figure, who shielded her eyes as she looked up.

'My son is coming up,' she called.

It seemed like an eternity that I remained facing that same few inches of rock, as I talked to Jess and prayed she wouldn't make any sudden moves. Finally, I heard rustling and footsteps from above, and a man's voice.

'Shout so I know where you are.'

'We're here,' I called. 'My dog's lead is hooked over a rock and she's clipped on.'

I felt a tug on the lead and peered up to see him leaning over the edge. His shaggy black hair hung like curtains around his face and when he brushed it aside his eyes struck me as the brightest golden brown.

'I'll pull you up first,' he said.

'No. My dog first. She's already clipped on.'

'But if I pull her up first, are you secure without the lead?'

'I think so,' I said, and searched the rock for something to grip onto. I slipped my fingers into a crease and edged my toes nearer to the rock face. 'I'm secure. Take her up.' I turned to Jess, knowing I mustn't move a millimetre.

'OK. Here we go, Jess,' he called down.

I watched as the lead pulled taut against her harness. Slowly she raised a few inches off the ledge, her legs hanging free, and as she did, she whined and turned to me. Her eyes grew wide and full of fear - mirroring mine.

'It's OK, Jessie.' I prayed her harness was secure enough to hold against her weight. Her side scraped against the rock but she didn't struggle.

Only moments later I heard.

'Well done, Jess. Clever dog.'

'Thank you, thank you,' I called and tears welled in my eyes.

'We're not done yet. You must stay still,' he urged.

'I've got the dog,' he shouted down to the woman below. 'Is she OK if I unhook her lead?'

'She won't be daft enough to fall again,' I replied and awaited further instruction.

'She's well back from the edge. Now I'm going to lower the lead to your left side. Don't make any sudden movements but take hold and secure it around your waist.'

When the lead appeared inches from my face, I raised my hand and grasped it. Carefully, I pulled the twine around my back then across my abdomen. I tied three knots so the twine was tight against the waistband of my skirt.

'Try to use your hands and feet to feel for knots in the rock.'

'There are a few. I've climbed this spot with ropes before.'

'OK. Don't rush or you'll slip.'

The lead pulled taut and with my fingers, I gripped the smallest crease with all my strength and with my feet I found a cleft in the rock. The twine dug into my belly as he pulled me up.

The twine tightened beneath my ribs and I gasped. When I looked up I saw the strain on his face as he hauled on the lead. The veins in his arms bulged and his teeth gritted together. He heaved on the lead and it was clear he struggled.

'You have to climb,' he called, with desperation in his voice.

'I'm trying.' And I stretched and grappled for a hold inches higher. And then my foot found another ridge and this gave me the leverage I needed. I reached up and when my fingers touched his, he gripped my wrist and dragged me up the final few inches. In seconds my belly scraped over the ledge and I was safe. I turned over and laid on my back, exhausted, breathless and feeling more relieved than I'd felt in my entire life before.

The young man stood over me, breathing hard.

When I felt the sweep of Jess's breath and her damp nose on my cheek, I wept and wrapped my arms around her neck.

I sat up and shuffled further back from the ledge. 'Jessie.'

He crouched down beside me. 'You took your time,' he said, still breathing heavily. But I saw the look of relief in his eyes. 'Are you hurt?'

I rubbed my abdomen with stiff fingers and fumbled to untie the lead. 'Not as much as I could've been.' I looked towards the drop and realised how close both of us had come to our deaths.

He looked into my eyes. 'However did you end up on that ledge?'

I wiped the dirt and grit off my skirt. 'Jess ran off chasing a squirrel. She fell.' I sucked in a breath. 'I don't know what we'd have done...'

'But you're both safe. That's all that matters.'

'I shouldn't be up here. My parents will kill me.'

He thought for a moment. 'Not if you don't tell them.'

'But I'm so late home.'

'Then hurry back and think of a plausible excuse.'

He was right. There was no need to tell Mum and Dad. No need to share the drama or the fact that I'd only escaped death by a whisker and with the help of a man - a stranger. I nodded and scrambled up.

He untied Jess's lead from the rock and clipped it onto her harness. 'Let's go, young lady.'

Amazingly, other than my tights being in tatters, I was relatively OK. I straightened my hair and clothes as we hurried back through the undergrowth and trees and to the main path that led back down the slope. I paused to check Jess over. Not a scratch on her.

'What's your name?' he asked as we picked our way back down the stony path.

'Orla.'

'And you live locally?'

'On the outskirts. Bramble Lane - Mum and Dad own Oaks Furniture on the High Street.'

157

'Yes, I know it. Will you be late for school?'

I thought for a moment. 'I'll tell them I had a dentist appointment.'

'That's the idea,' he said.

'I've forged mum's signature before now,' I said, feeling emboldened by my adventure.

'Have you now?' He stooped lower and said, 'White lies and scheming are a sign of intelligence.'

I giggled. 'Really? I'll remember that.'

'My mother's down here.' He stopped walking and turned to me. 'You mustn't pay attention to anything she says.'

'Oh, OK,' I said, and wanted to ask why.

He continued talking as we walked. 'Mother tends to overreact in all situations - even if we run out of tea bags or bread. She sometimes gets confused, too.'

When we rounded the base of the rock, his mum scurried towards us. The first thing I noticed was her ruddy complexion beneath wild grey curls and how spindly her legs looked beneath her woolen skirt.

She placed her hands on my shoulders and her eyes blazed into mine. 'Thank God you didn't fall.' She began to weep. 'And your sweet little dog.'

The man put his hand over hers so that now, both their hands were on my shoulder. 'Everything's fine, Mum.'

I ducked and stepped back.

She reached out and took my hand. 'Are you hurt, my dear?'

'Only scratches,' I said, and looked down at my tattered tights. I peered into the man's face. 'You saved my life. Jessie's too.'

'I'm only glad I was able to.' He smiled thinly. 'Anyone would have done the same.'

The woman kept hold of my hand. 'What were you doing on that ledge? You shouldn't be taking such risks.'

'I walk Jess every morning before school and she fell. I couldn't leave her.'

'But you're only a child. Your mother or father should be with you.'

'It's OK, Mum,' said the man. 'Orla's going home. She has school today.'

158

'But she should be checked by a doctor.'

'No, really,' I said. 'I'm nearly fifteen and I'm fine.'

'Let us walk you home then,' she said.

'There's no need to,' I said and looked at the man.

'I don't think Orla wants you to hold her hand.'

Reluctantly, she let go. Jess pulled eagerly at her lead, none the worse for her ordeal.

The young man, who I guessed was in his late teens - early twenties, chatted as we walked, the way adults did when they wanted to make a child feel at ease.

'I'm studying Science at Manchester Uni. Going back tomorrow as it happens.'

'He could stay home for longer if he wanted to,' his mother said as she walked close beside me. 'But he needs to get back, apparently.'

'I've been home for weeks, mother. You'll have more time for your books and gardening.'

'You mean I'll have more hours to fill, alone.'

'Anyway,' he said, and turned to me. 'What's your favourite subject?'

I didn't hesitate. 'Sport and science, especially Chemistry and Biology.'

'Do you know, Orla, our world will always need great scientists. Medical discoveries have saved and improved millions of people's lives. People who might have died young but instead went on to live long and productive lives.'

His mother made a strange gulping sound, which might have been a cough, but I couldn't be sure. I glanced quickly at her but she looked down at the path as she walked.

'I've not decided what I'll study yet, but either science or sport.'

'I'm guessing you also like climbing?' His brows raised and his smile flickered.

I nodded. 'I do. I did. I'm not so sure how I'll feel in future.'

He stopped, turned around and looked back up the hillside. 'Can you see your ledge? Right up there.'

I followed his gaze to where I'd clung only moments ago, perilously high and sheer, and I felt my legs sway.

He took hold of my elbow. 'Steady there.'

159

I straightened up and took some breaths.

'I'd keep Jess on a lead next time you venture up.'

'It's what Mum always says, too,' I said, and bent down and rubbed Jessie's ears. 'I don't know what I'd have done if she'd fallen and died.'

'A dog isn't the same as a child,' the woman snapped.

'Mother. Orla is only relieved to be safe,' he said.

We walked on but the woman seemed reluctant to keep up with us.

He leaned closer. 'Don't worry,' he said. 'She doesn't mean to speak harshly.'

When we reached the theatre by the lake, he said. 'I'll let you go on now. I need to stay with Mother.'

I looked back but couldn't see her. 'Of course. And thank you again.'

He gave me a final wave. 'See you around sometime.'

Strangely, although I'd walked in the shadow of Whispering Crag hundreds of times since then, I couldn't remember the last time I'd even thought about this dramatic event in my life. I wondered if I'd all but blocked it out, like people sometimes did when terrible things happened. Perhaps my head injury, or my memory loss and subsequent return, had triggered its recurrence today. And even more peculiarly, when I saw in my mind's eye the man who had peered over the ledge and swept his black hair aside, his face seemed familiar to me. Twenty plus years was a long time ago. His words, 'see you around', struck me as odd because given the size of Keswick, I don't think I had seen him again. He'd never approached me in the town to say hello or ask how I was. And his mother, too. She was a small but distinctive figure. Maybe I'd passed her shopping in the supermarket or the street market held there twice a week. Maybe they'd moved out of the area. Maybe she'd died. Anyway, it mattered little who they were. That they'd been there and that Jess and I had been saved was all that mattered.

I left the path, and walked down the slope and through a breeze scented with lake shore - pebbles, sand and water - and onto the beach where the waves lapped over stones, one watery breath after another. I stopped a couple of feet from the water's edge and listened to the movement of the water as it shifted the stones and gravel back and forth in a soulful rhythm. A flurry of wind snatched my hair and I brushed it off my face and looked out across the water to the woodland and Cat Bells Peak on the far side. Even from this distance the sunlight reflected off the rocks and when I turned away, the light strobed each time I blinked in ever diminishing intensity. Oddly, I'd noticed that following the accident, my eyes had become increasingly sensitive to light and I'd taken to wearing sunglasses, even when the sky was overcast. I made a mental note to ask about it at my next checkup and to have an eye test to see if there was an underlying problem or explanation.

I bent down and picked up two stones - flat, smooth and pale grey. Drew and I had often come down here and competed to see who could skim a stone with the most bounces. I rarely beat Drew and on the few occasions when I did, he'd argue that I hadn't. I was never sure if he was doing this to wind me up or if his competitive nature had taken over. Certainly he was one of the most competitive people I knew - in a way that was fun rather than aggressive. He couldn't hide his true self from me, but I'd seen him in action in conversations, often trying to get one up on a colleague or a friend with his clever wit or solid facts. But that hadn't so much been a negative, in my view, but rather it had made him more engaging, interesting and exciting to be with. It was this competitive streak that had given him the impetus to work hard to succeed in his medical training and in working his way into a senior position. Fortunately, I was no walk over - and I'd never taken his competitive streak too seriously. If anything, this trait had rubbed off on me and made me more determined to succeed. From that perspective, we'd made a perfect match. I'd never have described him as a chest-beating alpha male, but his intelligence and confidence definitely attracted me to him initially.

I held one stone in each hand and felt their smoothness between my fingers. I bent my knees, swung my arm back and threw the stone across the surface of the water - scalloped and dazzling in the sunlight. On the second bounce it caught a small wave, and disappeared beneath the surface. I transferred the other stone and launched it. It flew in an arch and skipped across the surface several times, though I couldn't keep a count before it sank below the surface. I heard some clapping and spun around. A tall figure in silhouette stood twenty or so feet away. I shielded my eyes from the sun. The figure walked towards me. 'Vincent.' I said. 'You saw my brilliant skim then?'

'I did. I'd be hard pushed to beat that.'

'It must be one of my best ever.'

'But I'm gonna try,' he added.

I lifted my gaze. 'OK. Good luck.'

He bent down and searched around for a flat stone. He picked one up but cast it aside. He picked up another. 'This one's a winner - or a runner upper.' He stood up straight and with a deadly serious expression he looked my way. 'I get one attempt to better your magnificent effort.'

'If you say so,' I said, and folded my arms.

He walked closer to the edge, turned to me briefly, then took his aim. The stone flew parallel to the water before it landed and bounced up again and then on and on until it must have skipped ten times and became a tiny dot.

'Oh my bloody God, Vincent. You've been practising, haven't you?'

He straightened up and shielded his eyes. 'Reckon it's reached that yacht by now.' And he pointed to the pale belly of a sail on the far side of the water.

I burst out laughing. 'How am I supposed to compete with that?'

'I shouldn't bother trying,' he said and grinned.

'I needed to get out today,' I said.

He walked nearer. 'How's it going back at work?'

I raised my eyebrows. 'Well, as you can see, I'm not there.'

'Are you going in later?'

'Hoping to. I need to talk to my colleague and boss.'

'Everything OK?'

Where to start, I thought. 'If you must know. It's been a disastrous couple of days. They've employed somebody in my place. She's supposed to be temporary, but she's sleeping with my senior colleague and it's obvious he wants her to stay on and me to shove off.'

'But surely now you're back, they'll no longer need her?'

'Unfortunately, there's a huge, whacking great spanner thrown in.'

'Sounds ominous.'

'It's a nightmare. I don't even know where to start.' I turned my face and looked out over the water, afraid that I might cry.

'Hey,' he stepped closer and put an arm around my shoulders. He reached into his jacket pocket and drew out a pack of tissues. I pulled one out and blew my nose. 'I'm sorry, but this week has been the worst yet. I feel better physically, but my memories are flooding back so fast I can hardly take them in. I've visited the graves, which threw up more surprises than I can begin to explain, and my boss sent me home suggesting I was hysterical and behaving too erratically to cope with work. They're insisting I see a counsellor who'll judge whether I'm fit to return. They'll have spoken to the counsellor first and what's the betting they find me unfit, and all because I challenged something potentially dangerous with a drug they're about to launch.'

He nodded in sympathy. 'Why don't we grab a coffee and croissant at Lava Java and if you want to, you can tell me everything, or part of everything. Who knows, I might even be able to help. And if I can't then at least you've let it all out.'

'I'd like that, Vince. If you've got the time?'

'I've got a day off, hence my being here. And anyway, what are friends for?'

The cafe was already busy, but I found a free table for two in the window.

'Sure you don't want a croissant?' he asked.

'Oh, go on then,' I said.

I checked my phone for new messages or emails. Still nothing. I gazed out of the window and felt frustrated with Jakob for stalling when he knew I wanted this resolved.

Vincent returned with coffee and croissants and my resentment receded.

'I've got jam and butter, too.'

'They do smell delicious,' I said, and lifted my cup and plate off the tray.

'I'm waiting on some information from my boss, so I've got a free morning.' He sat down and rested his elbows on the table edge. 'Not often I get one.' He propped his chin on his hand.

163

'I'm seriously feeling I might no longer have a job at all,' I said. 'And I need the money and just as importantly, I need a distraction.'

'They can't simply get rid of you,' said Vincent. 'If they try you can take them to a tribunal.'

'I know, but imagine the stress of that. I love my job, at least I did, but now it seems too much has happened for me to slot back in.'

'Do you feel OK for being back full time?'

'Definitely. And like I said, my memory's back in full. I remember everything including things I'd all but forgotten and archived from years ago.'

'Sounds positive.'

'It is mostly,' I replied.

'So what's the other serious issue with work, other than Jakob behaving like a bastard and sleeping with your stand in?'

I looked around, then leaned forwards. 'I'm not quite sure where to start.'

Vincent took a sip of his coffee. 'Take your time.'

'Did I tell you about the drug, Hexprin, we're working on?'

He nodded slowly. 'Remind me what it does.'

'It's rather like Viagra but for women with low libido. Not only post menopause. It's potent and it's going to be huge. Huge on profits and publicity. So you see, it's a critical moment for BioMedica. They, we, cannot afford to get it wrong.'

'And you think there's a problem with it?'

'I know there is - potentially. My problem is that Jakob and his lapdog Melanie have it all set up to go to production and market. They've tried but failed to cover up the latest research from me and are blaming my head injury for my alleged hysteria,' I said. 'Last night I snuck into work and found the research findings.'

'At the dead of night wearing a balaclava?' Vincent asked, with a quizzical expression.

'Pretty much. That particular episode is a whole other story.'

He raised his eyebrows.

'I'll tell you sometime,' I said. 'Anyway, the last set of research results showed inconsistencies and adverse reactions.'

'Don't most drugs have those issues and risks?'

I nodded. 'They do, but these particular reactions are dramatic and undoubtedly terrifying and dangerous for the recipient. Potentially, although they signed a confidentiality clause, they could go to the press, and imagine the damage that could do?'

'If the drug is dangerous then they'd have every right to. I'd encourage that.'

'But most of the women were cock a hoop after taking the drug. Some said they'd never experienced lovemaking like it. And some had never climaxed, but after taking the drug were multi-orgasmic. Seems their partners were chuffed too.'

Vincent considered me and his eyes grew wide. His mouth opened as though to speak, but then he closed it again.

'What are you thinking?' I asked.

'I'm thinking that this is huge. Like you said. You could be about to put a damn great spanner in the works and they can't afford for you to hold them back.'

'As far as I'm concerned, there's the ethics to consider. I won't approve, endorse or market a dangerous drug.'

'Yet they're quite prepared to. I could take this to the national press and they'd love the story. So would the British public.'

'Mmm. Now there's a thought. Let me think about that,' I said.

'Yes, do. And you needn't be implicated.'

'I do live in the flat below you, remember. Anyway, I'm meeting with Jakob and Dan to talk about it. I don't want to confront them, but I do want them to take a fresh look at what they're doing. Plus, I really want to keep my job so I'm going to have to tread carefully.' I split open the croissant and spread a layer of jam. I took a bite. 'These are tasty croissants,' I said, and took another bite.

'I always have one here. I'm a man of simple pleasures.'

When I looked upon Vincent's face and into his grey eyes that looked back at me, and as he scratched absently at the stubble on his chin, I felt an unfamiliar but pleasurable jolt. A sensation I hadn't experienced in some time. He was thoughtful and seemed to care about the issues with the drug, and more importantly, what I was going through.

'I'm enjoying it, too,' I said.

His eyes glinted. 'That's grand.'

He shifted in his seat and as he did, I felt his leg brush against mine. He put his elbow on the table and rested his chin on the heel of his hand. His eyes fixed on mine, but he didn't immediately speak.

'I wonder what it would be like to take the drug,' I said.

'From what you've told me, I'm not sure I'd want to risk it if I were a woman,' he replied.

'Maybe you wouldn't need it though,' I said, unable to take my eyes from his.

'That's a valid point.' He pressed his lips together and his eyes had a definite twinkle. 'Were the testers only women who had problems with desire or arousal?'

'Yes, and honestly, some of them were so excited about the drug afterwards. I'm not sure they would be if they'd heard about the negative side effects.'

'It's the sort of thing they say in the leaflet - x% suffered serious side effects.'

'Unless they do another research trial to suggest 0% suffered serious side effects,' I said.

'Most likely people don't read those leaflets anyway. Not if they're recommended by their GP.'

'I read them, on any new medication I take. But I'm programmed to do so.'

'I can't say I do,' he said.

'And you're probably the rule, and I'm the exception.'

We chatted and drank our coffee until my phone vibrated in my pocket. I read it and looked up. 'Text from Jakob.'

'And?'

'Says he and Dan can see me at five today.' I put the phone away. 'Now, I need to work out what I'm going to say.'

# Chapter 23

Talking to Vincent and having his support had lightened the shadows that pervaded my mind. And, I thought, being an investigative journalist, he could be helpful in more ways than offering his friendship. I texted Kim to find out if there'd been any further decisions on Hexprin or any news on Jakob and Melanie.

She replied promptly.

*'Melanie has gone into full throttle dictator mode. She doesn't ask, but demands. And she was vague when I asked her when you'd be returning, and when I asked Jakob he said he was worried about you and flatly refused to say more.'*

I texted back. *'Thank you! I'm coming in at five to talk to Dan and Jakob. Wish me luck.'*

Kim replied. *'Shall I come in with you? You're allowed to have someone as support.'*

I wasn't sure how to reply. I didn't want Kim or her position compromised, plus if they didn't know Kim was my confidante they may be prepared to share more confidential information with her when she asked questions.

*'That's kind of you,'* I texted, *'but I think you'll find out more if you're not seen as supporting me. What do you think?'*

Her reply said, *'You're right. Smart thinking, Bat Girl. I'm in full sleuth mode. Stay strong.'*

*'You're a brilliant friend, Kim. I'm OK. I can get through this.'* Fighting words from someone who was feeling decidedly wobbly.

I rifled through my wardrobe. What to wear? A trouser suit? No. I lifted out a burgundy suit - dress and box jacket that I hadn't worn in a long while. The dress had felt too tight after I'd had Harry, but it would fit now. I took off my clothes, changed into fresh underwear and zipped up the dress and paired it with black heels and a pair of sheer tights. I pinned up my curls into a neat bun and applied foundation, eye makeup and lilac lip gloss. It was a look I only took time over when I had an important presentation to give or if I was meeting a client.

Today could be the turning point.

The sun had been beaming through the window for a while and the room felt pleasingly warm. I sat at the window seat and stretched my legs along the cushion. For ten minutes or so I wrote down notes on what I wanted to say to them, then I stood up and rehearsed it to my reflection in the mirror over the fireplace.

I couldn't know how they'd respond so beyond what I needed to say I'd have to adapt and play it by ear. How far did Jakob have Dan under his thumb on this? Or maybe Dan was in it just as deep and willingly as Jakob. I watched the people on the street and I pondered how the meeting might play out and pictured various scenarios. Two managers against one with a head injury, residual memory loss, grieving for her husband and baby, surely not fit to return to work yet, who bordered on hysterical about a long awaited drug they were launching. Yes, some of that was true. But my mind grew more alert each day and most importantly, the serious side effects of Hexprin were only too real. To ignore them seemed unethical not only for the recipients of the drug, but also for expecting employees to produce, market and sell a drug that could do a huge amount of damage to unsuspecting users and ultimately to employee's careers. If someone had only stepped in to halt thalidomide, which wrecked thousands of children's lives from a single generation, and Hexprin hadn't even been tested on pregnant women. We knew no pregnant woman would willingly take it and certainly no doctor would prescribe it to them, but what if their heightened sex drive and frequency of having sex boosted their fertility? It seemed a logical progression that it could.

I pulled up in front of the security gates where staff were already driving out. I wondered if the barrier would lift as I waved my pass. It did and the security guard gave me a nod.

I parked and looked in the sun visor mirror. In this light, my amber eyeshadow looked too vivid and my lipgloss gaudy. I pulled a tissue from my handbag and wiped my lips dry. As I stepped out of the car, I had the strongest sensation that I was being watched and I looked up at the second floor and to Jakob's office window. The blinds moved. Of course, he'd been looking out for me to arrive. I felt sick and wanted to turn around, get back in the car and drive home. Both of them had worked in the business for longer than I had. They'd seemed to respect me up until the accident, but now they wanted me out and Melanie in. At least, Jakob did. I'd heard about this sort of thing going on in workplaces but never imagined that it could happen to me. And, here I was in that exact precarious position. And it felt horrible. I opened my audio app, selected record and slipped the phone back into my jacket pocket. If the meeting went badly, I might need the recording as evidence.

I took a deep breath and set off towards the entrance. When I walked into the main office Kim looked up.

She walked across, hugged me briefly and spoke in a whisper, 'Go get 'em sister.' She stood back, and appraised me. 'You look amazing, by the way.'

'Do I? It's probably the make up.'

'It's the suit. You'll definitely make Jakob stop in his tracks if only to gaze at your power and beauty.'

'Stop it, Kim, you're making me more nervous.'

'Sorry. You can tell he's got sex on the brain and now you're single, you could be the next candidate. Better to be aware.'

'Have you forgotten about Melanie? Not only is she more glamorous than me, she's smarter. At least that's what Jakob implied.'

'Don't worry about Melanie. You, my friend, are one smart and savvy woman. And determined not to be pushed out of her job.'

'I can't help feeling that Melanie, as a newbie here, is being manipulated to do and say exactly as she's told,' I said.

'I think you're right. And obviously complicated because she's besotted with Jakob.'

'Sure to cloud her judgement,' I said. 'She might actually be the victim as much as I am.'

'Except that she could have your job. Your income.'

'True.' I nodded. 'I need to think this through - about Melanie. First, I need to see how this meeting goes.'

'Orla.'

I turned around and saw Jakob standing just feet away.

'Jakob,' I replied.

'Want to come through?'

I looked back at Kim, grimaced then turned to follow Jakob who was already headed towards Dan's office.

I followed him in and clicked the door shut behind me. Jakob sat next to Dan in the easy meeting chairs and I took a seat opposite.

'Good to see you, Orla. How are you?' asked Dan, and he gave me a warm smile.

'I'm doing well,' I said, determined to remain confident.

'I hear you're seeing our HR counsellor tomorrow?' Dan asked.

'That's right,' said Jakob. 'He's going to Orla's house to save her a journey.'

'I look forward to meeting our head of HR,' I said.

'Good,' said Jakob. 'Now what was it you wanted to talk to us about so urgently?'

'Obviously, I want to be back at work asap. But in the meantime I've been reading through all the papers and correspondence on Hexprin. Given that it's at a critical stage.'

Jakob tilted his head. 'Critical?'

'It is, isn't it? About to go to production?'

'Everything's running to plan,' said Jakob. 'And we can thank Melanie for that.'

'I'm sure she's been a great support to you in my absence,' I said, and watched his expression.

'Then what is it, precisely?'

'Melanie or you failed to send me all of the trials data and reports, but I've found the results I knew were missing.'

Jakob sat up and his eyes bore into mine. 'What missing results?'

'The previous trial. The one you neglected to forward to me.'

'But we sent you everything.'

'No, you didn't. And I have proof.'

Jakob stood up and walked across to the window. He turned around and with legs braced and arms folded, said, 'OK. Where did you find this alleged missing information?'

'I'm only interested in what it told me. And you should be, too. And especially you, Dan,' I said, turning to him.

170

The room fell silent. Neither of them spoke, but I watched Jakob's face redden and his eyes looked decidedly twitchy. I waited for what seemed like eternity for one of them to speak.

Finally, Dan said, 'Do you have these results with you?'

With a lurch in my stomach I looked down at my empty hands and realised I'd forgotten the damned file. I felt my face flush and my heart juddered. 'It seemed wiser to leave them at home,' I said. 'But I'll scan them and email them to you both.'

How could I have been so stupid and forgetful? And here I was fuelling their doubts that I was mentally unfit for work. Before setting off I'd felt so nervous that I'd dashed back to the toilet. I could picture the file sitting on top of the laundry basket.

'Let me tell you what they said. Though, I'd have thought you're already well aware.'

Jakob came and sat back down. He rubbed his hands slowly up and down the tops of his thighs and leaning forwards looked intently into my eyes. His pupils widened above a tight lipped smile.

He turned to Dan and his features softened. 'Now do you see why I'm so concerned about her?'

Dan nodded.

'I'm absolutely fine,' I said.

'No,' said Dan, 'it's clear that you're not. You've been through an horrendous ordeal which you're still coming to terms with. You shouldn't be concerned with nit picking at drug trials that have been fully assessed by us and other experts, and scraping around for results. You should be taking time to recover.'

'Do you want to hear my concerns?'

Neither of them replied.

I waited, but when the silence grew too awkward, I continued. 'Why do I feel like we've had the exact same conversation a couple of days ago? When instead of listening to me, you told me I was being hysterical and sent me home.'

'Because we don't want to unsettle you more than you already are,' said Jakob. 'Please, Orla. Go home until you've been properly assessed.'

Now I knew they wanted to shut me up because they didn't want to hear my concerns. And, it was clearer still they knew my concerns were bona fide.

'I know,' Jakob continued. 'Let me follow you home and you can show me the results you're so concerned about. We'll read them together and then I'll talk with Dan tomorrow.'

His patronising tone filled my ears, and I saw the blindingly fake sympathy in his eyes. I became aware of a growing tightness in my chest and throat. 'What about you, Dan?'

'I trust Jakob to check this out thoroughly,' he said, dryly.

I looked at Jakob, who gave me another phony sympathetic look.

'I need to have a quick word with a colleague and I'll meet you down in the car park,' he said.

'And would that colleague be Melanie?'

'Is it relevant?'

'Because she's your girlfriend,' I said, bluntly.

Dan stood up. 'This is getting ridiculous, Orla. You're being paranoid and making a fool of yourself. And this won't help get you back into work.'

'It isn't paranoia when something is really happening. And because I'm prepared to speak the truth, which isn't convenient for your business plans, not to mention your personal plans.' I turned to Jakob who glanced arrows back at me. 'Then you'd prefer to diagnose me as paranoid. Neither of you are my doctor, nor are you psychologists.'

'You're wrong. We care only for your welfare,' said Dan. 'Of course we also care about the business and what we've all worked so hard to achieve with Hexprin. Now I suggest you go home, put your feet up and when you've seen the counsellor we'll decide next steps.'

'So you refuse to take my concerns seriously? Even when they could come back and bite far harder than I ever could, with lawsuits and damning publicity?'

Dan stood his ground. 'I don't share your concerns and the final decisions are down to me. Is that clear?'

'Then why try to cover up any of the results?' And I added mentally, damn you men sticking together.

'Here we go again.' Jakob stepped in. 'You're not being rational. We've been through the results.' Jakob turned to Dan who nodded slowly.

I felt infuriated. 'Let me email these results tonight and I'll come in tomorrow morning and we'll discuss them line by line,' I said.

'It's better if I come to yours and read them tonight,' said Jaokb. 'Then perhaps I can put your mind at rest and keep the launch on track.'

I walked across to the window and took some slow breaths to gather my spiralling emotions. I looked out over the houses and to the hillside beyond. I swallowed my frustration then turned back to them. 'How long have I worked here?'

'Since October, five years next month,' said Dan, with a frown.

'And how many times have I got anything wrong? How many times have you not trusted my opinion and judgement?'

'No one's right about everything all of the time,' said Jakob. 'But the important point to remember, Orla - and I'll keep on repeating this until you understand - is that I'm thinking of you. We're all thinking of you. You have been through a trauma and it's clear to everyone here that you're not ready. It's blindingly apparent.' He continued, softer this time. 'Your head and your heart must be allowed to heal, and you need to come to terms with your losses. If I were in your position, I'd take the time and be content to be paid for it.'

'You mean, put my feet up like a good girl.' I laughed. 'You've lost it, Jakob. You're not me. And I know how I feel better than either of you can.'

Dan folded his arms. 'Please go home. Jakob will come too to read through those results with you. See the counsellor tomorrow morning.'

Again I wondered about Melanie's part in all of this. Did she know or care about the risks? Was she being manipulated by Jakob?

'OK. I'll leave. All I ask is that you properly consider my concerns and perhaps when Jakob and I have talked through the results, you'll understand why I insisted we talk about them.'

'Of course. I always listen,' said Dan. 'I value my employee's opinions.'

I couldn't repress a shot of laughter. 'Dan, if you valued my opinion we wouldn't be in this bizarre situation with me feeling like I'm fighting for my job when I've just lost my husband and my son.' I looked from him to Jakob. 'You're making me feel like I've done something wrong, when all I'm trying to do is to protect BioMedica from business busting lawsuits. Not least protecting the end users of the drug.'

'Let me see these results you're concerned about,' Jakob interjected. 'Dan and I will discuss them tomorrow. You have our word, right, Dan?'

When Dan looked into my eyes and said, 'Of course.' I knew they were doing so to shut me up and get rid of me.

When I walked out of Dan's office I turned off the audio record on my phone and feeling too angry and tearful to stop and talk to Kim, I marched down the stairs and out to my car without a backward glance. I presumed that Jakob would follow, but I didn't wait to see.

I drove up the hill out of Penrith and looked up at the black clouds that raced over the peak of Blencartha. The wind had picked up and it rushed against the car, causing me to grip the steering wheel to hold it straight.

I ran through the conversations which felt like deja vu. Dan's words were - '*Of course. I always listen. I value my employee's opinions*'. More like, put your feet up and shut up.

Placating words. Hollow words. Nothing more.

I felt furious and let down by both of them. However hard I tried, nothing I said was going to make them sit up and listen. As far as they were concerned, I was in the way. And what happened to obstructions, I thought?

By one means or another, they got removed.

# Chapter 24

*Thursday evening*

Luckily, I found a space in the parking bay at the bottom of the street and walked back up the slope still cursing Jakob and Dan, and even myself for forgetting the trial results. When I looked up, I was startled to see Jakob already waiting on the top step to the house. He leaned against the stone pillar and looked down at me with his black curls framing his features. The sun peeped over Cat Bells and the light reflected off his mirrored sunglasses. His face and physique looked leaner, gaunt almost, but there was no doubting he made a striking figure in his tweed jacket, waistcoat and silk tie. The country gent look didn't appeal to me but there was no doubting his handsome face and dress reeked of masculinity and money. No wonder Melanie had fallen for him. Most of the single women who started at BioMedica, and even some of the women with partners, sought him out or hovered like butterflies.

He lifted his glasses onto his head, and his gold eyes pierced mine. 'What took you?'

When his fringe flopped down over one eye and he swept it away with his fingers, my vision staggered with a suddenness that made all about me fold inwards. A memory that before today had been long buried within the riverbed of my mind now rose to the surface. And the young man leaning over the crag looked down at me. Twenty two years slipped by in a flash. I gripped the railing at the bottom step and sucked in my breath. Slowly my peripheral vision stopped moving and I looked back up at Jakob - a polaroid print from my past.

'You OK down there?'

'Fine,' I said, but remained still. Oddly, from the moment I'd walked into my interview at BioMedica, Jakob had struck me as vaguely familiar, as though I'd known him from childhood. I'd always imagined I'd seen him around Keswick - a bar or a restaurant somewhere. But up until this moment that was as close as I'd come to realising where I'd met him before.

Here was the young man with black hair and golden eyes who'd peered down at me and Jess trapped on the ledge up at Whispering Crag. I'd never made the connection.

He must have known full well who I was from the moment he'd interviewed me. Maybe even from the moment he'd received my application. If only I'd realised, too. But I knew why I hadn't - the trauma of getting stranded on that ledge, combined with blocking out the memory of that day.

Jakob had that way about him. I wouldn't have called him charming, exactly. He was more subtle than that. When he spoke to me or from what I'd observed with any woman, or man for that matter, he had a way of making me feel as though I were the only person in the room, even if the room heaved with other people. I think it was his eyes. The closeness of his gaze and how he always appeared attentive to what I had to say. He'd show concern and seemed keen to hear my opinions. I wondered now if that had always been a clever ruse to reel me in. To trust him. Yes, he may be here now, willing to read the results I was so concerned about, but he certainly hadn't shown respect for my concerns in the meeting with Dan. Neither had Dan, for that matter. No, I knew full well this was not genuine interest in the drug's safety, or my views on it.

My recent memory loss and its subsequent return had kickstarted a memory long shelved in the recesses of my mind.

I walked up the steps and slotted my key into the front door. 'You must have driven quickly.'

'Not especially. I drove a shorter and faster route, that's all.'

Of course, he would know all the shortcuts as his family home lay between Keswick and Penrith. Maybe he'd overtaken me - I doubt I'd have noticed, so distracted was my mind.

I listened to his footsteps as he followed me up the stairs and across the landing.

My fingers twitched as I raised my hand and twisted the key in the door.

Feeling his breath on my neck, I turned around.

Jakob stood close behind me. He wore a scowl, but his face instantly softened and he looked upon me with steady eyes.

Adrenaline fired through me - my hands trembled at my sides and I knew instinctively that I shouldn't let him in. But how could I refuse now that he'd driven out here because of what I'd wanted to show them?

I felt lightheaded as if I'd run up several flights of stairs, but still, I opened the door and walked through.

Jakob followed me in and he swung the door shut behind him.

Normally I'd offer a cup of tea, as one would any visitor, which up until now was how I'd always viewed Jakob.

I turned to him. 'Please, wait here.' My voice croaked and I felt certain he would sense my fear.

I walked into the bathroom and pushed the door softly behind me. I leaned against the wall, pressed my fingers against my eyes and tried to slow my breathing. If only I could act normally, I'd get through this and he'd soon leave.

I had an idea. I picked up the report on the wash basket, opened the lid and dropped it inside. A cop out, but at this moment, a crucial cop out. Something in my gut told me I shouldn't confront him about this alone. Not here. Not now.

I opened the bathroom door.

Jakob leaned back on the sofa, his knees spread wide and he looked about as relaxed as I was hoping to feign. He clasped his fingers together and stretched his arms out in front. His knuckles clicked. Then he cocked his head to one side and then the other as though easing a crick in his neck. 'So, where's this damning report?'

I made a show of looking for it on the dresser and bookshelf then leaned against the dining table and gripped the edge to steady myself. 'It's not where I left it. My memory's playing up again.' I tried to keep my voice level and thought that if I had the report in my hands, I'd be tempted to ram it down his throat. 'I'm sure when you've gone where I left it will come back to me. I'll scan it and email it to you and Dan, along with my concerns. We'll talk about it tomorrow.'

He sat forwards and his eyes locked on mine. 'We'll look together. Now.'

'I'm sure you'd rather get home.' I took a step towards the front door and looked at the wall clock. 'It's getting late.'

Jakob stood up and walked across the room, his eyes scanned the bookshelves and coffee table. He reached out to a pile of papers on the dining table and picked it up. He looked over. 'This looks like work stuff. Mind if I?' And he rifled through the pages without waiting for my answer.

'Those are a few papers I printed out,' I said quickly. 'It's not in there.'

Without looking up, he continued leafing through. Eventually, he placed the pile back down on the table. He walked up to me. 'Do you understand why I'm concerned about you?'

My heart battered against my ribs and I stood my ground. 'But I know I'm OK.'

'Let's allow the expert to be the judge of that.' He paused, then added. 'Hexprin is what I'd class as a life enhancing drug. It's a life changer for some women. You know this.'

My mouth felt dry, and I nodded.

'You've probably never had the need for such... stimulation.' His gaze dropped and his eyes lingered unashamedly on my chest. Then slowly, he raised his eyes to meet mine again. 'Were you and Drew always...' he paused, 'passionate together?'

'Mostly,' I said, but I was barely able to move my tongue.

'Even after Harry?'

My breath caught in my throat. 'I can't talk about Harry.'

'Of course. Insensitive of me.'

I suppressed a response and tempered my tone. 'In time I might find it easier.'

'I wasn't sure how you were feeling. With not remembering everything.'

As he spoke, I felt his breath upon my face and I stepped back. 'Like I told you, I remember so much more.'

He drew his bottom lip up over his top lip. 'But not where you left the research paper?'

'It'll come to me.'

His eyes narrowed. 'Perhaps you'd like to talk about Drew? I only ask because sometimes friends avoid talking to those who're grieving because they don't want to upset them further. And I don't want to fall into that trap.'

I didn't know what to say. I only wanted him to leave.

'When Priya died,' he continued. 'People I thought I knew well became experts at avoiding the subject. Not you, Orla.' He reached out and patted my shoulder. 'You always encouraged me to open up.'

I flinched. 'I never got the feeling you wanted to talk about her.'

'I didn't always. But isn't it better to be asked than to have something so important ignored? Swept under the carpet as though it didn't matter?'

'Maybe.' My legs felt unsteady. I turned away, pulled out a dining chair and sat down. 'But in other respects perhaps we're better left alone with our memories so we can deal with them how and when we want to. However long that takes.'

'I only want you to know you can talk to me about Drew and Harry. I'm your friend. I hope you consider me so.'

'Of course.' I didn't want to share anything with him. Ever again.

He persisted. 'How was it visiting the graves?'

'Horrible,' I said.

'I didn't tell you this, but I went to their graves last week. After I'd visited Priya's.'

'Oh?'

'Yes. The odd thing was that I felt more pain standing before Harry's grave than I did in front of Priya's. Why is that?'

I wondered where he was going with this. 'I don't know.'

'Is it because he was a baby?' he said.

A sob escaped me and my hand flew to my mouth.

Jakob didn't appear to notice my distress and continued. 'And Drew. Can I be honest with you about something?' He continued. 'He might have been an anaesthetist, but I never felt he was worthy of you. I remember you saying how exhausted you were, and you might never have said it aloud but I got the impression he wasn't pulling his weight. That he was neglecting you. That Harry was being neglected.'

'Harry was never neglected,' I said.

'That wasn't what I meant,' said Jakob.

'It was Drew's work,' I said. 'He often had to fill in when people were off or for emergency surgery. He was dedicated.'

'But I imagine you wished he'd been more dedicated to you?' Jakob enquired.

His concern seemed fake. He was prying - even baiting me to react.

'Am I right?' he said.

'I loved Drew and he loved me.'

'Did you really though?'

His questions were too intrusive. 'I'm tired. Can you please go?'

But he went on, regardless. 'I occasionally got the impression there was someone else.'

My voice rose. 'Are you implying I was having an affair?'

'Not you.'

'You think Drew was?'

'Maybe. He had an eye for the ladies.'

'You think so?' Perhaps Drew had said something to him in confidence.

'You didn't see that?' he asked.

'Not at all.'

'It's so often the wife or girlfriend who never suspects their man of having an affair. It's denial of what would be too painful to accept.'

'I thought I could trust him.'

'But how was your sex life? Still passionate after Harry came along?' He didn't wait for my reply. 'I suspect not. You hinted at that, too. And lack of sexual desire can trigger an affair in either partner.'

I began to shake. 'I don't know. If he was he didn't let on.'

'It can be after a spouse's death that we learn the truth about who we were married to.' Jakob nodded and turned to the window.

Had he seen the fresh flowers and the card beside Drew's grave?

'Did that happen with Priya?' I asked.

He turned his face to me. 'I'd rather not discuss her,' he snapped.

'I'd rather not discuss Drew either,' I replied.

Jakob only wanted to make me mistrust my memories of Drew.

'What would you like to talk about then - the trial results?'

I looked towards the window trying desperately to figure out how to get him to leave.

'I know,' he said. 'Relax and I'll make us a drink. Then we can talk.'

'I should have offered you one,' I said.

His questions were too probing and I became conscious now of the sweat prickling my back and between my breasts. 'In fact, Jakob, I have an appointment to go to.'

'What appointment?'

'I'm meeting a friend - we're thinking of setting up a book club.'

'What time and where?'

My voice stuttered. 'Not decided yet. I'm going to ring her.'

Undeterred, Jakob said. 'I'll fix us that drink and then I'll leave you to your arrangements. OK?' He walked away to the kitchen without waiting for my reply.

It was clear that he didn't believe me. I never was a convincing liar.

He returned carrying a tray - an opened bottle of red wine and two half-filled glasses.

He set the tray on the coffee table and sat down on the sofa. 'Please. Come and sit down. You seem so uptight.'

I walked across to him and he handed me a glass.

'Of course I'm tense,' I said. 'I want to come back to work and you and Dan are putting obstacles in my way.'

He patted the sofa for me to sit beside him. 'There's no rush. And of course you'll return when you're ready.'

I sat down at the other end. 'I'm ready now.' I knew I was wasting my breath. 'And what about Melanie?'

'What about her?'

'She's a yes woman. Though I can hardly blame her for that. She's new and inexperienced.'

'She's a smart girl.'

'And you and her seem to get on well,' I said, and watched closely to gauge his reaction.

His eyes narrowed. 'Why have you got it into your head that there's something going on between me and her?'

I took a mouthful of wine. 'Is there?'

'Has somebody suggested so?'

'It's a feeling I get.'

'Not jealous are you?'

'Far from it,' I said.

'Let me tell you something about Melanie. And when I do you might be more kind towards her.'

'Go on then.'

He took a breath. 'Melanie has a brain tumour.'

I nearly spat out my wine. 'What?'

He nodded and his eyes shuttered. 'She found out recently it's inoperable, but slow growing. She's had it for two years and wants to carry on working and living a normal life for as long as possible. So if you think I'm being kind to her then you'll understand why.'

'Doesn't she get horrific headaches and other nasty symptoms?'

'Of course, but she won't allow them to interfere with her work.'

'Does Dan know?'

'Not yet. Melanie told me after she'd suffered a terrible headache at work. She asked if I'd keep it confidential.'

'So why are you telling me?'

'Because I want you to have some sympathy and respect for her, whilst she is managing your workload in your absence and facing a terminal illness.'

'So you're not in a relationship with her?'

He shook his head. 'God, no.' He responded with force. 'I think you need to look at yourself and ask why you're seeing things that aren't there.' He drank a mouthful of wine. 'But I do understand.'

'Maybe you're right.' I thought for a moment about Melanie, and Jakob's words. 'Yes, of course you are.'

'Now let's try to relax.' He reached across the gap and rested his hand on my knee.

I twitched his hand away.

'I don't find Melanie in the least attractive. I only feel sympathy and respect for her.' He leaned towards me and raised his glass. 'It's a decent wine, Orla. Cheers.'

I let his words sink in. Was this revelation about Melanie bullshit or the truth? I'd ask her when I next saw her and she'd know Jakob had told me. Nothing to lose there. He continued talking about things other than work - some improvements he was planning to the family house. 'Mother wants a new bathroom and most of the electrics are unreliable and dangerous. It'll cost, but what choice do we have?'

I decided not to say much or ask questions. That way he'd get the message I wanted him to go. As he talked, I sipped my wine. I set the empty glass onto the coffee table and Jakob reached over and topped up both glasses.

'Better not have too much. Since you're driving,' I said.

'Don't worry. I'll make a coffee before I leave.'

'That won't stop you being over the limit.'

'Come on Marjorie Proops. I could do without a lecture.'

'Marjorie who?'

'An agony aunt, slash puritanical killjoy. Before your time. She might even be dead.'

'I wouldn't want you to lose your license.' Maybe I wasn't such a bad liar after all, I thought.

'I'll have this one and it's only a few miles,' he said, and sank another mouthful. 'Not as if the police are going to pull me over.'

I'd never visited his family home although I'd seen the occasional photograph. The Hall looked huge and was set amongst ancient trees and acres of rhododendrons. The gardens looked wild although they apparently had a gardener who'd been with them for years and lived in a cottage on their land. Jakob's father had inherited the estate and had made millions himself through logistics and transport. Yet all of his success didn't prevent him from leaving his wife for his mistress but later returning to the family home and hanging himself in the stable block. From what I understood, the business had fallen into bankruptcy and Jakob's father had to sell his life's work for a pittance. After that he'd given up on life as well. His death, when Jakob was twelve, must have affected him and his mother in terrible ways. I knew too well how losing a parent, in my case both, forever left a gaping wound. Jakob explained that was the reason he spent so much time with his mother and why he often lived in the house with her for weeks on end. He'd confided once that when he left to go to his own home it would always be traumatic for his mother. At least I didn't have those problems to deal with.

Maybe life would have been easier if I'd died along with Harry and Drew, I suddenly thought. I felt sick and with an unbearable ache inside for my baby. It felt as if a stone lay lodged in my heart - squeezing my breath and suffocating my life and soul. It seemed that only now I'd begun to endure the full force of my grief. But I would never deny Harry or Drew their part in my life - in my memories. They were as much a part of me today as they had been when they were alive, only now I couldn't talk to them. I could no longer hold Harry against me and kiss his soft, plump cheeks. Inhale that divine baby smell that only a mother or father knows. But I wouldn't allow myself to crumble beneath the weight of my grief. Sylvia deserved more than that from me. Perhaps even I deserved more.

Jakob's voice murmured in the background and I realised I'd barely heard a word he'd been saying. My mind had drifted - awash with pain and blurred memories. When I looked up and around the room it was as if I was seeing it for the first time.

'What day is it?' I said, but my voice sounded distant and muffled.

'Orla?'

I turned to his voice and tried to sit up. 'What day...?' My words slurred.

'Thursday, of course.'

And I felt a warmth wash through me, and my legs and arms felt oddly leaden.

Jakob grasped the bottle by its throat and poured some into my glass. 'How's that?'

I sipped and the warmth of the wine seeped ever deeper. I stowed my glass between my knees. 'I've felt so confused this week. Everything...'

'I understand.' Jakob put his arm around my shoulder. 'Come here.'

I wanted to say no, but my tongue and lips felt numb. Instead I leaned and rested my head against his arm.

'You've been through so much...'

His words faded into nothing and I closed my eyes.

# Chapter 25

*Friday. The Early Hours*

My eyelids flickered and a sound fizzled in my ears. Daylight had gone and I was on my back, and looking up at the ceiling, at a hole in the plaster that blinked down at me. This was my living room - Flat 2, Windmoor House, Featherbed Lane. I turned my head and tried to regain focus. The standing lamp shone on the far side of the room. Out of the corner of my eye I spotted a pair of legs - black shoes, trousers. I tried to sit up, but it felt like a boulder lay on my abdomen. My eyelids drooped, like pebbles sinking in water.

I tried once more to sit up but I fell back again, defeated by an all pervading weakness.

I felt confused and disorientated. 'Who's here?' Even to me, my voice sounded too faint. 'Who are you?'

I heard movement and a figure crouched beside me. 'Ahh. My sleeping angel has awoken at last.'

'Jakob?'

Why was he here? My fuddled mind scrambled for details.

I looked towards the window. The curtains were drawn but I saw the muted glow of the street lamp outside.

'I'm so tired.'

'You had a drop too much wine,' he said, and his eyes looked distant and empty.

·I felt damp between my legs and reached a hand down. 'I want to sit up.'

Jakob stood up and as he reached down his hands slid against my breasts and under my arms. He pulled me to a sitting position and propped a cushion behind my back.

'Better?'

'How long have I been asleep?' I looked down at my skirt.

His eyes followed. 'Ahh, you spilled your wine.'

And I thought, thank God that was all.

'I didn't like to leave you in case you threw up,' he said.

'How much did I drink?' The words stumbled from my mouth.

'I guess it doesn't take much to affect you.'

'I'm so sorry. You must go.'

'It's OK. I slept in the armchair.'

'What time is it?' I looked over at the wall clock but my vision blurred.

He glanced down at his watch. 'Twenty past three.'

'I've been asleep all this time?'

'You must have needed the rest.'

Memories of the evening came flooding back. Something horrible had happened to me. Between Jakob and me. 'I have my counsellor meeting in the morning,' I said, remembering how important that was.

'Don't worry. I won't tell him you've been on the razzle.'

'Please don't.' What a fool I'd been. Getting drunk when so much was at stake, and in front of Jakob, again, of all people. 'I feel sick and dizzy.'

'Go to bed and get a few hours sleep. You'll be fine by the morning.'

I flinched as he hooked my arm. When I stood up my legs felt like jelly and the walls seemed to fall inwards.

'Let's get you into bed.'

He gripped my arm too tight and all but dragged me to the bedroom.

I tripped and he lifted me to standing.

'Shall I help you?'

'No.' I had the presence of mind to say. 'I can manage.'

'If you're sure?'

'Yes. Just go.' There was a desperation in my voice as I sat down on the bed.

He stood too close. My body began to shake and I felt sweat seep from my pores. I couldn't bear to look upon his face and I remained still and waited for him to leave.

After some moments and with reluctance, he turned to leave. 'I'll call you later,' he said, and he left the room.

The moment I heard the front door click shut, I let out a sob and forced myself to stand. I stumbled to the front door, and tripped twice along the way. I bolted the lock, then leaned against the door to ease the spinning in my head.

I floundered my way back to bed, curled into a ball and pulled the duvet up to my chin.

Within moments I felt the numbing opiate of sleep pull me under. A sleep filled with memories that seemed at once vivid and horrifyingly real.

# Chapter 26

*Friday morning*

I awoke to the sound of buzzing.

The front door bell. At this early hour? I sat up and pushed back the duvet. The blood pulsed in my ears and for a few moments my head reeled and a blanket of whiteness filled my vision.

The door buzzer brayed again, and I stood up carefully and walked barefoot across the floorboards and through to the living room. I pressed the intercom. 'Who is it?'

'Mark Winters. I'm from BioMedica.'

Shit, I thought. I pressed the door release. 'Come on up.'

I stumbled to the mirror above the fireplace. My eyes were streaked with mascara and my hair a tangled mess. I hurried to the bathroom and with a wet flannel I wiped my face clean. I grabbed a brush and ran it through my curls, then swigged a mouthful of Listerine, gargled and spat it into the sink. I was desperate for a wee, but I'd have to wait.

I gulped another mouthful of water and walked to the front door. I glanced at my watch. How had I managed to sleep so late? I turned the latch and opened the door. I recognised Mark from our website.

He gave a weak smile and his brow grooved with wrinkles.

I forced a smile and stood aside. 'Please, come in.'

He walked in and turned to me. 'You were expecting me this morning?' His manner felt brisk and business-like.

'Of course. I'm sorry, I was cleaning the bathroom and didn't hear the door. Can I make you a coffee?' I tried to disguise the brain fog that enshrouded my head.

He sat down on the sofa. 'Please. Milk, no sugar.'

I left to fill the kettle. Thank God he wanted coffee. My need for caffeine was far greater. An unpleasant odour wafted up my nostrils and I looked down at my skirt. There was an obvious dark stain and smell. A whirlpool of memories from the night before flooded my mind. I could hardly make an excuse to change now. I carried the cups into the living room and with shaking hands placed them on the coffee table. I sat down on the armchair opposite him, only too aware how unkempt I must have looked.

From what I knew of Mark, he'd worked for BioMedica for years and was head of Human Resources. If he was interviewing me, then I knew I was a serious case. He wasn't what I'd consider to be a counsellor though. I'd seen his team members come in to conduct various employee interviews or help recruit, but never Mark himself. He looked more like a city banker than an empathic counsellor - clean shaven, with neat, slicked back grey hair, navy pinstriped suit and high-voltage glasses. He wore the shiniest black shoes I'd ever seen. He set his briefcase on his lap, unclipped the catch, reached in and pulled out a manilla file.

My file. My stomach turned a somersault.

He set his briefcase squarely on the floor then lifted his eyes to mine.

'How are you feeling today? I understand you've had a difficult few weeks.' His words of sympathy didn't sound remotely genuine.

'I'm feeling fantastic, thank you.' And how ludicrous my words sounded to me and I felt a sudden urge to giggle.

He gave a tight-lipped barely there smile and nodded slowly. 'I understand you went back to work this week after several weeks away?'

'Yes. I'm ready to.'

'And how did you find it being back and with your colleagues?'

'Fine. Great.' I knew he'd have been given plenty of background. 'But it seems that because I have questions about the new drug, Hexprin, that I've... upset Dan and Jakob.'

'I hear you got quite distressed and accused them of withholding information from you.' He continued. 'And that you weren't pleased about having a marketing manager in to help.'

'Actually, I was told Melanie was managing the Hexprin launch. And that was because I questioned its safety.'

'But we have product managers who are responsible for the safety of any drug.'

'My role is to manage research and assess outcomes. As a team we're all responsible for safety. What's our company strapline?'

He paused and his brows lifted, but he didn't reply.

I assumed he was testing my memory. 'Helping you to live the life you deserve,' I said.

'Of course.'

'Then why the problem?' I asked.

He looked across at me and his eyes lowered to my skirt. He inhaled deliberately through his nose. 'I think we also need to have trust in and respect for those we work with.'

'Do you mean not to question when told to be quiet?' I asked. 'I'd have thought any employee who cared about the business, should in theory question everything. As Managers, we're not paid to follow orders. We're employed for our expertise. Our knowledge and our experience.'

'I see you've been with BioMedica for about five years. Yes?' He sniffed again.

I nodded.

'Dan and Jakob have been with the company for twice as long, and more. Dan has final say and I think it's important, especially when one is not quite oneself, to take a step back and have trust in our colleagues.'

'How will you deem if I'm fit to return to work?' I said, and realised I was up against the same barriers I faced with Dan and Jakob. Yesterday evening swirled in my brain and I knew for certain I could never trust Jakob again. Strobe-like flashes of what happened became ever more vivid and vile in my mind. I wanted this man to leave. I needed the toilet. I wanted to check myself over. I wanted a bloody hot steaming bath.

'Have you been feeling depressed or anxious since the accident?'

What a ridiculous stock question, I thought. 'Well, I have lost my son and husband. So yes, naturally. But do you think that's enough to stop me from returning to my job - a job I've been excelling at for five years?'

'We'll see,' he said, jotting down more notes. 'I have a few more questions and then I'll write up my assessment.'

I stood up. 'Please excuse me a moment.' I couldn't wait a moment longer.

I walked from the living room, into the bathroom and closed and locked the door behind me. I lifted my skirt, pulled down my pants and sat on the toilet. There were spots of blood against the pale blue cotton. I hadn't had a period since the accident although I didn't have any of the familiar cramping. Had Jakob touched me as I slept? And I could picture his face next to mine. Asking me if I was tired. He'd laid me down. Pulled up my skirt, touched my legs and pressed his fingers against my skin. What after that?

Shaking, I flushed the toilet and washed my hands. I went back into the living room and knew that the counsellor had already marked me unfit.

Unless I could convince him otherwise.

'Everything OK?' he asked, and peered at me beneath heavy brows.

'Let me assure you, Mr Winters, I am perfectly fit for work. I have another check up in a fortnight. In my last appointment my consultant told me I'd made incredible progress, given all I've been through. She tested my memory with current affairs and wrote a full emotional assessment too. She concluded that I am and will still be grieving for my child and my husband, but that returning to work would be a positive step towards my recovery. Would you like to speak to her?'

'By all means give me her number if you'd like to.'

I walked to the sideboard to pick up my phone. It wasn't there. 'I just need to find my phone for her number.'

'Orla.'

I turned to him and he pointed beneath the dining table.

'Oh!' I crouched down and retrieved it.

He stood up. 'Do you mind if I use your bathroom?'

'Of course.' I pointed. 'First door on the right.' I jotted my consultant's name and number on a slip of paper.

Mark seemed to be taking his time in the bathroom but finally he returned and sat back down.

'There is one more thing we need to talk about,' said Mark.

'Of course,' I said, and passed him my consultant's details.

'I spoke with Jakob first thing and he showed me a message you sent to him last night.'

'But I saw Jakob last night. I haven't messaged him since. What did it say?'

His eyes didn't waver. 'I think you know.'

'If I knew would I be asking?'

Mark held out his phone. 'Jakob sent me a screenshot of your message. Sent last night at 10.25pm.'

My heart thudded as I stood up and walked across to Mark. I took his phone and looked down at the screen.

I read the words. 'I did not send this!'

'Why don't you check your own phone - WhatsApp?' He paused. 'I'm afraid it wasn't only a text you sent, although Jakob didn't show me the photos.' He paused again. 'He said he would if it proved necessary.'

My heart raced ever faster as I tapped on WhatsApp. Top of my messages was a text to Jakob. I'd never even messaged him via WhatsApp - only regular texts.

I opened the message - the exact same wording. Below the text were two images - of me. One close up and intimate, the other of my exposed breasts. Not including my eyes because they'd have been closed. I stared at them and the phone fell from my hands. I ran to the bathroom, leaned against the sink and retched over and over again until there was nothing left inside of me. Sweat poured down my face.

As I washed and dried my face, anger surged through me. I stormed back into the living room where Mark sat composed and with a pen poised above his notepad.

I reached down for my phone. 'I did not send these. He was right here - plying me with wine. He opened my phone whilst I was asleep and sent the message and the pictures to himself. I'm appalled. He's a revolting monster.'

How could he do this to me? A million thoughts scattered through my mind. Jakob was a vile pig. How could anybody think I could send those words to a colleague? He'd physically abused me while I was unconscious. As soon as Mark went, I'd report Jakob to the police. This had gone beyond anything I thought him capable of.

'So are you saying that Jakob stayed here late last night?'

'Didn't you ask him what time he left?' I said. Of course Jakob would have lied about that.

'Yes, we discussed that. He told me that after coming here to look at some files he returned to his mother's and it was a while later when he received your messages. He said you'd tried to, how can I put it, persuade him to take your side while he was here?'

'All lies,' I said, raising my voice. 'And you'd better check with his mum what time he got in, hadn't you? What's more, taking intimate photos of me after spiking my drink and saying he's prepared to share them with you is a criminal offence. If he does so he's an accessory to the crime. He's fully responsible anyway. You can tell him I'll take him to court and he'll be given a sentence. He'd do well to admit to his crime and keep the images to himself. I'll send off my phone for DNA evidence - you can tell him that too.'

Mark pressed his lips and steepled his fingers. 'Given the nature of the images he insists you sent to him I don't want you returning to work until we have this matter resolved. This is serious sexual harassment and there are strict processes for dealing with it.'

'And who do you believe is the harasser?' I asked.

'Do I really need to answer that, Orla? This isn't looking in your favour.'

My mind raced. 'There's CCTV outside and I'll get a copy of the recording that will prove he was here, and more importantly, what time he left.' It was unlikely that the CCTV up the street reached the front of our building but it wouldn't hurt for Mark and Jakob to think it might.

'Yes, that may help. But it doesn't alter the fact that you sent him those explicit messages.'

'But I've told you, I didn't.'

Men always stuck together against a woman that hindered their plans. My fists clenched at my side and I fought to contain my rage. 'I want you to leave.'

He stood up and said calmly. 'Whilst I decide next steps, I advise you to stay away from work and especially from Jakob. Do not send further messages or call him. Is that clear?'

What could I say? If I told him I had every intention of confronting Jakob about this then Mark would likely report me to the police and get a restraining order taken out against me.

'Jakob was here all evening and until the early hours,' I repeated once more. 'And not because I wanted him here.'

'Why was he here?'

'You already know it was because he wanted to see some research that I believe compromises the safety of Hexprin.'

'And what did he say about the research?'

I hesitated. 'I didn't show him - I felt threatened and wanted him to leave.'

'And yet I hear you and he shared a drink together.' He gave a heavy sigh. 'I shall be making all the necessary checks. I'm sorry this is hard for you right now and I can see you've been through a lot. But I urge you to take a step back and not do anything that could further damage your position and reputation.'

I wanted to scream that I'd done nothing fucking wrong, but I knew I'd be flinging myself into a deeper hole. Better to stay quiet and let him leave.

I needed time to think. To make a plan to expose the truth about Hexprin and the truth about Jakob.

# Chapter 27

I watched Mark walk down the front steps and onto the cobbled pavement below. He paused, turned around and glanced up at the window. He saw me watching him, and without acknowledgement he swung back round and walked briskly away up the street.

I waited until he'd turned the corner then I bolted the front door and went to my bedroom. If I'd been any nearer to recovery this felt like a giant kick back down again. I'd never thought of Jakob as manipulative, sadistic or a pervert. What he did to me was revolting and sick. And all because he didn't want me asking difficult questions.

Only a week ago I'd thought him kind for helping me back to my flat after I'd made a drunken fool of myself at the dinner party, and then on the Sunday for rescuing me and Sylvia from those vile rapists. And it suddenly struck me how coincidental and convenient it was that he was there at that precise moment when I needed him. So that he could step into the breach with his gun like the super hero. Had he been following us and taken advantage of a situation that no one could have anticipated? He can't have known where we were going or that I'd climb the branch and fall into the water. And he'd been carrying a gun.

But why follow me?

As I tore off my clothes more flashbacks rippled through my mind - like taking the glass of wine from Jakob. Watching him top up my glass at every opportunity.

There was no further blood in my underwear. Naked, I went to the kitchen, tore off a bin liner from the roll under the sink and shoved last night's clothes into it. I felt abused and used. Had he penetrated me - raped me? I don't think he had. I had no memories of him entering me or inside of me. But I did have memories of his mouth close to mine, the odour of his breath, his fingers unbuttoning my blouse and pulling at my bra as I lay there unable to move. His mouth over my nipples and his hands groping my breasts. Had he touched my intimate parts?

Of course he had.

There was no tell-tale smell of intercourse. And if he hadn't had sex with me, which gave me some relief, then there would be nothing of him for the police to use as evidence against him. When I pictured him touching me and getting off on it, I felt sick and like an idiot for allowing myself to fall into that position. I should never have accepted the wine. I should have thrown him out at the first chance.

And did I really want to go through an intimate forensic examination?

Jakob was a despicable pig, but he wasn't a brainless pig. Yes, he'd touched me and abused me whilst I was out of it. He'd drugged me too - how I felt now was far worse than any hangover. I should get a blood test to check for whatever substance was in my bloodstream. That could be real evidence and less traumatic for me to undergo than a physical examination.

I grabbed my mobile and rang the surgery. After two minutes I'd convinced the receptionist that I needed a blood test. She'd booked me in for later and in the meantime a doctor would call me back.

Then I remembered the glasses and the bottle. That could be evidence, too. I returned to the kitchen but felt enraged when I saw only one wine glass washed and dried on the worktop. I sniffed the empty bottle - no alcoholic aroma. He'd rinsed that out, too. He wouldn't have bothered if he hadn't spiked my glass.

I ran a steaming bath, poured in some scented salts and scrubbed my teeth again.

After the past two months I feared this might tip me over the edge into pitiful victimhood. And yet somewhere deep within the recesses of my mind I knew I was strong enough to overcome this. That being the case, I wasn't going to let Jakob get away with what he'd done to me. Nor those men who would have raped Sylvia and I. And if Jakob had drugged me, which I was in no doubt about, then that was the evidence I needed to incriminate him. To put him away, even. Unless his mother gave him the alibi, which she might well do.

Either way, I knew exactly what I was up against and as last night continued to unfold and reveal itself in my mind, a madness and a bitter thirst for revenge built up inside of me. Jakob who'd revealed his true nature, the danger of losing a job I'd once loved, Hexprin and the problems this might cause, my darling son, and Drew. I could either become the victim or I could fight for what was right, and to make Jakob pay for what he'd done to me. That way I'd be better able to face the future without my baby.

# Chapter 28

*Friday*

I lay back in the steaming water as it swirled in mists around me. A doctor from the surgery had rung me straight back and I'd explained I was convinced my drink had been spiked. She'd urged me to report it to the police and when I said I didn't want to yet, she urged me to come down for a check over. But I insisted I didn't want to and I hadn't been raped. I sensed she doubted my judgement, but she let it go after saying I should seek help if I felt unwell or if I remembered more and wanted to take it further.

I reached for the soap and lathered it up in my hands until a foamy froth dripped from my fingers. I felt defiled and dirty. Jakob had made me feel this way. A sob broke from me as I scrubbed away the feeling of revulsion he'd left on my skin and inside of me.

I tipped the shampoo bottle, squeezed some into my palm and scrubbed it through my hair until my scalp hurt. Then I laid back, and with my toes I twisted the tap and topped up with more hot water. I closed my eyes, weak from the heat and the after-effects of whatever I'd been drugged with. I fell into a daze where my mind drifted between reality and something beyond that, and before long Harry's image appeared in my mind - sitting here with me in the bath before bedtime. He loved it when we bathed together and we'd play games with plastic pots and water whistles - tipping and pouring the water back and forth. The memory of delight and wonder on his face filled me with an intense and unimaginable sense of solace mixed together with unbearable loss and deep regret.

'Sweet, sweet Harry.'

Drew would sometimes come and sit on the toilet seat and sip his wine and chat to us, or he'd kneel down by the bath and join in our games. Harry would gaze round-eyed at his Daddy's face - delighting in the amusement and relishing our undivided attention and love. If only Harry were here with me still, my life would feel complete even without Drew. The void now seemed too vast to climb out of.

The accident. The fucking accident.

Before Harry, Drew and I had been quite the adventurers - we'd go hiking with our backpacks, sleeping bags and a two man tent. We'd plan our route but sometimes take a detour and end up somewhere unexpected but no less scenic for the change of plan. We didn't care that we had no washing or toilet facilities. We'd sieve fresh water from the stream, cook on an open fire and simply enjoy one another's company and the majesty of nature that surrounded us. In those days we'd made love almost every night, unless we were apart. Drew made me feel as though I were the most desirable woman on the planet. I felt loved and adored and that I was precisely where I belonged.

On one camping expedition we'd walked and camped along the edge of Windermere. It was an unusually warm and muggy evening and neither of us could sleep.

'I'm going for a dip,' I'd said finally, and pulled aside the flaps of the tent and crawled through. The moon was almost full amidst the cloudless night and the lake shimmered like a silver platter beneath.

'Can I watch?' said Drew.

I'd giggled but didn't reply. I pulled my nightdress over my head and draped it over the ridge of the tent. Then I walked down the grassy bank and onto the pebbles at the water's edge. The water lapped over my feet - caressing and cooling.

'It's so cold!'

The only way to swim was to boldly take the plunge. With my arms outstretched for balance, I took four strides in and when the water reached the tops of my thighs, I dived into the black water leaving a trail of bubbles in my wake. I lifted my face above the surface and gasped for breath at the shock of the cold on my skin.

I heard laughter bouncing towards me across the surface of the water, and turned to see Drew at the edge with his phone poised.

'Swim for me, my mermaid.'

I felt carefree and daring, and I pushed my feet off the lake floor and jumped high. I fell with a splash and jumped again but spun a full circle in the air. My wet hair slapped across my face and I laughed with abandon.

'You're the sexiest mermaid I've ever seen,' called Drew.

'How many mermaids have you seen before?' I called back, and with my arms outstretched I fell backwards with a splash.

'Only you. You're the only one I will ever want, my love.'

I swam further out. 'Swim with me.'

But I knew he wouldn't. Drew was athletic in many ways but a reluctant swimmer, even when we holidayed somewhere hot and sunny. He continued videoing me in still and watchful silence as the chill began to seep into my skin and bones. I swam towards him and walked out of the water.

He grabbed my hand. 'You're shivering. Come - let me dry and warm you.'

And he led me back up to our tent and did precisely as he said he would, then he kissed and made tender love to me.

The following morning he played back the video.

'I feel so silly. You must delete it,' I'd said, looking over his shoulder.

'You're beautiful and I won't. Not until I've watched it a million times first,' he'd insisted.

That was the Drew I wanted to remember, but those free and easy times felt like another life. It seemed as though he, or maybe both of us, had grown into completely different people. Maybe I'd grown up. Maybe I should have stayed childless and carefree.

All of the magic we'd shared seemed to vanish after those first euphoric moments when Harry came into our lives. No wonder couples split up or filed for divorce. Sex held couples together and if that went, what was left other than companionship and a building resentment and ever diminishing memory of a life they no longer shared? I'd loved having Harry and being a Mum, but I couldn't give up a sex life for long. And I'm damn certain that Drew couldn't either. Yes, he must have been seeing another woman and no doubt a woman without a baby for her to bestow her love and attention. Had Drew really been such a cliche? Or maybe he no longer found me attractive. Attraction couldn't be forced. I had put on a few pounds with Harry, but I don't think that had been the problem. Anyway, I'd never know and thinking about it all in retrospect was hardly going to help me to get over him any quicker. We'd grown apart, that much I did know. And in contrast, the bond between Harry and me had deepened day by day until the day his life was snatched from me.

My phone buzzed from the top of the wash basket.

I used my toes to pull the plug chain. The water gurgled and the level lowered. I lay there looking down at my long, slim and pale limbs as though I'd been cocooned indoors for months on end. I should get outdoors again. When I met Vince down at the lake yesterday, I realised how much I'd missed being near the water and the smell and sight of the surrounding fells. Walking had always helped me think through and resolve problems in my mind so that I'd inevitably return with a solution or a quieter mind. Maybe I'd ask a couple of friends to come along, too. Sylvia might join me. Kim at work was a reluctant walker. Vincent - I felt certain he'd be keen.

As the last dregs of water swirled and trickled down the plug hole I slid back up the bath and with my hands against the rim, pushed myself to standing. I turned and looked at my reflection in the mirror and raised my arms. There were black tufts of hair in my armpits and my pubic hair looked about as unruly as it had ever been. Still, I didn't dislike how I looked. I felt natural. And what need did I have to impress anyone right now?

The message was from Sylvia. I felt relief. She wanted to know when she could pop round. I slipped into a sleeveless cotton summer dress and cardigan then called Sylvia. She answered at once.

'Orla. Are you OK?'

I let out a long breath. 'I don't know. It's been the strangest couple of days and so much has happened. I should have rung you. I'm sorry.' I exhaled. 'But I do need to talk to you.'

'I'll come over,' she replied.

'Aren't you working?'

'Yes, but...'

'I have an appointment I can't miss, so how about tonight, and I'll cook us dinner?'

After reassuring her I'd survive until tonight, I checked my emails. Nothing from work - no surprises there.

After taking my blood, the phlebotomist advised me to ring the surgery for my results the following Tuesday. 'They may arrive sooner, but Dr. Turton will ring you if it comes back positive.'

I nodded.

'Considering this is a small town, I've done a few of these tests recently.'

'Really?' I said, surprised.

'I probably shouldn't have said anything,' she said, with a grimace and popped the plastic tube into an envelope.

'It's not something I've worried about since my nightclubbing days,' I said.

'Which bar or club were you in?' she asked.

'I wasn't in a bar,' I said, and let my guard down.

'Is it someone you know?' she said. 'This happens more than you'd imagine.'

I hesitated. 'If the result comes back positive then rest assured he'll be convicted.'

I could tell by her expression that she wanted to ask me more and her sympathy made me want to sit back down and tell her all about Jakob and what a conniving bastard he was - that he was supposed to be my colleague and friend. But what I needed first, was concrete proof that he'd done this.

'I'll be OK,' I reassured her before I headed out through the door. But I knew I wasn't. It was still only 3pm and Sylvia wasn't arriving until six. I walked to the Go Store on the High Street and bought some chicken and fresh vegetables to make a casserole, and a loaf of crusty bread. It was one of Sylvia's favourites and we'd often cooked it during our college years.

I flashed my debit card over the payment reader when I heard a familiar voice behind me.

I turned around. 'Vincent.'

'Glad to see you're looking after yourself,' he said.

I picked up my carrier and stepped aside. He placed his basket on the counter.

'Sylvia's coming for dinner,' I said, and paused. 'Hey, why don't you come, too?'

He pulled a twenty pound note from his jacket and handed it to the cashier. 'Won't I be intruding?'

'Please. I'd really like your thoughts on something important.'

We left the shop together and headed back up the High Street. The afternoon sun beamed overhead and feeling hot and lightheaded I slowed right down.

He turned to me. 'Are you all right? Here, let me carry your shopping.'

I felt grateful and handed him the bag 'I'm shattered, actually.'

'Are you sleeping OK?'

I shook my head and said quietly, 'Not so well last night.'

'Oh?'

I felt my tears threaten. 'I can't talk here.'

He held both carriers in one hand and hooked my arm. 'Come on. I'll catch you if you fall.'

Back in my flat I lay down on the sofa while Vincent nipped upstairs to put his groceries away.

I was almost asleep when he came back down.

'We could order a takeaway tonight if it's easier?' he suggested.

I nodded. 'I'll see how I feel in a bit.'

'Do you want to talk now? Or would you rather rest?'

I propped myself up. 'You know how I was telling you about Jakob and work and all the problems there?'

He sat on the armchair and leaned forwards. 'Actually, I've been thinking about that a lot.'

'Things have got worse. A lot worse,' I said, and bit my bottom lip, which trembled.

I relayed my meeting with Jakob and Dan, and tried to be as factual and balanced as possible.

'Was it preying on your mind last night?' he asked.

'Worse. I hardly know where to start.'

Vincent listened attentively as I explained how Jakob came here after the meeting and how he'd refilled my wine glass. How I'd blacked out and awoken in the early hours. The terrifying images that had been sparking and replaying in my mind.

'What a complete wanker. You should prosecute him. First for abusing you but also for this whole Hexprin cover up,' Vincent said, and nodded. 'He's hiding something.'

'I need to get my results back first. I'll take it from there.'

'Of course. I'm pleased you told me.'

'As I slept he hacked my phone, somehow. Then sent a filthy text, and more horrifying still, two intimate images of me, to himself, from my phone. Now the HR counsellor who is 'checking if I'm fit for work' thinks I'm a psycho sex stalker.'

'When it's completely the other way around. Jesus. What a fucking weasel. You must feel sick and angry.'

'I do, Vince. I feel violated by someone I used to think I could trust. If he came here now…' I stopped and felt a tight knot of fury in my stomach.

'I understand. And if I see him again I'll have words to say, too. With your permission, of course,' he added.

'Feel free. He deserves it and I'm not afraid to tell everyone now. I need some water.' I stood up. 'Do you want a glass?'

'Thanks,' he said. 'Mind if I nip to your lav?'

'Course,' I said, and headed to the kitchen.

I placed Vincent's water on the coffee table and sank into the sofa. I felt lightheaded and dehydrated and drank back the whole glass.

When Vincent returned, he held a small white box in his hand. He looked down at it for a moment before saying quietly. 'I found these in the bathroom.' He held out the box in his palm.

I didn't recognise it. 'What are they?'

'Tranquilisers.' He paused. 'From BioMedica.'

I stood up and held out my hand. 'Those are not mine.'

He placed them in my palm. 'Might explain why you're feeling groggy.'

'You don't think I took these willingly do you?'

His mouth twisted but he didn't reply.

'Vincent?'

'I don't know. It would be understandable if you were tempted to. Though I'm sure your doctor would prescribe something if you told her you were struggling.'

I opened the box and pulled out a foil square of small white tablets. I looked directly at him. 'These are not mine.'

'Surely they keep a tight control of stocks and notice if any go missing?'

'Of course they do. It's like Fort Knox. We must sign every item and quantity out and countersign with another member of staff.'

'So maybe you could prove that someone else signed these out?' he suggested.

I nodded. 'Hopefully. And I know someone who can check for me.'

'Excellent. Ask them to photograph the signature and date.'

'Where did you find them?'

'On the bathroom shelf. In plain view. I wasn't prying but I recognised the name of the drug.'

My legs felt weak and I sat back down. 'I should ring Jakob and confront him.'

'Put him on speaker and I can listen to his reaction, too.'

'Wait. First I need to think through how to approach this.'

He nodded. 'That's wise. Why don't you rest for a couple of hours and I'll come back when Sylvia's here.'

'I do feel shattered. In every sense.'

'What time do you want me?'

'Seven?'

'Great. And if Jakob turns up, text me or yell.'

'I don't think he'd dare after what he's done. I could seriously murder the bastard.'

'Keep that anger. You're going to need it.'

'Don't I know it,' I said, and gave a wave as he headed out.

Feeling angry still but physically drained, I lay back down and within minutes I'd nodded off.

Some time later, a buzz from my phone stirred me from sleep. I reached for it. 'Sylvia.' I checked the time - 5.45pm.

'How are you?' she asked.

'I've been dozing.'

'Sorry if I woke you. Listen, Amy's got a tummy bug. She's been sick twice since I picked her up and Rick has had to drive over to his mums - a burst pipe or something.'

'Don't worry, Amy's more important. Hope you don't get it, too.'

'I'm sure I will. I wanted to talk to you though. What's been happening?'

'Crap work stuff - they've signed me off sick and Jakob's being an absolute bastard.'

'What's he done?' I heard the concern in her voice.

I didn't want to worry her and so only told her about the meeting at work. 'I've invited Vincent down for dinner, too, so I won't be on my own.'

I heard her release a sigh. 'That's great Orla. I feel less guilty now.'

'Hey you. Quit the guilt.'

Sylvia laughed. 'OK. Call me later if you like or I'll call you tomorrow?'

'Thanks, Sis. I love you.'

I got up and splashed my face with water then went to the kitchen to prepare the dinner. I peeled and chopped the vegetables, diced the chicken, mixed the sauce and shoved it in the oven. I brushed a couple of jacket potatoes with olive oil and a sprinkle of salt and placed them beside the casserole. It wouldn't be ready 'til eight, but I wasn't in the least hungry.

I went into the bedroom, sat on the bed and dialled Kim.

'Hey, Orla.' She sounded pleased to hear me.

'I need to ask you a favour.'

After explaining that I needed the signatures for the tranquilizers, she asked why, but I said it might be better for her if she didn't know just yet. I felt bad enough involving her but what else could I do? I couldn't go into work nor jeopardise my position further. I'd always had the utmost respect for Dan, but not any more. Although how I felt about Dan didn't come near to how angry I felt towards Jakob. Each time I thought about what he'd done to me - spiking my drink, groping and abusing me, taking intimate photographs, I wanted to punch his smug face in. If he ever released these photos into the public domain they could destroy me. He must know what he'd done was a criminal offence, or was he so incensed by my questions, and focused on keeping me from the truth, that he'd lost all rationale for his actions?

I hung up with the promise that first thing on Monday morning Kim would check the signatures for signing out drugs and hopefully get back to me with evidence.

The aromas from the casserole drifted through as I headed for a shower. I still felt defiled - Jakob had done that to me. It was the sort of trauma that could put a woman off sex and men for life. I thought back again to when Jakob helped me home after the dinner party. Had he drugged me at the party and then touched me when he got me home? I felt sick and dizzy at the thought and realised I'd probably never know.

I stepped into the shower and the water threw icy darts onto my skin until the heat came through. I pressed my palms against the tiles and hung my head beneath the flow of the water. My hair blocked out the light as all that had happened fanned through my mind. I'd read accounts of women being drug raped and sometimes with the sort of drugs BioMedica produced. I remembered one trial where a judge commented that as the woman was unconscious during the sex act, then at least she hadn't been raped while fully conscious. The judge had gone on to lose his lofty position. And rightly so.

I was approaching thirty-seven, a widow, I'd lost my only child, was probably about to lose my job and had been abused whilst sedated by tranquilizers and alcohol. It seemed as though some sinister force was out to destroy me completely. And if I did get through this mentally intact, what if I could never trust a man again - enough to have a normal sexual relationship again?

There was no going back to feeling normal, only a new reality to live with. A reality where I needed to take back control and become the driver.

# Chapter 29

*Friday evening*

After my shower, I flipped through the coathangers and picked out one of the dresses I'd recently bought - a sleeveless denim dress. As I changed I thought about Vincent. He was one of a handful of people I felt I could trust right now and he was interesting company too - precisely what I needed in a friend. He was right to ask me about the tranquilizers - I'd have thought the same if I'd spotted them in his bathroom. But I could also see he'd realised I was telling him the truth. He had that quality about him. An honesty he couldn't hide in his features. He seemed intuitive and unafraid to speak openly about how he perceived things. It was why he was so engaging to talk to and easy to open up with.

I felt much better after a rest and I blow dried my hair, applied a sweep of mascara and some lip gloss. I looked at the perfume bottles on my dressing table - all of which I'd received as gifts from Drew for various birthday and Christmas presents. The odd thing was that I'd rarely worn perfume unless we were going out for a special occasion. I'd sometimes dropped hints for gifts I'd rather receive, but he either never listened or didn't want to buy what I'd hinted at. The Christmas after Harry was born I'd asked if he'd like to buy me some lingerie. When he'd handed me a small wrapped box and I realised it was yet another designer perfume, I couldn't hide my disappointment. 'You know I still have quite a lot of perfume left?'

He'd looked bemused. 'You're going to love this one. It comes highly recommended.'

'By the saleswoman?' I'd asked.

'No, someone at work.'

As I recalled that conversation from the attic of my mind, a thought hit me. Had Drew wanted me to wear the perfume because it reminded him of that particular colleague? And more importantly, was she the same colleague whose name began with S? Had Drew gone to my dressing table and picked up the bottle whenever he wanted to summon her? The thought made me queasy, crazy as it seemed - but could there be some truth in it? Maybe the knock on the head had kicked some bloody sense into me - the last day or two I'd understood things, previously hazy, with a surprising new clarity.

I looked down at all these barely touched bottles and it seemed excessive as well as a waste of money. And especially so if they had been bought to satisfy some weird fixation. I opened the top drawer of my dressing table, scooped the bottles into my arms and placed each bottle at the back. I'd see if Sylvia or Kim wanted any of them and if they didn't, they'd go to the charity shop. One thing was certain, I'd never wear them. I felt convinced this was more evidence Drew had been sleeping with another woman. Had he wanted me to smell like her? No. I knew that wasn't the case. Months ago he'd turned his back on me physically. Perhaps I should have made an effort to exercise more. Maybe worn more feminine clothes. I'd lived in denim shorts and vests, or jeans and T-shirts at home, and suits and low heeled shoes at work. Drew would probably approve of the new slimmer me, and of wearing a short fitted dress I'd only have worn pre-Harry.

What ridiculous thoughts, I told myself. I knew I was clutching at anything that might have prevented our relationship from withering away.

I stepped into a pair of wedge heeled sandals and stood in front of the mirror. My reflection could be of any woman getting ready for a night out or a date. And like it or not, I was a single woman who'd lost her beloved child. I'd become what I didn't ever want to be. But my life was about to start over again. And what choice did I have?

I hung up some clothes and folded a pair of jeans and added them to the pile in the wardrobe. I spotted the research report alongside the strips of Hexprin I'd tucked to one side and pulled them out. I'd show the full report to Vincent - hear his thoughts.

With the report and the most recent strip of Hexprin tablets in hand, I went and sat at the window. I drew my legs up and stretched them out the length of the seat. I stared down at the tablets and ran my finger over each hard lump before pressing and popping one pale yellow tablet into the middle of my palm. So small and harmless looking. As a rule, I'd always avoided taking medicines - and maybe this was in part because of the industry I worked in. But mostly it was something my mother had always talked to me and Sylvia about. Mum would suffer period pains or a migraine rather than take painkillers - she'd opt for relaxation, meditation and yoga before she'd give in. Ironic that I'd ended up working in this particular industry.

I rolled the small tablet across my palm then held it between my thumb and forefinger before popping it onto my tongue. For a moment or two I left it there before saliva filled my mouth. I tipped my head back and swallowed. With a sense of calm, I turned and looked out onto the street - a view that never looked quite the same with shoppers and tourists who I rarely recognised, but loved to watch. This evening, couples and small groups of people headed out to the bars and restaurants - typical for a Friday night. A gaggle of teenagers stood clumped together directly below - talking and laughing. I thought back to when most weekends, Drew and I would head out for drinks with friends, or straight to a restaurant where we'd inevitably drink too much wine but laugh and talk about anything and everything. That easy intimacy had changed even before Harry was born.

A couple, who looked about the same age as when Drew and I first met, walked up the street towards the flat. They weren't talking, but their expressions were relaxed as they turned and gazed into shop windows or round at the other people as they walked. She was pretty with long sleek brown hair and wore a red blouse with jeans. My eyes were drawn to the man's face. He had black hair, shoulder length and stylishly messy. Even from here I could see the deep blue of his eyes and the blackness of his lashes and brows. His lips seemed impossibly red and full and when his tongue protruded slightly and licked his bottom lip, I felt a jolt in my lower abdomen. I knew well that it wasn't the Hexprin - the tablet took at least an hour to begin to kick in. The couple stopped in the street and the man put his arms around the woman and leaned in and kissed her. The kiss was slow and I could tell by the way her body cleaved towards his that she responded with love and longing. How lucky she was. How lucky both of them were. Their love and their bond looked intense - any onlooker could see that.

Drew and I had once been like that. I'd felt and been confident of his love every single day. He'd ring and text me if we couldn't meet up and when we did, he'd shower me with loving words and affection. His feelings and desire for me were never in any doubt. And he'd been that way until we'd married, which was why I'd never doubted that our marriage would be anything but blissful and long lasting. I'd never felt jealous when Drew talked to my friends or spoke of work colleagues, and if anything, he was the one who grew jealous of other men I knew or worked with. Not so jealous that he'd make me feel worried or that he'd stop me from doing things on my own, but jealous enough to reassure me that he wanted me to be his and his alone. Anyway, I wasn't the least interested in other men. How could I be when I'd felt so loved and adored, and in return had felt a love so deep and powerful towards him?

Pre-Harry, there was one colleague and friend of Drew's, Zack, who made it blatantly clear he found me attractive and hinted that if the opportunity arose, would want to spend time with me alone. I knew it was all a flirtatious act to bolster his humongous ego but one night he went too far. Zack had a girlfriend, Claire, and Drew and I would spend evenings and the occasional weekend away together. When Zack told me he liked me it came as no surprise - I already sensed this by the attentive way he'd talk to me and his behaviour when we were in company. After that I'd noticed his smooth charm in action with other pretty women, but despite his wandering eye he'd stayed with Claire and they even talked about moving in together. His flirting made me feel awkward and upset for Claire who clearly adored him.

One night, when the men were preparing after dinner drinks Claire got up off the armchair and came to sit beside me. 'Mind if I ask you something, Orla?'

'Of course, anything,' I'd replied, already sensing by the intimate tone of her voice that her question was going to be a tough one to answer.

She took a breath. 'Did Zack try to play footsie with you under the table, during dinner?'

But I hadn't expected such directness and I felt my face begin to burn.

I hardly needed to answer her question but she deserved better - better than Zack.

I nodded. 'I'm sorry. I've made it perfectly clear I'm not interested and never would be.'

She gave a sigh. 'So this isn't the first time?' I watched the tears pool in her eyes.

I shook my head and took her hand, fighting back my own tears.

'I didn't think so,' she said. 'I appreciate your honesty.' And she knocked back what was left in her glass, stood up and walked to the door. She unhooked her handbag and jacket from the coat rack.

'Please don't go, Claire,' I said. 'Let's have it out with him.'

She shook her head. 'No point. Tell Zack not to bother calling me. It's over.'

What could I say? I'd have done the same, only I'd have given him a belly full of my anger first. 'He doesn't deserve you, Claire. You're beautiful and could have your pick of anyone.' My voice broke. 'Let me walk you home?' I stood up.

'No need. I'll be OK. I knew this was coming.' She nodded, tearful.

'I'll call you in the morning,' I said.

She opened the door and closed it quietly behind her. I was left to ask Zack to leave our flat and never to return. When Drew discovered Zack had been flirting with me, he turned his back on him too.

That was the way some creeps behaved. Eager to make a play for other women, right under their girlfriend's noses, even when they had a girlfriend they adored. I could never continue loving a man who juggled women's hearts as though they were assorted sweets to pick and choose from as the mood took them. Now, in my naivety, I realised I had probably done just that, whilst Drew had turned away from me and given his love and attention elsewhere. And I knew it wasn't only men who did this - women were just as capable of playing with men's hearts. But this wasn't me, and it never would be.

My mind returned to the present and my gaze remained on the couple as they kissed - unable to take my eyes away. What they were doing in full view was entirely natural and innocent, but the reaction it provoked in me felt anything but innocent. It felt deliciously voyeuristic. I felt one heartbeat chase another and my breaths seemed unnaturally heavy.

Finally, they pulled apart and with his arm about her waist they continued up the street and out of sight. My hands trembled as I glanced at my watch. Almost seven o'clock and Vincent would come down soon. Earlier, I'd heard the bass of his music, a distant rumble that came through the floorboards, but all seemed quiet now. As I sat and waited, I became aware of a warm feeling that spread through me and extended all the way down to my fingers and toes. I felt an arousal in my core and stretched out my legs and ran my fingers down the backs of my calves. My skin felt smooth and soft and I continued moving my hands up my inner thighs where the touch of my own fingers upon my skin made my breaths come faster. I felt exhilarated - and I loved the feeling. I knew I'd taken a risk with Hexprin - but then I thought, sod the damn risk. This was a way to test the drug's safety, and God knows it seemed to be working to full effect.

There came a knock at the door and I felt a rush of energy. I ran across the floorboards and opened the door.

Vincent broke into a smile and held out a box of chocolates.

'I figured wine wouldn't be the best dinner gift tonight.' He smiled again, the fine lines fanned out around silver-grey eyes that shone.

'You figured right,' I said, and led him through to the living room. 'Cup of tea?'

'Perfect. How are you feeling now?'

'I did manage a rest and actually, I feel completely better.'

'Wow.' Vincent's face grew serious and he nodded in agreement. 'You certainly look a lot happier.'

He sat down and crossed his legs. I stood and watched and it seemed as if his limbs stretched forever as he sank back into the sofa. He'd made an effort, too. His scrub of thick brown hair looked damp and a lock flopped down across his forehead. I could see he'd shaved and put on a pressed shirt that clung perfectly to his chest and arms. I smelled his aftershave and inhaled. Generally, Vincent had a disheveled look, but that did nothing to detract from his attractiveness. If anything, it enhanced his appeal, for me. I moved to sit beside him but then changed my mind and sat down on the armchair. Even from a distance I caught waves of his aftershave and I couldn't help but stare as he knitted his long fingers and rested them together between his thighs.

My eyes were drawn to his mouth - his lips, red and with a sharply defined cupid-bow. 'Sylvia can't make it,' I said. 'Her daughter has a tummy bug.'

'That's a shame. I expect she might get it, too.'

'I expect so,' I said, and felt a rush of regret. Harry had so often caught bugs which meant taking time off work to look after him and then to recover myself whenever I succumbed. Now I'd do anything to have him back with a tummy upset that created endless loads of washing and sleepless nights. I should have been more grateful when any illness gave me extra time with him, instead of wishing him better so that I could get back to work.

'Dinner smells delicious,' said Vincent.

'I hope you're hungry as there's masses now Sylvia's not coming.'

'I'm starving. How about you?'

I was beginning to feel ravenous, although not for food. I could hardly share that snippet with him. Hexprin was taking effect and I was feeling intensely aroused - my nipples tingled and I felt flutters between my legs. Not that I was going to do anything about it. I hadn't taken the drug to seduce Vincent. I'd only wanted to see how it made me feel in a man's presence. There was no denying its potency and on top of that its ability to boost my energy and my mood.

'Let's listen to some music?' I said, and tapped my music app. 'Do you know Azana - she's new?'

'No. What sort of music?' he said.

'She's from South Africa, sings in Zulu and English,' I said.

'Cool. Let's listen.'

I got up and hurried over to turn on the speaker. 'This one's called, Your Love. It's amazing.' I swayed to the music as I walked back to the sofa.

'She has a beautiful voice.'

'She does. You can sing though, Vince,' I said.

'I like to think so but I'm never going to sing on her level.'

'Don't be modest,' I said. 'You have a gorgeous tone and depth to your voice.'

'You're flattering me.'

I sat on the armrest of the sofa and swung my legs gently back and forth. 'Not at all. I don't do flattery unless it's completely justified.'

I sang along to the track, just loudly enough to be heard.

Vincent turned to me, his eyes wide. 'You know Zulu tongue?'

I laughed. 'Sadly, no. But I did look up her lyrics and learn them by heart. In fact, I did this before my accident.' I continued to sing until the end of the song and I knew Vincent watched me.

'I'm impressed,' he said. 'You too have a lovely tone.'

'Kind of you to say, Vincent, but do you know, I was rejected from the choir in Year One and have never fully recovered?'

'Then your choir mistress must have been tone deaf.'

'Funny how little things like that can knock your confidence early on,' I said.

'Equally, rejection can spur us on to prove someone wrong. Don't you think?'

'Yes, I think you're right. Anyway, it's never stopped me from singing.'

I felt so buoyed up with spirit that I jumped up and danced and sang along to the next track.

Vincent watched me, and drummed his knees to the beat. He hummed along too, and in perfect harmony. When the song ended, I remained standing there and gazed at him.

'You seem kinda different tonight,' he said. 'It's nice to see.'

'I feel oddly fantastic. Let me serve dinner and make you that cuppa.'

'Shall I help?'

'OK.'

Vincent followed me through to the kitchen and as I lifted the casserole from the oven, he filled the kettle.

'Where are your cups?' he asked.

I opened a cupboard door and stood aside.

Vincent reached up and as he did I noticed how tall and broad shouldered he was and how well fitted his jeans were against his slim hips and buttocks.

I think I sighed.

When he placed the two cups onto the worktop he glanced my way. He gave me a quizzical look. 'Do I have something on my face?'

'Oh, no!' I said quickly. 'Not at all.'

For goodness sake, get a grip, I thought.

He rubbed his lips together.

'Sorry.' I turned away, picked two plates from the rack and ladled out the casserole. I wasn't in the least hungry now. Not for food, anyway. I split and buttered a jacket potato for Vincent.

We sat down opposite one another at the table and as he talked, I could barely take my eyes off his mouth. Flickers of pleasure welled up within me like a flame rising and taking shape.

'I'm interviewing homeless people in Manchester next week,' he said. 'It's preliminary research for a documentary highlighting the downward spiral some people get caught up in.'

I rested my knife and fork on the side of the plate. 'I hope our government will sit up and listen. They make lip service and fund shelters but the reality is funding has been cut in real terms and people are falling off the radar and dying needlessly.'

'I didn't vote them in. And I'm sure you didn't either.'

'Not a chance,' I said. 'We have one or two homeless men here in Keswick. You could interview them if they're willing.'

'I've actually just interviewed a girl turfed out by her parents for taking drugs.'

'When your own parents throw you out, that must be the pits,' I said.

'I think there were deeper problems. I liaised with Shelter and they've found a young person's residence for her - albeit temporary.'

Vincent's thoughtfulness shone through in a way that was rare amongst many of the men I knew. He genuinely cared about people and fairness and equality for all. I found it hard to believe his ex, Sadie, had found another man anywhere near as fascinating, intelligent or as handsome as he was.

216

I leaned on my elbows and cupped my chin in my hands. 'Can I tell you something?'

He looked at me as he chewed. 'Of course. Anything at all.'

Without thinking, I reached over and placed my hand upon his. 'I think I like you.'

He swallowed. He turned his palm around and cupped my hand. 'Do you remember that time we kissed?'

I bit my bottom lip. 'How could I forget?'

'I've thought about that a lot since then,' he said. 'Though I tried not to.'

'And did it work?'

'I failed,' he replied, maintaining eye contact.

His eyes were unblinking, with the blackest and widest pupils I'd ever seen. I pushed my plate to the side and gazed at his face. 'I'm really not hungry.' I couldn't take my eyes away.

He straightened his spine. 'Do you have no appetite at all?'

'I think I do.' I twirled a lock of hair through my fingers. 'For you.' I realised this was true. I think I'd suppressed the memory of kissing him the night Harry choked on that pound coin, and how that kiss had made me feel, both at the time and afterwards whenever the moment returned to me. No doubt, guilt had played a part in this.

He pushed back his chair and stood up whilst maintaining eye contact and keeping a hold of my hand. He walked to my side of the table and slowly he pulled me to my feet. For a moment we stood face to face and energy and excitement fired through me and when he leaned down and cupped my chin, I lifted my face to his and parted my lips. I felt his arms as he wrapped them around me and when his lips touched mine, gently and then firmly, we were locked together. I pressed myself against him and felt the jut of his hip bones against mine and the strength of his chest and heartbeat. His breaths came fast and the butterflies inside of me darted ever faster. Our tongues touched and I heard a moan that could have belonged to either one of us. His hands, caressing, moved down my back and he lifted the back of my dress, and slowly, he ran his fingers inside my underwear. I lifted one leg and hooked it around his as he clutched my bottom and lifted me to him. I wrapped my other leg around him and he carried me to the sofa.

'Are you sure?' he said. 'What about last night?'

'I've already forgotten last night.'

He laid me down on the sofa and knelt over me. 'Let's take our time.' He gazed down at me. 'I want to taste you, savour you, every beautiful inch of you.' He leaned down and kissed each of my cheeks in turn, so tenderly that I almost wept.

I looked up at him, drunk eyed with desire, and laid a hand upon his forearm. I felt the flow of his muscles as he undid the buttons down the front of my dress.

He pulled the material aside and his eyes lifted to mine. 'You're an incredible woman, Orla.' He shook his head. 'And if I'm honest with myself, I've wanted you for too long.'

I ran my finger along the waistband of his jeans. 'I'm realising the same.' I longed for his touch - for all of him. 'The way you kissed me that time, and here now...I can hardly believe it.'

Without speaking, he bent down and with a silken touch his mouth brushed my lips, so gently at first - so soft and warm. He parted my lips with his tongue and I pulled him closer.

He cupped the back of my neck with one hand and with his other he reached behind me and with a swiftness of fingers he unhooked my bra. He caressed my breasts and teased my nipples in turn all the while flicking his tongue against mine.

'Vincent,' I murmured.

He stood up and as he unbuttoned his shirt then unzipped his jeans I pulled down my knickers and cast them onto the floor. I pulled my dress over my head, flung my bra over the back of the sofa and laid back down. Vincent was an Adonis in the flesh - how had I resisted him until now?

Still in his underpants, Vincent looked down at me, his eyes wide. He appeared alarmed. 'You have a rash.'

I peered down at my chest and abdomen and saw the angry splashes of red skin. I sat up. 'I didn't have this earlier.'

'I couldn't see it two minutes ago. Is it an arousal rash?'

I sat up and pressed the skin which went white beneath my fingers. 'I don't get them like this.'

'You don't think it's because of what Jakob might have given you last night?'

I clasped my hand to my mouth. 'Oh my God!'

'What is it?'

'I've done something really stupid.'

He sat beside me and took my hand. 'Have I rushed you?'

'No, no. I wanted to.'

'Then what?'

I looked down again at my breasts and saw the red patches were joining together. 'I took a dose of Hexprin.'

He stared at me, his eyes round with disbelief. 'Are you serious? But why, when you know it could be dangerous?'

I shook my head. 'To see how it affected me. I wanted to test it.'

'But you know the risks. You told me so yourself.' He let go of my hand and stood up. 'Let me call a doctor. Your neck is turning red too.'

I grabbed his hand and turned to him with desperation. 'We can't. I shouldn't even have them in my possession.'

'You mean like the tranquilizers?'

'I didn't steal those. I already told you.'

'So you wanted to test Hexprin out, on me. Is that it?'

'I should have told you.'

'Yes, you damn well should. But that's not the point and you know it.'

'I should take a cold shower.'

'I should go. Do you feel OK in yourself?'

I laughed lightly. 'Not really.'

'Then I'll stay.'

'Honestly, Vincent. It's probably safer if you go.'

'Not if you feel ill.'

'I don't so much feel ill, though this rash is worrying.' My brow furrowed and I gave a kittenish smile.

'Bloody hell, Orla! I thought you fucking fancied me.' His features tensed. 'How do you think that makes me feel? And don't bother answering. I'll be back in an hour to check you're OK. OK?'

I fidgeted awkwardly. 'But I do like you.'

He snatched up his trainers and jeans and without bothering to dress he headed for the door.

He turned back briefly. 'Call me if you feel ill.' Then he clicked the door shut behind him.

'Bloody hell and damn,' I said, and hurried to the bathroom. The blotches were now all the way down my arms and legs. I felt panicky and my heart pounded wildly as I turned the shower dial to cold. I stepped into the flow and gasped and shuddered beneath the freezing spray.

My appetite had been well and truly doused. And what would Vincent think of me now? I did like him. I liked everything about him. He was intelligent, kind and interesting - not to mention, gorgeous. And his voice and accent, too. I'd managed to destroy any possibility of us becoming anything together. He must be feeling completely used. Never in my life had I thrown myself at a man so wantonly. Shame livewired through my mind and body. And Drew, only eight weeks dead. Had Hexprin made me lose all sense of rational thought, and to lose control of my sexual desire which should always be tempered with what the other person wanted or didn't want, instead of running headlong to seek gratification? It was wrong, even if he did like me a bit.

The moment the drug had begun to take effect, I'd felt aroused at the mere sight of an attractive man in the street, after which I couldn't drag my eyes away from Vincent - a friend who'd been kind enough to look out for me. The potency of the drug was huge and beyond what I'd imagined, but I felt sick and ashamed at my behaviour. When Vincent returned, if he dared to, I'd apologise and at least try to keep him as a friend and to pull back a little self respect.

No wonder the testers of Hexprin had talked of it as some kind of wonder drug. With the right man - a partner or lover, the experience could be truly immense. One of the remote side effects had mentioned blotching of skin - but this had been explained as an orgasmic flush. I looked down at my arms and inner thighs. Never had I experienced a sexual flush in those areas. I ran my palm over my chest, which felt hot and tender to the touch. The red welts looked unsightly, too. Hardly an aphrodisiac for a woman's partner.

I turned the temperature dial down a notch and remained there for some minutes and hoped the rash might fade. Eventually, when I couldn't bear the biting cold a moment longer, I stepped out of the shower and reached for a towel. I swallowed two paracetamol, drank back a glass of water and stood in front of the mirror. The rash had maybe faded a little. I dressed in loose cotton shorts and vest and opened all the windows to allow fresh air to flow through the flat. Other than the rash, physically I felt fine. A slight pressure headache, but nothing too painful. Arousal sensations were returning but I felt so guilty about throwing myself at Vincent that I repressed these urges. I remembered the blood pressure monitor I'd bought when pregnant and I went to fetch it from the bathroom. I fastened it around my wrist, pressed the button and watched as the readings rose. Normally my blood pressure was on the low side. But now, my systolic reading continued to rise up and up. I watched with increasing alarm until it eventually stopped at 180 - at least fifty points higher than my usual reading. No wonder my head ached and my heart pounded. My diastolic reading was 105 - again, worryingly high. I found the trial report to look at the blood pressure results. Some of the trial users had tested with high blood pressure but again that had been attributed to making love and climax which automatically raised blood pressure. They'd only taken one reading after making love and no further readings to check that their blood pressure had gone down. Thank God we hadn't actually gone as far as making love - that may have sent my blood pressure skyrocketing and putting me at risk of stroke or cardiac arrest.

I lifted my vest and felt relieved to see the blotches looked less angry. I hurried to get my mobile and took several photos. I should have taken some when it first appeared. Vincent would be back down soon to see how I was and I threw on a baggy shirt over my cropped vest which on its own left little to the imagination. I didn't want it to look as though I wanted to seduce him again. After checking my blood pressure once more, which had gone down a little, I lay on the sofa and checked my social media. It was the usual family and holiday photos, but I read a couple of articles - one about Trump destroying sacred Indian sites to build his Mexican wall and another about plastic pollution choking whales and microplastics in sea creatures. This left me feeling even more annoyed and wretched than before.

Outside, the street lamps flickered on and a refreshing breeze rushed through the open window and cooled my skin.

Again, I read the message I'd allegedly sent to Jakob. The one I knew he'd sent from my phone after drugging and molesting me. How bloody dare he make me out to be some kind of hyper sexed stalker desperate for his body. I tapped the telephone icon and listened as it rang out. Nine-thirty pm. Was he out with Melanie or at home working? He always banged on about working late into the evenings and he'd often sent me emails past midnight. Presumably, Melanie was the recipient of all these additional communications now - and no doubt with plenty of pillow talk involved.

I called again and this time he answered on the first ring. 'Orla.'

'Jakob,' I said, and paused. 'Mark Winters told me not to call you, but we both know you have no reason to be fearful. Don't we?'

'I'm not scared of you, Orla. Only concerned for your welfare and mental health.'

'I should report you. Why did you drug me and then photograph me with my phone and send it to yourself?'

'Shhh. Careful what you're saying.'

'Why? Are you worried someone you're with might hear what you've done to me? You don't want Melanie to know what a lying, disgusting monster you are.'

'You've lost your mind. Mark's already spoken to me saying you need mental health support and medication.'

'And what about last weekend when you helped me home from the dinner party? Did you drug me and touch me up then, too?'

I could hear a female voice in the background, then crying. 'Who are you with?'

A door slammed somewhere.

'I'm on my own,' he said. 'It's a play on the radio.'

He could conjure a lie in an instant. 'You're with Melanie, aren't you?'

'It's Friday night. Presumably Melanie's at home. As am I.'

In the background I heard muffled voices again and a woman shouting.

'Wait a minute,' he said.

I heard a knock as he placed the phone down and movements. Then I heard a door opening and closing, and again faint voices.

He came back on. 'I have to go,' he said. 'Don't call me again.'

'Wait. We need to talk. Face to face.'

The line fell silent.

'Jakob?'

I pressed call again and it rang out for a few moments before the tone went dead. I felt frantic and furious and I called again and again but all I got was his answer message.

'Ring me back,' I said. 'We have to talk. I'll go to the police.' But I knew he wouldn't return my call. I hung up and threw my phone onto the sofa. 'You bastard!'

And then it dawned on me that I shouldn't have called him repeatedly. He'd no doubt screenshot that and use it as more evidence for my 'stalking' him.

But I'd prove he was the orchestrator of this mess.

There was a knock on the flat door.

Vincent.

I hurried over, opened the door, smiled and stood aside. 'Come in.'

But he remained out on the landing.

His expression was neutral. 'How's the rash?'

'Definitely going down.'

'How do you feel?'

'Like a fool.'

He gave the slimmest of smiles. 'But you feel well? No headaches or racing heart?'

'My head hurt earlier and my blood pressure was raised.' I'd probably hiked it up a whole lot more during my calls to Jakob, I thought.

'You should go to A&E,' he said. 'You don't have to tell them what you've taken. Show them the rash. They'll check you over. I'll drive you there.' His tone remained clipped and I knew he was upset with me.

'I'm OK. I don't need medical attention.'

'Fine. I'll leave you to rest. Take care.' And he turned, hesitated for a moment, then walked away.

I watched him until he'd climbed the stairs and disappeared onto the landing above. I closed and bolted the door then walked slowly to my bedroom and flung myself onto the bed.

# Chapter 30

All Saturday I remained indoors, moped around and felt about as pathetic and miserable as I could ever recall feeling. I watched, 'Sleepless in Seattle', which had always been my pick me up movie, but every time a poignant scene came on, my own emotions came to the fore. Watching 'The Holiday', I fared no better although Cameron Diaz and Jude Law did make me smile a few times. Sylvia rang and I lied and told her I was heading over to Penrith to go clothes shopping and would meet up with Kim for tea. I knew Sylvia felt concerned, and I didn't want her to rush over and find out what a prize idiot I'd been. I never could hide things from my big sister.

There's something to be said for keeping your thoughts close to your chest, I thought. And I knew that was where I'd gone wrong. I should have been more secretive and cautious with Jakob and Dan instead of wading in and expecting them to listen to and support my concerns. Years of working with them and trusting them had led me into a false sense of security. That Jakob had been so caring and thoughtful after the accident led me to believe he genuinely cared and felt concerned for my welfare and future. If I'd known how devious, sadistic and manipulative he was before now, I could have avoided being ostracized from work and the whole bloody nightmare I'd been sucked into.

In the flat above, Vincent seemed unusually quiet and I only heard the occasional door close or footsteps on the floorboards. I didn't hear any music, or him talking on the phone. I realised I missed hearing his deep Scottish tones. I was desperate to go up and talk to him, but it was obvious he didn't want anything further to do with me. He hadn't been back down to check on me, but had sent a brief text, to which I'd replied, said I was fine, and apologised once more. I'd had no messages from him since and I didn't want to force anything with him.

By Sunday morning as I dressed I felt relieved that my rash had all but faded away with only a few pale pink blotches here and there. My head felt clearer and my heart beat at a normal rate. I hadn't stopped fixating on Vincent, although I couldn't work out if that was because of Hexprin lingering in my system or if I really did like him. I felt certain it wasn't the drug. I cooked a breakfast of poached egg on toast then measured my blood pressure which had returned to normal. Now that I'd experienced the full effects, as well as some nasty side effects of Hexprin, I felt even more convinced it was a loose cannon and nowhere near ready to be prescribed. Friday night had been the first time I'd taken it and the results had been dramatic in every possible sense. If a woman chose to take this regularly, who knew the damage it could do to her body or the longer term psychological effects.

My phone buzzed beside me. A text from Kim.

*'I decided to nip in to collect some 'extra work', and while I was there I found the evidence you were looking for. I won't ask what it's all about but PLEASE CALL ME if you want to talk about it. Your loyal friend, Kim xx.'*

I zoomed in on the image she'd sent. Date, last Monday - my first day back. It could be my exact signature, if I didn't know better. And counter signature by Melanie Evans. Was that even her signature? If Jakob had faked mine he may well have faked hers, too. Or maybe he'd persuaded her to do it - for the greater good, or some other hogwash reason.

Either way the removal of the tranquilizers implicated both Melanie and me, whereas Jakob remained innocent.

I messaged Kim. *'Can't thank you enough! I owe you big time. Orla xx.'*

She replied. *'I want you back here. That'll be more than enough repayment.'*

At least one person was still rooting for my sanity and my return.

I sipped my umpteenth coffee of the day and ran over last night's call with Jakob again. Why had it taken me until now to see him for what he really was? I'd always thought we'd made a great team - we'd usually come to an agreement on things which helped with projects we were working on and he'd almost always supported and praised my ideas whilst he offered constructive feedback and criticism. He'd made me feel secure about my abilities and as a result, my confidence at BioMedica had soared.

225

As far as I was concerned, he'd seemed the ideal colleague. When others I worked with had moaned about him, I'd been quick to defend him. I now suspected he'd hidden his darker side from me only too well. Maybe Kim had been right about him fancying me. Perhaps that was the reason he and I had gelled, although I'd never encouraged him in that respect. We may have flirted a little. Or had he flirted a lot and I'd not been aware? When I thought back, I realised it was often the older women or those nearing retirement who disliked or had complained to me about Jakob. Was he a man who only liked women he found attractive or could flirt with? I could think of at least a couple of other women who he seemed to have a close working relationship with and he could sometimes be found chatting to Natasha on reception.

But what I found most disturbing and which only dawned on me now was how much of a coincidence it was that the speedboat accident, which Jakob had organised, had not only destroyed my family but had also been the catalyst for shattering our working relationship at a crucial time for BioMedica. I suspected now, as memories of recovering in hospital flooded my mind, that Jakob had played the guilt-ridden victim only too well. I couldn't believe he'd shed one genuine tear. Oh, he'd made a great pretence at doing so, and even taken a few days off work to recover. He'd told me this as he'd sat on the end of my hospital bed with a pained expression whilst he covered his face with his hands and made a theatrical performance of mopping his eyes and blowing his nose. I'd even felt pity for him, as I did for myself. I'd reassured him that it hadn't been his fault, even though I'd wrestled with this in my mind over the cause and how the sequence of events had unfolded. Of course, it would be understandable for Jakob to be devastated by the accident, if he hadn't intentionally planned the whole thing, which is what I now strongly suspected and feared. The inquest had said the fault on the boat was unusual but possible. Jakob was seeking to sue the boat manufacturer. They'd attributed the locking of the accelerator to one cable coming loose and getting caught up with another. From what Jakob had told me of the accident, and unsurprisingly, his was the only account we had - there were no other witnesses on or off the water. When we'd raced nearer to the shore and he realised he had no chance of stopping the boat from crashing, he'd urged Drew to jump overboard with Harry in his arms. Had he known Drew wasn't a confident swimmer? He'd have known Drew wasn't wearing a life jacket.

Somehow, I'd fallen and been thrown around and Jakob hadn't been able to drag me out of the boat before it careered into the shore and tumbled into the rocks beyond. I'd been thrown from the boat, and Jakob had landed in the water - conveniently.

My memory of the accident was still too much of a blur.

How had the accident really happened?

I suspect nothing like the way Jakob had described.

An overwhelming rage towards Jakob built within my mind, and my head buzzed with thoughts of what I wanted to say to him. My fingers trembled as I poured myself a glass of cold water and gulped it back.

I needed to get out of the flat - breathe some fresh air - think things through. For the briefest moment I thought about running up and knocking on Vincent's door. I pushed the thought aside and grabbed my denim jacket off the coat rack. Rather than head into town I set off down to the lake again which had always been my refuge during difficult times. I saw two couples on the pavement outside the cinema and I stepped into the road to walk around them.

I overheard one of the women say. 'I love Keanu Reeves. Let's see when it starts.'

'It's a chick's flick,' one of the men replied, grudgingly.

I looked up at the cinema front. 'The Lake House' with Sandra Bullock and Keanu Reeves. An enchanting and cleverly told love story and exactly the sort of thing that I could lose myself in. I jogged up the steps and through the doors. The foyer heaved with people milling around with drinks and buckets of popcorn.

'Do you have any seats left?'

'Just the one?' he asked.

'Yes please.'

The young man on the counter handed me my ticket and coffee cup and asked if I wanted a free promotional bag of jelly beans. I declined and headed into Screen One and down the aisle to find my seat in Row D. The couples I'd seen on the pavement came in and sat along the same row. I heard one of the guys muttering - something about wanting to go on a boat ride instead. When the overhead lights dimmed and the curtains in front of the screen opened fully, I stretched out my legs and placed my cup in the holder. The audience hushed and only the odd whisper and rustle of sweet wrappers broke the silence. I had nobody on either side of me and I draped my jacket over the armrest. I'd originally watched this movie when I was a student and it was one of the first dates Drew and I had been on together. How my life had changed since then. If I could have gone back to that time and done things differently, would I have? I don't think I could have. I'd fallen headlong in love with him and I couldn't have pulled away then unless he'd finished with me. We'd slotted together naturally and our relationship felt right from the very start. After a year we'd shared a room in a student house and life had seemed exciting, yet at the same time easy and uncomplicated.

Up on the big screen, as Dr. Kate Forster walked back from her car to leave her first letter for Alex Wyler in the mailbox outside The Lake House, my phone pinged - I'd forgotten to mute it. A woman behind me tutted her disapproval. I shielded my phone beneath my jacket to see who'd messaged.

The text read, *'BOO!'*

Unknown number.

My heart shuddered. Was it a wrong number or meant for me? I turned the volume down and left the phone on my lap. I tried to relax and enjoy the film, but I felt uneasy. What a horrible, creepy message. A few minutes later I jumped when the phone vibrated against my leg. I tried to resist looking but curiosity got the better of me.

*'I said, BOO TO YOU.'*

I texted back. *'Who is this?'*

I stared down at the screen and waited for a response, but nothing came. I continued watching the film and when I'd finally relaxed and become immersed, my phone vibrated once more.

*'I can see you.'*

I turned my head left then right to see if anyone was looking in my direction, then I twisted around towards the dimly lit faces in the auditorium. Every instinct told me this wasn't a hoax. Someone was here and watching my every move.

228

My phone buzzed, and only seconds later, again.

*'Are you losing your mind?'*

*'Are you imagining things?'*

I looked across the auditorium, but everyone else remained seated with their eyes fixed ahead at the screen. Then, in the opposite corner, just beneath the green fire exit sign, I spotted a tall figure, a man, deadly still and facing my way. It was too dark to make out his features, but there was something familiar about his height and shape. Whoever it was, and I had my suspicions, I'd confront him, right here in the cinema.

I felt the perspiration on my face and chest and I stood up, grabbed my jacket and squeezed past jutting knees and feet to the end of the row.

But when I looked up, the man had already disappeared.

No doubt through the side door. I hurried back out through the foyer and down the steps and onto the street. It was even busier than before. There were groups of people that wandered up and down, to or from the lake. I ran across the road, and darted between people and through the gates to the public gardens. I continued running down the slope towards the putting green.

Was he coming behind me? My mind raced. Should I wait and confront him, or run home and lock the door? Yes, better to lock him out. I felt sure my phone buzzed again and I ran, breathless and desperate to get away. The grass, trees, hedges and people seemed to blur and merge into one and the last thing I recalled was a buzzing in my ear, strobes of light and my world turning over like a folding blanket.

I opened my eyes and a pair of brown shoes came into view, then more pairs of legs appeared in my field of vision. I turned my face upwards. A low tide of voices and indistinct words surrounded me. Several faces, with concerned expressions looked down at me.

A middle aged woman knelt and spoke softly. 'You fainted, dear. Moments ago.' She put her hand against my forehead. 'What's your name?'

'Orla. Orla Safian.'

'I saw you running. You kept looking back, terrified.'

I tried to sit up and she hooked my arm.

'A man. In the cinema,' I said, the memory of him returning.

'Sit still for a minute.' She touched my cheek. 'You do feel warm. Are you unwell? Pregnant perhaps?' she asked.

'No.' I looked around. 'He might be nearby.'

'Orla, are you OK?'

I recognised the voice and turned my head.

Vincent crouched down beside me.

'Someone followed me to the cinema,' I said. 'They sent horrible texts.' I moved to stand up and Vincent and the woman each took an arm.

I stood on trembling legs. 'Can you help me get home? I know he's here, watching me.'

'Did you see who it was?' asked Vincent.

'I couldn't see his face, but...'

'Might it have been Jakob?'

'Maybe. But whoever it was texted me anonymously.'

'Are you OK to walk?' he asked, and gripped my arm tighter.

'I think so.' And I took a hesitant step forward. I turned and thanked the kind woman and the crowd around me dispersed.

'I felt so freaked out that I panicked,' I said.

'I'm not surprised, after all you've been through and what Jakob's done to you.' He paused. 'If it was Jakob, he's seriously psychopathic.'

Vincent kept hold of me as we headed out of the park and my racing thoughts began to settle.

'I'm sorry, Vincent.'

'It's him who should be sorry.'

'I meant, about what happened the other night. I feel terrible.'

He turned and gave me a slim smile. 'I'll admit I was disappointed and even shocked. But I think you did it with the right intentions.'

'It was idiotic of me.'

'It was a little foolish. But don't worry about that now. Seems there are more pressing things to worry about.'

We walked across the cobbles of Featherbed Lane, and I felt shaken still. The cinema stalker had to be Jakob - who, it seemed, had taken one step further in his attempt to intimidate and control me. It was working, too. Even so, his actions made me more determined than ever not to allow him to beat me into submission. He wanted me out of the way by whatever means he could find. I refused to submit and give him that satisfaction. I wanted my job and I wanted to do what was the only ethical thing with Hexprin - expose the dangers so that anyone under the illusion that it was safe to use, knew the risks. The truth was, in its current state, it should never be made available for public use.

Vincent didn't let go of my arm until I was safely sitting on the sofa.

'I'll fetch some water,' he said, and headed off into the kitchen.

Moments later, he placed a glass in my hand.

I took a long mouthful of the cool water. 'Should I phone the police?'

Vincent thought for a moment. 'I'm not sure. From what you've told me, the evidence might look worse against you if they questioned him.'

I considered this. The tranquilizers in my bathroom that had supposedly been signed out by me and Melanie, the intimate photos and texts I'd allegedly sent to Jakob, Mark Winters' assessment who was most definitely on Dan and Jakob's side, and on top of all that, I'd been forced to go on leave from work which would most likely make me appear bitter and vengeful. Jakob would only need to mention my head injury and memory loss to cast further doubt upon anything that I said.

'I need to think this through,' I said. 'What about the anonymous texts?'

'But did anyone actually see him at the cinema or in the park? You said yourself you didn't know who it was. You told me he came to yours and Sylvia's rescue when those men attacked you both, and that he saw you safely home after you got drunk at your friend's dinner party. The police will already know about Jakob holding those van drivers until they'd arrived on the scene, and your friends at the party will have seen Jakob being kind and supportive. I realise it's not the case, but it might appear as if he's on your side, not against.'

'But the whole Hexprin thing. Shouldn't I be allowed to flag up safety issues?'

'Of course you should. But you said they've already done further trials which on the surface suggest it's safe. This could

231

weaken your arguments. And you can hardly admit to having tried it yourself.'

'Why can't I? If it stops them launching it, it might be worth it.'

'If you admit to that, you'll be unemployable by pharmaceuticals. As a journalist, if I took it, that might be more easily justified. We're expected to take risks in the name of searching for the truth, but your career could be sunk. You mustn't admit to taking it, Orla - ever.'

'You're right. And of course, I wish I hadn't.' I felt stuck in a bloody great hole.

'I know you do. And I can almost understand why you took it.'

He gave me a lopsided smile and I felt my cheeks redden.

I wanted to ask for his help as a journalist, but I sensed by his body language that he felt uneasy being alone here with me. I could hardly blame him.

'You go, Vincent. I'm sure you've got things to do. And I appreciate you helping me home. I'm sure it was only stress that made me panic and faint.'

He nodded. 'Might also be the after effects of Hexprin. I wouldn't discount that,' he said.

'I hadn't considered that,' I said.

'Listen,' he said, 'will you phone me or come up if Jakob or anyone sends you anything suspicious?'

# Chapter 31

*Monday*

On Monday morning I awoke from a deep sleep to my phone buzzing on the bedside table.

I reached across. 'Kim?'

'Sorry, were you asleep?'

'I shouldn't be.'

'I need to talk to you.' Her voice sounded quiet but urgent.

I sat up. 'What's happened? And why are you whispering?'

'I'm in the stationery cupboard.'

'Why?'

'Because I don't want anyone to overhear. I've been talking to Melanie. I found her crying in the toilets.'

'Did she say why?'

'At first she was too upset to get any words out, but when she eventually calmed down, she said her boyfriend had dumped her - or she'd dumped him. Anyway, they've split.'

'Did she elaborate?'

'Yes, she did.'

I waited for her to continue.

'She confessed she'd been desperately in love with Jakob - past tense, I hasten to add. And that she'd started seeing him before working here. She refused to say what they'd fallen out over but became quite hysterical when I suggested I'd fetch him so they could talk.'

'Is Jakob in the office now?'

'Of course. Head down at his desk. I suggested Melanie say she felt ill and she's just gone home. I've got to tell Jakob. No doubt he'll know full well why.'

'Interesting developments.'

'How are you doing?' she asked.

'Surviving. A bit of a mad adventure yesterday which I won't go into, but otherwise trying to relax and read.'

'Well, I'm curious to know about your adventure but I'll be patient. Listen, I'd better go and talk to Jakob.'

'I'm grateful for you letting me know,' I said.

I propped the pillows behind my back. Did their break up have anything to do with what happened down at the cinema? It had to have been Jakob, and the texts too. I reread them and a chill shuddered through me. He was sick and I was fuming at the way he was treating me, plus all that bullshit about Melanie having a brain tumour.

On impulse I rang him.

I knew he'd pick up and I sat and stared at the screen. He wouldn't ignore me this time. He knew I knew it was him at the cinema. He also knew I knew that he'd drugged me. I'd already warned him that I'd go to the police and there's no chance he'd risk that.

He picked up. 'Orla?'

'I need to see you,' I said.

'OK. Cedar Hall. Tonight, 8pm.'

'OK,' I said.

The line went dead.

To the point, but it was enough. The thought of confronting him on his own territory filled me with horror, but equally, I knew I had no choice. We'd reached a point of no return. Maybe now that he'd split with Melanie, for whatever reason, I'd be able to get my job back. But now that all trust had gone, could I ever work with him again? Absolutely not, it was either him or me.

# Chapter 32

*Cedar Hall*

I'd never visited Jakob's family home.

I knew where it was because I'd driven past the entrance a few times, although it was on a backwater route rarely used unless people had lost their way. Their house was virtually unseen behind woodland, but one wing of the Hall and the tall chimney tops were visible from the lane. I'd see it from the top of Castle Fell, but even from that distance it appeared an isolated and austere building. Jakob had talked about its history and a few of his ancestors, but forever complained that it cost the earth to maintain.

The pulpy sun laid low in the sky and the long shadows of the trees slashed through the fading light as I pulled into the drive that led to the Hall. I peered up at the two stone pillars either side of the original gated entrance, topped with weatherworn figureheads - a horse and a lion - symbolic of the days when the family had been part of the wealthy elite. The gates were missing now - only a faded sign to inform visitors, 'Entrance - Private'.

Jakob's wife, Priya, had died before I'd had a chance to get to know her properly, although they'd been to ours once for dinner and I'd talked to her at a couple of work functions. Jakob had never invited Drew and I for dinner in return, as was the usual way with couples. Not that this had concerned me. Priya was British born, but her ancestry was Indian and she was slim and charming in a delicate and unshowy way. Well spoken, too, but a non drinker and in some ways she seemed reserved. I recalled that she was very well read. Her features came alive with any opportunity to talk about literature and she confessed she aspired to becoming a writer one day. She'd written poetry and even recited one during dinner, after I'd asked if she'd let me read one or two of them. It was a poem about a woman, a painter, exploring the grounds of Cedar Hall and collecting samples as she walked to later sketch and paint. It seemed to me to be reminiscent of an Emily Bronte poem - with the themes of solitude, sensual expression and immersion in nature. At that time, Priya had worked her way up to becoming a senior in a solicitor's firm but I got the distinct feeling she wasn't in love with her career. She was respectable and intelligent and I saw why Jakob had married her. The one thing I did notice about them together, was how they seemed so much more like friends than a married couple newly in love. I never saw any cuddling or flirting or any talk of sex, which Drew and I were often inclined to.

After Priya had died tragically in a car accident during heavy rain, Jakob sold their cottage in Braithwaite and moved back in with his mother. I knew he felt lonely, and Drew and I invited him to accompany us on walks or if we were having friends over for dinner. Jakob and Drew seemed to get on well and it was often Drew who asked Jakob over and then let me know. I got the impression Jakob's relationship with his mother was strained because he'd since bought a flat in Portinscale and seemed to split his time between the family home and his flat.

I checked my phone to see if Vincent had replied to my last minute text letting him know I was going to Cedar Hall to talk to Jakob. It had seemed a prudent thing to do. But there was no reply and right here, no mobile reception. Hardly surprising, given the remoteness of the house and the height of the surrounding hills. I had serious last minute doubts about heading down to the Hall. After realising first-hand what Jakob was capable of, I knew well I shouldn't be going anywhere near him, especially alone. He was unstable with a dangerous and vicious streak. If I hadn't lost so much as a result of him, I'd be counting the loss of my job and trying to move on. But I wanted answers and if nothing else, I felt determined to prevent the sale of a drug that could do serious damage to innocent women in need of some support and love.

I drove between the pillars, then followed the gentle curve of the drive through the woods where oaks and elms predominated with faded foliage and decaying leaves. I slowed down at the speed ramps and steered around the worst of the potholes.

Jakob had once told me his mother kept a horse for driving a trap, although they'd had to give it up after the horse had spooked and bolted, which resulted in the cart turning over with his mother inside. She'd broken her arm and suffered a concussion. From what I gathered, his mother wasn't an easy person to be around and was prone to making unreasonable demands on her only child, Jakob. And the vague memories I had of her from the day Jakob pulled me and Jess to safety on Whispering Crag, only confirmed my perception of her.

When the car emerged from the woods, the grounds opened out in front of me with vast lawns and clusters of pine and cedar trees, elegant and shapely, in front of the house. I pulled up on the gravel, stepped out of the car into the shadow of the Hall and felt daunted by the sheer size of it. There were two wings either side of the large central block, three floors and countless windows. The ivy that covered almost the entire front only served to intensify the Hall's mystery as though it held secrets inside. The ivy grew wild and thick enough to almost cover some of the windows like black lace curtains. It looked grand and magnificent from the outside and I imagined the interior to be full of antique furniture, ornaments and paintings. I hesitated for a moment at the bottom of the steps and then walked on up to the front door. As I was about to knock, the latch clicked and the vast wooden door creaked on its hinges.

Jakob clasped his hands together. 'The lady graces me with her presence.'

My heart pounded. 'Jakob.' Not a chance of my replying in kind.

He stepped aside and motioned for me to enter. 'I won't apologise for the mess. Mother is as disorganised as ever.' He said this as though it were something he'd long learned to live with.

'Is she here?' She might be odd, but I hoped she'd be present.

'Around somewhere.' He flicked his eyes upwards. 'Probably in her bedroom reading, A Room of One's Own, again,' he said, and rolled his eyes.

'Not a bad choice,' I said.

But Jakob didn't acknowledge my reply and there seemed to be something unnerving in his mannerisms and demeanor which only heightened my unease.

The entrance hall was cavernous with wooden panelled walls to the floor above. On one wall I noticed a row of bells - Master Bedroom, Study, Bathroom and so on, once used by the owners to summon a servant to add logs to the fire or bring tea. This was no ordinary family home and even if he and his mother no longer had the wealth of yesteryear and previous generations, their long ancestry here was sure to have had an influence upon their sense of entitlement and authority over those who worked with and for them.

'We'll talk in the lounge.' Jakob turned and walked across the tiled floor.

Our footsteps echoed as we passed the main central staircase and on through a doorway into a seemingly endless corridor, that despite the tall windows had a claustrophobic feel. As I followed him I felt the pulse in my neck beat fast and hard. If he made any move to touch or hurt me, what would I do in defence? I felt both of my jacket pockets in turn. One with my mobile phone, and the other, a personal alarm, should it prove necessary. But who would hear the alarm, other than his mother?

Without speaking, he led me to a room. He turned in the doorway, flicked a switch and a grand central chandelier lit up the space.

I walked in, took a breath and looked around.

The walls were full of framed paintings, mostly faded watercolours of landscapes and birds and some formal looking portraits which I imagined were of their ancestors. I followed Jakob between piles of journals, newspapers and leather-backed books piled feet high, and wicker baskets full of more books and papers. Some of the piles looked thick with dust as if they hadn't been touched in years. The aroma of old books, musty fabrics and the breath of burnt wood filled the room. The central marble fireplace looked as big as a sepulchre.

I wondered how anyone could sit and relax in such a vast but cluttered space. 'Your Mum is quite the collector,' I said.

He turned to me. 'Most of this junk belonged to my father. When he first left us Mother refused to get rid of anything and she gathered up piles of his stuff and placed it in here where she'd sit and rifle through and talk about Dad as though he was still here with her. Pathetic to see. Over the years she's added more piles and said he'd be pleased we were making good use of them. Like he'd give a shit. She's barely looked at them the past decade but refuses to let me store them in any of the empty rooms.' He snorted with derision, and I caught a definite whiff of alcohol on his breath. 'I'd incinerate the damn lot if I could. Then there'd be nothing left of him in my memory.'

If he hated it so much, why had he brought me into this particular room instead of another one? Did he want my sympathy - my understanding?

He gestured for me to sit on the sofa - a chesterfield which sprouted tufts of hair through cracks in the leather. I sidestepped in, moved a woollen blanket aside and sank into the sofa. There was just enough room for me to cross my legs. I looked down at my hands which felt iced and awkward. I clasped them together and rested them on my knees.

'Jakob?' A woman's voice echoed from a distance. 'Jakob!'

'I'll see what she wants and fix us a drink.'

He was raving mad if he thought I'd touch anything supposedly edible he offered me, but I didn't comment as he weaved his way back across the room. Being here with Jakob felt wrong in every possible sense. Why couldn't we just say what we needed to say then I could leave? My nerves bubbled away as I pulled out my phone. Still no service.

I'd seen programmes about hoarders when life coaches were brought in to declutter their homes. Inevitably, there was some deep underlying reason for the individual to hold onto things from their past. On top of the pile of encyclopedias closest to me sat some drink coasters with worn out pictures of Victorian children. Other than the sofa and armchairs, the rest of the furniture seemed overladen with clutter. Vases filled with fake flowers - their silken leaves paled by years of sunlight, candlesticks dripped and misshapen with wax, even a large pile of logs - not beside the fireplace but stacked up against an old dresser.

How could anyone live like this? In contrast to the clutter around me, Jakob had always looked smart and impeccably dressed. And perhaps because of this I'd imagined his family home to be neat and clean and full of tasteful antiques. Maybe beneath all of the clutter there was something of what the family home used to be.

I sat alone for a few minutes trying to frame what I would say to Jakob, when the sound of crying startled me.

A young child. The crying continued. Not desperate, but in bursts echoing from somewhere in the house. I stood up and moved towards the door to listen. Did Jakob have a child - a child he hadn't told anyone about, or did they have visitors?

I hurried back down the corridor and through to the entrance hall where the sound of the cries grew louder. I inclined my head. They seemed to be coming from upstairs.

It wasn't my imagination. But then as suddenly as the crying had started, the house fell to silence. I paused, not daring to breathe lest I disguise more cries. I jogged across to the staircase, took two steps at a time, then paused at the top to listen.

The crying began again and following the direction it seemed to come from, I jogged along a corridor, dimly lit and with closed doors on either side.

'Hello,' I called.

The cries reminded me of Harry waking at night, alone in his room. I never could leave him to settle himself and I felt the same sense of urgency to find this child. A child who needed comfort and reassurance.

I came to a steep and enclosed stairway that led to the top floor and I stalked up the first few steps, my palm damp against the bannister rail. The cries that drifted from a distance compelled me onwards and I hurried up the remaining steps. The ceiling seemed lower and the passage narrower and confined. The crying ceased once more, and I stopped still. To my left lay a short flight of steps which I sensed must lead to the wing. To my right a narrow corridor.

Instinctively, I turned left and ran up the four steps and then along another passageway - unlit and as silent and shadowed as a black and white movie. My senses prickled. I was getting closer and I stopped outside the first door. The whimpers came again, softer at a distance, and the memory of the sounds tore at my heart.

How was this possible? Was I finally losing my mind?

A sob escaped me.

The barely perceptible cries led me to the end of the passage. I turned to the door on my left and as I twisted the handle, the crying intensified.

I threw open the door and stepped inside. The blinds had been drawn, which left the room in near darkness, but the crying persisted. Where was the child? Barely visible, on a table beside a single bed stood what looked like a radio. As I approached I recognised it as a cassette player which played the cries I'd been searching for.

What sick joke was this? And it dawned on me then that these cries had been laid as a trap to lure me up here. I heard footsteps closeby just as the bedroom door slammed shut behind me and a key twisted in the lock.

# Chapter 33

I ran and turned the door handle. 'Jakob?' I slammed my palms against the door panels. 'How did you record Harry? Is he alive?'

I heard movement on the other side of the door, but no reply came.

I kicked the door and banged it with my fists. I swung around. The room appeared striped with a strange, half-light, like the bars of a cage. I hurried to the window and felt for a cord to open the blind. I hoisted it up, but by now only the dregs of dusk remained and twilight hung in the air. I dashed back to the door and the light switch by its side. I snapped it on. No light, and no lightbulb.

'Jakob!' I screamed. 'Do you have Harry?'

I waited a few moments. 'Is he here?' My tears streamed and my mind reeled with a mixture of desperation and hope.

I stood back from the door and breathed hard. 'Tell me,' I begged. 'Is Harry alive? If you give him to me, I'll do anything. Anything you want.'

A woman snarled; her tone bitter. 'You don't deserve him.'

I pressed my ear to the door.

Then came Jakob's voice, in a raised whisper. 'Wait in your room. I'll handle this.'

I heard a tussle followed by a slap and a small cry.

There came the rustle of paper.

'Under the door,' he said.

I saw a note at my feet. I reached down and unfolded it. It had been typed and the words were barely visible in the faded light.

*'We have Harry. He's safer with us and deserves someone who will love and be with him.'*

My legs weakened and I fell to the floor. Harry was alive.

My body shuddered with relief. Nothing else mattered. I couldn't catch my breath knowing my baby was still alive. Joy flooded my body. But panic, too. I had to find him and get away. Be with him. Protect him from Jakob and his mother, who I knew to be deranged and capable of anything that served their sick motives. My mind felt wracked with questions as to why he had Harry. What could he want with him?

'I'll give up work. I'll leave BioMedica. I want nothing from you but my baby.' I paused. 'Do you understand?'

'Too late for excuses,' came his eventual and clipped reply.

I slipped my phone from my pocket and the screen sprung to life. One bar of signal. I switched on my data and wifi, but even if they had connection up here I'd never guess the password. I jumped onto the bed and raised my arm to the ceiling. Still no messages. I ran to the window, pressed my phone against the window pane and checked it once more. I peered out to the ever dwindling light and down to the ground below - a profusion of rhododendron bushes twenty metres or so below. I pulled and wrenched the widow catch and with a creak of wood, I flung it open.

A breeze rushed in and I took some hurried breaths. There were no doubts in my mind that Harry was alive. Now I understood why his body had never been found. Jakob had been the only one to witness the aftermath of the accident and his reports had been lies from the outset. Had he engineered the whole accident to attempt to do away with both me and Drew so that he could steal Harry from us? Drew and I had even made Jakob, Harry's Godfather. He'd bought him expensive gifts - even for no special occasions. He'd offered to babysit too, but something had always held me back from taking him up on his offer. Jakob's crazy mother was in on this, too. Harry was young enough for them to conceal here for a few years and he'd forget Drew and I. Children adapt. He'd think Jakob was his Dad and Jakob's mother his grandma.

'Orla?'

His voice startled me and my phone slipped from my fingers and plunged into the bushes beneath. 'Jesus Christ!'

I ran to the door. 'What do you want from me?' I pleaded. 'You have Harry.'

'Yes, I have almost all that I want,' he said, slowly.

'Is he hurt? Was he injured in the accident?'

'A few bruises, but he's settling well.'

I slammed my hand against the panel and pressed my face to the door. 'But he should be with me. He needs me,' I cried.

'That is the problem I have,' he said. 'You never stopped moaning about him keeping you awake. You came back to work - full time.'

'That doesn't mean I didn't love and adore him.'

'Anyone can see you're not the motherly sort. You don't deserve a baby. You'd rather be at work than with him.'

'Please, Jakob. I need to see he's OK. Then I'll leave.'

'We can't risk that. You'll go to the police. Trust me. Harry will be fine.'

'You're leaving me in here?'

I waited for his reply but only heard the sound of footsteps retreating.

I hammered the door and screamed. 'Talk to me.'

I ran to the window and looked out. Beyond the rhododendrons I saw a lawn - and beyond that, visible in outline, an ornamental pond. In the middle was a fountain with what appeared to be four statue figures with arms outstretched and surrounding a larger figure on a plinth. Beyond the ornamental pond was the top end of Ullswater, and the shore lined with trees, and further still, if my bearings were correct, must be the road I'd driven down only twenty minutes ago.

The sun had sunk below Rosset Peak and the Western sky had turned magenta. The remaining light waned fast and soon it would be too black to see anything, inside the room or out.

I picked up the cassette player and watched the tape turn around but no longer with any sound. I pressed rewind. Eventually, the machine clicked and I pressed play. After only a couple of seconds Harry's cries filled the air and my breath caught in my throat. My stomach heaved at the sound and I leaned over and clutched my hands to my belly. These cries could only belong to Harry. So distinct and memorable to me. Why hadn't Jakob or his mother tried to soothe him? I heard no words of comfort to ease his tears and his wails continued. To hear him again evoked both pleasure and pain - sensations that swirled into a whirlwind and spun through my mind. It felt like a miracle knowing he was alive, and yet, hearing his tears filled me with despair.

I turned and looked around at the walls, and the sections beneath the eaves, with damp patches and peeling paint. Were they planning on leaving me in here to die? It wouldn't take long without water and it was unlikely anyone knew I was here to come and search for me. Vincent hadn't received my message. Sylvia wouldn't have a clue. And even if someone did eventually come, would I still be alive? Jakob and his mother would conceal Harry, and believing him to be dead, he'd be forgotten by the outside world.

My mouth already felt dry, and a sense of panic blazed through me. My head and neck pricked and burned and my hands and arms trembled at my sides. My breaths came faster - heavy and rasping. Feeling a desperate need to get out, I ran to the door and hammered it with my fists.

I twisted and yanked at the handle, then I sat on the floor and kicked the door panels with all my strength. The walls wavered and the room spun around slowly at first and then in ever quickening circles, squeezing and closing in on me. I lay down and pressed my fingers against my eyes and in the background Harry's cries faded into silence.

Some time later, a light broke through the shadows and I blinked to see a tall figure against the light from the doorway.

A beam of light swerved into my eyes and blinded me for a moment. I turned away.

Jakob stood over me with a wide stance. 'Stand up.'

I rolled onto my side, then slowly rose to my feet. I looked his way and he lowered the torchlight, shut the door and turned the key with a click. I watched him slide the key into his trouser pocket before he leaned against the door with one leg crossed in front of the other.

'Where's Harry?' I said.

'Be quiet,' he said. 'When I want you to speak I'll ask you a question. OK?'

When I didn't immediately answer, his eyes flared and bore into mine. 'Is that clear?'

My voice wavered. 'Yes.'

'Do you want to see Harry?'

'More than anything...' My breath shuddered. 'Is he well?'

'My terms!' He spat the words. 'Do as I say or you'll never see him again.'

Jakob drew the key from his pocket and turned and unlocked the door. He slipped between the gap, closed the door behind him and the key sounded in the lock.

The room turned to darkness, but I stepped up to the door and pressed my ear against it. Was he fetching Harry? His footsteps dripped into silence and I remained still and listened. The sound of his footsteps soon returned and I backed away from the door, picturing Harry in Jakob's arms. If I played along with whatever he wanted - if I was clever and cunning, I could escape and run away with Harry. The anticipation of being reunited with my baby steadied the fear that rushed through my head. Above all else, I knew I must remain rational and calm. I heard the key in the door and the light poured in. Jakob walked through.

I wanted to charge for the door, and wrestle him out of the way but my feet remained fixed to the floor and my legs trembled beneath. 'Where's Harry?'

Jakob held a pile of clothes. My immediate thought was that they must be Harry's.

He looked back at me but didn't reply.

'Where is he?' I couldn't disguise the torment in my voice.

Breathe - I repeated to myself, and I stepped back as he locked the door once more.

He walked across to the bed, placed the clothes onto the quilt and turned to face me. A pair of heels lay on the top. 'Take off what you're wearing and put on the silk slip and shoes. I want to see you in them.'

I shook my head. 'What? No!'

'Do as I say.' He crossed to the corner of the room to a wooden stool where he sat down squarely and fixed his eyes upon me.

'You're insane - you've lost your mind,' I said. 'I'm not getting undressed or dressing up for you.'

He jabbed his finger at me. 'Do you want to see Harry, or not? You said you'd do anything.'

'Not that. Not after what you did to me the other night.'

'I think we both know that it is you who has lost her mind. You're a fantasist. You make stories up.'

'I told the police what you did to me. They believed me, too.'

'Nah.' His upper lip curled. 'I don't think so. If you had and they even suspected you were telling the truth, they'd have approached me by now. So, do as I've told you, there's a good girl.'

'Why should I?' I leaned down and picked up the slip. The blood was racing around my body so fast that I went lightheaded. I straightened up and the dizziness passed. The slip was deep red and made of silk. I knew only too well why he wanted me to put it on, but I asked anyway. 'Why?'

'Because it's feminine. I like my women to dress according to their sex.'

I took a sharp breath. 'Your women? My husband died two months ago. You have Melanie. I'm not yours. I'll never be yours.'

'I've already told you, Melanie and I are nothing to one another. She never was.'

'Are you sure she knows that?'

'Quite sure,' he said, but didn't elaborate. 'I find it hard to believe you're too modest to undress with me here, but I'll go and fetch you something to eat and drink. When I return I expect you to have changed.'

'And if I don't?'

He narrowed his eyes. 'Like I said, do as I say and you'll see Harry. If you refuse you won't see him alive again.' He paused. 'And no underwear.'

'But I can't see with the door closed.'

He held out the torch. 'I have another room prepared for you. It has lighting, an ensuite and is more comfortable. Let's see how we get along first.' His eyes lingered on me, with the nightdress still in my hand. 'You have a sensational body. I want to see it. And why waste it now that you're free?'

'Hardly free, locked in here? And you know I've never looked at you that way.'

He walked to the door, unlocked it, then placed the torch on the floor.

'That's because you were married. We both know we have a connection - an attraction that neither of us can deny.'

'You were married to Priya.'

247

In the torchlight I watched his lips set in a straight line. 'I told you. I don't talk about Priya.'

'What really happened to her, Jakob?'

He ran a finger across his lips. 'It's better to move on.'

'But we can't deny we loved someone because they died.'

'You think I care about her?' He twisted round and rammed his fist against the door before opening it and leaving.

Jakob was insane.

Locking me in here - did he expect me to dress up to satisfy some weird fantasy? He was a predator and I feared he'd even engineered Priya's accident. She'd died driving over a precipice and landed on rocks below. She'd been alone in the car, but something suspicious had happened, I had no doubt. Priya hadn't produced a child, an heir for Jakob and a grandchild for his mother. I recalled how Jakob had once come in to work in a foul mood - said he'd argued with Priya and threw in that she was infertile. I hadn't asked more about it because he'd only wanted to rant about their argument, not for me to sympathise, and certainly not to offer advice. But at the time it had seemed a cruel thing to get angry about. Even if she was infertile, it was hardly something one blamed one's partner for. Plus, it might have been him with the fertility problem. In her late thirties Priya was no longer useful to Jakob - that seemed a logical conclusion now that I knew what he was capable of towards women.

But should I act passively and go along with whatever he had in mind, or fight back and risk being hurt and never seeing Harry again? And if I did go along with what he wanted, might he harm or even kill me anyway?

Murder the victim and have done with the evidence - that's what happened in books. It's what happened in real life.

Think. Breathe. He might be evil and conniving but if I kept my cool I could outsmart him. I picked up the torch and my insides cramped and twisted. I leaned over and couldn't move until the pain subsided. I undressed whilst keeping one eye on the door. Then I pushed my clothes under the bed and pulled the slip over my head and down over my hips. It hung mid thigh, and the silk clung to my skin. He'd also left a lacy red blouse and black silk pencil skirt, both my size, and a pair of patent red stilettos, size 6. So, he'd checked out my size. And I felt the bile rise in my throat. Jakob might not be physically unattractive, but his mind was sick, and his thoughts warped and I knew now what he was capable of in his pursuit of getting what he wanted. I walked over to the window. The half-moon came free of clouds and sent a shimmer of silver over the tops of the trees and across the water in the pond and the statues at its centre. I saw a light in the distance through the woods – a farmhouse perhaps.

I'd long known Jakob liked to be in control and that he had a close but strained relationship with his mother, but I'd never imagined he could be capable of anything as extreme and depraved as this.

I sat on the bed and awaited his return. My body shook and I rubbed my hands up and down my arms to try to calm myself. Whatever I went through tonight didn't matter as long as I survived and could hold Harry close to me once more. Once I had him with me, I would do everything in my power to get away.

The key turned and I pulled up a strap that had slipped off my shoulder. I folded my arms over my breasts. The torch beside me beamed towards the door and Jakob walked in carrying a small wooden tray. He placed the tray on the floor, locked the door, slipped the key into his jeans pocket then picked up the tray and set it on the bedside table. He lifted the torch and directed it at my face; blinding white.

I turned away.

'Stand up,' he ordered.

I stood up.

'Put your hands by your sides.' He paused. 'Please.'

Without looking his way, I lowered my arms. I heard his breaths quicken as he took a step closer and beamed the light from my face, slowly down the length of my body to my feet. If only I'd been wearing boots I'd have kicked him in the balls. But despite the thundering of my heart and my legs shaking, I remained as still as I could. I wished I'd put on the stilettos.

He stepped closer and placed his finger beneath my chin. 'Look at me.'

I lifted my eyes and as I did he ran his tongue slowly across his bottom lip.

He moaned. 'You really are too exquisite. You have a body that every man wants to touch with his hands, and his tongue - to feel your skin against his. The core of you holding him.' He moaned again and his eyes lowered. 'You have curves a man cannot resist but to see and touch in the flesh. Your beauty is like the edge of a knife - enticingly sharp. It's what makes you so utterly alluring. It's why I must have you.'

'I'm not a body. I have a brain and feelings.'

He gave a half-smile. 'Of course. You had an outstanding brain, too. Before your accident.'

'I'm the same person,' I said, but the cracks in my voice exposed my fear.

When he angled his head from one side to the other, the veins in his neck stood out. 'No, my dear Orla. You're not. Dan and I had a long and intimate talk and he said exactly the same. He never wanted you back at work. Not once he saw how you'd changed.'

His words hurt and I wanted to retaliate. But no, I'd go along with whatever he had in mind. Only so I could see Harry again.

'How do I know Harry is here?'

'You've heard his cries. How else could I record him?'

'How do I know he's still alive and that you haven't hurt him since?'

He pulled his phone from his back pocket. 'I'll show you.'

I could barely breathe as Jakob searched on his phone then sat down beside me.

He turned the screen to me.

I reached out to take it but he drew it to his chest.

'Look, don't touch.'

Jakob edged closer until I felt his thigh press against mine. He turned the screen and when I saw Harry's sweet face, tears fell down my cheeks. He was standing in a cot, his small hands clutched the rail and he gazed into the camera lens. His eyes appeared dewey and troubled. But his skin looked clear and unblemished and the pale blue babygrow appeared clean and dry. My eyes fixed upon his face and I wiped my eyes to see him better.

I gasped and swallowed. 'Does he climb out of his cot?'

We'd only recently moved Harry into a cot bed without sides because he'd refused to remain inside once he realised he could clamber out at night and come and find me.

'He stays in... most of the time.'

'Have you been kind to him?' I said without taking my eyes off Harry.

'You were right when you said he cried a lot. Though I'd say that was your doing for being too soft.'

'I imagine he's cried more because he's missing me and Drew.'

'Oh, I told him I was his dad. He adores me and Grandma. He's well fed and cared for. But mother and I both feel that life here could be even better with you. Harry and I will love you, and Grandma can step in to help whenever you need a rest or if we have another baby.'

The tick tick of my blood pulsed against my eardrums and my limbs tensed in readiness. Here was a crazed fantasist and what he suggested, with all the seriousness of someone who believed it possible, was utter madness. Stranger still, but infinitely more wondrous, was that Harry was alive. I couldn't drag my eyes from his face.

Jakob drew the phone away and tucked it back into his pocket. In the torchlight his features appeared distorted in a way that I barely recognised him from the colleague I'd worked with for five years. All along, I'd been blind. I'd been a fool, and here I was locked in a room with him and about to be subjected to whatever depraved acts he thought he could subject me to.

His gaze lowered and I saw the saliva pool on his tongue as he pushed out his bottom lip.

I felt his breath on my face as he moved closer and cupped my breast and squeezed.

I froze as he fingered my nipple, but unable to bear it a moment longer, I swiped his hand away, sprang up and ran to the corner of the room. I pressed myself against the wall, breathing hard.

'No! I need to see proof that Harry is safe. For all I know, you might have recorded him and taken his photo weeks ago.'

Jakob got up and I held up my hand. 'Don't you dare come closer.'

In the torch-light it seemed as if Jakob's eyes were aflame. But was it fury or lust? Great golden orbs - wide and luminous against olive skin, pierced my eyes - goading and threatening me all at once. His mouth opened to speak and I waited, neither wanting to prevent or preempt his next move. I remained still, hardly daring to breathe, yet my body and senses felt fully wired and emboldened, ready to respond in an instant.

'I want Harry,' I said. 'You'll get nothing from me without a fight until I do.'

Slow and deliberate, he took two steps towards me and the shadows sunk into the hollows of his cheeks. He nodded at the tray. 'Drink. Eat.'

'Why - what's in them?' I said. 'Hexprin or rohypnol?'

He marched the final few steps and his hand gripped my neck.

For some moments I felt the pressure of his fingers and the blood hummed in my veins. I grappled at his hand to pull him away. My breath left me and pressure and terror rose in my throat as he ran his other hand down my breastbone, yanked down the slip and exposed my breasts. Finally he released his hold on my neck and I gasped for air.

He slipped his other hand into the front of his jeans. 'I will fuck you. I've waited long enough. And you'll plead for more because I know you want me to.'

With shaking hands and a thundering heart I pulled the slip up to cover myself. 'I'm surprised you didn't rape me when you drugged me.'

'Oh, that would have been too easy. Trust me, I took my pleasure.'

My mouth filled with saliva.

'But I want to see your eyes when I fuck you.' He continued, and his eyes lasered into mine with lust, and something else too, loathing.

Adrenaline powered through me. His strength and madness combined could overpower me. I stared back into the wildness of his eyes and my mind reeled with options.

I moved my hand to his trousers and pulled at the button. 'Let me.'

I pulled down the zip and knelt at his feet. He was only a body. I could detach myself from the man. When I took his hardness in my hand he moaned, and I felt his fingers upon the back of my head urging me closer.

But my plan would only work if he was lying down and not watching me.

I looked up. 'Why don't we lie on the bed?'

He nodded, with lips loose and eyes drunk with lust.

Every fibre of my mind and body fought against what I must do, but I took his hand and led him across the floorboards to the bed.

Jakob lay down and his eyes fixed on me as I straddled him and pulled his trousers further down. My stomach rolled as I held my breath, shut my eyes and took him in my mouth. I moved my lips and tongue slowly and at the same time stroked the top of his thigh with one hand and felt my way towards the right pocket of his jeans.

He moaned, and again I felt his hand on my head pushing me to take him deeper. In my mind, I tried only to see Harry's face and how much he needed me.

Jakob's breath quickened and already I felt his body tense beneath me.

I glanced up and saw his neck arch backwards. I eased my fingers into his pocket and found the bow of the key. I gripped it between the tips of my fingers and drew it into my fist. As I felt him shudder towards his release, I leaped off the bed and hurtled towards the door. With fumbling fingers I slipped the key into the lock and heard Jakob grunt and move behind me. The key turned and I yanked it out at the same time as I turned the door handle. I glanced round and saw him lumber towards me. The look of madness on his face only fuelled my desperation to get out. I opened the door, slipped through and pulled it shut.

But something caught in the way.

Jakob's hand.

His fingers gripped the edge of the door as I tugged harder. An immense fury burned inside of me - what he'd made me do to him so that I might be reunited with my son.

And I yanked on the handle again and again with superhuman strength.

He yowled in agony and the tips of his fingers withdrew.

I slotted the key into the lock and turned it with a resounding click.

This key had secured my fate and I hoped, my son's.

# Chapter 34

I raced along the passageway and I heard a commotion as Jakob screamed obscenities and battered the door. I didn't look back, but clasped the key in my hand and stopped at the top of the stairs. Harry's room could be on the floor below. Or then again, if they'd aimed to conceal him, he might be hidden away up here.

I paused and listened.

Where was Jakob's mother? I knew she'd be lurking nearby, and waiting to see what happened. She might already know that I'd escaped and locked Jakob in the room. What if there was another key for the room? I didn't know how long the door would hold him and time was running out. I hurried along the top corridor and at each of the doors I came to, I stopped and turned the handle. I found each door unlocked and each room appeared dark and empty. When I checked the room at the end of the corridor I heard a faint noise coming from somewhere close by. It sounded like water pouring down a drain. Perhaps a toilet flushing.

I retraced my steps and looked again into the room I'd just passed. It was small with a bed in one corner and a dressing table against one wall. On top of the dressing table I spotted a gilt edged vanity mirror and reflected in the mirror a thin line of light. I took a step closer to see where the light came from. I turned around and below the skirting board on the opposite wall, a strip of light, a door's width, escaped through. There appeared to be no door handle but I saw in the light cast from the corridor the outline of a door.

A hidden closet?

I walked across and pushed. The wall seemed thin and rattled. I heard a gasp from close by and I felt all down the edge of the door and squeezed my fingers into the gap. It seemed to be bolted from the inside, but I could feel the door beneath the wallpaper was no thickness at all. I stood back and rammed my shoulder against it. A pain ripped through my arm, but I stepped back and slammed into it again with my full weight. The door swung open. I staggered through, stumbled onto the floorboards and looked up.

In the far corner of the room, with her back to me, an elderly woman with wild grey hair looked over her shoulder – Jakob's mother. She clutched something to her and a shadow of panic passed over her face.

I scrambled up and rushed over, and when I saw Harry pressed against her, I reached for him. 'Give me my baby.'

'Get away,' she screamed, cradling Harry tighter and turning her back to me.

I reached my hands around Harry's waist. 'Give him to me. Now!' I couldn't believe the steadiness in my voice, when my gut instinct screamed at me to punch her in the face.

She made a move towards the door.

I grabbed the waistband of her skirt and pulled her back.

She swung around and slapped me, full force on my cheek.

My head rocked and for a moment I felt disorientated.

'Harry...it's Mummy.'

'Mumma.' He turned his face to me, reached out his arms and cried. 'Mumma.'

'Please,' I begged. 'He needs me.'

She squeezed him tighter. Too tight. 'He doesn't need a mother who goes out and leaves him with people he barely knows.' Her words were laced with bile and bitterness.

My patience snapped. I reached forwards and with the key in one hand prized my fingers into her armpits. I gouged the key into her skin and dug with my fingernails.

She squirmed and yelled, and Harry fell from her grasp.

I reacted instantly, caught him in my hands and scooped him up. I sobbed with relief and clutching him to me, raced back through the bedroom and onto the landing.

The old woman scurried behind me, 'Jakob!' she screamed. 'She's taking Harry.'

Thunderous crashes echoed from the locked room. I charged back to the main flight of stairs, and hoped she couldn't keep up with us. I had to make it out of the house.

Harry whimpered in my arms.

'It's OK, Harry. You're safe.'

255

I didn't dare pause to look back and I raced on down the stairs and across the hallway.

Harry gripped my shoulders. 'Gramma coming.'

'We're going home, Harry.' I prayed the front door wasn't locked.

'Mumma.' His voice trembled.

'Hold tight my darling.' I grasped the door handle. It turned but was locked. Thank God the key was in the lock and I moved Harry onto my hip and wrestled with it. I twisted it one way, then the other and it clicked open.

A bony hand gripped my arm. 'Harry belongs with me.'

I jumped away and spun around to face her.

Her wild eyes flared. 'Harry belongs here.'

She reached out her arms and pulled at Harry but he pressed himself tight against me.

My fury raged. 'Get away from us you mad bitch.' I swung my arm back and with a force I hardly knew I possessed, I thumped her in the mouth.

Her scream resounded through the house, and she staggered and toppled backwards.

Footfall reverberated through the floorboards above and I glanced up. Jakob had broken out. I hauled the door open, dashed through and hurried down the steps and out into the night.

The air felt chilled and I pulled Harry close to keep him warm.

My car stood only feet away, but I hadn't had a chance to grab my keys, which were in my jeans pocket, in the attic room. To run up the drive would leave us too exposed. No. We needed to find cover, and fast.

I kept close to the side of the house. I barely felt the stones beneath my feet in my desperation to reach the shelter of the woods some way up the slope of the lawn. The overgrown grass and thistles scratched against my bare legs as I bore left and out of immediate view from the front of the house. If Jakob had any sense, he'd know I'd head for the road, but hopefully he'd think I'd run up the drive. I kept running, but with the incline my breaths came fast and heavy. Harry fell silent - no doubt terrified and in shock. But I knew that if I didn't get away now, they'd imprison us here and we might never get out again, or stay alive.

When I reached the trees I heard a voice bellow from some distance behind.

'Got you!'

A gunshot split the air and instinctively I cradled Harry's head and ducked. The trees were only yards away - I had to make it there. If he wanted Harry why shoot, other than to frighten me into surrendering?

I ran between the trees and stumbled over stones and bramble stems that tore at my skin. I struggled to breathe and my lungs screamed for reprieve. I scrambled behind a broad tree trunk, and gasping for breath leaned against it.

Harry lifted his face to mine, and even in the darkness I saw his eyes widen. He reached out his little hand and touched my face in wonder. 'Mumma,' he said so softly and my heart swelled with immeasurable love.

I kissed his cheek and whispered, 'I'm here, sweetheart.' I could hardly believe he was alive, with breath, warm skin and in my arms again. But right now I would take nothing as permanent.

I pulled him to me then peered around the trunk. I couldn't see or hear anyone approaching, but I knew Jakob couldn't be far away. I stepped forwards and continued in what I sensed and prayed to be the direction of the road. The undergrowth felt thinner underfoot and I set off running once more. The night appeared black, but with my eyes accustomed, I could see the outline of the trees and any large bushes. Darting left and right I hurried around them and Harry clung tight.

Somewhere behind us and over the sound of my rasping breaths and footfall, I heard movements and the snapping of twigs and rustling of undergrowth. Terror fuelled me and I increased my pace. Jakob had an advantage over me - shoes, and with no child to carry. A gun, for God's sake.

Up ahead, a hundred yards at most, I saw a flash of headlights and the sweep of a vehicle as it passed. I hurried on. There might be more cars. If we reached the road someone would stop to help us. We were only yards away when I pitched forwards. I landed awkwardly and felt my cheek crack against Harry's head and he let out a wail. It took me some moments to scramble back up and I scooped Harry up against me as he continued to scream.

I looked up at the edge of the ditch we'd fallen into. Movement. A shadow. Then I saw him.

Jakob glared down at us. He aimed his gun. 'Don't fucking move.'

I wasn't going anywhere.

As though sensing the gravity of our situation, Harry fell silent and turned his face to Jakob. I placed my hand protectively over his head and turned away, so Harry was out of the firing line.

'Please, Jakob. Think of Harry. If you let us go, I won't tell a soul. I'll never return to work.'

'And how will you explain Harry's sudden reappearance?'

'We'll think of something - you and I. We'll talk.'

'I want you both. You're staying and you'll feel grateful to be here with me.'

Harry's cries started again.

I heard another car approaching. Might they see us, or hear Harry? But I knew from the crazed look in Jakob's eyes that to make any move to get their attention would be my death sentence.

'I only want what's best for Harry,' I said. 'You must know that.'

'What's best for Harry is to be with me and Grandma. And you, you'll see.'

'I know Priya and you wanted children, but I didn't know it upset you that you hadn't.'

'You think I share everything with you?'

I stroked Harry's head and his crying eased. If I could keep him talking, he might see reason. 'What really happened, Jakob?'

He gave a scornful laugh. 'You don't care.'

'Yes, I do,' I said.

He remained stock still with the gun aimed at my head.

And I saw in his eyes how he fought with himself between holding back and needing to talk.

Eventually he spoke. 'I had a twin brother. But he drowned.' Jakob paused. 'I, we, never got over losing him.'

'I didn't ever know you had a brother. How old was he?'

'Eight,' he said quietly, and took a deep breath. 'Christopher. We were skating on the pond at the back of the house. The ice seemed solid, or so I thought. I ran in to fetch us some gloves and when I came back, Christopher had gone, along with Jack, our labrador. When I spotted the hole in the ice I ran to get Mum. We had to drain the pond which took hours. By then Christopher had died. But the medics still tried to revive him.'

He stopped talking and in the silence that followed some details and missing links came together in my mind.

The young boy's name, Christopher. Chistopher Jones. The same surname as Jakob. The boy Christopher who laid in the grave beside Drew's. The boy whose small decayed hand broke out through the coffin and the soil. Which was why Jakob had been so enraged about it after the funeral.

What a bizarre and horrible coincidence.

'Mother never recovered,' Jakob continued. 'Dad was already distant and Christopher's death only sent him into a deeper retreat. He was barely ever at home - shagging his mistress, Mum said, which only made her cry more. I was left to fend for myself, and for weeks I didn't go to school. Not even after the school and social workers visited. Mum, when she did start talking to me, often screamed and blamed me for leaving Christopher alone. Except I didn't leave him alone - Jack was still with him. So I got blamed for both their deaths.'

I saw how this had destroyed Jakob. Destroyed the entire family, but Jakob had chosen to hide this from everyone at work.

'Go on,' I said, and hoped that the more he talked, the less likely he'd be to make any sudden or dangerous moves.

'Christopher was shy and had learning difficulties and I was outgoing and smart, so I was always expected to be the responsible one. I thought I was being responsible by coming in for gloves when our hands were freezing.'

'You must leave here, Jakob. Have your own home. Your own life.'

He shook his head. 'But now we have Harry everything's all right again.'

'But Harry should be with me. You know that.' I pleaded for him to see reason.

'You're no good for Harry on your own,' he said, bitterly. 'When I saved you and your dog from the crag all those years ago, you showed then you couldn't be responsible for an animal, let alone a child. Mother often said so and she was right. No. Harry will stay with us and you will too.' He looked at me in silence for a moment and his eyes penetrated mine. 'Did you ever work out that your hero on Whispering Crag was me?'

I nodded. 'But only recently.'

He cackled. 'You can't imagine how my knowing we'd already met whilst you remained blissfully ignorant thrilled me each time I saw you - from the moment I saw your name and photo appear on the job application. My little secret. You in your navy school skirt, rolled up to your thighs. Revealing your stockinged legs like a gazelle's, even at such a tender age.'

My stomach heaved. 'I was a child. Like you were when Christopher died. If you were a parent, you'd know that when you have a child - they become our whole life - our whole reason for existence. I'd rather give Harry freedom and you lock me in that attic room forever, than leave him here with you.'

He jerked the gun. 'I'm taking you home - both of you - where you belong. Refuse and I will shoot you. You won't go anywhere then.' He angled his head to one side and then the other. 'What if I miss you and kill Harry?' He jabbed the gun again.

I shuddered and had no doubt that he'd follow through with his word. The madness in his eyes exposed his true capabilities.

'Move!' he said.

I had no choice. I wouldn't risk Harry's life or my own. Defeated, I turned around, climbed out of the ditch and stepped carefully back through the undergrowth. Harry rested his head on my shoulder.

A voice echoed through the trees. 'The police are on their way. Let them go, Jakob.'

I knew the voice well.

Jakob swung round to see where the voice came from and he aimed his gun to shoot.

'Stay back!' I screamed. 'He has a gun.'

But Vincent charged through the undergrowth towards Jakob, zigzagging left and right to avoid a bullet. Two shots rang out, but Vincent kept on running. When he was only feet from Jakob another shot blasted the air. Vincent lurched forwards and collapsed into the ditch at Jakob's feet.

I sat Harry on the ground then rushed down the bank, and leapt onto Jakob's back. I grabbed him around the throat and dug my nails into his skin. We collapsed to the ground and I watched the gun fall from his hand.

Vincent struggled to get up and he reached out his hand to clasp the gun, but Jakob was on it too and they wrestled for it.

I scrambled up and looked about me. I groped around on the ground until I found a rock the size of my palm. I ripped it from the soil and jumped up. Jakob and Vincent were a mass of thrashing limbs, but I dived upon Jakob, raised my arm and brought the stone down with a sickening crack on the back of his head. I lifted my hand, and with fury, I brought it down once more.

In that instant, Jakob fell deathly still.

# Chapter 35

Two days after our escape, the night where Vincent had received a shot that by some miracle had only skimmed the skin of his thigh, the night when I'd knocked Jakob out and he'd received a fractured skull and a severe concussion, Dan came to visit me at the flat.

We sat opposite one another, and as Harry sat at my feet and played with his cars across the floorboards, Dan told me that Hexprin was to be delayed and would go before BioMedica's International Drugs Committee.

He told me he'd discovered Jakob had remortgaged the family home and invested a considerable sum of money into Hexprin but in another name. This was against business policy, whereby all stakeholder investments had to go through a strict approval process first.

Dan also admitted that Jakob had purposely poisoned him against me - and he felt ashamed that, like a deluded fool, he'd fallen for Jakob's many lies.

I'd told Dan about the date rape drug Jakob had given me, confirmed by the results of the bloodtest, and Dan confided that Melanie had also approached him to say she had been bullied and coerced into lying and hiding research that threw into question the safety of the drug. Dan couldn't have been more apologetic and promised, in writing, that when I was ready my job would be open for my return. He also said that I could work two days from home to help take the pressure off me as a single parent.

'Let me think about it all, Dan. I do want to return, but right now Harry has to be my priority.'

Feeling understood finally, I'd broken down in tears and Dan gave me the warmest hug that showed he understood entirely.

'Jakob duped and deluded us all,' he'd said. 'He and his mother are under investigation. It'll go to court.'

'You'll know they're reinvestigating the boat accident?' I said.

Dan froze and his eyes closed momentarily. 'I feel sick that I didn't suspect something.'

'I know.' I nodded, realising I'd have to face the court case in time. 'That's how Jakob worked. He's a master manipulator, and, I believe, a murderer, too.'

# Chapter 36

*A Fortnight Later*

Harry reached out his hand to catch a falling leaf - crisp and yellow. A breeze swept a pile of leaves into a swirl and they spilled across the path in front of us.

I stopped and stepped round Harry's pram. 'Do you want to get out?'

Harry pulled at his straps. 'Yes, Mumma.'

'I'll help you,' I said, and unclipped the straps.

He wriggled his arms free and I took his hand as he climbed out. He was walking well now and each day grew more reluctant to stay in his pram for the duration of our walks. He giggled as he kicked at the leaves which crunched beneath our feet.

'I don't think speedy here will be needing the wheels for much longer,' said Vincent, who pushed the pram beside us.

We walked through the gateway into the cemetery and started up the slope at Harry's meandering pace - pausing every few steps to examine a twig or a stone. The moment felt surreal as I thought back to only a few weeks ago when I'd laid flowers at Drew and Harry's graves. The funeral director had confirmed that Harry's headstone had been removed and no evidence of any flowers remained on that plot. Even after two weeks of being reunited with Harry I had too many moments of disbelief when I looked at him playing or sleeping. And I sensed that he did too. Since bringing him home, he'd slept in my bed at night and each time he'd awoken, he'd see me beside him and reach out and touch my cheek, then smile, reassured, and close his eyes again. I'd lie still and watch him breathing next to me and hardly believed he was alive, safe and home with me.

Memories of the night we escaped from Jakob and his mother returned to haunt me. But I reminded myself that Harry had had to endure so much more - the trauma of the accident, on top of the confusion he must have felt at being taken to Cedar Hall and looked after by virtual strangers. Thoughts of how they may have mistreated him tore me apart. He hadn't any bruises or nappy rash and he was saying a few words now, but he'd been especially needy since I'd brought him home. I kept him close to me at all times, unless he toddled off to play or to pick up another toy. But he'd soon return and sit beside me, and look up at me every now and then, almost as if to check I was still there.

As we neared Drew's grave, Vincent took my hand. 'Do you want to go on alone? I can stay with Harry.'

'Thank you, it's probably too much for him to digest anyway,' I said and paused. 'Did I ever tell you about the mystery flowers and card on Drew's grave?'

He gave my hand a gentle squeeze. 'You did.'

'Sometimes I'm still not confident my memory is quite back to normal.'

'You seem sharp as a pin to me,' he said, and smiled. 'In the nicest way possible.'

I leaned in and kissed him on the lips. 'I'm glad you think so.'

I bent down and kissed Harry on his cheek before I headed on alone up the path.

To distract Harry, I heard Vincent say, 'Come on, let's see who can find the biggest stick.'

As I reached the brow of the hill I felt a rise of butterflies and my mouth felt dry. Drew was alone here - not that he could feel or know anything now. After losing my parents I'd given up any idea that there was an afterlife, and this thought comforted me. Life was rich, varied and wonderful and at the other end, painful, sad and pitiful, until ultimately, we came to rest. But for me, that was all I saw. When we'd lost Mum and Dad, well-meaning relatives and friends told us that they'd gone somewhere better, that they were looking down on us still. But I strongly sensed that wasn't true. If God existed, there was no way in heaven or hell he'd have left two teenage girls to fend for themselves - to have torn away the two most precious people from them.

Only weeks ago, I thought I'd never feel joy again, but having Harry back had reawakened in me a new energy and lust for life. Harry was the reason for my going on. My new beginning. For waking up each morning and smiling as he lay sleeping beside me. Not Hexprin, not even my job, although that came not too far behind. Harry gave me the motivation to launch myself into the world of the living again. And, there was Vincent. He'd been my rescuer, though he'd insisted we'd have got away somehow. I wasn't convinced. The moment he'd got my message he hadn't hesitated to come to Cedar Hall to find me. And he was my rescuer in other ways, too.

The sun was already low in the sky as I looked down at row after row of gravestones. There were one or two people down the slope and I shielded my eyes from the sun to see more clearly. A woman knelt at a grave. I felt certain it was Drew's and for a moment my step faltered. She had her back to me and I didn't recognise her, but she had long fair hair and wore a black leather jacket. A small brown dog sat at her side. Even from here I sensed by the way she leaned over that she'd been crying and I watched as she lifted her face and wiped her cheek. I walked down the slope with purpose. She didn't appear to hear me as I approached but when I stopped beside her, she looked up at me.

Her cheeks were wet with tears, and her eyes and mouth turned down with sadness.

'I'm Orla,' I said. 'Orla Safian.' The words staggered off my tongue.

She stood up and brushed the grass from her knees. She seemed reluctant to look me in the eye. 'I'm sorry. I worked with Drew.'

She was the doctor from the hospital website. 'You're upset.' God, why did I state the obvious? I was upset. 'You knew Drew well?'

Her cheeks flushed, and tearful still, she picked up the dog's lead and turned to leave.

'Please.' I touched her shoulder. 'Don't go.'

She turned back to me, slowly. And as she did, everything about her struck me as fragile and small - even the delicate lashes that fringed her tear soaked eyes.

'Have we met before?' I asked.

She nodded. 'Once over Christmas drinks with work. We were never formally introduced.'

'You know Harry is alive?' I said.

'Yes. I cried when I heard.'

'And you're crying now...'

She looked down, and her discomfort felt palpable.

'I saw the flowers you left for Drew,' I said. 'What's your name?'

She looked up. 'I'm Suzie. Drew and I were friends.'

'Is that all you were?' Did I imagine I caught a waft of her perfume - a familiar scent?

She considered me for some moments before finally speaking. Her voice sounded gentle. 'We were close. Though he never said he loved me so I'll never know.'

My legs weakened and I took a breath.

'I knew he was miserable,' I said, and my eyes pooled with the emotion I could no longer contain.

'Did you know he was taking antidepressants?' she asked.

'No. But Drew gave up speaking to me about anything that mattered. I should have known he was having an affair.'

'It wasn't an affair.'

'You didn't sleep together?' My tone sounded accusatory despite my knowing I shouldn't blame her.

She paused, reluctant, then nodded. 'Yes.' Then quickly added, 'But only a few times. He had to work out what he wanted.'

My legs crumbled and I sank to the ground.

She crouched down beside me, her eyes full of shame. 'I'm so sorry.'

'Don't be. He barely slept with me after Harry was born.'

She knelt down on the grass beside me and I saw she felt no animosity towards me, only, pity. 'His GP said he had postnatal depression.'

'So why didn't he talk to me?'

'I don't know,' she said. 'He seemed to not want to talk about home at all.'

'You mean he wanted to pretend he wasn't married or a dad?'

'He wasn't well,' she said, as though that excused him.

'You know he slept like a baby,' I said. 'Which is a joke because Harry didn't. Did he ever tell you that?'

'No, he didn't. I'm sorry.'

'No need. Our marriage was over and he'd have left me soon enough. For you.'

'I didn't ask him to.'

'But you wanted him to? I can see you were in love with him.'

She didn't reply and I knew that sooner or later I'd have lost Drew to her. But I didn't feel anger towards her, only a deep sorrow knowing that I'd lost Drew even before he'd lost his life.

'I came here to say goodbye to my husband. I was wrong to think it might make me feel better.'

'If I'd known you were coming, I'd have stayed away. And I haven't told anyone about me and Drew.'

'Then you should,' I said. 'What's the point in lying? He left me and Harry months ago, I just didn't realise it.'

'Some men, some people don't cope well with responsibility.'

'He was a consultant anaesthetist. Responsible for people at their most vulnerable.'

'Maybe there's the answer,' she said. 'Too much on top of what he already had to deal with.'

She reached into her handbag, pulled out a notebook and pen, and wrote something down. 'Please call me if you want to talk. I'd like us to, if you think it might help.'

I took the piece of paper and tucked it into my jeans pocket. I nodded. 'I might.' And I knew it would match the number I'd already discovered in Drew's messages.

She turned and as she walked away, I felt an agonising pain claw through my insides. I knelt in front of Drew's grave and felt confusion and frustration all rolled into one. I'd loved him. I'd bloody well loved him. If only I could have had one final but real and honest conversation with him? But he was lost to me now and I don't think I could have done anything to have changed him or his feelings towards me.

As my tears soaked my cheeks, I traced my fingers over his name in the stone. *'Andrew Marcus Safian, Much loved Husband, Father and Son...'* and, I thought, an irresponsible, cheating bastard.

I heard a squeal and giggles and I wiped furiously at my eyes then turned around. I watched Vincent scoop Harry into his arms and lift him over his head. Then he sat him on his shoulders and both of them smiled as they came across the grass.

Here was my future, whatever that might hold, and I stood up and walked to meet them.

'OK?' Vincent looked into my eyes with concern, and lifted Harry down from his shoulders.

I nodded, too full of emotion to reply. And he put his arm around my shoulder and we turned to face one another. When he leaned down and kissed me tenderly on the lips, I knew that I would be OK and more importantly, so would Harry.

# Chapter 37

I'd been excited but nervous about taking things further physically with Vincent after my disastrous experiment with Hexprin. With characteristic generosity, Vincent had made light of it and said it had taken every ounce of his willpower to walk away from me that night. I hadn't yet invited him to sleep over because I'd focussed all of my energy on settling Harry back in and I didn't want to rush anything.

What surprised me most was how peacefully Harry had slept almost from the first night home. Far better than I had - as I watched and listened to his every breath. Granted, he now had all of his molars and wasn't awoken by sore gums, but I also wondered if he felt relief and contentment to be home with me again.

Once or twice I'd tried to encourage him to talk about his time in the big house with Jakob and his mother, but he simply didn't have the vocabulary to express himself. Maybe that would come at some point. With relief, I'd seen how he was relaxed and playful when I bathed and changed him, and he'd put on a bit of weight, so I knew he'd been fed well, and only time would perhaps reveal if he'd been mistreated or traumatised in any way during his abduction.

Even looking at and being close to Vincent made me yearn for his touch - for far more than that. I longed to hear his voice and be in his presence in a way I couldn't ever recall experiencing with another man, not even with Drew. And I knew that Vincent wanted me too. The scent of him, the way my head fit into the curve of his neck, made him seem so familiar to me already - so right for me, and I hoped - me for him. When we kissed or held one another, I'd feel a great stabbing desire for him, and I knew it couldn't be long until we'd allow ourselves to succumb to what we both wanted. What we both needed from one another.

'It's so good to see you,' I'd say, unnecessarily whenever he came down to my flat or I went up to his. And at the same time I'd know that I was in love with him, even though neither of us had said these words. It seemed too soon. Not that I felt any guilt. No, Drew didn't deserve that.

I adored how Vincent would take me into his arms, and gaze at me with his wide grey eyes, before kissing me. He began with gentle lips, and perhaps a stroke with his fingers against my cheek and neck - lightly and with the promise of so much more. He'd run his hands through my hair and sigh and hold his body against mine. We'd sometimes draw apart and drink one another in with our gaze, then kiss again, our breaths merging and our kisses growing more urgent. With a pricking, burning ache inside, my mind and body responded with a yearning I hadn't experienced in so long. The sensations and feelings Vincent aroused in me seemed equally as intense as when I'd taken Hexprin, if not more so. The difference was that I felt this for him alone, not for some handsome stranger walking up the street.

Whenever Vincent returned to his flat, I'd catch the occasional trace of his unique scent in the air or on my clothes - his essence that seemed so deliciously rousing and sensual.

As I ran Harry's bedtime bath, I thought back again to our visit to the cemetery only days before. It all seemed so unreal. The only positive that had come from it was that at least I'd found some resolution to what had been the most distressing time of my life. More painful even than losing my parents. Or perhaps that was the passage of time which had softened the blow of that event in my memory.

After Harry's bath, I dressed him in fresh pyjamas, gave him a beaker of warm milk then tucked him up on Drew's side of the bed. I picked up a framed photograph in which Harry was seated in front of Drew on the seesaw in the park.

'Do you know who that is, Harry?' I sat on the bed beside him and asked him gently.

Harry looked at the photograph for a moment before touching Drew's face and nodding. 'Dat Dada and me.'

I almost wept at his words. And when Harry took the picture in his hands and planted a kiss on Drew's face, I shuddered and drew him into my arms and held him close. 'That's right. And Dada loved you so much.'

Harry didn't ask where Drew had gone and I didn't try to explain. That would all come in time.

I placed the photograph back on the dressing table and picked up Harry's toy monkey from the floor. He took it from me and hugged it against his chest. We snuggled up and I read aloud, The Tale of Peter Rabbit, before I closed the book and kissed him goodnight. I switched off the bedside lamp and the nightlight gave out a warm glow. When I turned to look down at Harry one more time, his eyes were already closed.

THE END

Printed in Great Britain
by Amazon